"Jayna Breigh delivers a debut that is on fire! on everyone's list and moved straight to the TBR'! A for-sure thumbs-up and recommend .

—JAIME JO WRIGHT, ECPA best-selling author of *The Lost Boys of Barlowe Theater* and *The Vanishing at Castle Moreau*

"An intriguing, action-packed romance that kept me turning the pages until the end. Jayna Breigh's style is fast-paced with no chance for a dull moment. The characters are quirky, compassionate, and compelling. I very much enjoyed reading *The Hunted Heir* and encourage others to do likewise."

—TRACIE PETERSON, *USA Today* and ECPA best-selling author of over 130 novels

"Jayna Breigh's brilliant writing in this outstanding debut exceeded my expectations! Not only does her legal expertise shine through, but her rich and deep characters drew me in from the first page. Nona is one of my all-time favorite characters. Wow. What a story!"

—KIMBERLEY WOODHOUSE, author of the Alaskan Cyber Hunters series

"What a dazzling debut! *The Hunted Heir* was an absolute pleasure to read. The characters are robust and believable, the plot layered, the dialogue smart and witty, and the redemption arcs fully satisfying. Jayna Breigh writes legal suspense with the authority borne from years of experience in the field, and with the maturity and skill of a seasoned and professional storyteller. I can't wait to read whatever she writes next."

—JOCELYN GREEN, Christy Award–winning author of *The Hudson Collection*

"Author-lawyer Jayna Breigh keeps her readers' pages flying with a tingling mix of danger, suspense, and amorous sparring in her romantic legal drama, *The Hunted Heir*. Private eye Nona Taylor is smart, sharp, and cheer-worthy. Same for DeMarcus Johnson, Ivy League lawyer-on-the-rise.

So is the modern plot, with surprising ties to the historic past, that keeps the story racing to its stunning, satisfying end. An exciting, don't-miss debut."

—PATRICIA RAYBON, Christy Award–winning author of the
Annalee Spain Mystery series

"A PI running from self-incrimination. An ex-jock turned cocky lawyer. And an odd inheritance case that threatens to take them down. Debut author Jayna Breigh deftly layers gritty, snarky, well-tuned characters over a twisty plot steeped in the historic divides of the American South. *The Hunted Heir* is a suspense lover's dream."

—JANYRE TROMP, best-selling and award-winning author of
Darkness Calls the Tiger and *Shadows in the Mind's Eye*

"Jayna Breigh's *The Hunted Heir* captivates! Her debut checks all the boxes: witty dialogue, mystery and intrigue, and just the right amount of romance. This faith-filled story will make you take a look at your own family tree and give it a good shake. Well done!"

—ROBIN W. PEARSON, award-winning author of
Dysfunction Junction and *A Long Time Comin'*

The Hunted Heir

The Hunted Heir

A ROMANTIC LEGAL DRAMA

Jayna Breigh

KREGEL
PUBLICATIONS

Published by Kregel Publications, a division of Kregel Inc., 2450 Oak Industrial Dr. NE, Grand Rapids, MI 49505. www.kregel.com.

Jayna Breigh is represented by and *The Hunted Heir* is published in association with The Steve Laube Agency, LLC, www.stevelaube.com.

The persons and events portrayed in this work are the creations of the author, and any resemblance to persons living or dead is purely coincidental.

"Glory, Glory, Hallelujah," "What a Friend We Have in Jesus," "I Will Trust in the Lord," and "Come, Thou Fount of Every Blessing" are public domain.

Scripture quotations taken from the (NASB®) New American Standard Bible®, Copyright © 1960, 1971, 1977, 1995, 2020 by The Lockman Foundation. Used by permission. All rights reserved. www.lockman.org.

Scriptures taken from the Holy Bible, New International Version®, NIV®. Copyright © 1973, 1978, 1984, 2011 by Biblica, Inc.™ Used by permission of Zondervan. All rights reserved worldwide. www.zondervan.com. The "NIV" and "New International Version" are trademarks registered in the United States Patent and Trademark Office by Biblica, Inc.™

Scripture taken from the New King James Version®. Copyright © 1982 by Thomas Nelson. Used by permission. All rights reserved.

Cataloging-in-Publication Data is available from the Library of Congress.

ISBN 978-0-8254-4886-7, print
ISBN 978-0-8254-6379-2, epub
ISBN 978-0-8254-6378-5, Kindle

Printed in the United States of America
25 26 27 28 29 30 31 32 33 34 / 5 4 3 2 1

To my husband and my children.
Thank you for your unwavering support and love.

Chapter 1

Another New Year's Eve, and Nona Taylor's prayer remained unanswered. Still. The digital clock on the microwave read 6:20. Five hours and forty minutes until midnight. Five hours and forty minutes until she begged God—again—to grant her one, her only, request.

The slow, pulsing ache behind her right eye required an immediate caffeine fix. Nona's gaze trailed toward her coffee station but jerked to a stop on the bill for her car affixed to the fridge by a Los Angeles Lakers magnet. The paper screamed "past due" in an all-caps, red-lettered font. Not possible to do her private investigation work without transportation, and the mountain bike propped in her guest bedroom's corner wouldn't cut it. Her gut clinched. Clipped behind the car bill were overdue notices for health insurance and townhome association fees, waiting like silent time bombs to annihilate the rest of her meager funds.

She scowled at her shepherd Lab mix, who lay sprawled on the floor, and snapped her fingers twice to get the dog's attention. "Move, Lady." Lady snorted, not ceding any ground. The throbbing behind Nona's eye intensified. One short yip from her Yorkie-poo, Bruiser, drew Lady out of the kitchen, giving Nona room to maneuver. Bruiser, the tips of whose ears didn't even reach Nona's knees, stood alert as a sentinel in the doorway. Lady outweighed ever-bossy Bruiser by sixty pounds, but Bruiser acted as though he descended directly from wolf stock. He gave Nona a yip as well.

Nona pursed her lips and filled her coffee cup to the brim with Italian roast. The smoky aroma wafted upward, and the first sip heated her mouth but did nothing to thaw the coldness in her heart. She downed the last few drops of her brew and placed the mug in the sink. Fully caffeinated, she walked to the front door of her townhome, averted her gaze from the full-length mirror in the foyer, and stooped to tighten the laces on her cross-trainers. Three clicks of her tongue called Bruiser, who skittered across the wood floor. She reached out and snagged his outdoor gear, squatted to his level, and worked him into his doggy jacket and step-in harness. He waggled his rump and gave a sharp bark, summoning Lady, who lumbered into the room so Nona could strap her into her control harness.

A pat on the head earned Nona a poke in the ear by Lady's cold, moist nose, and a lick.

Nona turned and nuzzled Lady. "I needed that." She blinked away the sting behind her eyes.

After confirming that her driver's and private investigator's licenses, along with her firearm permit, were inside the front pocket of her concealed carry leggings, she double-checked the manual safety on her Ruger MAX-9.

A windbreaker hung from the door handle of the coat closet. She donned the jacket, zipped it up, and yanked the scrunchie off her wrist. With a grunt, she wrestled her mass of thick dark-golden curls into a bun at the base of her neck and yanked a baseball cap low on her head.

The door to the downstairs guest bedroom opened on a swoosh. Her brother, Lemar, stood barefoot in the doorway, wearing a vintage Run-DMC T-shirt and athletic shorts. He scratched at the two-day stubble sprouting on his dark-tan face. He'd grown out the scruff for a potential acting role in a techno-thriller.

"I see a few gray hairs in that weed patch you're calling a goatee, bro." Four years her senior, Lemar didn't look a day over twenty-five, even though he'd celebrated his thirty-third birthday a few weeks prior.

"I see you're wearing your ninja costume." Lemar gave a soft smile. "Working a case?"

Anonymity was the goal of the black tights, black shoes, and black hat. Keeping a low profile was second nature in her line of work. "Nope. Taking the dogs out."

"I can walk them if you want to get some miles in or shoot some hoops."

On any other day, she'd jump at the offer to get in some time on the basketball court or take a run. She turned her head to the side, blinking a few times. "Not today."

"You going to be okay?" His gentle voice was almost a whisper.

Warmth generated by her brother's care tried to work its way into the numb space in the center of her chest. With his primary base in New York, Lemar flip-flopped between coasts, auditioning for roles, working gigs, and taking acting classes. She'd given him a key to her place years ago and told him he could crash anytime. His work was steady but low paying. He couldn't afford two apartments. But the arrangement worked well for both of them. He got a free place to live, and she got occasional company exactly when it seemed she needed it. Always protective and encouraging, he did whatever he could to arrange his schedule to spend the last days of December with her—he knew what it meant. She appreciated his efforts and his unconditional love, but no one possessed the strength to lift the boulder of guilt and shame that crushed her.

She drew in a long breath and pushed out a tight smile. "Yeah, I'll be okay."

Bruiser scratched with desperation on the front door's brass plate. The sound clawed at her strained nerves. Grabbing the leashes off their hooks, she drew in a long breath.

"When you get back from walking the dogs, pick up some takeout from California Pizza Kitchen. I'll treat." He gave a gentle smile, but the shadowing around her brother's eyes showed this ten-year anniversary of their family's loss saddened him as well.

"Sure." Nona tried to match his expression but gave up. She stooped and snapped a leash on each dog's harness, opened the door, and treaded out on legs weighed down with grief. Hoping to clear her head. Dreading the hours leading up to the stroke of midnight.

*　*　*

As desperate as Bruiser had been to get out, he and Lady took their time smelling random sidewalk litter and pawing at flowers on the median strip as they walked down the street of her live-work-play community tucked away in Old Town Pasadena. Darkness shrouded the shops' interiors, but uplighting showcased the merchandise immediately behind the glass. She stopped in front of Papier's Fine Pens & Stationery while Lady watered a square of grass at the edge of the walkway. Punctuating the Christmas display in the window were signs that read Bonne Année and 50% Off.

Her smartwatch vibrated, and she glanced down. Ken Fuller? Surely he wasn't trying to convince her to go out with him again. Last week, he'd asked her to some cheesy ball drop celebration. Since his company was her biggest—actually, her only—client right now, she'd let him down gently. Apparently, she'd cloaked her rejection in too many niceties. Besides, there was no way to tell him her plan was to ring in the New Year at a church's Watch Night service, like she had for the last ten years. At Watch Night, the church members thanked God for the blessings of the past year and committed the year to come into his hands. Nona would sit in the sanctuary feeling like a weed hiding among the wheat, hoping this was the year God would finally forgive her.

Bruiser strained his leash, urging Nona to continue their outing.

She double-checked her surroundings. Too exposed. She gave the dogs' leashes a gentle tug, shuffled backward into a storefront alcove, and faced the street.

"Sit." Nona clicked her tongue and pointed at Bruiser. She removed her phone from her pocket, and Bruiser showed Nona his backside. At least Lady obeyed and took a seat. "Ken. What's up?"

"I'm stuck at the office until later this evening, cleaning up a few things to close out the fiscal year." The flicks and flutters of rustling papers cut into the call. "Then, you know, off to that party." Ken gave an awkward chuckle.

She sighed inwardly and searched for yet another way to reject his offer without risking her bread and butter. She never revealed to Ken, or anyone else besides family, the significance that Watch Night held for her. "Well, Ken, like I said before—"

"Um, Nona." A muffled cough echoed from Ken's side of the line.

Ken was normally an overtalker, but now he was fumbling to put a sentence together. An itchy sensation crept up her neck and spread over her scalp.

"There's no easy way to put this. And I hate to do this on New Year's Eve, but the company is bringing all security and investigations in-house. Cost-saving measures. I've had to remove you from the books, Nona. Tonight."

She could not formulate words. The blood in her temples resumed pounding like a hammer striking an anvil.

"Nona, did you hear what I said?"

Her stack of bills. Now this. Tonight, of all nights. She held back a groan and forced her mouth to compose a sentence. "I understand."

"I'm really sorry. We'll get a check out to cover your last invoice as soon as possible. Sorry again for having to do this tonight. Um, happy New Year."

The phone cut off on Ken's end. Anger wrestled with anxiety and shame, jostling for dominance in the battle of emotions. She checked her watch. Couldn't justify putting off getting ready for church any longer. She turned to head back home, but her dogs resisted, still enjoying the fresh air. "Come. Now," she barked at them, her voice louder than necessary. Always the empath, Lady nuzzled Nona's fingers with her nose. Nona propelled herself back home, every step taken with compulsion and dread.

◆ ◆ ◆

Impending financial disaster hung over Nona's head like a wrecking ball poised to smash a table set with fine china. But as she stood in front of her closet, she willed herself to shove the monetary crisis aside to focus on choosing an outfit to camouflage the emotional mess she was inside—something that masked the pain and guilt she still felt after ten years. Something that covered the dread, laced with thin hope, that pressed and kneaded her heart, squeezing and twisting.

Her minimalist wardrobe contained few acceptable outfit choices. Most people would be at church to celebrate and would dress accordingly. She opted to make do with some dark-wash jeans and a maroon V-neck. She slipped her feet into some half boots and exited the closet, each step across the room made with legs that felt encircled by ankle weights. Tugging off the scrunchie, she raked her fingers through her hair, then gave her head a few shakes to bring some semblance of order back to her curls.

Nona eyed the mirrored jewelry box in front of her, perched on top of her bedroom dresser in silent judgment—daring her to work up the courage to open it.

After a calming breath, she reached forward and slid a finger over the lid and down to the pewter-colored closure that sealed in the memories. The small latch gave way, and she lifted the top. A porcelain ballerina emerged. Eternally on pointe, arms in first position, the figurine made a slow twirl as the melancholy notes of "Clair de lune" plinked out.

Her gaze fell to one of the two items inside.

A pristine photograph sat tucked on the underside of the lid. The darkness of the music box's interior had preserved the exquisite sun-kissed face she hadn't seen in person in a decade, the amber eyes and the perfect lips of Tyson Foster, the betrayer. She kept the picture to bear witness against herself. A reminder of exactly how far she'd fallen. How far she could fall again if she failed to keep every emotional defense fortified.

She shifted her attention to search for the second item. It lay undisturbed where she'd placed it last New Year's Day. She took a moment to steel herself. This would be the tenth year she repeated her ritual.

She lifted the slender gold chain from the box, but the attached charm remained behind like an anchor, revealing itself only when she pulled the entire necklace free.

A delicate, cursive letter N emerged. N for her sister, Nikki, not for Nona.

Nona's fingers shook as she pushed her hair aside and fastened her sister's necklace around her own neck. Her scarlet letter. Her mark of Cain. She wouldn't even make it to the Watch Night service if she started thinking about everything now. The raging argument she'd had with Nikki. The spiteful words inflamed with jealousy that she'd hurled and could never take back. Everything in Nona's life spiraled downward from that moment, that New Year's Eve. She needed to barricade the emotions within herself and get to church. Then she could pour it all out. Nona strode to the front door and grabbed the brown leather jacket hanging in the coat closet.

She stared down at the N nestled on her chest, but then forced her eyes upward to peer into the hallway mirror she'd been avoiding all day. She squeezed her eyes shut and tried to blank out her mind. Maybe this year, if she prayed hard enough, if she was sincere enough, God might forgive her, and the constricting bands of guilt choking out any semblance of peace might fall away.

She forced her lids open and locked on the face staring back. The same ebony eyes as her sister, Nikki. Every feature an exact duplicate of Nikki's face. Identical twins distinguished only by a small mole on Nona's cheek. Same lips, same cheekbones, same nose.

And the eyes of Nikki's killer.

Chapter 2

WHAT A PATHETIC little church. What a stupid time to hold a service.

Ten o'clock on New Year's Eve, and the meeting didn't start for another hour. Zeke Steele's target sat wedged between a Quicky Mart and a hookah bar in a strip mall in the Crenshaw area of Los Angeles. Even if he believed the stuff being spouted inside that building, he'd never heard of a Watch Night service. A ridiculous waste of time on a night made for booze and partying.

Movement near the church's entrance caught Zeke's attention. He lifted the night vision goggles to his eyes. An old man held a key, which he used to unfasten the padlock securing the chains around the sliding metal gate in front of the building. The man pushed the gate back from the left and right sides of the door, fiddled with another lock, and entered. Probably the minister, Hosea Grant. This shoestring operation couldn't have any other staff.

Ancient fluorescent lighting sparked to life inside, and a sign awoke. Mount Zion Missionary Baptist Church blazed out in flickering red neon.

Zeke had scoured the internet for intel on the church's hours, pictures of the interior, and personnel stats. The church's Facebook page featured an old posting about a Labor Day potluck. They had posted nothing else until right before Christmas, when a grainy announcement about tonight's service appeared.

His phone vibrated in the cupholder of his rental car. He seized the device and jabbed the red End button, sending Councilman Gavin Calloway's call straight to voicemail. Micromanager. The notification badge now showed three new messages. The councilman didn't trust Zeke to do the job he was paid to do.

Zeke snorted. "Don't trust you either, Calloway." His derisive words pushed from between his lips along with a cloud of cigarette smoke.

Hard to imagine that this bent-over pastor of a hole-in-the-wall, inner-city church stood to inherit land worth millions from the estate of old Millie Carter and didn't even know it. Zeke shook his head and chuckled. The lawyer he'd scratched up to help him run this scheme called it a "laughing heir" case. The beneficiary was a relation so distant from the decedent in the family tree that instead of mourning the decedent's death, he'd laugh all the way to the bank to cash in the windfall.

Zeke tossed the still-lit butt into his half-empty coffee sitting on the dash. This was his last late-night stakeout. No more shaking down businesses and bribing contractors to line Calloway's pockets. If Zeke played his cards right, he could fund his own operation.

The clattering of his burner phone once again snagged his attention, and he swore. After snatching it up, he stabbed the Talk button with his finger. "Listen, Calloway, I'm tired of—"

"It's me, Zeke. Baby, it's me." The shrill voice of his girlfriend, Kitty, cut through his tirade.

Clamping his forehead between his index finger and thumb, he gave a squeeze. "Hey, darlin'. I'm on stakeout. What's up?"

"I'm missing you, is all," Kitty drawled.

A phlegmy cough rattled out of Zeke, and he fished around his breast pocket to find another smoke. It had taken his otherwise ditzy girlfriend only seventy-two hours to track the old pastor down after Calloway had turned over what little information he'd had. She loved those genealogy detective TV shows. A week later and here he was, two thousand miles from Alabama, sitting in a cramped Kia, staking out an old man who didn't know he was set to hit the jackpot. Kitty was probably calling him to keep tabs on him, same as Calloway, but she only knew what Zeke wanted her to know. Like his bootlegging granddaddy taught him, never trust a woman.

He readjusted himself in his seat. "That's sweet. Don't forget, when I get back, I'll get you that mink coat you've been going on about."

"I'd rather have a ring." Her voice trilled up hopefully.

"Sure, baby. Whatever you want." He choked back his snort. She wasn't getting a fur or a ring.

Kitty sighed. Silence ticked over the line for a beat. "Saw Big Zeke today."

At the mention of his father's nickname, heat flamed inside Zeke. He reached for his coffee cup, then clunked it down in disgust, remembering the extinguished butt he'd tossed in. "Where'd you see him?" He kept his voice neutral, but there were only a couple of places Kitty could have seen his daddy. When Zeke Sr. crawled out of his hole at night, he was either holding court at the bar—sloppy drunk and spinning lies about his glory days of college football—or staggering down the street trying to make it back to crash with his woman of the month.

"Saw him coming out of one of his usual places. You know your daddy."

Sure did. Revulsion at having to live in Big Zeke's shadow fueled the desperation inside him to make this con game work. The physical blows stopped years ago, but now it was a nasty word, a request for a handout, or both from his daddy. Zeke couldn't wait to disappear from his old life and his old man. And with the money he had coming, he would. He'd move into a sweet high-rise apartment in Vegas.

The plan was simple. Zeke would sucker Pastor Grant into selling the property to Calloway for a low five-figure amount. He'd given the codger a fake ninety-day deadline to ratchet up the pressure. Then Calloway would keep Leisure Zone Holdings dangling on the line and eventually sell to them for the millions the land was worth. With both the old pastor and Leisure Zone in the dark about each other, there'd be a six-figure windfall for Zeke and Calloway.

Burnt Water wasn't big enough for two Zekes, and Calloway sickened him. Zeke couldn't wait to put his hometown in his rearview mirror for good. "Gotta go, darlin'." He pressed End and worked to calm the boiling sludge in his gut. Once he lifted the binoculars back to his eyes, he pursed his lips and made a low wolf whistle. "What have we here, sports fans?"

A slim woman in a leather jacket tried the front door of the church, peered inside, and held up her phone. She turned to face the street. What a looker. She had a wild head of honey-colored curls framing her face. He let out a little growl. What was this she-cat doing at a church at this hour? She put the cell phone to her ear. The pastor let her in after a second.

So the old saint had a pretty young thing on the side. Figured. What man of the cloth wanted his dirty laundry about girlfriends aired to his congregation? This low-level gospel pusher didn't deserve to inherit millions of dollars' worth of land.

Zeke mentally added *blackmail* to his list of things to do. He'd get the preacher to trust him to handle all the arrangements to secure the inheritance. Next, Zeke would have the man sign away his rights, so the parcels would automatically flip to him and Calloway. Then Zeke would bleed the man dry, taking every penny the pastor had in exchange for keeping his mouth shut about the she-cat. A double take.

A chuckle slipped out. Didn't know where the idea had come from to take this shakedown for a percentage like an ambulance-chasing attorney instead of charging Calloway his normal hourly rate. It chafed Zeke's hide that Calloway claimed a bigger share of the proceeds, but the dirtbag had insisted that since he had pieced together all the necessary tracts of land and had manipulated the zoning commission votes to build the entertainment complex, he deserved the bigger cut.

No matter. With the property, Zeke's 25 percent take of seven figures would be ample seed money to set up shop down in Vegas, earning him the respect he deserved. He was done living under the thumb of any man, Calloway or his daddy. Zeke cycled through all the things he planned to do and buy. He'd drop Kitty for a high-class girlfriend. He'd get a Cadillac SUV, veneers, a twenty-footer to take out on Lake Mead. It made him smile thinking about it. Finally, everyone would take him seriously.

Zeke figured a week—two tops—out in LA to get the old pastor to sign on the dotted line. Zeke would be rolling in the dough a few months after that. He took a drag, reclined his seat a few inches more, and hoped the ridiculous New Year's church service wouldn't last too long.

"You're doing this, Steele. All the way." He glanced at the flickering neon cross on the storefront, flipped down the visor, and stared hard at his reflection in the mirror. He'd show Calloway and Big Zeke. His grandaddy had the right idea. He always said, "*If you really want it, do what you gotta do to get it.*" Zeke gave a nod, sealing his promise to himself. The bigger the money, the bigger the risk. If somebody had to die for him to cash in, so be it.

Chapter 3

Nona plopped into the guest chair in Pastor Grant's office. She watched the pastor while he shuffled around, trying to find some papers. In the years since she'd known him, his stature had diminished. Perhaps the effects of carrying other people's most painful burdens—like hers. But his movements remained sure. A ring of short white Afro hair circled a shiny brown bald spot dead center on the back of his head.

She'd left his voicemail message in her inbox for several days before guilt and the red notification badge on her iPhone made her cave and listen to his plea to come early to talk to him about an urgent personal matter. Pastor Grant called from time to time to check on her, but this whole thing better not be a ruse to have some sort of heart-to-heart. He knew better than to ask her to attend service any time other than her annual Watch Night pilgrimage.

As Pastor Grant bustled about, she took in the bookcases jam-packed with books. The spines on some said *Commentary*, while others had the names of the apostles on them. She recognized Billy Graham on another. Who didn't know him? All the books bore evidence of frequent usage. She shook her head, forcing herself to turn off her inclination to catalog and mentally record information. Hazard of the trade.

"Found it." He waved a manila packet in the air, sat on his seat, and slid the envelope across the desk toward her. "Tell me what to make of this."

She noted the return address: Javit, Blatt & Steele, Birmingham, Alabama. She slid several papers from inside.

We are an heir hunting firm and specialize in locating people who are unaware of their potential inheritance. This is to notify you we believe you are one of the legal heirs to the estate of an individual who died in Alabama. Because of the expense involved in locating and representing heirs, the law does not require us to disclose the name of the decedent or the potential amount of any inheritance until after you have entered into a retainer agreement with our firm. Time is of the essence. If you do not file notice with the court within ninety days to secure your claim as a beneficiary, any inheritance to which you may be entitled will escheat to the State. Please contact our office immediately to secure your valuable claim.

"I've done some skip tracing but never any heir hunting. Have you considered hiring an attorney?" She flipped the papers over. On the back were blank lines for Pastor Grant to enter his identifying information.

The old preacher took off his glasses, ran a hand over his face, and resettled the spectacles. "I don't have an attorney, plus I want someone I can trust. Don't want to give out my personal information, birth records, driver's license, to any ole body. I didn't want to call them, because this may be one of those identity scammer things to steal my money." Wrinkles of worry creased his brow. "I can't pay you now, but I can give you a percentage out of any inheritance. After paying off a few bills, I'm going to give the rest to the church."

Her thoughts flashed to the past-due notices on her fridge. This thing might eat up more time than she could spare. She needed a paying job immediately, and she needed to search starting on Monday. On the other hand, if this law firm was legit and there actually was an inheritance, it could be quite substantial. She bit the inside of her cheek and reexamined the front of the letter carefully. Hesitation and the urge to help wrestled in her brain.

Pastor Grant gave a small cough, and she looked up. His filmy eyes regarded her with kindness.

She sighed and ran the mental calculus one more time. She wasn't a member of his church and only attended once a year, but he had officiated Nikki's memorial and done some grief counseling with her family. He always sought her out, year after year, on Watch Night to offer a kind word and to tell her he never stopped praying for her and her family. Over the years, even in their brief interactions, he'd somehow created a safe place in his sanctuary for her. One without judgment. Sure, she could sink a ton of time into this all for nothing, but how could she not help someone who had always been so nice to her?

She shook off her indecision. "Tell you what. I can do some preliminary investigation and see what I turn up. If this firm seems legit or I'm able to uncover information that shows you are an heir of an estate in Alabama, we'll decide what to do from there."

Voices carried into the pastor's study.

"Oh dear." Pastor Grant peeked at his watch. "I need to pray and get ready to preach."

Humming and singing drifted into the room.

"I hear the deacons are starting up with devotions." He stood. "Let me make a copy of these papers so you can take them with you." Pastor Grant moved to an ancient Xerox machine in the corner and ran the pages through.

She stood by the door, ready to leave.

Pastor Grant handed her the papers and squeezed her shoulder with his hand. "Thank you, Nona. I can't tell you how much this means to me."

"You're welcome. See you in service."

She exited into the small hallway. Resignation and sadness slid over her. For the few moments in his office, she'd been clinical, weighing pros and cons, but now the guilt and shame that drove her to seek absolution during this night's service reached out with their dead fingers and squeezed her heart in their cold, unforgiving grip. New Year's Eve, ten years ago, she'd started everything by hurling at her sister venomous words designed to inflict maximum emotional damage.

Tyson told me he loves me, not you. I'm the one he wants, not you. You know what? I wish I never had a sister.

Hot recrimination mortified her. Tyson was cheating on Nikki—with Nona—and fool that she was, Nona had desperately hoped Tyson would dump Nikki and pick her. She had crushed Nikki with those hateful and untrue words, and her sister had fled, leaving behind the smack of the slamming front door and the grinding of their car's engine. The last glimpse Nona ever had of her twin alive was of Nikki's retreating back. Nona could never forgive herself for her wicked treatment of her sister, and neither would God.

Chapter 4

WELL, OLD LADY, you win.

DeMarcus Johnson picked a parking space for his baby under a light fixture and as far from other cars as possible—no dings, no dents, no damage—and readied himself to make good his promise to his beloved grandmother, G'Mama, to attend church once during the calendar year. He scanned the row of storefront businesses across the street. A couple of dudes in gang colors stood in the doorway of a store right beside the church. Fortunately, DeMarcus's C-Class convertible didn't have the distinctive Mercedes hood ornament, because that crew gave off a vibe like it might want a souvenir. Didn't matter. He'd let them know the deal before he went inside the church.

He loved G'Mama, but she played dirty. Said she wouldn't cash another one of his monthly money orders until he made good on his repeated promises to go to church sometime this year.

"And it better be a Missionary Baptist Church too, 'cause how else I'm gonna know it's a real gospel-preaching church?" she'd told him. *"And I want proof. Send me, what you call 'em? A selfie. Send a selfie showing me you there."*

Busted. She'd mastered the texting feature on the senior citizen cell phone he'd sent her for her seventy-fifth birthday, so there was no way out of it.

No one would believe it if they heard he planned to spend New Year's Eve inside a church. Not his boys back home in Baltimore, not his teammates from Princeton, and not the attorneys at his law firm. He'd trusted Jesus as a kid. Got baptized too. Even prayed occasionally. God knew his heart. There'd be time for all the church stuff in the future, but right now, he wasn't ready to settle down and play by all of God's rules. He flipped his wrist to check the time. December thirty-first, five minutes till eleven. Promise kept.

He smoothed his fingers over his mustache and down around his goatee. He lifted his phone, angled to the side to make sure the church's neon sign lined up in the center of his screen, snapped a pic, and texted G'Mama. A chuckle escaped. He wasn't worried about disturbing her. She'd be up to pray at four o'clock anyway.

He was going to lose the facial hair come Monday as he dug in for his bid to make partner at his firm. His boys would call him corny, but to make partner he'd dial back on his swag and channel Steve Urkel. As soon as he'd grown old enough to shave, his granddad had clued him in.

"A real man wears a mustache."

He'd fallen in line with his grandfather's admonition and grown it out, marking his entry into adulthood. But now? He'd miss his mannish fashion statement, but business was business, and the partners at this firm liked things on the traditional side.

Another time check. Service started in three minutes. Good. Didn't want to be even one minute early for church. He slid off the watch and locked it in the glove box. His TAG Heuer might tempt someone. After clicking the key fob to activate the security system, he dodged a Prius as he jaywalked toward the Quicky Mart.

He eyed the trio in front of the store. Younger than his first guess. Maybe thirteen, fourteen years old. Old enough to get into trouble but too young to call the shots for their crew. Spotters. If G'Mama hadn't filled his every waking hour with school, basketball, and church, he'd have had his own assigned corner to guard when he'd been their age.

He shifted his face to neutral, approached, and gave a slight nod. "Sup, fellas?"

"Like your whip," one of the crew with a do-rag and sagging pants called out. "Let me take it for a spin. Promise I won't break nothing."

He smiled at the kid's bravado. "I'll think about it."

The boy's friends scrunched up their faces and jostled each other as he squeezed by.

The smell of nacho cheese and pine-scented car air fresheners permeated the store. He snagged some Tic Tacs, broke a twenty-dollar bill instead of using his credit card, and fisted the change. Organ music pushed through the wall that adjoined the church. Time to stop stalling.

The crew still loitered around the entrance. He strolled over and addressed the one who'd spoken to him earlier. "Watch my ride." He stared at the boy and extended his hand with the folded bills sticking out discretely.

The kid slapped his hand, gave it a shake, and took the money. "You got it, player."

He pivoted from the kid and walked toward Mount Zion to get it over with. *Only for you, G'Mama.*

The front door opened into the sanctuary. No vestibule, no warning. An elderly man in a black suit approached and handed him a program. "Welcome to Mount Zion's Watch Night service."

DeMarcus looked around and oriented himself. Bodies packed all the folding chairs aligned in neat rows of ten, broken in the center by an aisle. At the front of the church, facing the congregation, a line of six middle-aged men stood, swaying and clapping.

Glory, glory, hallelujah, since I laid my burdens down.
Glory, glory, hallelujah, since I laid my burdens down.

One of G'Mama's favorites. The organist improvised and riffed. One woman lifted a tambourine and started slapping it against her wrist as the medley of hymns continued.

I'm gonna stay on the battlefield.
I'm gonna stay on the battlefield.
I'm gonna stay on the battlefield till I die.

The clapping intensified, and the tempo increased.

At the name of Jesus every knee will bow.
At the name of Jesus every knee will bow.

Man, this took him back. The church's most senior and respected women, all in white. The old songs.

Someone pressed close to his elbow. "Let me help you find a seat."

The music slowed while the usher led him up the center aisle. Near the pulpit, a thin man in a suit knelt beside a chair and began singing, chanting, praying, and moaning all at once. A second gentleman, wearing a gray shirt and a red bow tie, stood beside him, hand on the first man's shoulder. Others—DeMarcus guessed deacons—flanked him, rocking back and forth slowly, tapping their feet. Some were nodding, giving forth a "Yes, sir. Amen."

The usher led DeMarcus about midway down the aisle and pointed into the row. DeMarcus squeezed past a woman holding a sleepy toddler and focused his eyes forward. It had been a long time since he'd set foot inside a church. His neck itched.

The moaning deacon at the front rose to his feet. Everyone else sat. A gentleman, who appeared to be in his seventies or eighties, was behind the podium and addressed the audience. "Turn with me, if you will, to the book of Isaiah, the fortieth chapter, and the thirty-first verse. Stand when you have it."

Furious rustling of pages began. The older ladies on the Mothers' Board popped up to stand first.

DeMarcus made a face. He'd forgotten about all the standing and sitting. Plus, he didn't have a Bible. He whipped out his phone.

"'Those who wait on the Lord shall renew their strength; they shall mount up with wings like eagles, they shall run and not be weary, they shall walk and not faint.'"

The pastor recited the text from memory, not even glancing at the page. "The Bible says . . ."

The Watch Night crowd gave a hearty amen to that.

"'For what profit is it to a man if he gains the whole world, and loses his own soul? Or what will a man give in exchange for his soul?'"

DeMarcus had only been inside the building for about fifteen minutes, but it already felt like an hour. His desire to pay attention cratered, and his ADHD flared. He swiped up on his phone. With luck, ESPN could occupy him until this whole thing ended.

◆ ◆ ◆

Mercifully, the sermon lasted twenty minutes. Only one thing left to endure—Watch Night prayer—and he'd have satisfied his obligation to

G'Mama. DeMarcus bowed his head. He could come up with a few things to pray about.

Movement in the empty seat beside him caught his attention. He angled his head to the right. A woman had slipped in while he was praying. He shifted, and she glanced at him. Women didn't make DeMarcus nervous. Ever. But the tear-spiked black lashes over near-black irises, plus the reddened nose and shuddering breaths, caught him off guard. He couldn't make himself stop staring. He felt sorry for her. What could make someone so sad on New Year's Eve? As he continued watching, her head tipped to the side, and a furrow appeared between the beautiful brows. The perturbed set of her mouth said sorrow had shifted to ire.

When prayer ended, the pastor dismissed the congregation, but DeMarcus held his seat. Time for a full-court charm offense.

"I'm DeMarcus Johnson." He extended his hand and waited.

The spikey-lashed eyes flicked down to his hand and back up to his face. The mystery woman returned to facing forward, clasped her hands together, slammed her lids shut, and began moving her lips.

More praying?

O-kaaay. Women had dismissed DeMarcus before, but rarely. Even four-time NBA Championship winner LeBron James shot a brick once in a blue moon. But dissed with prayer? *Well, whatever.*

She resembled that princess girl married to that redheaded dude, but with a thicket of crazy-curly hair. DeMarcus's distracted mind shifted to England. He snorted. What a waste of airtime on ESPN. Their stupid tennis match used up two precious weeks of prime post-draft NBA coverage. *Focus, dude!* He wrestled his brain back to the interior of the church.

He tucked his phone inside his pocket. Gentle organ riffs covered the chatter from the churchgoers enjoying each other's company, and crying girl still sat beside him.

He chanced another glance. Her eyes remained closed, so he may as well take his time and check her out as long as he'd like. What was she doing here anyway? Mount Zion wasn't some international feel-good Los Angeles church, but a straight-up, down-home, Sunday hat–wearing Mothers' Board, anyone-with-the-title-*pastor*-invited-to-sit-in-the-pulpit Black church. This girl, with her golden-brown ringlets cascading down her back, was . . . what . . . biracial? Brazilian, Hispanic, or something. He couldn't tell.

The crowd in the sanctuary thinned out to a handful of people. The girl beside him kept on praying, and now tears rolled down her cheeks. Women. He slid his phone back out and tapped Google to find the route from Crenshaw to Sunset Boulevard. As soon as he found the directions, he was out of here. Still plenty of New Year's left.

◆ ◆ ◆

This had been the last empty seat when Nona had returned to the sanctuary. She hadn't even looked at the dude beside her when she sat. She felt his presence and smelled his cologne but kept her eyes shut tight. Who wore Drakkar Noir anymore? Must be some teen who borrowed his dad's—scratch that—his granddad's cologne. She squeezed her lids together more tightly, not wanting to see or talk to Drakkar Noir Jr. Her seat jiggled in time to his bobbing leg.

Tears still wet her face. Arms crossed, she rocked herself forward and backward. She rubbed her hands up and down her forearms to ward off a chill. But it wasn't cold. Not even by Los Angeles's standards. Still, her innermost soul felt frozen solid. When the clock struck midnight, one more year would have passed since Nikki's death. One more year since Nona's careless words ripped her sister's heart from her chest and sealed it in a box Nona didn't have keys to open. She had made her annual pilgrimage to church to cry out to God and ask why. But what was the point? She'd come to ten years of Watch Night services. Ten years of silence. She hadn't given up on God. He'd given up on her.

She cracked open one eye to glance at her row-mate and spied a giant Italian loafer–clad foot bobbing up and down on its toe. Drakkar Noir had the "jimmy leg." Figured. Chancing a slightly higher glance, she spied deep-brown hands with manly, blunt-cut nails and a huge class ring on one of his fingers. So juvenile.

Church had ended. Why didn't he leave already? The guy cleared his throat, and she peered up at his face. Chocolate-browns stared back at her. Hard.

Oh my.

She rolled her eyes at him, stood, and walked back toward Pastor Grant's office.

◆ ◆ ◆

A kid in the row ahead of him dropped a Hot Wheels car that landed at DeMarcus's feet. He bent over to pick it up and hand it back, and the kid rewarded him with a gap-toothed smile. He glanced to his side. The diva with the tearstained face and don't-talk-to-me attitude had disappeared. Whatever. Time to get out of this church. After picking out his next move of the evening on Google Maps and checking to make sure no reservation was needed, DeMarcus stood to leave. A glow of light caught his eye. A phone lay on the chair vacated by trouble-in-heels. He surveyed the room. She was nowhere around, and the place had emptied quickly.

He turned to a deacon, who stood, keys ready to lock up. "Did you see a woman, about five eight, long curly hair?"

"Nope. We're closing it down. I'm locking up as soon as the few people in here leave."

I'm going to regret this. Palming the phone, DeMarcus headed for the door. He'd get the phone to her somehow.

◆ ◆ ◆

DeMarcus's eyes flew open at the frantic barking and blaring of "Who Let the Dogs Out" coming from somewhere in his bedroom. He thrashed about, trying to find the source of the racket, then remembered. Stretching out his arm, he used his fingers to fish about on the nightstand and picked up the lost phone. His bedside clock said six thirty in the morning. The display on the phone said "ICE Lemar."

"Hello." His morning voice pushed out gruffer than he'd intended.

"So you *did* steal my phone."

DeMarcus shook his head. It wasn't ICE Lemar. "What?"

"I said"—the voice spoke slowly, as if to a small child—"You. Did. Steal. My. Phone."

Everything tumbled into place, and he sat up, wide awake. "Woman, I did not steal your phone."

"If you didn't steal it, why do you have it?"

"I have it because you carelessly left it." He growled. "The sun isn't even up on a Sunday morning. Why are you up in my grill?"

"Up in your grill? A giant class ring on your finger, and the best sentence you can come up with is, 'up in my grill'? Did they teach you that at Princeton?"

She *had* checked him out. And she'd noticed his ring. He shifted to smooth mode. "I take it you liked what you saw?"

"Look, DeMarcus . . ."

"And you remember my name . . ."

"I don't have time for this. What I need is to get my phone back."

"Meet me for Gospel Brunch at the Blues Café, and I'll give you your phone there. Nice public place. Nothing to worry about."

"Nuh-uh."

"Why? ICE Lemar can't be the holdup. I mean, yeah, you're calling from his phone at oh dark thirty, so something's up. But what dude lets his woman go to Crenshaw by herself on New Year's? Plus, I didn't see a ring, so Lemar's asleep at the switch."

DeMarcus rolled onto his side. He enjoyed talking to—still didn't know her name. That's all right. He had a name for her.

"You don't even know what you're talking about."

"Oh yeah, Sassy. I definitely know what I'm talking about. So about brunch."

"Like I said, not gonna work. You know what, I'll report it lost and get a new phone Monday."

"Hold on, hold on." This wasn't going as he expected. "You lose your phone. I save it for you. You call me on a Sunday morning, wake me up, and now you dismiss me."

He heard a sigh on the other end.

DeMarcus pressed ahead. "Tell you what. I live off the 110, north of downtown. Are you anywhere near there? I'll bring it to you personally."

There was a loud bark followed by some yipping in the background. He heard some muffled talking. "We'll go outside in one minute."

It was hard to understand, but he figured it out.

"My office is in Pasadena. Can you be here at ten?" She gave DeMarcus an address.

"I'll see you at ten."

◆ ◆ ◆

Lemar had rolled his eyes when Nona told him a guy she'd met a day earlier was coming with her phone. She could handle herself. The man's outfit had screamed "lawyer" in all caps. He'd had several thousand dollars' worth of clothing on his back, and he was in church on a Saturday night. Lemar was home, Lady and Bruiser were on guard duty, and there was no way for DeMarcus to know her street-facing office doubled as her home on the backside. Besides, worst-case scenario, she'd shoot him with her concealed handgun.

Nope. Not worried.

She'd try to be nice and thank him, then dismiss him. She grabbed some disposable bags and jangled the leashes. Ready for their midmorning excursion, Lady and Bruiser rushed her at the front door.

The video doorbell rang, and Nona eyed DeMarcus on the monitor. Lady and Bruiser continued their fracas. Okay, he was extremely handsome, albeit doused in cologne at Watch Night. A tapered haircut. A short-sleeved button-down and khakis offset by brown, brown skin. Not a blemish or imperfection in sight.

Lemar sidled up beside her, pausing in his preparations to leave for a callback in Studio City. "You going to get it, sis, or do you want me to?"

"I'll get it. You finish getting ready."

A few more seconds and Bruiser was going to piddle on the floor. She steeled herself and opened the door.

DeMarcus stood angled sideways with his hands in loose fists. He slowly opened them, revealing two dog treats. *The gall!* Lady and Bruiser inched forward, and each lapped a snack from a hand. He patted them on their heads, then fixed his attention on Nona. Those dogs were absolute traitors. Chomping on the treats DeMarcus had given them, they made their way to their favorite bush growing in the patch of grass next to her door.

"So, Sassy. Were you going to have your dogs eat me after I gave you your phone back?"

Nona tried but couldn't suppress a smile. "How'd you even know I had dogs?"

"Normally a magician doesn't tell his secrets, but I heard you talking to them when you called me."

The dogs wandered back to Nona's side. DeMarcus crouched down, reached into his pocket, and extracted a cellophane bag. He offered the dogs more goodies. "What are their names?"

"Lady and Bruiser."

DeMarcus patted the giant shepherd Lab on the head. "Hey, Bruiser."

He reached for her tiny Yorkie-poo. "Hey, Lady."

Bruiser growled.

"Most people assume my big dog is the male." She gestured to the smaller dog. "That's Bruiser."

Bruiser stuck his tail straight in the air and widened his stance.

DeMarcus stood. A resonant laugh, smooth as honey, rolled out. He was tall. She guessed six foot three or four. If she were in heels, he wouldn't loom over her five-foot, nine-inch frame. Wait. Why was she thinking she'd see him again?

Lemar came up beside her. "Hey, man. I'm Lemar."

"DeMarcus Johnson. Nice to meet you."

"Thanks for returning the phone. You want a reward or something?" Lemar reached into his back pocket.

DeMarcus waved him off, slid the phone out of his pocket, and handed it to Nona.

Lemar faced her. "I gotta go. You good?"

"Yes. I'm fine. See you tonight." She leaned in. Lemar kissed her on her forehead and hustled down the walkway.

She trained her attention on DeMarcus. He'd drawn his eyebrows together and made a slight shake with his head.

"Sorry I was so . . ." She swiped an errant strand of hair from her face. "Rude?"

"Yeah. Sorry I was so rude. And thanks for returning my phone."

"You're welcome . . ." DeMarcus held his hand out, indicating she should fill in the blank.

"Nona. My name's Nona."

"You're welcome, Nona." DeMarcus palmed the back of his neck and scuffed the bottom of his loafer on the stoop. "So, take care, Nona."

"You too. And thanks again."

"Oh, here." He handed Nona the bag of dog treats.

"Thanks." She checked out the gourmet dog chews. Not the usual peanut butter–flavored Milk-Bones within her budget.

DeMarcus stepped down, took a couple of backward steps, turned, and strode to his car.

"Come on, you two." Nona snapped her fingers, and the dogs followed her back inside. She locked the door and watched DeMarcus drive off on the video feed.

♦ ♦ ♦

DeMarcus reran his brief interaction with Sassy Nona. She was even lovelier when she wasn't crying or snarling at him. Lemar. What was up with that dude? A woman as gorgeous as Sassy? She had perfect lips, and Lemar kissed her on the forehead like an uncle? Not buying it.

The gift of hyperfocus had saved DeMarcus's life on the streets of Baltimore. It had also turned him into a star on the court. Was the shooter going to take it to the hole? Post up and shoot a jumper? Did that head fake mean a pivot to the left or right? He watched their eyes, not their feet, not their hands. The eyes never lied. That quick check to the side showed the opponent's true intentions. Was this corner safe? Whose tag was on that building? What color was the guy on lookout wearing? Had he crossed the line onto a different turf?

He would give Lemar his props. Bro was tall and built. Women would call him handsome. But DeMarcus really only needed to know one fact about the guy. Was Lemar Nona's man?

DeMarcus shook his head, trying to dislodge the woman from his thoughts. What intrigued him so much? Why couldn't he kick her out of his mind? She'd played the church girl last night but was torn up about something. Lemar? Or something else? Well . . . DeMarcus had a street address and a first name. Didn't know how, but he'd figure out some way to see her again.

Chapter 5

THE MOUTHWATERING AROMA of fried food and baked goods greeted Nona from the sidewalk before she even entered Mama's Chicken & Waffles. Pastor Grant had asked her to meet the first Monday of the New Year to discuss the letter from the heir hunting law firm and had suggested a famous soul food restaurant well-known by locals and Hollywood types. She'd need to put in some extra miles on her bike this week because she planned to have sausage links and bacon with her order.

Nona was grateful Mama's kept the vibe mellow for the breakfast set. It was too early for the upbeat Motown classics that greeted the raucous crowds packing Mama's after regular restaurants shut their doors and comedy club gigs let out. Pastor Grant had requested a seven o'clock meeting, and the smooth jazz floating down from the speakers helped ease Nona into full alertness.

"Can I get you something to drink?" A woman with blond braid extensions and glowing skin the color of pristine sand jutted out her hip and applied the tip of a pencil to a small pad of paper.

"Coffee please, black. And water, no ice."

"Want to order now too?" The waitress tapped her pencil eraser against the pad in time to the music from the speakers.

"No thanks. Waiting on someone."

"Back in a second." The waitress and Pastor Grant crossed paths as he made his way to the table.

"Sorry I'm late. Sister Jones called me this morning at six to tell me her aunt back east passed away." He sat, unrolled the napkin from around his fork and knife, and rubbed his flatware against the tissue before placing the napkin on his lap.

The waitress reappeared to take their orders, and Pastor Grant asked a half dozen questions about the different combo platters. "I'm going to need a minute to decide. Could I get some iced tea to start?" He pushed his glasses farther up his nose and studied the menu.

Nona swallowed small sips of the scalding hot coffee, willing the caffeine to kick in instantaneously. Out of nowhere, DeMarcus Johnson floated through her consciousness and prickles crawled up her neck. After the nuclear fallout from Tyson's betrayal and Nikki's death, Nona had shoved all thoughts about dating into a mental closet with a locked door. She tried to swat down the image of DeMarcus's smile like an annoying gnat, but his cocky mug buzzed back around. Remembering his expression when Lemar kissed her goodbye . . . Was DeMarcus interested in her? Self-recrimination slammed her back to reality, and she frowned at her mental slipup. She had no right to think about any man in that way after what she'd done.

"Who was that young man talking to you at the service, Nona? Never seen him at a Watch Night before."

The old pastor wore quarter-inch-thick glasses, but he didn't miss a thing.

"Some guy. I don't know him." *Liar, liar.* She knew tons of stuff about him. That's what Google was for. Pastor Grant didn't need to know about DeMarcus's LinkedIn page. Or his squeaky-clean Instagram with all the outfit-of-the-day posts, still shots from his Princeton glory days on Throwback Thursdays, and endless pictures of basketball shoes. He was always squinting and plastering on that infernal smile, which didn't fool her one bit. A man even handsomer than DeMarcus Johnson had caused her to turn on her womb-mate and best friend. She'd never let a pretty face and smooth words deceive her again.

"He had on a sharp outfit. Handsome. Was in church on New Year's Eve too. Can't be all bad."

Wrong again. Pastor Grant had no clue how bad a person sitting at Watch Night could be. She, with her bloodstained hands, was exhibit A.

"Wish I'd had a chance to greet him." But whatever he said next slipped past her.

"I'm sorry. What was that?"

"I said you look like you're thinking about something serious." His warm eyes held nothing but patience.

Even with the pain burning as fresh as it had ten years ago, she had no intention of turning this breakfast into a psychoanalysis session. Plus, early that morning, the bill from her internet service provider pinged into her inbox. Only a first notice. Not past due, but still. The quicker she shifted this conversation to the inheritance case, the closer she was to a potential payout.

The waitress reappeared with the tea and her order pad, leaving Nona a graceful exit from the difficult conversation she never planned to have with Pastor Grant. "I'll have two eggs, sausage, and bacon." She'd save the waffles until her bank account stood on more solid footing.

"No waffles? Nonsense," Pastor Grant interjected. "That's what this place is famous for. Not as good as my wife's. Whoo-whee, she could cook." He winked at the waitress. "Add a side of waffles to that. On me." He gave the waitress his order as well.

Unexpected stinging made her eyes water, but she would not, could not, let any moisture gather. "Thank you, Pastor."

As soon as the waitress departed, Pastor Grant peered at Nona. "Any thoughts about the inheritance?" Traces of expectant hope emanated from his caring face.

She regained her composure and smoothed on a pleasant expression to cushion her words. Best to give it to him straight. "I've done some research on the Javit, Blatt & Steele law firm." She dug her phone from her bag and opened the Notes app. "They handle personal injury and minor criminal cases. Drunk driving, shoplifting, low-level drug possession. Nothing on the internet to indicate that their routine caseload includes probate and estate matters."

Pastor Grant's countenance fell. "You think the letter is a scam?"

The remaining hope in his eyes made her temper her words. "I'm not saying that at all. There is a possibility of a lucrative upside for a firm that handles an heir hunting case. Maybe the firm is new to this area and is starting to take on these sorts of cases."

The waitress returned with a huge tray stacked with their food. She placed fried catfish, scrambled eggs, and a waffle in front of Pastor Grant, and delectable toasty waffles, along with the sides, in front of Nona.

"Thank you, Miss"—Pastor Grant stared at the name tag pinned below the waitress's collar—"Crystal." He gave the woman a smile. "I'm a pastor. We'll pray for you when we say grace."

Unexpected tears welled up, clumping the woman's lashes. "Thank you so much, Pastor. Nothing for me, but please pray for my boy, Jamal. He has a custody hearing next week." She swiped under her eye. "He's a good son and a better daddy to my grandchildren."

"We will." Pastor Grant gave Crystal the type of smile a loving father gives his daughter.

The waitress departed, and Pastor Grant clasped his hands together. "Let us give thanks." He bowed his head.

Hot shame burned behind Nona's closed lids. Grace and bedtime prayers had been daily occurrences during her childhood with Nikki and Lemar. Sunday school. Youth camp. Even in her early teens, she'd clung to the certainty that God loved her and had forgiven her sins.

But not anymore.

As her mother told her when she misbehaved, *"God don't like an ugly attitude."*

The words Nona had said to her sister the night she'd driven her out of the house to her death went beyond *ugly* all the way to *hateful.* Jealousy and envy had filled her heart and loosed her tongue like a fire and set her on a path to hell. She'd been fooling herself all those years during her youth, when she thought she was safe and secure in God's arms. Oh, she still believed in God, but there was no way he wanted anything to do with her.

"Amen."

At Pastor Grant's benediction, she opened her eyes and lifted her head, and the bile of remorse backed up in her throat. She'd been so caught up in herself that she hadn't even prayed for her food. Such a simple act, yet more evidence she was lost. Her appetite vanished. The waffles and fluffy scrambled eggs looked like bricks. She pushed the plate away and settled her phone in front of her, hoping Pastor Grant overlooked the sudden turn in her mood.

"While you eat, I have some questions. I think we can reverse engineer your search for the estate." She swallowed another sip of her coffee. "We'll go back through your family history and see if we can find potential relatives who are the right age and who lived in or moved to the right location."

Steam rose from Pastor Grant's catfish as he cut into it. He held the fork aloft and nodded in agreement before plopping the forkful into his mouth. He chewed a couple of times. "I didn't toss that inheritance paper as soon as I opened it because of the Alabama return address. My family goes back generations down there somewhere. Wish I knew where."

"We'll work on piecing it all together. Let's start with your history. What were your parents' names?"

"My father was Booker Grant, and my mother's name was Florence."

"And do you know your mother's maiden name?"

Pastor Grant scratched his head. "I want to say it was Hall, but I'm not 100 percent certain."

"That's fine. We're simply gathering facts." Nona typed the information into her phone. "Were you born in Alabama? If so, your birth certificate would be very helpful."

"No." He shook his head. "I was born in Mexicali, Mexico."

She coughed, choking on her drink. "Really?" After locating her napkin, she pressed it to her lips and coughed again.

"Seems odd, but the way I remember the story—" He took another drink. "At some point during the war, Daddy had been a driver helping supply fuel for combat vehicles. Something called the Red Ball Express." He tipped his glass, drained his tea, and gave a satisfied grunt. "After the Red Ball Express ended, he was shipped off somewhere else. He returned stateside in the spring of 1946. I guess Mama turned up pregnant with me soon after. He never really talked about the war much. One thing he did say, when I was coming up, was that after being in France, he'd vowed no child of his would grow up under Jim Crow."

He chewed a bite of his eggs. "My memories get fuzzy on some points. I think I remember Daddy telling me he'd picked California so he could work in the shipyards in San Diego. It took them a while to make the trip across the country, because their car kept breaking down. Daddy would pick up daywork here and there to pay for repairs. By the time they were close to California, Mama was ready to burst. Closest doctor who would see her was across the border, so they went there."

"Are you a US citizen?"

"Absolutely. Born to two parents who were US citizens, but my original birth certificate is in Spanish."

Crystal approached the table. "More coffee? Refill your tea?"

"Yes, please." Pastor Grant gripped his glass to steady it.

Nona pushed her mug closer to the edge, so Crystal wouldn't have to lean in. "Do you have a copy of your birth certificate somewhere? That would be helpful."

"I do, but I need to figure out where I put it. It's been so long since I needed it. Think the last time I saw it was when I showed it to someone when I signed up for Medicare about fifteen years ago. Maybe my wife stashed it somewhere. When cancer hit her, she said cleaning helped keep her from dwelling on things. She cleaned up my office so good, all my important papers disappeared." A half sigh, half laugh escaped from him. "Besides, by the time you reach my age, no real reason to prove you were born anymore. The numbers people are more worried about are the measurements for the suit they'll wear when they're on the way to glory."

She winced. He'd been there with her as she stood over Nikki's closed casket. At the time, his words of comfort had rolled off her like rain sluicing off a newly waxed car.

"Whether or not you like it"—the pastor's voice tugged Nona back from the most horrible day of her life—"death is coming for us all. The only question is, are you ready to meet the Almighty?" He removed his glasses and used his tie to clean them. A sheen of moisture covered his cloudy eyes. "Sometimes it seems like just yesterday my sweet Elsie passed, rather than thirteen years ago."

As always, when Elsie's name entered a conversation, emotions overcame Pastor Grant. Nona envied his freedom to mourn his wife's loss without guilt or recrimination. The years since Nikki's death had come and gone in the blink of an eye. All the laughs and secrets and their twin bond lived in her heart as fresh today as they did before she'd let a man step between the two of them.

Nona squeezed down the acid churning in her stomach, stamping out the discomfort by shifting her thoughts back to Pastor Grant. "With the ninety-day deadline in the letter from the heir hunting firm, if you can't find your birth certificate in a day or two, I'll research how to get a new copy from Mexico. Did your parents ever talk about where they were born?"

He regarded her but said nothing about her rude pivot in the conversation. She steeled herself and zeroed in on the present. He needed help, and she needed the money. While this inheritance case wasn't instant cash, it might be in the thousands, and she could really use a hunk of money like that coming in at one time.

"Nona, I'm sorry. All of this happened so long ago. My parents never returned to Alabama. From time to time, Daddy talked about possibly going back home. Mama would get glassy-eyed or stare off into the distance. Lips pressed together. Shoulders stiff. He and Mama fought about it two, maybe three times. In those days, children were seen but not heard, so I kept my mouth shut."

"That seems odd." She tilted her head to the side.

"You have to understand the times." Pastor Grant pushed his chair back from the table and folded his hands over his belly. "When I was about nine or ten, Daddy came to me one day after work with tears streaming down his face. I'd never seen my daddy cry. He sat me beside him and shook and shook. Then he stared dead in my eyes and said, 'Emmett was visiting from Illinois. Not even from Alabama. If something like this can happen to a boy from up north . . .' He never finished his sentence. My parents never talked about going back to Alabama again. I found out from some of the other children at school about Emmett Till being lynched. All that happened back in '55."

Nona recalled the gruesome picture she'd seen in middle school during one Black History Month. To have lived through those times must have been so scarring.

She pushed away the horrid thoughts. "Do you have any family still living out there we could talk to?"

"I was an only child. Lost Daddy back in the '80s, and I believe he had a couple of brothers who died before him. Mama passed a few years later, in '91. I know Mama had a sister, who she called Lizzie, and a niece, whose name I can't recall. Mama's nephew died in Vietnam. One day, Mama pulled out what she called her family Bible, and she mentioned him. Told me she was writing his name in there. Called him Skip. I remember that, because I always thought it was funny. Probably just what he went by at home. Not what his birth certificate said. But that's just a guess. Saw her shuffle some other papers in the front of that Bible, but we never talked about the past. I only caught snatches. I think it hurt my parents too much. Now I wish I'd asked more questions or at least glanced at the papers in her Bible. I'll try to find that too."

"At this point, we don't even know if the inheritance is on your mother's side of the family or your father's side."

"You know, I never thought about it that way. Here I was, assuming it was on Daddy's side."

"Any reason? Was there some money or land that you knew of on your father's side?"

"I recollect something about sharecropping and some parcels. Don't know why that's in my head. I heard my parents talking about a plantation one time, and I remember that because we'd studied the Civil War in elementary school. I didn't ask questions. You know my generation. Stuff like that would come up at school, and I wanted to slide down in my seat and disappear. People didn't talk about history in the right way. I always felt small and less than, even though I didn't live in those times."

"Well, do you remember them mentioning any city or town?"

Pastor Grant stroked his chin for a moment and chewed his top lip. "I know they were from the same town. Also, I remember thinking as a child that my parents came from someplace funny, something involving nature or water. Crooked Creek, Black Water, River Head. Not sure."

A faraway expression clung to his face. "It's like there's a big hole in my childhood. My family shook the dust off their shoes and never looked back, but I don't know exactly why." His chin quivered.

Why was she only now realizing this might be painful for Pastor Grant? The elderly man was all alone. A widower without children. She'd been so caught up in her own pain and financial worries that she'd never focused on the fact that he'd been grieving as well. She reached over and squeezed his hand lying on the tabletop. "I didn't anticipate all the memories this search would dredge up for you."

He used his free hand to pat the top of hers. "The pain of losing loved ones never goes away, Nona. The world is fallen. We are fallen. As a result, death stings. But the Lord's been faithful and has sustained me all these years. And one day, I will see him, plus my family, face-to-face." He lifted his fork again but paused. "What other information do you think you need right now?"

"Anything you can find will help. Obituaries or funeral programs your parents may have saved. We need to figure out where this estate is and who the decedent might be."

"As soon as I get back to the church, I'm going to find my birth certificate and that Bible." He wagged his finger.

"Those two items will help us piece together a family genealogy and track down the estate."

The attentive waitress handed Nona a to-go box and slid the check on the table. "Pay up front. Take your time. And thank you again, Pastor."

"Of course."

Nona reflexively reached for her purse, but Pastor Grant held up his hand. "This is on me."

Relief mixed with mortification swept over her at his gracious financial gesture.

Pastor Grant fumbled in his wallet, removed a five-dollar bill, and placed a card on top with his name and the church's number on it. "Always like to leave my card with the tip. Never know when someone might need to talk." He scooped up the tray holding the check and signaled Nona to exit ahead of him.

Outside, the bright sunlight drove Nona to reach into her handbag for her sunglasses. Fumes from a passing Metro Bus caused a sneeze. Pastor Grant escorted her to her car, gave a small wave, and made his way to his vehicle across the street. Somehow, he'd been able to piece the broken shards of his own heart back together since his wife's death. He was still getting around, still driving himself. He held on to hope and kept pressing forward, so close to the very end. The thought of carrying around the shame and weight of her guilt for another fifty years felt like an anvil on her chest. She tossed her breakfast in the trash can beside her car, slid into the vehicle, and drove off. Would working so closely with Pastor Grant rip the wounds in her soul wide open?

Chapter 6

A GUSH OF chilled air blasted Nona's face at the front door of the Automobile Club of Southern California. Restlessness to get up close and personal with her research on the heir hunting case had driven her out of her home for this field trip.

Days of searching the internet had failed to yield any clues. Pastor Grant still couldn't locate the Bible or his birth certificate. Without the name of a town or a county to narrow the search, she might as well throw a dart at the map of Alabama and start there. And that was the rub. She needed actual maps. She wanted to scan them with her eyes. Mark them with a pen. She could wait at home for five days for Amazon to deliver the maps she needed, or she could burn a few gallons of gas and get them herself. Impatience won the battle.

A pang of nostalgia caused a sting inside her nose and behind her eyes. Dad had loved everything car related. The haggling for a good deal. Killing a couple of hours washing and waxing his vintage 1971 VW Super Beetle. Visiting the flagship Automobile Club of Southern California close to downtown for maps and TripTiks to plan family vacations in the summer. And driving by the one-hundred-year-old Moreton Bay fig tree, with its gnarled, exposed roots, at Christmas to see the lights.

She stepped aside to allow two spritely senior citizens wearing matching tennis visors to exit the building. While the women bustled each other down the stairs, Nona scanned the meticulous landscaping and historical architecture of the massive three-story Spanish Colonial Revival–style building. Her entire body felt laden with weights, and she swallowed a lump in her throat. The trips to AAA ended when her parents' marriage dissolved not in fiery drama but in icy silence. Nona remembered the day she came

44

home from school and her father was gone. He simply left, never to return. The best explanation her mom could conjure was that he needed to "find himself."

Without Dad, they'd clung together the best they could. But heartache and regret caused walls to go up, closing what had been open avenues of communication. Days of stilted talk turned into weeks of the barest conversation. Right before Nona's sophomore year of college, the rest of the family collapsed in slow motion. Traces of Nikki's life haunted every crevice of the hollowed-out ranch house, and Mom couldn't stand it. She moved back east to be closer to cousins, aunts, and uncles when Nona returned to UC Irvine that fall. Lemar went off to New York to pursue his dream of acting.

Nona entered the Auto Club's lobby, and the convex-domed ceiling, with its gold inlay design, caused the voices of the customers inside to bounce off the walls. The racket drew her back from the past.

A sign pointed her to a waiting area on the right, and she queued up behind a man in walking shorts and a pastel T-shirt. He peeled off and walked forward to an open customer service agent.

"Next customer." An efficient-looking man with a glistening forehead fringed with receding hair gestured her direction.

She stepped forward, extracted her AAA card from her wallet, and slid it across the counter to him. "I need a statewide map of Alabama and any Alabama city maps you have."

"Planning a trip back east? It's a long drive. We can compile a TripTik for you." The name tag on the man's AAA employee shirt read "Paul."

"Not a trip. Helping a friend with some . . ." She rummaged around mentally, searching for the right word. "Genealogy research."

"Oh, I love genealogy." Paul's eyes widened, and based on the gulp of oxygen he sucked in, he was winding himself up for a long speech.

Nona flipped her wrist over and gave her watch a pointed stare. "Maybe next time, Paul." She pasted a smile on her face, clinching her teeth to hold her terse words behind them.

"Right, right." Paul's fingers danced over the keyboard in front of him. He held up a finger. "I'll be right back."

The song "I Don't Want to Wait" slipped its way inside her brain as it emanated from a speaker hidden somewhere in the room. True divine irony, as restlessness jabbed and poked her insides. She wouldn't be able to keep that song from playing on mental repeat for the rest of the afternoon. She and Nikki loved watching reruns of *Dawson's Creek* in high school. Sweet nostalgia rose inside her at the memory. Nikki had been Team Pacey, while she'd been Team Dawson. Joey had ended up with Pacey, leaving Dawson in the cold. Nikki had ended up with—

"Here you go." Paul thrust his findings toward her.

At his words, she pushed away the hurt and guilt from the past and corralled her attention back to the present.

The stack included maps for Birmingham, Montgomery, and Mobile, a statewide road map, plus a brochure entitled "Plan an Alabama Getaway." Exactly what she needed.

"Thank you very much." A genuine smile worked its way onto her lips.

Remorse gripped her as she watched the discomfort drain off Paul's face. She'd been rude, and she'd hurt his feelings. She didn't want to be this way, but since Nikki's death, her emotional reserves ran on empty and her brittle patience crumbled at the slightest inconvenience. Every day, something reminded her that the person she'd been didn't exist anymore and had been replaced by the hollowed-out shell of a woman. All the fond memories from visiting Dad's happy place evaporated, while dejection, heaviness, and cold, laced with recrimination, nagged at her conscience. Her hands tightened on the reason for her visit, crumpling the maps. Her grasp loosened, and she straightened her back and turned to leave.

She picked up her stride and exited toward the parking lot, squinting as the ever-bright Southern California sun reflected and radiated off every available surface. She'd commandeer a table at a coffee shop and begin her search. Determination kicked in. Did she need the money? Absolutely. But it was more important to find Pastor Grant's family. She'd help him win his inheritance, which he'd use for his church. Then, maybe, somehow, the scales measuring the weight of her failures with God would tip back to even.

The always-present smoky sent of ground coffee beans mixed with toasting cheese lured Nona toward the Starbucks counter.

"What are you having?" The barista's spiky fuchsia hair poked out from the front of a slouchy beanie.

Caffeine, definitely. But hot or cold? She eyed the menu board, and a caramel-drizzled, whipped cream–topped concoction made with blended iced mocha called her name. The prices were sky high, but the indulgence might lift her spirits. She added a butter croissant to the order, paid, and scouted out a table where she could keep her back to a wall and charge her phone. She plunked the maps down to save her spot and parked herself at the pickup counter.

"Jane," the barista called.

Nona stepped forward and picked up her items. Baristas always received an alias. Jane Doe, Miss Marple, Sydney Bristow. Didn't matter. Snack in hand, she sat down and unfolded the entire Alabama state map. Google had been a waste. It had been fruitless trying to reverse engineer a city name without knowing if the ones Pastor Grant had suggested were even in the ballpark. Circling and highlighting on the internet were impossible, and she wanted to keep track of her progress. Pastor Grant needed something to jog his memory. A list compiled from her visual grid search of an Alabama map would pick up city names, river or creek names, or any other data that might help narrow down the potential hometown of his family.

After locating the northwesternmost corner of the map, she refolded the entire thing so only one four-by-nine-inch section faced her. While a chewy piece of the croissant occupied her mouth, she found a pen in her bag, left it capped, and began methodically running the tip across the page, guiding her eye to the name of every town, waterway, county, and city in that rectangle.

In the background, the rhythmic bongo of Toto's "Africa" competed with the loud hissing of the espresso machine.

Nothing in the first quadrant. She reopened the map accordion style and positioned it so she still had a view of the northernmost portion of Alabama, but now the next rectangle to the east was her focus. After depositing another bite of buttery goodness in her mouth, she scanned the page, tracking with the pen to avoid overlooking a potential location. Again, no likely targets.

Forty minutes later, after all the folding, unfolding, and refolding of the map, she had a list of weird and funny names that had popped out at her. She spread out the map, located her highlights, and made sure she'd compiled in her Notes app all the promising candidates. She scanned her entire list again. Double Springs, Paint Rock, and Burnt Water. Odd names for towns. She'd keep them on the list. The unincorporated city of Burnt Corn south of Tuscaloosa and Little Ugly Creek almost due east from there might jog Pastor Grant's memory. Murder Creek southwest of Montgomery and Puss Cuss Creek near the Alabama–Mississippi border could also be strong candidates. Finally, near the bottom of her list was No Business Creek northeast of Birmingham.

She typed the church's fax number into the Fax app on her phone and hit Send. She pushed aside her mild irritation with Pastor Grant for still living back in 1999 and dealing in hard copies, not digital content.

At this point, she and Pastor Grant had only burned about a week of the ninety-day deadline listed in the heir hunting firm's letter. Her goal was to circumvent Javit, Blatt & Steele and help Pastor Grant secure the inheritance himself, but right now there was so little to go on, and she didn't know if Pastor Grant could even remember the town. Plus, she wasn't a lawyer. How was she going to prepare and file the papers in Alabama? She shook the ruminations away. She'd cross that bridge when the time came.

◆ ◆ ◆

"Sorry, lady. Your name's not on the list."

The beefy man with a military-style crew cut stood in front of Nona and held a clipboard as he guarded the entrance to the ballroom at the Beverly Wilshire like it was Fort Knox. The earpiece jutting from the side of his head connected to a wire, which disappeared into his collar.

Looking beyond him, Nona made out a series of sparkling chandeliers, and the strains of "Y.M.C.A." being played by a DJ drifted to her ears. "I know I have that invitation somewhere. Can't you double-check one more time? It's Nona Taylor. That's Nona with an N, not Mona with an M."

The guard rolled his eyes but began methodically running his finger down the top sheet of paper in his stack.

While Gigantor scoured the list for her name, she considered diversion scenarios, casually turning her head from side to side to scout out alternative entrances to the ballroom. She pretended to rummage in her purse for the nonexistent invitation and shifted to her right to get a better view over the man's shoulder.

She *had* to get inside. Pastor Grant had called her within an hour of receiving her list of Alabama towns and waterways. He'd latched on to the name Burnt Water with near 100 percent certainty, but he'd said the reason for his assurance kept eluding him.

One website clocked the population of Burnt Water and the surrounding area at fewer than ten thousand people, but the city had access to a major highway and was about an hour away from Mobile. She'd run Burnt Water through various search engines. Tingles crept up her neck when an article popped up in the Lifestyle section of the *LA Times*. This had led her to an online press release for a company based in Los Angeles. While the bouncer continued paging through the guest list, she sneaked a peek at the printed copy she'd shoved in her purse to make sure she'd burned the faces of the CEO, COO, and chair of the board of Leisure Zone Holdings into her memory.

Leisure Zone Holdings is proud to once again co-sponsor this year's HeartSpark Hands for Change Valentine's Charity Ball, which raises funds to support after-school care, summer bridge programs, and scholarships for students in Title 1 schools. Joining us are dignitaries and officials from various states where we have operations, including the governor of Arizona; state senators and representatives from Texas, Utah, and Missouri; and Councilman Gavin Calloway from Burnt Water, Alabama, who is spearheading our latest venture in family entertainment destinations, which will be located outside of Mobile, Alabama.

Pictures of various men making power poses in conservative suits accompanied the press release. She hadn't figured out the connection between Burnt Water and California yet, but the fact that Burnt Water was smaller than some suburbs in Los Angeles and yet garnered a mention in the Lifestyle section of the *Times* had caused a clinch in her gut. The information had spurred her into purchasing a dress she couldn't afford to crash a glitzy society party without an invitation.

Time was slipping away on Pastor Grant's claim. According to the letter from the heir hunting firm, he had a little over six weeks left to sign their retainer letter to secure his rights. For her to locate the estate, Nona needed more than the name of a town. She also needed the identity of the right decedent. Burnt Water did not have any digitized local papers with obituaries, and Pastor Grant still had not found the Bible. If she couldn't get this thing solved in the next few weeks, it might force him to take his chances with the heir hunters.

The giant tank blocking her way moved farther to her left to speak with someone from the hotel staff, and she had an unobstructed view into the ballroom. Attendees swirled around on the parquet floor as waitstaff deftly maneuvered through the crowd and delivered nibbles and cocktails. Wait, what? Did her eyes deceive her? A mere twenty feet away, she registered a quick glance of a man's profile. A precise tapered fade, the posture of an athlete, a glint of light—that ridiculous signet ring. *Bingo.* The cockiest man in America, DeMarcus Johnson, surrounded by a quartet of corporate honcho types, threw back his head and gave a laugh. Whatever amused DeMarcus ended, and he turned and sauntered into the crowd.

She tugged the guard's jacket sleeve. Adrenaline pushed her mouth ahead of her brain. "My fiancé's in there." She pointed toward DeMarcus. "His name is DeMarcus Johnson. He's with . . ." She hesitated. *Come on, think.* She rummaged around in her memory. "Livingston, Meyer & Kendrick." She sidled up beside the man, reached out a hand, and flipped a few pages. "There." She stabbed her index finger on the paper. "There's his name. Can I go in now?" She dipped her head a bit and peeked at him through her lashes.

Lurch narrowed his eyes.

She blinked a few times to appear as harmless as a baby deer.

"Fine." He grabbed her wrist and fastened a band reading "HeartSpark Hands for Change Foundation" around it. "Have a great time." He dismissed her with a wave of his hand, his voice signaling he hoped she had anything *but.*

She entered the ballroom, spotted DeMarcus at her three o'clock, pivoted, and moved in the opposite direction. She scanned the lush interior for her targets. Votive candles twinkled atop crisp linen tablecloths. White fabric swathed the chairs encircling the tables, and chiffon sashes tied into bows behind the seat backs secured everything in place.

She eyed her Donna Karan sheath dress, picked up for a steal on consignment. The stress knot in her stomach loosened. The peachy-gold draped material fit in with all the full-price designer gowns floating around. She'd march the dress right back to the shop Monday morning and put it on consignment herself. Hopefully, someone else would snatch it up quickly and she'd recoup most of the expense. Couldn't keep it. The price obliterated her budget.

Somehow, she needed a dance with someone from Leisure Zone Holdings or the city councilman, so she could chat them up. The wall-to-wall bodies made finding them difficult. What seemed like a good plan while hunched in front of her computer in her living room now might turn out as a hot mess. What had she been thinking?

A hand clasped her upper arm in a firm grip. *Please, please, please don't let it be the guard.* She turned in the offender's direction. Not the guard. A balding man, probably early forties, with bags under his eyes, pushed into her personal space.

"Dance with me, pretty lady?"

Stale breath reeking of tobacco assaulted her nose. The guy wore a tuxedo like the other men, but the pants showed an inch of ankle, and he'd dribbled some cocktail sauce on the front of his shirt. He had the battered visage of a once-handsome ex-jock trampled over hundreds of times by heavy defensive linemen.

"There you are." DeMarcus appeared on her other side.

Relief and irritation at DeMarcus's sudden apparition dueled it out inside her. She didn't want to talk to him right now, but the man in front of her gave her the creeps. Nona returned her gaze to the stranger. "Sorry." She darted a glance at DeMarcus. "This fine gentleman has next dibs."

"How 'bout the next one?" A smarmy smile worked its way over the guy's lips.

"He's my fiancé. I'm sure he wants me all to himself." She trained a direct stare into DeMarcus's eyes and used mental waves to plead with him to play along. The fake-fiancé lie had ushered her into this ballroom, and now she'd use it to break off from this whack job without causing a scene and getting herself bounced.

DeMarcus slid his hand around her waist and drew her close to him. She could smell his signature scent. For some bizarre reason, it soothed her jitters. He clasped her to his side and turned to the guy. "Sorry, man. Her dance card's full tonight."

Without another word, DeMarcus ushered her through the throng on the dance floor to an area to the side, which hosted several standing bistro tables covered in tablecloths capped with vases of orchids. The DJ shifted into a popular Michael Bublé song, and a crowd swelled close to DeMarcus and Nona's space.

She readied a grudging thank-you to DeMarcus for his rescue and steeled herself to force gracious words from her mouth.

His eyes—hypnotic and smug as all get-out—shone back at her. "I know you're into me, but stalking?" He tsked, amusement clear on his face. "Doesn't seem like your style."

She stepped back. "I'd planned to thank you for helping me out of a jam, but . . ."

"And now we're engaged as well. You're moving pretty fast, don't you think?" A slow smile, at once humorous and dangerous, graced his infernal mug.

Why did his teeth sparkle? Why did his tuxedo have to fit so well? His broad shoulders filled out the black suit like a Calvin Klein model. He'd eschewed a cummerbund but had a black bow tie with orange shields on it. She squinted. Princeton!

"So you are here at this event because . . ." He tipped back his head and gave a molar-revealing smile, which no doubt caused other women to fall in love within seconds.

It made her want to smash a plate of canapés into his conceited face.

"I'm working on a case. I'm a private investigator, and I needed to gather some information without tipping off anyone about my reasons. It's all good now, so thanks. I have things to do."

"Not so fast, Sassy."

No one had ever burrowed their way under her skin and annoyed her as much as DeMarcus "Big Head" Johnson. The childish thought made her laugh.

"Something funny?"

"It's nothing." Her frustration cooled a few degrees. "Thanks again."

"You owe me a dance, woman."

The music crescendoed, and a man dipped a lady right beside them, almost knocking them over.

"It's the least you can do, seeing as how we're engaged and all."

She shot him a withering stare. "Fine."

He placed a hand on the small of her back and steered her farther into the crowd. Bublé gave way to the "Macarena," and DeMarcus launched right in. His long-wingspan arms folded and unfolded over each other as he patted his shoulders, then his stomach. He slapped his rear, which forced a laugh out of her. Not a shy bone in the man's entire body.

She glanced across the room and caught sight of the bozo in the too-tight tux who'd tried to get her on the dance floor. He was talking to the councilman from Burnt Water. Ashtray-Breath had access to the very men she needed to investigate, and she'd turned the guy down. Unbelievable. Now what? She stalked off the dance floor and marched to the powder room to gather her thoughts without giving DeMarcus a backward glance.

Chapter 7

THE PERENNIAL GEEZER tune "Celebration" by Kool & the Gang lured all able-bodied attorneys, spouses, and guests to the center of the dance floor to shake their collective groove thangs. DeMarcus hovered by the punch bowl, back turned to the crowd, hoping he'd blend in enough to avoid the hit his reputation would take if anyone saw him dancing to his grandmother's favorite song. He still reeled at having agreed to a fake engagement five minutes earlier only to watch his newly minted fiancée dash to the bathroom before he could compose himself.

He needed a moment of solitude to gather his thoughts. He wanted Nona to return so they could come up with a plan. But no time for either, because job one for all the attorneys at the firm was mixing, mingling, and otherwise wooing potential clients under the guise of supporting HeartSpark Hands for Change. His thoughts spun in a dozen different directions.

"Oh, DeMarcus . . ."

Not now. The warbling trill of Sylvia Meyer's voice carried over the din of the party. Of all the attorneys' spouses, he liked Sylvia the best, but his insides clamored for space to think, and *chatterbox* was the woman's middle name. He arranged his expression into an agreeable mask and turned to face the managing partner's wife.

What he wouldn't give for one of the other associates to arrive at the punch bowl so he could implement a backdoor screen play, cut behind the serving table, and avoid talking to Sylvia. No such luck. "Oh, hey, Sylvia. May I get you a glass of punch?"

"Absolutely not." She waved her hand in the air in an aristocratic and dismissive manner. "Kool and the Gang is playing. I *have* to get out there.

Mitch is talking business with some client or another, and he's left me all alone." She gave a slight sniff.

Can't win if you don't play, Johnson. He gave Sylvia his Colgate smile. "Of course. I'd love to."

He escorted Sylvia to the dance floor and began his law-firm two-step. Side to side in rhythm. Discrete finger snaps, but no head bobbing.

"You're a won-der-ful dancer, DeMarcus." Sylvia's dance motions mimicked either rowing a boat, churning butter, or both.

"Thank you, Sylvia." He gave a genuine smile. She always treated him with motherly concern.

The song faded out. He gave a nod to Sylvia to exit the dance floor, but the next instant, the DJ dropped Sinatra's "I've Got You Under My Skin," and she latched her arm over his shoulder. Fine. Some schmoozing happened during a golf game, some under the hoop. But the best time to curry favor with the wives of partners occurred over cocktails or on the dance floor. Once he placed Sylvia a safe twelve inches away, he secured her left hand in his and placed his right hand high on her back, making sure that every surface of his hand touched fabric.

He pushed back his impatience. Nona had reemerged and now stood in a corner. She appeared to be lurking or eavesdropping. Her hair framed her face like a coiffed lion's mane. Curls and swoops gave her the appearance of a fierce queen. The dress was tasteful dynamite. Nothing inappropriate, yet the shimmering, almost glowing, material fit and moved with her in a way that drew second and third glances. This fake engagement needed resolution ASAP.

"Did you hear what I was saying?"

He dragged his attention back to Sylvia. "I'm sorry. Thought I saw someone I knew on the other side of the room."

Sylvia gave a quizzical look. "You're not fooling me, pretending you see an old friend."

He pulled a face. What was Sylvia talking about?

"Congratulations on your engagement, silly."

"What . . . I . . ."

"She's lovely, DeMarcus. So glad you've finally settled on one."

How? He scrambled mentally.

"If you could see your face." Sylvia gave an affable titter. "I heard you two on the dance floor. Jim Jeffries tried to dip me right beside you." She gave his arm a pat. "And you two, trying to keep it all hush-hush." Sylvia winked at him. "Does Mitch know? I want to be the one to tell him. How exciting!"

His brain glitched, and no words formed in response. Until this moment, the existence of the fake engagement remained between himself, Nona, and the loser who'd tried to drag her onto the dance floor. Now, his split-second decision to play along with her had escaped its containment barrier and spilled over into his real life. Time for a scramble defense.

"Sylvia, it's all so new. We're keeping it quiet for now."

"Nonsense." Sylvia patted him in a motherly fashion. "I've never told you this before, DeMarcus, but you're my favorite associate at the firm. I don't have a say in partnership decisions, but . . ." She hesitated. "The legal profession is full of sharks. They're quick on their feet with sharp elbows, if you know what I mean." She dropped her arms, stopped dancing even though the song continued, and gave him a frank and appraising stare.

A couple bumped into their immobile bodies, and he steered her from the dance floor over to the hors d'oeuvres table. "Sylvia . . ."

"I'm not done." Softness came into her eyes, and she continued. "I've watched you over the years. You're respectful of the partners, gracious with their wives. Mitch has frequently mentioned you are a team player. You work hard but don't seek the glory for yourself. I've always thought to myself that beneath all your charm and bluster, you're a decent young man. So I'm thrilled that you're settling down."

As much as his ego wanted to meditate on Sylvia's compliments and what they meant for his partnership chances, he was desperate to escape this conversation. A sentence formed, but a flare went off mentally. Under no circumstances would he risk Nona's cover. He'd agreed to play along, because her Iron Lady exterior had slipped for a moment, and he'd seen genuine fear in her eyes.

A bright smile tipped up Sylvia's lips, and she gestured in a come-hither manner to someone behind him. He turned, and his gaze clashed with Nona's, the object of Sylvia's excited summoning.

"Really, Sylvia, there's no need to . . ." His words died in his throat as Nona started in their direction. How could he stave off the impending train wreck? It was one thing to play engaged to keep Nona undercover. Another for him to come out as engaged to the partners and staff at his firm. Nona glided with feline grace toward them, the look on her beautiful face as blank as a high-stakes Vegas poker player. He had no clue what thoughts swirled inside her.

He'd been a shot caller on the court, running the plays. Time to take charge.

"There you are. I've been looking all over for you." The moment Nona stood close enough, he reached out, snagged her hand, and nestled her close to his side. She rounded on him, and he gently squeezed her fingers and intertwined them with his. "Babe, this is Sylvia Meyer. Her husband is Mitch, one of the senior partners." He gestured with his free hand toward Sylvia. "Sylvia, this is my fiancée, Nona." Yikes. He still didn't know her last name. Sweat broke out under his tux. He gave Nona's hand a few more squeezes, hoping she'd pick up his signals.

"Mrs. Meyer, so nice to meet you." Nona cut a suspicious glance at him.

Sylvia seemed oblivious to the awkwardness. "Oh, hush, dear. Call me Sylvia."

The music died off, and someone onstage announced an intermission for the DJ. Without the loud music, the clank of forks on dessert plates and background chatter filled the room.

From out of nowhere, Mitch sidled up to his wife and gave her a kiss on the cheek.

"I hope DeMarcus hasn't been boring you with shoptalk, sweetie." Mitch's eyes twinkled, his glass of zinfandel the probable cause.

DeMarcus felt Nona's attempts to extricate her hand from his, but he gave another squeeze. They'd hash out this whole thing after he could ditch Sylvia and Mitch.

"No. Mitch, I have the greatest news." Sylvia's breathless voice caused DeMarcus's gut to clinch. "DeMarcus is engaged, dear. Isn't that wonderful? This young lady here is his fiancée, Nona."

Mitch's attention bounced between DeMarcus and Nona, his mouth slack with incredulity. "I don't believe it." Mitch gave a snort and slapped

DeMarcus on the back with his free hand. "I'm delighted. Where did you two meet each other?"

"We . . ." Moisture beads broke out on Nona's neck.

". . . met in church." He finished her sentence for her and angled a glance, daring her to refute the stone-cold truth.

Nona started coughing beside him.

"Do you need some water?" Concern crossed Mitch's face.

"No, I'm fine." Nona gave a sniff.

Yet again she tried to remove her hand from DeMarcus's. He didn't let go. He was certain she hated it, which made him smile. She'd ensnared him in this mess. She'd have to gut it out.

"Let go of her hand, DeMarcus. I want to see the ring." Sylvia fluttered and fidgeted with excitement.

"Well, actually . . ." Nona started.

"Don't be shy, Nona." Sylvia reached for Nona's left hand, which he still gripped in his own.

"I just popped the question tonight." He set Nona away from his side and peered into her eyes. The ink-colored irises with the dark fans of lashes hypnotized him. She squinted a bit with a hint of snark behind it—a challenge. He held in a laugh. Her sass made her even more beautiful. "She looked so gorgeous tonight. I knew I wanted to ask her to marry me on the spot. I couldn't wait to do all the prep for a proper proposal, so I called an audible. She floated out her front door, mesmerized me, and I dropped to one knee." He trained all the megawatts of his smile at Nona.

She gave a look that held a hint of menace.

"Aw. That is so romantic. Don't you think, Mitch?" Sylvia squeezed her husband's arm.

"You bet, sweetheart. Plus, nothing I like more than an associate with a spouse and a mortgage. Those are the kinds of attorneys that work the longest hours and bill the most."

"You are shameless." Sylvia gave Mitch a playful swat. "He's kidding, De-Marcus."

"Only a little, sweetheart." Mitch laughed.

Mitch's words struck a chord. The possibilities of the fake engagement paraded before DeMarcus's eyes in real time.

He needed to execute a trick shot. Right now. He worked his Princeton ring off his finger and snagged Nona's left hand again.

"Nona, babe. Until I can get you the ring you want, this will have to do." He slid his Princeton ring onto her thumb. It fit like it was custom made. Her eyes now shot deadly electron beams as if she were a Marvel superhero. He lifted his hand, brushed a curl away from her ear, leaned in, and whispered. "Don't lose my ring, woman."

Sylvia let out a squeal. "Oh, Mitch. Isn't that romantic? Reminds me of high school. He gave her his class ring." She clutched her clasped hands to her heart.

The DJ returned and spun up a slow love song.

"I want to talk to you on Monday, Johnson." Mitch stroked his chin. "I have a case that's"—he gave his wife an odd look—"popped up. I think you're the right one for the job." He thrust out his hand for DeMarcus to shake, then turned to his wife. "Let's give the lovebirds a moment to themselves, shall we?"

Mitch whisked Sylvia off to the dance floor. The moment they dissolved into the crowd, Nona rounded on him.

+ + +

Nona forced her thoughts into compliance. DeMarcus Johnson could do some serious emotional damage to any woman. Sylvia almost melted into a puddle in his presence, and a shiver had zinged down Nona's spine when he'd pressed his lips to her ear. She gave herself a mental shake. The only reason she'd crashed this party was to gather intel for Pastor Grant's case. She'd tried eavesdropping, but nothing had materialized from her efforts.

She angled her body so she could scan the ballroom. At a corner buffet, the Burnt Water councilman dipped a huge shrimp into a dish of marinara. She ticked her head in his direction.

"Do you know that man at the table with the ice sculpture of a swan?"

DeMarcus flicked a glance that way. "Never seen him before. Want me to do some digging around?" He moved slightly away from her.

"No." She reached out a hand and yanked on his arm, her voice pitched several decibels higher than necessary. He'd blow everything. "I meant, thank you. I have some other means of investigating."

Besides, no matter how obnoxiously handsome he might be, smart, smooth, tall—whatever—she'd fallen for the charm of a man like him once before. Her sister had died as a result. She'd never trust a man like him again.

She pointed toward the lobby of the hotel in a silent order to follow and wheeled around to stalk away. They'd have it out in a private corner, end this crazy charade, and she'd figure out a new angle on Pastor Grant's case. A gentle hand on her arm drew her up short.

"They're playing our song." DeMarcus squinted down at her and smiled.

In the background, she heard a female gently cooing the song "So This Is Love." Her sister had made her watch *Cinderella* only fourteen hundred times. She glared at him.

He tipped his head to the side and mouthed, "Someone's watching."

She shifted her gaze in the direction of his nod and noticed Sylvia giving them a fingertip wave and showing all her teeth with glee.

Someone on the dance floor jostled them, and DeMarcus moved in closer to her.

"I haven't bitten anyone since kindergarten, Nona. And my grandma gave me an old-school whooping when she found out, so you're safe." DeMarcus placed a hand on her back and gently cupped her right hand in his left. "See. Nothing dangerous here." He led her in a chaste swaying back and forth in time to the music.

He'd dialed his Drakkar Noir way back for tonight. Maybe he'd spilled some on himself New Year's.

"Look, Johnson. I'm on a tight deadline. Besides, do I even look like a woman who wants to date you, let alone marry you?"

He drew back and stared down at her. "You absolutely look like someone who wants to date me. In fact, you look like you want to be on a first-name basis with our kid's kindergarten teacher and chair of the PTA."

A laugh burst out of her mouth without her consent.

DeMarcus laughed too, then his smile dropped. "My boss thinks we're engaged, and I'm up for partnership." Lines creased his forehead. "Our worlds are overlapping here at this dance. Maybe there's something I can do for you. Legal assistance, research. All I'm asking for is some time to finesse this mix-up so I don't come out with egg all over my face and lose my shot . . ."

She ran through a mental list of reasons she should walk out the door and never talk to DeMarcus again, but her conscience gave a tug. The entire thing was her fault. She'd crashed the party with a lie, and she'd ensnared DeMarcus in her web of deceit. Worse, this engagement was sidetracking her from her mission. The song died out, and someone announced it was time to gather to hear how much money the charity ball had raised.

DeMarcus dropped his hands and looked warily at her. He kept his lips pressed in a firm line, leaving the ball in her court.

She hadn't intercepted her target tonight, and she was ending the evening with a fake fiancé. She needed to get her investigation back on track and gracefully shed DeMarcus as soon as possible. "I'll think about it."

✦ ✦ ✦

Zeke squinted and peered across the hotel ballroom. Glasses were unnecessary. He'd recognized that tigress the minute she'd slunk in. Never seen anything like her hair back in Burnt Water. And that dress. Everything was in the right place. The next girlfriend he found would be a fine young thing in her twenties like the she-cat. Not a mousy, weak woman like his mama. Mama never had the backbone to throw Daddy out on his ear. Never protected Zeke like a mother should. Took whatever garbage Daddy dished out. Nobody ever looked out for Zeke. High time he started looking out for himself. He'd upgrade his entire life. An upgrade on his girlfriend. An upgrade on everything he owned. Only the finest things for him when he finished this job for Calloway.

His mouth watered for a cigarette, but in California, it was hard to find a spot inside or out where he could steal a few drags. He slurped a sip of the hoity-toity wine from the stupid, skinny glass and choked it down. Tasted like spoiled grapes. What he wouldn't give for a cold one. He kept his sights set on the minx while she stayed glued to her fiancé. It had been reckless to ask her to dance, but he'd wanted to get up close and personal with the gorgeous tease.

Wait. Why was she here? Her fiancé clearly was some sort of corporate muckety-muck—all decked out in a Poindexter suit. She must be his arm candy. Plus, he recognized the guy from that stupid New Year's Eve service. He drove a nice Mercedes and had talked to some gangbangers. Dollar signs ran through Zeke's mental calculator. Might get himself a Mercedes too. Best car his daddy ever owned was a Ford. He tugged at the stiff jacket of his rented tuxedo and dismissed the vixen's presence as coincidence.

Breath smelling like cheese reached his nose. He turned his head.

Councilman Calloway stood beside Zeke's elbow. "Why haven't you closed the deal?" Calloway's voice pushed out in a harsh rasp.

"Like I told you, he won't meet with me." Zeke eyed the dude and his chick again.

"It's been two weeks now."

"I know." Every time he called the church, the old pastor put him off with one excuse or another. Wouldn't even set up an appointment to meet with him. Zeke had burned up two round-trip tickets, trying to get the pastor to sign and return the retainer agreement. The clock was ticking. If the old man didn't step forward and the property went back to the state, there was no way Calloway could get it at the cut-rate price they planned to chisel out of the pastor. It would go to the highest bidder at auction.

"You told me not to worry, you could handle it." Calloway cut Zeke a hard look. "I don't know why I put up with you, Zeke." He made a dismissive gesture with his hands. "You've always been soft and dense. Couldn't take a few licks from your old man, couldn't take a hit on the field, and you couldn't find two thoughts to rub together if you tried."

Calloway's words hissed hot and ugly in Zeke's ear, scorching him like molten lava inside his skull. Calloway always resorted to being nasty when things didn't go his way. Zeke's breathing became short and labored, and the urge to smash something, anything, roared to life inside him.

"Now I want you to listen closely to me . . ."

A flurry of thoughts scrambled inside Zeke as Calloway flapped his gums. Blows from his father, the missed block in college football that ended in a compound fracture for him and a concussion for the quarterback. The humiliating visits from Child Protective Services. His mother's cover-ups and lies to protect his worthless, drunken daddy instead of her own son.

He'd learned never to trust a soul. He forced himself to refocus and respond to Calloway. "I *can* handle it. It's under control."

"You better." Calloway stalked off without a backward glance.

The she-cat and the tall dude walked in his direction. Zeke turned his back, but a waiter with a huge tray stood in his way, making escape impossible.

"Excuse me."

Zeke glanced over his shoulder. The guy had jostled him trying to get by.

"No, excuse me," he murmured. Zeke ducked his head and scurried for the exit.

An old, beat-up pastor stood between him and his new life. He swore under his breath, clenched his hands into fists, and shoved them in his pockets. Hosea Grant was out of time, and Zeke wasn't putting it off any longer. He wasn't leaving California this time without the signed retainer in his pocket.

Chapter 8

DeMarcus opened his office door and eyed the basic, low-budget filing cabinet and the two generic guest chairs stacked with boxes of case files. His office lacked style but not for long. If he played his cards right, he'd move upstairs to Partners' Row and could outfit his office any way he liked.

The Valentine's Day event had messed with his flow, pushing his weekend work onto Sunday—his chillax day—and he still wasn't caught up. To beat Monday traffic and have a moment to himself, he'd arrived at seven thirty. The combination of the noise-deadening low-pile carpet and the minimal number of staff and attorneys cut out unnecessary stimuli and limited distractions. Maxine was in, but she knew if he came in early not to bother him. He hoped to use the extra time to get into a groove and on top of his work.

He withdrew a chilled Red Bull from his briefcase and drained the can in a dozen gulps. Had to get it down fast. The stuff tasted like a kid's chewable vitamin with ten added tablespoons of sugar. He fired up his computer and opened the brief he'd spent all yesterday finalizing. He forwarded the finished draft to Maxine for her to format when she had a moment. Next on his agenda, preparing for an afternoon client meeting.

"Knock, knock."

Who was in the office this early to bother him?

His door opened, and Mitch stuck his head around the doorjamb. "I saw your light. Do you have a second?"

No. "Of course." DeMarcus waved Mitch in.

DeMarcus rose to clear the mess from one chair so Mitch could sit.

His boss shook his head. "I'll grab a corner here."

The senior partner propped himself on the edge of DeMarcus's desk, one foot planted on the ground, the other leg swinging. Mitch must not be meeting any clients today. The dress code was suits for client meetings, but sports coats and even high-end khakis were okay otherwise. Mitch's brand of casual was to ditch his tie.

"Wanted to follow up on the case I mentioned at the event Saturday night."

"Right." Thoughts about the case had tantalized him all weekend. Mitch had hinted it could be something big. DeMarcus's prospects might turn on how he handled it. He grabbed a legal pad from a drawer and a pen from the cup on the desk. "Shoot." He nodded his chin to prompt Mitch.

"This is a two-million-dollar case, DeMarcus." Mitch ran a finger down the crease in his pant leg. "And the outcome is extremely important to me."

DeMarcus's gut clinched. Three seconds on the clock, and the entire game hinged on him. Time to take his shot. "Whatever you need, I'm the guy."

"Good to know." Mitch turned his head away and stared into space.

Normally Mitch shot straight from the hip. Now he seemed evasive. Squirrelly. Fishy.

"I know real estate isn't your forte . . ."

Spit it out already. "I'll do whatever research I need to figure out how best to handle the case."

"Sylvia put me up to this, but I know you're the guy to keep this matter private." Mitch coughed. "There's a piece of real estate that overlooks the Pacific. Sixteen years ago, the purchase price stood at just over six hundred thousand. The view was two-thirds of that value."

"Must be some view."

"Oh, it is. The prior neighbors put in a hedge of juniper trees along the back fence line. They always kept it trimmed, and because of the way the house sits, the trees didn't obstruct the view of the ocean."

DeMarcus stood, removing the power imbalance of sitting lower than Mitch. DeMarcus paced to the corner of his office and sat on the window ledge. He gave a few nods of his head to show Mitch he was tracking along with him.

"A while ago, the owners of the house had a falling-out with the current backyard neighbors. Stupid and avoidable in hindsight, but water under the bridge." Mitch gave a wave of his hand. "To retaliate, the neighbors stopped trimming the junipers. Now they are almost thirty feet tall, and the property no longer has an ocean view. The house is worth three million, but the real estate agent says two million will be lost without the view."

"Wow. Aren't there firms that specialize in this area? Property law? A tree law firm? The homeowners' association?"

"Don't want an outside firm handling this." Mitch rubbed his forehead, sighed, and dropped his hand back to his side. "It's our house, DeMarcus. This case is for me. Can't get our weak homeowners' association to do anything. The neighbors have a reality show they film out of their house. They're influencers on the internet, whatever that means. YouTube. Instagram. I don't follow either. The association chairwoman is starstruck and intimidated, so I'm taking the bull by the horns."

DeMarcus schooled his face to neutral. "Wow, Mitch. I don't know what to say." This case would not advance his partnership chances. A quicksand time suck, more like it. And if he lost, what would Mitch do?

"Sylvia and I raised our girls there, and now we want to downsize to a nice ranch in La Cañada or San Marino, sock the excess proceeds away in trust for our grandchildren, and get on with our lives. The market is blazing-hot right now, but my financial adviser is telling me he sees a correction in the next month or so. I want to unload the house now for the maximum profit." Mitch swiped his hand down his face. Deep-set fatigue wrinkles framed his boss's eyes. "This can't hit the gossip rags. It will drive away potential buyers. All I want is for this headache to go away."

"I . . ." DeMarcus clamped his jaw shut to keep from saying anything stupid.

"DeMarcus, two million dollars is two million dollars. You're charming. You're hardworking. It's not quite a personal favor, but I want you to be the guy. I won't make you take this case, but I'm asking you to do it."

So much hung on this case for Mitch. Funding his grandchildren's trust funds, he'd want the maximum returns. Mitch had rich-people problems. DeMarcus looked at the man who held in his hands the future of DeMarcus's partnership bid. "Not a prob, Mitch. Consider it handled."

Visible relief rolled over Mitch, and the furrows left his brow. "Thanks, DeMarcus."

◆ ◆ ◆

DeMarcus reread California Civil Code Section 841.4 on spite fences to fix the elements in his mind.

> Any fence or other structure in the nature of a fence unnecessarily exceeding 10 feet in height maliciously erected or maintained for the purpose of annoying the owner or occupant of adjoining property is a private nuisance. Any owner or occupant of adjoining property injured either in his comfort or the enjoyment of his estate by such nuisance may enforce the remedies against its continuance.

He flipped open the copy of *California Appellate Reports* lying on his desk and turned to the decision he wanted to review. Only maritime law eclipsed tree law for the title of "Most Obscure, Counterintuitive, and Super-Niche" legal specialty. He might have even taken a skip day the one time the prof covered it in law school.

The hardest thing to prove in Mitch and Sylvia's case would be the malicious intent of the current owners in maintaining the tree height. The prior neighbors had pruned the trees, as had the current neighbors until the falling-out. DeMarcus had to show that they stopped pruning on purpose with the intent to annoy Mitch and his family. Since only a fool would own up to erecting a spite fence if asked straight-out, he needed to find someone other than the property owners themselves who could testify about the neighbors' state of mind.

He snatched up an ink pen from a repurposed Princeton coffee mug and began clicking the retractable end over and over. His brain whirled—a nanny, exercise-class friend, stylist, yoga instructor, masseuse. He stood and paced. The landscaper, the nursery where they purchased the trees. A housekeeper. A maintenance man. A jilted friend? He needed someone with loose lips willing to gossip or with a grudge. He jotted down his thoughts on potential witnesses.

The phone on DeMarcus's desk gave a warble. Maxine's name scrolled on the caller ID, and he stabbed the speakerphone button.

"Go."

"DeMarcus, there's some woman named Nona Taylor at the reception desk. She claims she's your fiancée, and she's demanding to see you."

Maxine knew good and well he didn't have a fiancée. Low-level panic crept in.

"Should I call security?"

Maxine ran interference for DeMarcus whenever he needed it. He tried not to take women back to his house, and he never brought them to his office. Yet, somehow, a few slipped through the cracks and tracked him down.

Maxine knew how to finesse them all. Old enough to be his mother, Maxine still dressed and wore her hair in a style one inch from being inappropriate for work. When he'd run into her in the break room the other day, he'd stared down a partner checking out her brown skin sheathed in a sleeveless dress and her feet showcased in stilettos. The weave cascading down her back in loose light-brown and blond waves belonged on a woman half her age. His pointed stare had caused the married man to cut his glance away. But no need to worry that she'd have an affair with any of the old, wedded partners. Maxine was a shameless cougar.

It was DeMarcus's good luck that Maxine's maternal instincts had kicked in as if she'd given birth to him, and she gloried in her position as his secretary, protector, and gatekeeper.

"No, she's cool. Let her come back . . ." His voice sounded lame even to his own ears. He'd left the charity ball with everything between Nona and himself up in the air. She'd summoned the valet and whisked herself away before they could sort everything out.

Maxine gave a small harrumph and ended the call.

Moments later, Nona stood at the door with Maxine right behind her.

He rose, unsure how to greet her.

"Your fiancée, Nona, is here, DeMarcus." The tone of Maxine's voice made it clear she'd be having a talk with him later in the day.

He eyed his desk. A jumble of papers lay strewn across the surface, and the boxes still sat on his guest chairs. He hustled to set some of the boxes to the side. "Thanks, Maxine. Hold my calls."

Nona entered his office, and he gave Maxine his winningest smile as he shut the door.

He squeezed the tight muscles in his neck. "This is unexpected." He focused his attention on Nona as he walked back to his desk. He lowered himself and watched her. She didn't fidget, but discomfort evidenced itself in the lines on the sides of her mouth and corners of her eyes.

She dropped her head and extended her hand flat out toward him. His ring rested on her palm. The glare from the office lights made the stone glint.

"I came to give this back." She leaned forward in her seat, moving her hand closer to him. "I appreciate your bailing me out, but we need to figure a way to get out of this mess. I have my case to work on. You have to do"— her perusal bounced over the stacks of paper on his desk—"whatever it is you do."

He leveled his stare at her. Her hair was smooth on her scalp, scraped to her nape, and held in place by a straining ponytail holder. A riot of corkscrew curls exploded from the elastic constraint.

Every time he was with her, he wanted to ogle her like a middle school boy with a crush. Another part of him wanted to give her a stiff talking-to for getting him in a jam with the fiancé lie.

The door burst open. Mitch entered with Maxine on his heels.

"I told him you were in a meeting," Maxine said.

Mitch gave Maxine a dismissive wave. "Nona," Mitch boomed, "excellent timing."

As she backed out the door, the daggers shooting from Maxine's eyes told DeMarcus that he had *a lot* of explaining to do.

"My wife put a dinner on the calendar for all the senior associates up for partnership. We're inviting spouses and significant others."

Nona's hand rested palm down on DeMarcus's desk, his ring trapped underneath.

"DeMarcus." Mitch tucked his chin and raised a brow, his voice firm and authoritative. "You still haven't put a ring on it, as the young people say?"

Heat pricked DeMarcus's back. He focused his eyes on Nona, hoping she could intuit what he was thinking. *Play along. Please.*

Nona lifted her hand and turned a sheepish smile on Mitch. "We were just discussing that." She slid the ring onto her thumb.

DeMarcus's shoulders relaxed. He shifted to offense. "I'm slammed here, so we haven't had time—"

"Nonsense. Make the time." Mitch rounded on Nona. "When I see you at the dinner next week, I expect DeMarcus to have given you a rock that sparkles so much it hurts my eyes." Mitch stood, swept from the office, then closed the door behind him.

At the snap of the door shutting, Nona's eyes flashed fiery sparks at him. "You say whatever you have to say to Mitch, but I'm not coming to his dinner party."

Impatience flared in DeMarcus like kindling hit by lightning. "Oh yes you are."

Nona screwed up her lips and glared at him.

He jabbed his index finger in her direction. "You owe me, Sassy."

Indignation scrolled over Nona's face, but he plowed forward.

"I returned your phone, pretended to be your fiancé to keep from blowing your cover, and I even agreed to help you with your case."

"First, I didn't ask for you to return the phone. Second, I've decided I don't want your help on my case." Nona's voice was firm.

He continued, undaunted. "I'm in this 100 percent now, woman. My boss thinks we're engaged. There's no way for me to back out of this before they make the partnership decision, so you're stuck with it. I saved your hide. Now you owe me a solid in return." Getting the words off his chest doused his ire. "Please, Nona." Nona didn't fit in the box where the other women in his life lived. He'd never asked a woman to do something he truly needed. "Let's make this a win-win. You scratch my back, I'll scratch yours. Besides, my charming company . . ."

Nona opened her mouth and stuck in her index finger like she was gagging.

A barking laugh burst from him, and he watched her suppress her own smile.

◆ ◆ ◆

Why couldn't she cut this joker loose? Every time she tried to get rid of him, he boomeranged right back. Okay, he didn't make her eyeballs hurt. In his charcoal-gray suit, crisp shirt, and tie with . . . what? Orange-and-black slanted stripes covered the tie. Princeton colors? He was over the top with the Princeton thing. But, defying all reason, he pulled off the standard Ivy League garb with class and style. Blemish-free skin. Rich, brown, and flawless. And without the razor bumps that plagued many. His chocolate eyes always appeared narrowed with mockery.

DeMarcus watched her like a child who wanted a cookie from his mother. "Maybe this will sweeten the pot. Mitch needs me to help him with a case, and I need an investigator. Since this case is for Mitch personally, and not the firm, he will give you a cash retainer. Up front."

Money was now on the table. She sat up straighter in her chair. The bills on her fridge marched before her mind's eye, and she performed some mental math on her budget. A fresh case plus a payout on Pastor Grant's estate could be the financial turnaround she needed.

"If your hourly rate exceeds the retainer, he'll pay that too. He'll also cover all your expenses."

She'd come to DeMarcus's office to break their fake engagement, but this could be the very thing that salvaged her precarious financial situation. Looking at his face sent up warning flares. Men as attractive and charming as DeMarcus had a knack for finagling themselves into a woman's life and heart and asking for more. Could she risk it? Her thoughts shifted to Lady and Bruiser, whom she'd been grooming at home to save money. Lady's eyes had traces of the milky covering that signaled cataracts. A huge vet bill would break her. Then there was the suspicious oily puddle growing in size where she parked her car.

"Earth to Nona. Come in, Nona."

She saw DeMarcus snapping his fingers, a hint of a smile playing around his mouth. Busted. She reeled her thoughts back to concentrate on his words and not the balance in her checking account.

"Like I was saying, after this case, I think I can even throw some future business your way."

Could she really believe all his pretty promises? She closed her eyes for a moment and decided to send up a quick prayer. What could it hurt? "What does Mitch need?"

DeMarcus slid a giant book toward her. "It's a spite fence case."

Nona read the statute in the California Civil Code and made a quizzical face. "How do I fit into all of this?"

He placed his elbows on the desk and steepled his hands. "The hardest part is proving someone's state of mind, that they held actual spite in their thoughts when they built the structure, planted trees, or refused to cut back trees that block a view. That's where you come in. I want you to investigate the neighbors, interview gardeners, manicurists, nannies. Track down someone who knows what was in the neighbors' heads at the time they stopped trimming the trees, and find a witness who will testify about the facts under oath."

"Why can't you do that yourself, with a subpoena or deposition?"

"The first step is the investigation phase. We need to uncover witnesses, facts, and evidence. I don't want to tip my hand and let Mitch's neighbors get to the witnesses first. Anyone willing to let a row of hedges exceed statutory limits out of spite might also tamper with witnesses. I need someone undercover who can find the witnesses and tell me what they have to say. Once I find out what they know, I will ask them to sign a sworn declaration, and if necessary, I will drop a subpoena on them to force them to testify in a deposition."

"But whatever I find out will be hearsay, won't it?"

"One step at a time. The hearsay objection only matters if we're trying to get a witness's testimony admitted at trial. Right now we just want to box people in under oath so they can't change their stories later."

Nona had treated DeMarcus like a clown, but he knew what he was talking about. She found his competence enticing. Squeezing her eyes shut, she gave herself a brief mental dressing-down to drive the unwanted thoughts away. Yet, somehow, like an insect on flypaper, she couldn't work her way free from this smug, albeit good-looking, guy. She brought her hand to her throat and fingered her sister's necklace, which she hadn't returned to the jewelry box like she had every year previously.

Resolve locked into place. Since he had done her a favor and not blown her cover, she owed him. She'd attend the partner's dinner but would have preplanned excuses at the ready in case any other social obligations arose. She'd help him with his case—charging full price, of course—stall him out from interfering with her own investigation, and she'd shed DeMarcus Johnson as soon as possible after that.

◆ ◆ ◆

DeMarcus spun his desk chair around to stare out the window while he called his grandmother. The adjacent high-rise reflected his own building. A temporary situation. Once he made partner, he'd get a south- or north-facing view. Mountains or the ocean. Either one, fine with him. Nona had left a scent, fresh and clean like detergent, behind.

The phone connected on G'Mama's end, catching her in midsentence.

"—Jamaria, shut that door. It's February in Baltimore. I ain't payin' to heat the entire block."

DeMarcus suppressed a chuckle. G'Mama was always fussing in love at somebody.

"Who is it?"

"It's D."

"DeMarcus, baby, how are you?"

"Good, G'Mama. You?"

"I'm blessed, baby. Lord woke me up in my right mind this morning. Blessed indeed. Hold on a minute. Jamaria!"

DeMarcus held the phone away from his ear.

"Need you to get on a plane and come out here. Put the fear of God in some of these knucklehead boys all buzzing around your cousin like drunken flies. She has developed into a poised young lady. Smart like you but pretty like you too. I ain't raising no more babies."

"I'll talk to her when we're done." Nerves kicked in. DeMarcus twirled his chair back around, faced his desk, and began bobbing his leg. "You see my text? I went to church, like I promised."

"Baby, it made my day seeing your text. So how was it?"

"You'd have felt right at home. I should fly you out here in your white dress, so you can sit with the other ladies on the Mothers' Board."

G'Mama harrumphed. "Boy, you know that's never going to happen. Aretha Franklin didn't fly. I read somewhere Whoopie don't fly. And I don't fly."

"I'm teasing you." His grandmother would endure any inconvenience to avoid an airplane. "That bus ride from Baltimore to Princeton for my graduation turned a one-hour flight into a seven-and-a-half-hour ride with a transfer."

"I still get Christmas cards from the lady I sat next to."

"I'm sure you do."

Silence stretched out.

"What's made you so quiet all of a sudden? Usually your mouth's running a mile a minute."

Not *what* but *who*. This thing with Nona. Faker than the Gucci bags being sold on the curb in front of his office. But his gut told him to have patience. "I met someone, G'Mama." He couldn't even hear her breathing. "Did you—"

"Boy, you know I heard you. Where'd you meet her? Not at the club, I hope."

"Not the club. Met her at church."

"Stop messing with me. Ain't nobody got time for that. The one day of the year you go to church, now you talking about, you done met somebody."

He chuckled. "Have I ever lied to you?"

He hadn't. Not that time he'd tried weed. G'Mama yelled for forty-five minutes, all with one breath. After that, she made the coach bench him for the first playoff game. Not that time DeMarcus thought he'd gotten a girl in trouble. She'd made him put on a suit and tie, and drive her ancient Lincoln—with her buckled in the passenger seat—over to the girl's house to talk to the girl's father and take responsibility. Turned out to be a false alarm.

She always said sin had consequences. *"But once you repent and apologize, move on. After King David sent that man Uriah to his death, and David stole Uriah's wife, Bathsheba, God made David's baby sick. David prayed and prayed to the Lord, but once the baby died, David got up, washed himself, ate some food, and moved on with his life."*

No matter what jam he found himself in, G'Mama fussed him out, made him do the right thing. Then she never held it against him again.

"No, baby, you haven't ever lied to me. Not. Like. Jamaria!" G'Mama screamed in his ear again.

"Chill. I told you I'd take care of Jamaria when we're done."

"So this girl, is she nice?"

"No. Not so much." He smiled.

G'Mama roared with laughter. "I like her already." A rattling cackle crossed the two thousand miles between them. "She's not impressed with your handsome face and your usual razzle-dazzle."

No. He didn't impress Nona at all. "I'm working this thing my way, G'Mama. Nice and slow." If he could call a fake engagement with the woman wearing his most prized possession *slow*.

Why even tell G'Mama about Nona? He shook his head. Until now, he and G'Mama had a silent agreement. He didn't ask her if she'd taken her diabetes medicine or whether she'd made it to her doctors' appointments, and she didn't ask him about the women he dated.

Why was he running off at the mouth, putting all his business in the street? Nona had him turned upside down, not thinking straight. She'd burrowed her way under his skin like nobody else. She infuriated him and intrigued him. Her beauty floored him. And she couldn't care less.

"I met her recently, but I like her. Don't even know why I'm telling you."

"You can't see it, but I'm smiling. I love you, DeMarcus baby, and I'll be praying for you."

"Thanks, G'Mama. Now put Jamaria on the phone."

"JAMARIA!"

He leaned back in his chair and prepared his lecture for his little cousin. It started with warning her about guys like him.

Chapter 9

DeMarcus slid his car into Mitch and Sylvia's horseshoe-shaped driveway. Nona's car eased in directly behind his. The bright-orange setting sun hung over the horizon like a basketball a second before it dropped through the net.

Nona had refused to let him drive her to the dinner, but he'd insisted they enter as a team. Sticky tape and gum held their fake engagement together, and with Sylvia acting as cheerleader in chief as the hostess, any signs of cracks in the union might send up a red flare.

The valet stepped forward to assist Nona, and DeMarcus put out an arm to stop him. "I'll take care of it."

He approached Nona's driver's side door and opened it. From his vantage point, her halo of curls obscured her face. Nona grabbed her purse from the passenger seat and removed the keys from the ignition. The slight movement caused the honeyed loops and swirls of her hair to shimmer and dance as if they were alive. She turned toward him and extended a hand, holding some folded dollar bills and her key chain.

"Please park it so I can get out of here quickly. I . . ."

Nona's gaze tangled with his, and he took her in like a man watching a dazzling fireworks grand finale. Flashes of information registered. Dangly hoops gracing her earlobes and a halter top tied behind her neck.

She placed one foot, encased in a high, chunky shoe, on the ground. He stood back, and she rose from the passenger seat with the grace and fluidity of a gymnast.

"Johnson." She flicked a dismissive inspection over him from his toes to his head. "You have a side hustle I don't know about?" She held up her keys and jiggled them.

Never breaking eye contact, he enfolded the money, keys, and her hand in his for a beat. Nona squinted at him. As he released her hand, he grasped the items and handed both off to the valet hovering near him.

Nona moved out from behind her car door to make room for the valet, and her full outfit came into view. Green like ocean waves, the dress moved and flowed. Not fitted or clingy anywhere, but mesmerizing. The bottom of the dress grazed the tops of her shoes. With those heels, she'd almost made up the six-inch height gap between them.

Nona's car backed out, leaving them standing in the driveway.

"Where's my ring?" His conscience twinged. He hadn't yet made good on his promise to Sylvia that he'd buy Nona a solitaire, although he'd found a place that rented luxury jewelry for Hollywood awards shows and movie shoots, but no time to follow up.

"Don't get all twisted around the axle, Johnson." She opened an envelope-sized handbag, produced the ring from inside, and pushed it onto her thumb. "Better?"

"Much."

She had on almost no makeup. Something on her cheeks resembled fine glitter, and her lips shimmered in the same shade. A woody, coconut smell wafted off her hair.

"In case I forget, you look . . ." More than *beautiful*, she looked *stunning*. Like his future wife.

"What?"

Her sharp tone drew him up short. She had him boxed up so tightly in the frenemy zone, it was cutting off his circulation. He scratched an imaginary itch on the back of his neck. "Nice dress." He let the moment pass.

"Remember, I'm not staying for the whole dinner. I'm making a polite appearance, then I'm out of here."

"Copy that." He placed his hand on the small of her back and guided her over the stepping stones, using the engagement ruse as a pretext for closer proximity to her.

No matter how many times he visited Sylvia and Mitch's house, the home never ceased to impress. He was loyal to Baltimore until the day he died, but after his stint at Princeton, he could now appreciate the beauty of fine architecture, high-end clothing, and luxury cars.

Decorative rocks and succulent-based greenery covered the front yard. Strategic boulders and flat flagstones marked out a path to the glass-paneled front door framed by the house's whitewashed wood shingles.

Nona shivered beside him.

"Cold?" He began shucking his suit jacket.

"No." She fiddled with the ring on her thumb.

He grabbed both her hands in one of his. "This is going to be fine. Think of it as another undercover operation."

Nona gave a short, affirmative jerk of her head.

He rapped twice on the door and pushed it open. The cocktail chatter of two dozen people surrounded them as they entered, and the smell of chardonnay and cheese hung in the air.

Sylvia materialized from among her guests. With her arms spread wide to greet them, her orange dress resembled an inverted Dorito.

"Nona. DeMarcus. So glad you both are here." Sylvia embraced Nona in a motherly hug, then patted him on the arm.

"Let's go outside for a minute to talk shop, shall we?" Sylvia skirted through various clumps of senior associates, partners, and their plus-ones until they reached a wall of glass doors. Sylvia threw open one sliding door, and they stepped onto the back balcony, which ran from one end of the house to the other.

"See what I'm dealing with, Nona?" Sylvia gestured with one hand, pointing at the expanse of trees behind her house. "If they trimmed those back five feet, we'd regain our clear view of the ocean. Our neighbors are simply unreasonable about the whole thing."

+ + +

The sun narrowly topped the juniper stand that ran behind Sylvia's house. The closely planted thicket with forest-green foliage blocked all but a sliver of the sparkling vista beyond.

Until Nona had seen Sylvia's neighborhood—and the obscured ocean view—the term *spite fence* seemed overblown and petty on Mitch and Sylvia's part. In her experience, the wealthy had little tolerance for even the slightest inconvenience. Now, with the huge evergreens, like an army of towering robots, blocking the view of the sun setting over the ocean, she embraced the injustice of Mitch and Sylvia's plight.

"I can see why you'd want to have these trees pruned. You'd have a clear sight line to the ocean from one end of this terrace to the other if the neighbors kept their trees four to five feet shorter."

"It all unraveled so quickly with our ex-friends, Mila and Arthur." Sylvia swiped under an eye with her finger. "Let's sit for a minute." She moved to a table with cushioned chairs around it.

DeMarcus hustled ahead and slid back both Nona's chair and Sylvia's. He gave Nona a wink and a smirky smile.

"I love the chemistry between you two. So sweet." Sylvia made moon eyes at them.

"Oh, there's chemistry. Formaldehyde and sulfur." Nona had agreed to the fake engagement, but she didn't have to like it.

Sylvia laughed and pointed back and forth between the two of them. "You're like Han Solo and Princess Leia. On the outside, it's fight, fight, fight. On the inside, it's love, love, love."

To escape Sylvia's mushy romance face, she turned to DeMarcus. The level stare he trained on her caused an unwanted thrill to snake down her back. She rolled her eyes. He winked, dragged his chair around the corner of the square table to sit parallel with her, and draped his arm across the back of her seat.

Keeping up this ruse taxed every nerve she possessed. Nona returned her attention to Sylvia and away from Cocky McJohnson, juris doctor. "So tell me more about your neighbors."

Sylvia pinched the bridge of her nose between two fingers and let out a sigh. "We could have avoided this whole mess if our neighbors stopped trying to manufacture a dramatic angle on every waking moment of their lives. Mila and Arthur Yacoubian. Famous for being famous. They've done it all. A skin care line. Clothing and accessories pop-up stores. Their latest venture, Très Chic Pet Boutique."

Mitch strode onto the balcony. On his heels trotted a snow-colored bichon frise with his head encircled in an Afro of fluff that rivaled the Jackson 5's in their heyday.

"Apollo." Delight laced Sylvia's voice. She made room for the dog and patted him lovingly, and Apollo thumped his tail on her lap. Mitch leaned over Sylvia and gave her a kiss on the cheek.

Mitch turned toward Nona and DeMarcus. "Syl giving you guys the background on the case?"

DeMarcus stuck out his right hand and shook with Mitch. "Absolutely."

"Good. She's the one who knows the most about this. We're counting on you, DeMarcus, to get us the legal authority to get those trees trimmed back and this house put on the market. Pronto."

"My trusty sidekick and I have the whole thing covered." DeMarcus draped his arm behind Nona's chair again, and he used the opportunity to pat her bare arm.

She wished she hated it, but she didn't.

"Great. I'll let you all get back to it, then, but not too much shoptalk. This is a party, after all." As Mitch opened the sliding glass doors to return to the rest of his guests, the crooning of Tony Bennett singing "Fly Me to the Moon" drifted out into the mild evening air.

"Where was I?" Sylvia said. "Oh right. Our neighbors Mila and Arthur. This is exciting, like *CSI* or *NCIS*. Espionage and investigation."

"I promise you, Sylvia, private investigation work is far less glamorous than it appears on TV." Nona smiled at Sylvia.

"Pishposh, dear. So modest." Sylvia's arms moved around in the air as if waving away something stinky. "Mila has long, midnight-black hair, exquisite porcelain skin, and almost olive-colored eyes framed with luxurious lashes and immaculately arched brows." She gestured with her hand to dramatize her words. "I'm so absolutely jealous. Mila's figure is to die for. She wears spandex tights almost every day." Her lips puckered. "Showing off the hours and hours she spends at Pilates and barre workouts.

"Anyway, Mila's husband, Arthur, has a face made for *GQ*. All chiseled cheekbones and broody. He has a ridiculously thick mane of chestnut hair that he wears in a messy man bun. This family was a reality show's casting call dream couple. I understand why they have hundreds of thousands of followers on social media."

Nona fished her phone out of her pocket. "What do they call themselves online, or what is their show called?"

"Ah yes. Their reality show is called *Yo, It's the Yacoubians*."

Using her private Instagram, Nona located their account. She scrolled up for a few seconds. Makeup, clothing, workout routines. Their lifestyle was the product they were selling.

DeMarcus leaned forward toward Sylvia. "Why do you think the relationship soured?"

"So sad." Sylvia sucked in her lips. "We'd been so cordial before. Supported everything their kids participated in. We bought magazines, we purchased Girl Scout cookies. Sponsored walkathons and bikeathons and whatever other -athons they pushed in front of us." She sniffed. "I mean, really, who even buys magazines anymore?"

A waiter slid open the door, entered, and silently offered everyone a round of water and hors d'oeuvres from a precariously balanced platter. Nona selected a plate of what looked like mushrooms stuffed with spinach dip.

"Sounds like you all were good neighbors to them." Nona leaned forward a bit, encouraging Sylvia to continue.

"I thought we were. We'd get their mail when they were away on vacation. They did the same for us."

Mitch returned, and Sylvia scooted over so he could perch on the side of her chair.

Mitch crossed one leg over the other. "They started filming their reality show in the neighborhood. Cops shut down streets for blocks all around. Catering trucks. Vans for the camera crews. Bright lights shining on the house exterior, front and back, day and night. People in the neighborhood started complaining. Sylvia and I complained. We also used to take Apollo to their grooming salon, Très Chic Pet Boutique, all the time."

"Apollo was even on camera." Sylvia drew her dog close to her face and made a kissy noise.

A hard look crossed Mitch's face. "Apollo received skin burns after they leashed him in a drying cage, but they refused to take responsibility."

"When was this?" Nona directed her question to Sylvia.

"I'd have to check my calendar for the exact date, but it was right before spring last year. I remember, because we'd already attended the HeartSpark Hands for Change ball, but it was before our annual ski trip to Boulder."

Apollo hopped down off Sylvia's lap and made his way over to Nona. He lifted on his hind legs and placed his front paws on Nona's lap.

"Who's a good boy?" Nona whispered and scratched Apollo under his chin. He rewarded her by licking her hand.

"Isn't he so adorable?" Sylvia cooed.

Apollo trotted back to her and resumed his perch on her lap.

"So did you sue them?" DeMarcus leaned back, and his hand brushed Nona's shoulder again.

"No, but we should have." Mitch grunted in disgust. "We left a one-star review on one of those sites where you can rate businesses. We didn't want anyone else's dog getting hurt in the same way and wanted to warn people."

Sylvia gave a vigorous nod. "Mila and Arthur were furious. They wanted us to take down the review and threatened to report Mitch to the State Bar. But they wouldn't compensate us for Apollo's vet bills. We don't need the money at all. It was the principle."

A waiter swooped in and relieved Nona of her hors d'oeuvre plate with one hand. He then turned to refill DeMarcus's water from a pitcher he held in the other hand.

"Thank you." Nona gave him a brief smile.

"We also posted comments on Beverly Hills Undercover. It's more of a local site. People looking for a nanny, a dog sitter, streets where parking enforcement is booting cars." Sylvia patted Apollo affectionately. "I simply recited what had happened to our dog. No embellishments. But the Yacoubians took swipes at us. Other people piled on about groomers in general. That led to a whole onslaught of posts about other dog salons, disputes about best practices and it went on and on. After a few days, the moderators closed the thread to further comments. And . . ." Sylvia trailed off.

"About that time, they simply stopped cutting their junipers, and here we are," Mitch filled in.

"Nona and I will devise a strategy and let you know what we've come up with. What do you think, Nona?" DeMarcus gave Nona's arm a gentle pat. She forced herself not to squint at him.

"I think the most logical starting point will be diving into the message board at Beverly Hills Undercover and seeing if I can find any leads. Next would be an in-person trip to the groomer."

"Thank you, both of you." Sylvia stood with Apollo cradled in one arm and hugged Nona around the neck with the other arm.

Mitch stood as well and shook Nona's hand.

They all made their way back inside the house. A woman with waist-length midnight-black hair and an elegant crew-neck dress sidled up next to DeMarcus and began prattling on about her billable hours. Nona used the opportunity to give DeMarcus the once-over. He wore a single-breasted navy suit that fit as though it were hand-tailored. His pants had that almost-too-short look guys wore these days. He'd paired the suit with wing tips, a brown leather belt, and a light-blue shirt, which he'd left open at the collar.

She needed to take two giant steps back from him like one did in the kids' game Mother, May I? so she could regain her equilibrium. "Mr. Johnson, want anything from the bar?" A brief frown crossed his face, and her lips twitched upward in satisfaction. Anything to put a chink in his impenetrable armor.

Before Nona could retreat, Sylvia fluttered around her and DeMarcus. "Isn't that so sweet? So formal. She called you 'Mr. Johnson.' It's like *Pride and Prejudice*. You're her Mr. Darcy."

Nona rolled her eyes at DeMarcus, making sure Sylvia didn't see.

Someone across the room waggled her fingers and snared Sylvia's attention, and she waved.

"You two lovebirds have fun. Looks like Thad Livingston's wife needs me." Sylvia dissolved into the crowd in her living room.

"More like Wickham," Nona muttered under her breath.

DeMarcus leaned into her space. His breath smelled like Tic Tacs. "Wickham? Girl, you know I'm Darcy."

She rounded on him. "What? How do you even know what *Pride and Prejudice* is?"

DeMarcus let out a long breath, interlaced his fingers with hers, and toyed with the giant ring on her thumb. Then he lifted their joined hands until her knuckles were almost at his lips.

Her breath hitched.

He stared at her intently. "Do I need to remind you . . ." He moved within an inch of the hand he held aloft, suspended between them.

That arrogant smirk that she'd come to anticipate appeared on his face and chipped away at her resolve to maintain an icy composure.

"I went to Princeton."

He gave a chaste peck on her knuckles, which burned like fire, and she snatched her hand away.

DeMarcus threw back his head and laughed.

She pursed her lips. She needed to work on this case because of the money. It didn't matter that Mr. All-American regarded her with eyes that held warmth and infernal confidence or that he flirted with her while conversing about Jane Austen. She couldn't let him in. Man, but she'd need to erect a mental firewall to keep DeMarcus Johnson from using all his charm and good looks to hack into her mind and heart like a computer virus.

Chapter 10

NONA WRENCHED HER steering wheel sharply to the right, backed up slowly, then whipped the wheel back to the left. Her compact Civic fit neatly into a parallel spot in front of Très Chic Pet Boutique. She killed the ignition and shot a glance back at her crew. Bruiser lay sleeping in his raised car booster. Lady reclined at an awkward angle inside her travel carrier.

Très Chic Pet Boutique sat nestled in a cute little strip of shops off the main drag in the tony and infamous Brentwood neighborhood. A black-and-white-striped awning protruded from the store's facade, and splotches adorned the pale-painted brick, mimicking Dalmatian spots.

She snagged her purse, exited the car, and made her way to the parking meter. After paying with a credit card, she took a picture of the meter to have Johnson's firm reimburse the expense. Every single part of today's undercover operation pushed her straining credit card balance to the limit.

Her purse emitted the annoying honk of a clown horn. Johnson. *Figures.* She leaned back against her car and fished out her phone to read the incoming text from DeMarcus "Big Head" Johnson.

> Don't forget, I need you to inspect the drying stations. Check to see if they use any chemicals to speed the drying process. Is water provided for the animals? Are they using high-velocity dryers? What temperatures are they using?

I've done undercover work
before. That's why you hired me.

Three dots danced on the screen, and Lady's cold nose poked her arm through the cracked window.

I hired you to keep the $ in
the family. Seeing as how
we're engaged.

She sucked back a snort. She never wanted to laugh, but somehow Johnson always worked his way around her defenses, straight to her funny bone.

Whatever, Johnson. I'll email my
report to you this evening.

Keep your head in the
game. Counting on you to
clock the W.

The unnecessary warning echoed around inside her. Mitch and Sylvia's dog had escaped with dehydration and mild surface burns. Lady and Bruiser could be burned, or worse, if things went south inside the salon. Nona wouldn't release the dogs to the salon's care until she'd satisfied herself they'd be safe. This might be the most thorough investigation she'd ever done.

She opened the car door, unzipped Lady from the carrier, and attached her leash. Bruiser, now wide awake, yipped, and Nona undid his attachment to the car seat and snapped on his leash as well. The pair tumbled from the back of the cramped car, causing her to teeter in her high-heeled, lace-up sandals. She'd chosen a sleeveless, emerald-colored, scoop-neck sheath dress accented with a chunky orange necklace to mimic what she hoped would pass for Westside money.

Even from the outside, the shop oozed class. At the front window, she spied an artfully arranged tier of stainless-steel doggy bowls and apothecary canisters of dog snacks. The tantalizing scent of oven-hot bread wafted from the gluten-free bakery located to the left of the boutique. A woman wearing disposable pedicure slippers hobbled out of the nail salon to the right.

With two dogs, strappy shoes, and a tight dress, Nona felt like Sandra Bullock gliding out of the airplane hangar after her transformation in *Miss Congeniality*. A sidewalk-smacking face-plant might happen as well—with each step toward the entrance, she had to focus on walking gingerly to keep from breaking her ankle. If she could survive the day with no gaffes, she'd send the entire outfit straight back to the consignment store.

She stepped into the shop, keeping Lady and Bruiser close in case they encountered any other dogs as they entered. The scent of cedarwood and the melody of guitar jazz with a distinctively French flair greeted her. On one wall, two tiers of built-in racks held pet clothing on little satin hangers. On the opposite side of the shop stood an expansive display unit with cute arrangements of grooming tools, squeaky toys, wrapped chews, and bones.

She approached the island counter in the center of the room.

"How may I assist you?" A thin brunette woman wearing a starched white shirt, capris, and ballet flats glanced up from her task. Her name tag in the shape of a dog's pawprint read "Jeannette."

"Yes, Nona Taylor. I have an appointment for two grooming sessions."

Jeannette zipped her finger over a tablet on a stand in front of her. "Yes, Lady and Bruiser are getting the full package today." The woman stood on her toes and peered over the waist-height counter at Lady and Bruiser. "Cute dogs." She made a face that belied her words.

Lady thumped her tail against the floor, and Bruiser sat in stony silence.

"Okay, they are getting nail clippings, lemon and tea tree detoxifying baths, followed by our exclusive gentle vortex dry cuts, a coconut oil treatment, and massages."

"Yes."

A heavy steel door opened behind the woman and the baying of dogs spilled out. The door slammed closed, and the jazz filled the room again.

"This is my first time here, and I'm a little nervous. Could you give me a tour of the back?" She looped the leashes over a wrist, put her hands in front of herself, and wrung them. Okay, she wouldn't win any acting awards.

Jeannette scrunched her face as if she'd sucked a lemon. "We have four point five stars on Beverly Hills Undercover and thousands of positive comments."

Well, none of those stars came from Mitch or Sylvia. Plus, while she hadn't seen anything in the comments directly connecting the junipers to the grooming injury, the level of vitriol in the Yacoubians' responses, followed by the immediate cessation of pruning, was a huge red flag.

"These dogs are my life. You can understand that, can't you?" Nona slapped on her most imploring face.

A sigh pushed out of Jeannette's mouth. "Fine, but we need to make it quick. We can't have any disruptions to our operations."

Nona followed Jeannette, who pressed a code into a keypad and pushed open the door. Bruiser and Lady needed coaxing to enter the raucous space. Nona mentally rehearsed the items DeMarcus told her had concerned Mitch and Sylvia.

More dogs' wails and yips assaulted Nona's ears, and Jeannette started moving to her left, toward the bathing stations.

"Can we start with the drying cages?" All baths Lady and Bruiser had ever taken transpired in the bathtub at Nona's townhome. A late-night cram session of YouTube videos and Google searches on dog grooming brought her up to speed on current industry standards and equipment.

Jeannette walked to the right and strode to a long wall of drying stations and cages. She gestured to the drying area. "As you can see, we take every precaution, using humane methods for the animals' care."

A handler stood next to a platform within arm's reach of a shivering poodle attached to a post by a safety restraint. Nona's stomach spasmed at the remembrance of the stories she'd read about improper leashing procedures causing injuries to dogs.

Beside the guy, a mounted blow-dryer extended over the table toward the dog. The groomer made methodical brush strokes over the dog's body. Given Nona's crash course in grooming, everything appeared to be in order.

Lady strained at her leash, eager to make friends with the retriever at the next station.

"Heel!"

Ever-obedient Lady complied, and Bruiser glanced around, bored at the whole scene.

Jeannette pointed to an adorable Irish setter with a glossy coat in a large cage. "That's an older dog who's a little skittish. We use the cage dryer to calm her nerves."

"Does someone man the cage stations at all times?"

"We use auto cutoff timers to ensure we don't overdry the animals."

"Do you use heated air?"

A wince flitted across Jeannette's face. "We transitioned away from heated dryers about six months ago."

So sometime this past summer. Made sense, since Très Chic Pet Boutique blocked Sylvia in the spring. Nona inched the dogs closer. A digital timer clamped to the front of the cage stared back at her, but no water bowls. She noticed they hadn't replaced the heated dryers, but according to Jeannette, they'd stopped using that function months ago.

"Do you ever use the heat on a dog? You know, to speed things up?"

"Never." Jeannette's discomfort sent off warning flares.

"What if I wanted you to use heat?"

"Well, for those customers that insist, we make exceptions . . ."

"And what's the max temperature?"

Anger sparked in Jeannette's eyes. "We will not be using heat on your dogs. Are you ready to proceed, or should we cancel?"

This chick. "I'm ready."

Jeannette snapped her fingers, and a dishwater blond emerged from a corner.

"What are your dogs' names?" The assistant looked like a college-aged girl with a gentle disposition. Exactly what her dogs needed.

Nona pointed. "Lady. Bruiser. Lady's a little ticklish."

"Okay. I'll take good care of them." The girl's cheerful, open demeanor unknotted the tightness in Nona's muscles.

"And maybe some water?" Her separation anxiety caught her by surprise.

"Of course." The girl gave each dog a reassuring pat.

Jeannette escorted Nona back to the lobby.

"We need payment of half before we start the services and the rest when you come pick up the dogs."

Nona fished her card out of her wallet. Not platinum, not titanium. Only a basic Visa with no frills. DeMarcus's firm had advanced the costs for this service, but her credit card carrier wasn't used to seeing this much action. *Don't decline. Please, please.* Disquiet cycled until the payment pad changed from Processing to Accepted.

The woman rotated the tablet to face Nona. "Check the 'consent for services' box saying you understand that even cosmetic treatments for pets carry some risks, then sign and press Enter."

Anxiety zipped up Nona's spine again, and she forced herself to calm down. Her dogs would be fine. The spa package she'd ordered did not involve heat. She checked the box, signed, and pushed Enter.

"It will be about two hours. We'll send you a text when it's time for pickup."

Jeannette pivoted and haughtily walked toward the back. After pressing in the code, she pushed the door, and barking and howling again rushed out. And—*poof!*—just like that, she disappeared from sight.

◆　◆　◆

An old-fashioned bell gave a tinkle as Nona entered Gluten Be Gone. The door shut behind her, shushing the midday hustle and bustle on the street. Small café tables filled the space between the front door and the two large bakery cases flanking a cash register in the back. The exposed woodwork in the ceiling matched the ebony floors, while a calming shade of caramel graced the walls, along with sepia-toned photos of espresso shots, hot cocoa, and a pitcher of milk. The scent of butter and vanilla swirled around her, propelling her forward to examine the pastries in the cases.

A plump woman appearing to be in her fifties emerged from behind a case. "Can I get you something?"

"What do you recommend?" The chocolate chip cookies were as large as bread plates and appeared to have oatmeal in them. Nona could freeze a couple.

"Our all-time favorites are the cinnamon buns." The woman tapped the top of the case, pointing to the treats on the first row. "We run batches all day long. These right here have only been out of the oven for about five minutes."

"Sold. I'll take one."

"Anything to drink with that?"

"Can you make a mocha here?"

"We sure can." The woman looked to her left, then right, trying to find something. "Shawn, get out here to make a mocha." The woman gave a sheepish smile. "New machine. Need my nephew to work it."

"How long have you been in business at this location?"

"My six-year anniversary comes up in June."

A dude in a flannel shirt and a blue skullcap slid out from the back and started Nona's drink.

She steeled herself. Time for some more undercover work. "I dropped my dogs off next door. First time." She made a show of chewing her bottom lip. "I'm a little worried. I heard something about a dog being seriously injured over there."

Shawn stepped behind his aunt and slid the mocha toward the cash register.

"There was a giant stink about a year ago." Shawn's gaze connected with hers from underneath the shaggy hair blocking his eyes. His timid, soft voice didn't match his grungy-Seattle-rocker style.

"Someone left a dog inside a drying cage. Overheated." He gave a disgusted grunt. "An employee burst in here, begging us for a bucket of ice." Shawn leaned his forearms on the counter. "She tells me the dog's gums and tongue are bluish gray and that the dog was vomiting, staggering around, and panting all over the place. Someone later told me the dog had collapsed." Shawn's lips pursed and turned down. "Good thing there's a vet close by. A few minutes after I gave that girl the ice, I see the owner come tearing out of the groomers', clutching something that looked like a spaniel and sprinting in the vet's direction."

Nona's insides roiled at the gruesome word picture Shawn created. This wasn't Sylvia and Mitch's dog, so the groomers had injured another one as well.

The bakery owner bagged up her cinnamon bun, put in a fork and napkin, then rang up the order.

"They fired the girl. I heard she works in a smoothie shop around the corner now," Shawn volunteered. "Did I forget anything, Aunt Phil?" He glanced at his aunt.

"I don't like to gossip."

"My two fur babies are over there, so anything you know would sure put me at ease." Nona stepped closer to the register. Bruiser might use one of her running shoes as a chew toy if he found out she'd called him a fur baby.

"As I recall, there was a big stink on the Beverly Hills Undercover message site. Turned nasty. I think they settled out of court. Wasn't the first time something like that happened either." Phil made a disapproving face.

"That'll be eighteen seventy-five."

Two times more than Nona's morning Dunkin' splurges, but with Johnson's firm footing the bill, she freed her card from her wallet, swiped it one more time, and stared at the screen until the payment processed.

She grabbed her bag and drink, and turned to leave.

"Come back anytime," Shawn piped up from behind the counter, smiling.

She gave a fingertip wave and exited the store.

Nona sank down onto a chair outside the café, glad to give her toes a rest. She massaged her temples. Once she lifted the lid off the mocha, she chanced a tentative sip. The exactly right temperature. She sighed. So as far as stakeouts and investigations went, working for Johnson had some perks. On the top of that list stood baked goods, the cost of which she'd submit on her expense report. Hopefully the sugar and caffeine would act as balms to her nerves, easing her worries about Bruiser and Lady and the fact the girl at the smoothie shop was her only strong lead.

Nona removed the napkin from the bag, laid out the still-toasty bun, and pinched off a bite. Her eyes rolled up toward the sky. Who needed gluten? The sweet yet spicy bread might be the best cinnamon bun she'd ever tasted. She followed with another swig of the mocha, and the chocolaty brew with espresso melted its way into her stomach.

Nona slid her phone from her purse and dialed.

"Livingston, Meyer & Kendrick, how may I direct your call?" The woman on the line spoke in a brisk, efficient tone.

"DeMarcus Johnson, please. This is Nona Taylor calling."

"One moment."

Discordant classical music filled her ear while she waited for DeMarcus to connect.

"Nona."

"Johnson." She didn't hear laughter, but something in his voice told her DeMarcus was smirking. When wasn't he? Unwanted, her lips inched up in a smile. She kicked herself mentally. "Two things. First, there's a police report you need to get ahold of."

"What? No 'how is your day, babe?'"

"Small talk? Aren't you at work?"

"You should know. You called me." More smirk-waves radiated through her cell phone.

"There's no need to pretend when it's only us, Johnson, and I guarantee I'm never going to call you babe."

"Oh, I see you've thrown down a gauntlet."

She snorted. "Stop using words you don't know."

"I have one word for you. Nine letters. P-r-i-n-c-e-t-o-n."

Laughter welled up and bubbled out. She felt rusty and out of practice at enjoying, well, anything.

"Plus, I need to stay in character. Not being careful is what led to this whole thing in the first place."

"Sorry to tell you the Beverly Hills Undercover angle is a bust. While it did get really nasty, and the timeline between the incident, the comments and the failure to prune fits nicely, it's not enough. The Yacoubians never mention the junipers. But I've learned about another incident at Très Chic. There's also a potential witness at a smoothie shop."

"Great job. Text me the info you have, and I'll do either a Freedom of Information Act request for the police report or a subpoena. Not sure."

"You don't know which one you need?"

"Nope. People don't expect a podiatrist to know how to perform open-heart surgery. I don't know why they expect every lawyer to know every nook and cranny of the law. Don't worry, Sassy, I'll figure it out." The clickety-clack of a ballpoint pen punctuated the call repeatedly. "That's what all the big books and the internet are for."

It occurred to her that some part of DeMarcus Johnson was always in motion. His leg, his hands, his mouth. "What gives with the jitters and the fidgeting, Johnson?" She rubbed her forehead. That wasn't supposed to come out of her mouth. At least not like that.

"Ouch. I thought you told me we weren't getting personal. You said everything is strictly business between us."

She remembered what she'd said in response to some remark or another he'd made, which had crossed the line into flirting. "I'm sorry." She ground the words out from between her stiff lips. "That was uncalled for." Apologies, to anyone, were so hard for her.

She didn't deserve the good-natured laugh he gave her. She really had been rude.

"I have ADHD. Diagnosed in high school." He said it in a matter-of-fact tone. He spoke without shame. "It's a learning disability, but it comes with the gift of hyperfocus, which has gotten me far in life."

"What's hyperfocus?"

"What it sounds like, really. For things I'm passionate about, I can drill down to the exclusion of everything else and concentrate for hours on end."

"Really?"

"Yeah, basketball was one of those things. As a bonus, all the conditioning and the workouts helped me tame the downside of ADHD—hyperactivity. I don't get as much exercise as I'd like behind this law desk. That's why I fidget."

"I'm sorry. I didn't mean—"

"No offense taken. My G'Mama used to always tell me, 'God gives everybody a basket of gifts and a basket of challenges. He wants us to serve him with both.'"

That he had a grandmother he listened to and respected touched her. "I bet your G'Mama is a wise woman."

"She is. She's hilarious too." A muffled knock reached her ears. "One second, Maxine. Finishing up here."

"I didn't give you my full report."

"That's all right. We'll talk later. Thanks again for all the hard work, and don't forget to email any invoices as they come in. I want the firm to stay on top of your reimbursements. None of that net-thirty stuff with your bills."

She was silent for a moment. It irritated her that he was always being considerate and attending to her when she didn't expect it.

"Later, Sassy." He hung up the call.

She opened her phone's Notes app to double-check the rest of her action points for the day. The noise of traffic and pedestrians faded into the background as she concentrated. Maybe this is what DeMarcus's hyperfocus felt like. Something at once sweet but uncomfortable cracked open an inch inside of her.

"Nona?"

At the bass timbre of a male voice coming from in front of her, she jerked up her head.

"Nona Taylor?"

Every nerve in her body sprang to high alert, and disorientation set in. In a city of nine million people, what were the chances?

"Nona. It's me."

Tyson Foster. There he stood, clad in a pair of gray joggers, and a matching gray sleeveless Nike shirt. Showing off his biceps had been his signature look. Seemed like he hadn't outgrown that. His once tawny curls now stood frozen in place in the stylish side-parted style all the guys sported on the cover of *Men's Fitness*. His skin, still perma-tan. A gift from his Sicilian grandmother. His devastating smile? Still heart-crushing.

She felt exposed and helpless. And with his height arched over her, she felt at a disadvantage. She stood, and the ridiculous heels brought her almost eye to eye with him and close enough to smell the CK One he'd always worn.

"Wow. Nona. You look"—he took her in from her crown to her toes—"amazing. Your hair, that outfit . . ."

In an instant, she saw herself through Tyson's eyes. She'd dressed like Nikki to fit in on this side of town. Her mass of curls, singed into submission by a flat iron, hung halfway down her back. She didn't even own a pair of heels when she'd first met Tyson. And the dress, totally something Nikki might pick out for a fancy brunch. In going for a Beverly Hills vibe, she stood before Tyson as Nikki's ghost.

"It's been forever." He leaned in and gave her an awkward hug.

Disbelief superglued her feet to the sidewalk. No, it hadn't been forever. It would never be long enough. Her mind careened backward like a car unable to gain traction while sliding down an icy hill. Thanksgiving of her freshman year in high school, Lemar brought Tyson home like a stray puppy. Both Lemar and Tyson were first-years at UCLA. With his family back in Philadelphia, Lemar's teammate became a fixture around the Taylor family dinner table during long weekends and holidays. He was exquisite. Caramel-colored eyes. Sandy-brown curls. Sun-kissed skin. Rangy but muscular. And a shooting guard for the UCLA Bruins. Lemar watched from the bench, while Tyson brought showtime to Pauley Pavilion.

Nona had fallen for him, headlong and utterly.

For a couple of years, Tyson had treated Nona and Nikki like little sisters, until they turned eighteen a few weeks before the Thanksgiving holiday of the girls' senior year. That holiday, he made jokes about how grown they both were. He spent the entire meal making eyes at Nikki over the turkey but sharing his hopes and dreams with Nona during a game of horse in the driveway.

Christmas break. A long weekend or two. Spring break came around, and he showed up on her TV during March Madness. His devastating smile shone for the entire world to see, and love for him wrapped Nona in a silken vise. But she'd also seen how Nikki sat transfixed in front of the screen, rapture scrolling across her face.

She and Nikki graduated from high school in the spring. In the fall, Nona entered her freshman year at UC Irvine. Nikki took a gap year, working at a coffee shop and teaching dance lessons to kids at a local studio. Tyson used an extra year of eligibility to play a fifth year at UCLA.

And the narrow rift caused by teenage squabbles between Nikki and herself ruptured into a chasm.

Nona had made furtive trips to UCLA's campus a few times to see Tyson. She'd slip away from home in the car she and her sister shared, always careful to conceal the clandestine trips and reveling in the thrill of dating an NBA prospect. She had pushed down the accusing thoughts caused by the sneaking around—and by the things they had done.

A teen on one of those annoying e-scooters whizzed by, tousling her hair and pulling her attention back to the man in front of her and not the specter that had haunted her past all these years.

"Such a hard situation, the last time we saw each other."

Really? That's how he described Nikki's memorial. It was a *situation*? "You could say that."

Scrambling extended family from the East Coast to attend a funeral for Nikki proved difficult, so after a private service the week after Nikki's death, the family held a celebration of life service a few months later. During that gap in the family's formal mourning, Lemar confronted Tyson about his relationships with both Nikki and Nona, ending his side of the heated discussion by smashing Tyson in the face so hard he broke Tyson's nose. But hardwired for sympathy and understanding, Lemar forgave Tyson before the knuckles on his fists healed and invited the betrayer to Nikki's memorial.

"Nikki would want us to forgive Tyson. He didn't cause her accident."

And he hadn't. Nona herself had. Still, Tyson's face in front of her caused heat to pulse in her chest, the intensity triggering the memory of the volcanic anger that had wrenched Nona's sister from her.

"I have a scouting business going and run a website ranking D1 basketball prospects. I host a tournament, do some work with kids in AAU basketball. All the stuff we used to talk about."

"All the stuff we—" A police siren *boop-booped*, jerking her attention from the clueless man in front of her. How long did he expect her to stand here as he skipped down memory lane, as if he hadn't crushed her heart into a thousand pieces, before she imploded? Rage warred with anguish and shame. Shame that she sacrificed her sister for him. Words, vicious and angry, sprang to the tip of her tongue. Half of her wanted to cut Tyson down, eviscerate him the way his betrayal had gutted her and left her the shell of a woman she had been. The other traitorous part was desperate to know why he had not chosen her. It was the *why* that had plagued her all these years. What was it about her that made men in her life run?

"What has you on this side of town? Lemar says you're living near Pasadena." His voice drifted up at the end of the sentence, as if he really cared.

She'd shared all her dreams with him in the past, about the home she wanted, the career. And he'd thrown it all away. He hadn't cared then, so she wouldn't give him any personal details to trample over now. "Working on a case. I'm a private investigator."

He snapped his fingers. "That's right. I forgot. Lemar told me that last time I saw him."

Wait, what? "When did you see Lemar?" Why was she even asking?

"The team had a little get-together celebrating the retirement of one of the coaches. In fact, I'm going up to the campus now, to interview for an associate athletic director position."

The one day she set up for this investigation was the day Tyson had a meeting eight miles away, in Westwood. There was no place in the metropolitan area to outrun Tyson and the memories.

Her phone pinged with an incoming text.

"I need to go. My dogs are ready." She pointed to Très Chic Pet Boutique.

"You have those dogs you always wanted. Cool. Cool." He bobbled in affirmation like a cheap prize from Chuck E. Cheese. Tyson was a joke. How had she never seen it before? "I gotta run too. Maybe we can get together one day and catch up."

All she could muster was a brief negative shake before she stalked away, leaving her spine, her nerve, and her pride on the spot she'd just vacated.

* * *

As soon as Nona entered her townhome, she unlaced the heels she'd been wearing, tossed her keys in the bowl, and unclipped Lady's and Bruiser's leashes. The new, glossy sheen on Lady's coat and the jaunty bandanna encircling Bruiser's neck did nothing to lift her mood. While relieved to see her dogs had enjoyed their spa treatments, she could not shake off her run-in with Tyson. Heaviness weighed her down. She moved like a robot, each step farther into the interior of her home wooden and forced.

Time had been unfairly generous to Tyson. In fact, he was handsomer now that he'd lost some of his boyishness. In the first year after Nikki's death, she'd wished him complete financial ruin and a debilitating illness. But then she realized she'd ultimately been the one responsible, so she moved past revenge fantasies. Not that she'd forgiven him.

Her phone pinged with an incoming message from Johnson.

> Good job getting all that
> information. If this looks
> like it's going to trial, we'll

depose Jeannette, the
kid at the bakery, and
the vet. There may be a
confidentiality clause in the
settlement with the owner
of the spaniel, but I'll dig
around in the court records
to see what I can find out.

Bruiser trotted off, no doubt to take a nap in his doggy bed. Lady stayed close by, poking the back of Nona's hand with her nose. Maybe it was her expression, some chemical in her perspiration. She didn't know how, but Lady could always sense her mood and would offer comfort.

Her phone dinged with another incoming text.

We need to meet to discuss
next steps.

She could not deal with any of her casework right now. She dropped her phone on the console, forced herself to climb the stairs to her room, and collapsed on the bed. Guilt and shame had been her constant companions for years, but she'd put the rage at Tyson behind her and moved to indifference—or so she'd thought. When would she be free of the shame?

She turned and mashed her face into her pillow, suffocating the pain. Seeing Tyson had been like entering a horrible time machine back to the absolute worst days of her life.

The last time Nona had seen her sister, Nikki had stood on the front stoop, arms crossed, the glow from the porch light sparkling in the highlights of her honey-golden hair. Normally Nikki was the peacemaker between the siblings. And her beauty radiated through her loving heart and her gentleness. But at that moment, Nikki was a fierce warrior, determination shining in her eyes.

The argument had started when Nikki had nagged Nona about taking care of the worn tires and asked her—again—to fill the tank like she'd promised. In a childish attempt to punish her sister, Nona had blown off

Nikki, hidden behind the half truth that her waitressing job barely covered her books and that she'd maxed out her credit card. In reality, Nona didn't care if her failure to fill the tank left Nikki stranded on the side of the road. Her anger made her petty, and her jealousy made her cruel. Why did Nikki deserve Tyson? Why wouldn't Tyson make a clean break from her? Why wouldn't he date Nona out in the open and aboveboard?

And then it all spiraled when Nona told Nikki she couldn't hold on to Tyson in the long run, because she was too much of a good girl and that he'd soon tire of her. It had been a low blow, but Nona hadn't cared.

"I'm not giving in, Nona. Not on this."

"You're so selfish, Nikki." Heat flamed Nona's face. *"Why can't I have this one thing? You're always first. First with Mom, first in school."* Even when she'd said the words, she'd known they were a lie. Nikki had always been the one to share when they were kids. Half of her dessert. Some of her allowance.

Nona and Nikki had squabbled over the years. What sisters didn't? But they'd never crossed the line.

"Nikki, I love him." It had humbled Nona to tell Nikki that desperate truth. The tears rolling down her face were proof of her humiliation.

But Nikki left in a flurry of emotion.

If she closed her eyes, Nona could still see the fury on Nikki's face and feel the acid-like burn of her own anger in that moment.

In the aftermath of the car accident—or more rightly, Nikki's death caused by Nona's betrayal—Nona's family had disintegrated.

Her mother had flatly rejected a viewing. She'd told Nona she'd done it for her sake. So Nona wouldn't see her own face, still and lifeless in death. But Nona knew the truth. Her mother was so distraught at losing her child, she couldn't bear to look—not for one second.

A twin herself, Nona's mother had told the story over and over about how she'd felt double blessed being a twin and having twins. She'd delighted in dressing her girls alike and giving them matching initials. She'd told them stories about the special communication bond she had with her own sister, the tricks they'd played on people, and how she and her sister were best friends even though Auntie lived in New York. They talked almost every day. And how Nona and Nikki should always, always be best friends.

Within a year, Lemar began searching for acting jobs in New York; Nona entered her second year of college, which somehow gave her mother permission to close her dance studio and move back east; and her absent father sent flowers and a note. Like a few scattered petals could heal a broken family.

Mom had asked Nona over and over to move to New York, to make a clean break and be with the extended family. Nona had refused.

She'd known she had to do the right thing. Stay put and let her family move on without her. To stop being a constant reminder to her mother of the daughter she'd lost.

Nona had remained behind. Enshrined in her pain. Walled off from love. Paying her penance.

The jingle of Bruiser's dog tags drew her back to the present. A small mercy that kept her from rehashing the events the rest of the evening. Nona's body screamed for her to take a quick shower, then put on some basketball shorts and a tank to relax. But her emotional overwhelm made physical exertion impossible. So she lay on her back, making wrinkles in the sheath dress, and let the tears slide from the corners of her eyes, down over her ears, and into the pillow.

Chapter 11

THE OLD PASTOR barely spent time at the church. Who would want to, given how run-down it appeared on the outside? After a week of tailing Grant to a food pantry, a nursing home, a car wash, and the barbershop, Zeke was no closer to getting that retainer agreement signed. He needed the fish to take the bait. After the big publicity splash at that HeartSpark thing, the word was out about Leisure Zone Holdings and their plans to build an entertainment complex in Burnt Water. They'd even sent their stupid press release to the *Burnt Water Herald*. Kitty had sent him a screenshot. If Calloway wasn't careful, folks would start sniffing around, trying to get into his pocket for no-bid contracts and long-term leases.

Zeke's back was up against the wall, and these stakeouts were a waste of time. Leisure Zone Holdings didn't need Calloway to seal the deal; they only needed the land. If the reverend let it escheat, there'd be a bidding frenzy to buy, cutting both Zeke and Calloway out of millions. The company's pockets were deep enough to buy the property in the old lady's estate at auction no matter how high the price went, but if that happened, for him, there'd be a giant goose egg. The property had to pass through the estate to the pastor so they could finagle a low-ball offer.

As of right now, the chumps at Leisure Zone Holdings had trusted Calloway to handle all details related to the underlying property. They had no idea that an estate claim worth millions stood between the company and the megaplex they planned to build. Calloway had assured them that all transfers of title were being handled expeditiously and that the city council was smoothing the road for them. If things continued dragging on, however, they would find out.

Zeke stared across the street at the church and fumed. Calloway was pressing him daily for an update. But since Zeke was fronting his own expenses, Calloway didn't have his normal financial leverage over him, and Calloway didn't like it. Good. About time he gave Zeke the respect he deserved. Mr. High-and-Mighty wouldn't even be a city councilman if his old high school buddy Zeke hadn't helped rig the ballot box for him. The man was an ingrate, and Zeke couldn't wait to cut him loose.

He fished in his front pocket to pull out a smoke, but the pack was empty. Zeke needed Grant's cell number. He was tired of racking up messages on the church's answering machine and had hoped to get the letter signed without having a face-to-face with the pastor. Less messy. Nothing to track back directly to Zeke. But the delay was forcing his hand.

He exited his car and shuffled to the adjacent convenience store. He'd get a six-pack of cold ones for later tonight and some smokes to tide him over. A bell above the door gave a jingle when he entered. The man behind the register looked up for a second, then resumed reading the paper spread on the counter in front of him.

After grabbing his favorite beer from the refrigerated case, Zeke slid the bottles across the counter. "Give me a pack of Marlboros too."

Without a word, the man turned to grab Zeke's request.

Sports chatter squawked from a speaker beside the cash register. To its left was an ancient bulletin board covered with flyers, take-out menus, and business cards for bail bondsmen. Zeke squinted. One notice had little strips cut at the bottom of the flyer, with phone numbers printed on each little strip. He saw a picture of Mount Zion at the top of the page. Under the name of the church, a box of text read, "Need prayer? Call 213-555-PRAY."

He tore off one of the little strips. He had the church number memorized. This number was different. "Gotcha."

"What was that, fella?"

"I said, how much?"

"That'll be eighteen dollars and eighty-two cents."

Zeke pushed his credit card into the machine, then signed on the pad. His mood had improved considerably. "Y'all have a great day."

The clerk quirked an eyebrow.

Zeke didn't care. He pushed his way out of the store with the beer tucked under one arm and the smokes and slip of paper clutched in a hand. He'd write out a little script, so he'd say the right words to get the pastor to sign, then he'd give the old man a call. As he made his way to his car, he whistled a tune. Time to reel that fish in.

* * *

Nona approached the church's back entrance. The stink from the Quicky Mart's dumpster assaulted her nostrils. It smelled like sour produce, and she held her breath while Pastor Grant fumbled with the lock from the inside.

"So glad you could come, Nona. I think the Bible might be here in the church somewhere, but I need your help lifting boxes. Not as young as I used to be."

"This might be the break we need." She'd been heartsick the day before. She'd had to tell him that after several hours of phone trees, English to Spanish conversations using Google Translate, and a spate of email messages, she'd learned that decades earlier, burst pipes and flooding had destroyed years' worth of birth records from the early 1930s to the late '40s. There was no way she could get a copy from the Mexican government. But she was holding out some hope that the family Bible would be the key to unlock the mystery of the estate's location and the name of the deceased relative. She also hoped to find the certified copy of his birth certificate tucked inside that Bible.

Pastor Grant stood back to let her pass. Even in the middle of the week and with no one at the church but himself, he wore a dress shirt with the sleeves buttoned at the wrists plus a suit vest with matching pants and a tie. Mount Zion didn't do megachurch business casual.

Nona followed him toward his office, and tinny, static-laced music emanated from the doorway.

O what peace we often forfeit,
O what needless pain we bear,
All because we do not carry
Everything to God in prayer!

The words cut her clear through. She'd been praying for ten years, carrying her burden to the Lord, like the song said, but the promised peace had not come. She shoved the thoughts into her mental bottom drawer so she could concentrate on the task before her.

Pastor Grant plopped in his seat and gestured to three cardboard boxes in the corner. "Found these behind some folding chairs in the storage closet. I was able to drag them in here by myself."

Nona moved closer to the stack that was resting on dark burgundy carpeting. Water stains marred the flap of the one on top. She turned the guest chair in front of the pastor's desk to face the boxes. "Can you hand me a pair of scissors?"

"How about this letter opener?"

Nona stretched out her arm and grabbed the lethal-looking tool, turned, and made a quick cut in the packing tape. A tiny, almost translucent spider scurried up the side of the box, and she flinched. Given how small he was and that he was in a church, she gave him a reprieve.

She folded back the flaps.

"See anything that might be a Bible?"

She began pulling out Sunday school materials, old church bulletins, and tithing envelopes. "No Bibles in here."

"I could have opened them without you. I feel bad dragging you all the way here for nothing, but I'd seen something on that show *Law & Order* about chain of evidence or something like that. My wife loved that show." A sheen covered his eyes. He took off his glasses and swiped away the moisture. "Police shows and gardening." A wistful smile hovered on his lips.

Tenderness for him pulled at her. "Did you mean chain of custody?" She returned the conversation to the matter at hand.

"Yes. Chain of custody. And I didn't want to mess that up."

He talked about his wife like she might come back from the store at any moment. Nona's shoulders drooped. What would it be like to have a love that lasted decades?

She cleared her throat, pushing down the emotions clogging her words. "That's not an issue. Chain of custody deals with making sure mishandling or tampering doesn't taint evidence. It's a crucial matter in many criminal cases. It can come up in civil matters as well, but not as often." She began returning the items she'd found to the box. "The courts need to know where something came from and who's touched it in between the time of discovery and the time it's presented as evidence at court. Since it's your Bible, the chain starts with you."

She cut open the next box. More papers, but something farther down caught her eye. She plucked up what she hoped was significant.

There was an index card with a photo attached to it by a paper clip. The date on the card, 1989, stood out in a sure cursive.

My Heart,

I found this buried in a box full of treasures. You are radiant. This is how I remember you. Young and happy, before the thing that drove us apart ever happened. All I have is the memory of you. I miss you so much. You are a part of me always.

Your Dearest Love

The sentiment on the card echoed the pain in her own life. She flipped the photograph over and read the words on the back out loud. "'Harvest Dance. Flo, Lizzie, Rose, Book, Eddie, Laurence, Dale. 1935.'"

She held out the photograph, which featured seven people. Two women in taffeta dresses, and a third who appeared to be wearing velvet. Behind the women were four men. One man wore a white dinner jacket, and the other three wore black tuxedos. The differently hued complexions spoke of the variety of shades in the Black community. The faces appeared to be of youths in their late teens, early twenties, but each one bore the maturity of a generation that had weathered the Great Depression.

Tears glistened in Pastor Grant's eyes as he reverently received the photo with one hand and maneuvered his reading glasses onto his face with the other. "That's Mama. Behind her, at her shoulder, to the left, is Daddy. I don't know who the others are." He reached out his index finger lovingly to touch the faces.

"Are you sure you don't recognize anyone else?" she pressed.

Brackets of sadness appeared at the corners of his eyes. "No, I don't think so. Like I said, my mother kept everything hush-hush about her family. No pictures— Wait." He sat up straight and fixated on the photo. "The woman there." He pointed. "She resembles my mama so much." He stroked his chin, then leaned back and squeezed his eyes shut in concentration. "Maybe this is Mama's sister. I'm certain I remember that name."

"And you're certain your mother only had one sister."

"As far as I can piece it together. What with my old-man memory and my family's silence . . ."

"It is puzzling that someone sent this note to your mother with the salutation, 'My Heart.' That sounds like an endearment between sweethearts."

"You're right. But it's not my daddy, because they ended up married, not torn apart like the note says."

"Look one more time. Are you sure you don't recognize any of the other men in the photo?"

Consternation marked his face. "No, I don't. Sorry."

Nona gave him a reassuring smile, but uneasiness poked at her. What if there had been a love triangle involving Pastor Grant's mother, one of the men in the photo, and her sister? Bile pushed up. She'd hate for that to be his family history. Her own heart bore the scars of a romance turned ugly.

She blanked out her facial expression to not betray her concern and upset Pastor. "Even the smallest clue is helpful." *Small* was too big a word. The clue was the size of a grain of rice. "May I take this picture? Search engines have facial recognition software. This photo is old, but maybe a high school yearbook will pop up. I'll also run variations of the name Elizabeth paired with the last name Hall in Alabama." Lizzie could stand for Elizabeth. The name Hall was also generic, but she'd work with what she had.

She turned and opened the last box. It contained nothing but old church records. "Do you want to get rid of these?"

"No. Never know what the next pastor might want to do with them."

"Next pastor." His words caught her by surprise. "Are you stepping down?"

"Oh, no. But everyone eventually leaves the stage, Nona. The time to get prepared for that is now, while you still have a chance." He paused a long beat. "Are you prepared, Nona?"

The discussion had taken a personal and uncomfortable turn.

"Going through this whole thing has shown me that old wounds can fester for years and years into the future." Pastor Grant looked wistful. "I never knew what exactly happened in Mama's family, but since we never visited or talked to any of them, they clearly had a break in their relationship. So tragic."

She turned away from Pastor Grant as she neatened up the boxes and prepared to leave. This whole thing hit too close to home, like a heavy capstone on top of her run-in with Tyson, causing a suffocating pressure in her chest. She needed to get out of the pastor's office immediately. She stood and brushed her hands down the front of her jeans to wipe off the dust and moved toward the door.

"I think we're done for today," she said.

"Nona." Pastor Grant halted her retreat. "I don't know all the details of what happened between you and your sister, Nikki, but please know, I am available anytime you want to talk. More importantly, God never slumbers, and he never sleeps. He's available twenty-four hours a day. He can forgive all your sins, even those you can't forgive yourself for. I've seen how hard things have been for you. Won't you lay your burdens at his feet?"

Pastor Grant was pushing her, more than he ever had. She wanted to run out of his office and not come back, ditch the heir hunting case and never see him again. Standing in the doorway, she turned to look at him, ready to tell him she'd find someone else to handle the case. His eyes radiated so much love and concern for her, she felt as though her heart would crack into a million pieces.

"Take some time and think about it. That's all I'm asking, Nona."

She bumped her hip against the doorknob, causing a shot of pain as she rushed to escape.

✦ ✦ ✦

Zeke dialed the number on the strip of paper. This had to be the old man's cell phone number. The phone kept ringing, stretching Zeke's already taut nerves to near breaking.

"Hello."

"Is this Pastor Hosea Grant?"

"Why yes, it is. How may I help you?"

"Pastor Grant, I'm so glad I finally reached you. This is . . ." Zeke scrambled to make up a fake name for himself. "John Smith, with Javit, Blatt & Steele in Alabama. I'm the paralegal assisting with your inheritance case." *Really, John Smith?*

"Oh . . ."

The old man didn't seem enthusiastic.

"I have the delivery confirmations from the post office, which show you received our letters about a possible inheritance."

"I see."

Why was this geezer being so cagey? "There are a few more relatives that stand to inherit your share if you don't come forward, and time is running out."

"How do I know this isn't an identity scam?"

So that was the holdup. Zeke would give the fish a little slack in the line, then yank when he bit. Zeke pulled out his notes. "I have your identifying information right here. Roscoe Hosea Grant, born 1946 to Florence Grant and Booker Grant. Currently, you live in Inglewood, California. You've been pastor of Mount Zion Missionary Baptist Church since 1971. Is this all accurate?" He'd plucked everything he'd told Grant from the internet. Not worried. His surveillance had revealed Grant used a flip phone. "We needed this information to confirm you are the rightful heir. Is it correct?"

"Why yes, it is. But don't you need my birth certificate and other proof of my relationship to the person who died for the court?"

"We need that eventually, but what we need first is for you to sign the retainer letter we sent you, so we can begin working up the case."

"Well, my friend Nona . . . I mean, I already have someone assisting me a little with this. She's helping me find my family Bible and . . ."

"I'm sorry, what was that?" Zeke strained to keep the clipped tone out of his voice.

"I mean. Oh dear . . . I'm not ready to sign right now." Grant coughed. "I still have some time, don't I?"

Sweat broke out on Zeke's forehead, and he flexed his finger around his cell in such a tight grip, his fingers hurt. Pieces started falling into place. Someone was helping the pastor, and Zeke would bet it was that she-cat who kept popping up. Her presence at the dance wasn't coincidence, after all. She was sniffing around. Besides, didn't matter what she'd said about having a fiancé. She might still be the pastor's girlfriend—a girlfriend who was trying to help the reverend steal Zeke's share of the money. A vein pulsed in his temple.

"Like I said, there are some other heirs who will take the inheritance if you don't come forward." He wouldn't tell the reverend the property would go to the state. Better to let him think others were champing at the bit to get their hands on it. Wasn't envy one of the seven deadly sins? Everybody wanted to have something they thought someone else was going to get. "Plus, I am authorized to tell you we're estimating a figure close to ten thousand dollars." Greed and the ministry went together like ham and eggs. *Chew on that for a bit, old man.*

"Oh my. Well, I'll need to get back to you, Mr. Smith. Let me write down your number."

Zeke called out the numbers for his untraceable burner phone to Grant. "Get back to me soon. Don't delay. Remember, there are other heirs waiting in the wings."

"Um, okay." The geezer's voice warbled. Frail and uncertain.

The time to yank the rod back and hook that fish would be any day now.

Chapter 12

DeMarcus drove up in front of the In-N-Out Burger right off the freeway and checked his face in the mirror. The absence of facial hair still caught him off guard, but no one else at the firm could pull off an orange polo shirt on casual Friday and get away with it. He infused the right amount of tailoring and style into his traditional khaki pants and loafers that he made it look cool and not like he worked at the corporate headquarters for Orange Julius.

His phone rang. He rolled his eyes as he answered. "I don't have time for this, Jamaria."

"What are you doing?"

"I'm meeting a colleague for a working lunch." No need to tell Jamaria anything about Nona. He'd never hear the end of it.

"You're turning into a geezer."

"Like I said, I'm busy, Jamaria. Is this an emergency?"

"No. I wanted to send you some pictures of that prom dress you said you'd buy me."

"You don't even have a date yet. The prom is months away. Why are we discussing dresses? I have a meeting—"

She cut into his tirade. "Everyone knows you have to get the dress early. All the good ones will be gone."

He huffed out a gust of air and clamped his forehead between his thumb and index finger. "Fine. Send the pictures and let me know the prices. I'll get back to you when I'm free."

"You're the best, D."

"You are correct. I am." He pulled his mind out of his phone call with Jamaria and spied Nona, already seated at an outdoor table. He'd been so distracted, he hadn't even seen her when he'd driven up. Her two dogs were lying at her feet.

He reached for the handle to open the door, and a half dozen incoming text notifications flooded his phone, disrupting his concentration. Jamaria had a horrible sense of timing. He snatched up his phone and opened the messages. *What in the world?* The first dress was only suitable for a woman working Julia Roberts's job in *Pretty Woman*. There was no way he was letting her buy that dress with his money, with G'Mama's money, or with her own money.

He scanned down to the next dress. It was worse than the first and flaming red. Jamaria had lost her mind.

Pictures three through five were variations on the same theme. Short, low-cut, and see-through. He didn't have time for this, but she was going off the rails.

He eyed Nona, sitting patiently.

Another text came in. Jamaria.

These dresses are in the
$100–200 range.

Will more money buy more
fabric? These dresses are
scandalous and completely
inappropriate. My little cousin
isn't going around dressed
like a cast member from Real
Housewives.

There is this one dress . . .

His phone dinged again. He tapped on the picture to enlarge it. A peach-colored dress, down to the floor, with a neckline above the collarbone. It had some sort of see-through, lacy material over the skirt and little sparkles on the top. His cousin would be the prettiest girl at the prom in this dress.

Now that's what I'm talking
about.

Awesome. I ordered it! A
bargain at $1500. Later, cuz.
AP Physics calls.

He just got played. She'd sent him all those ridiculous dresses first, knowing she really wanted the last one. It was a good thing Jamaria lived on the East Coast. He grabbed his tablet and his legal pad from the passenger seat and exited the car to join Nona, mad at himself for letting his cousin distract him.

Nona's outfit was nondescript. She wore a pair of jeans topped with a navy windbreaker. She'd combed her hair back into a misshapen bun, but wild tendrils floated about, some across her forehead and others around her neck. He'd never met someone like Nona. She didn't usually wear makeup or accessories. Yet she was the prettiest woman he'd ever seen.

"Glad you could make it, Johnson. Were you watching me from your car?"

He flipped his wrist and checked the time. "I'm on time."

"Didn't say you were late."

"And I had a phone call. Are you busting my chops for sport?"

"Absolutely." She smiled, and his irritation at Jamaria evaporated.

"I see you brought your protection with you. I can order for us, since you need to watch the dogs."

"Um, sure. I'll have a number two with onions and a Coke, two hamburgers, no buns for Lady and Bruiser, and a cup of water." Her response was tentative, like no one ever offered to get her food. "Thank you."

"Onions. What, no kiss for your fiancé?"

"Never. Get the food, so we can get this meeting over with."

He laughed and walked inside to place the order.

DeMarcus plopped a couple of trays on the table. He divvied up the spread of food in front of them, then bowed his head and said a quick silent prayer.

When he opened his eyes, her brows arched in incredulity.

"Didn't take you for the praying type."

He gave her a disbelieving scowl and tsked. "Woman, you *did* meet me in church." He couldn't explain why, but he'd started saying a short grace before meals after the Watch Night service. Sometimes he'd bow his head. Sometimes he'd close his eyes briefly. G'Mama's admonitions were finally sinking in. He could hear her now. "*You can't make any crops grow. You don't bring rain, and you can't control the seasons. Thank the Good Lord for the food that keeps you alive.*"

"We didn't meet at church. It wasn't a date. I happened to be there. You happened to be there."

"I didn't say date. You're the one bringing up dating . . ." A smile tugged at his lips. "I got no problem if we date. I think you'd like it too."

"Stick to business, Johnson."

"I thought you'd want to flirt with me. You know, to make our relationship more believable."

She rolled her eyes, then shoved ten fries in her mouth at once. Her cheeks puffed out like a chipmunk's. It was absolutely adorable.

"Ready when you are, Alvin."

She laughed, slapping her hand over her mouth to avoid spewing her lunch. Lady and Bruiser made quick work of the burger patties and lapped up water out of the collapsible water bowl she'd extracted from her handbag.

DeMarcus ate his lunch, not feeling the need to fill in the silence while Nona enjoyed her food.

He pushed away his tray, stacked with burger wrappers and the residue of his ketchup pile, and stood.

"Probate is not my specialty, but I think I've figured out what's going on with Pastor Grant's case." He stood and moved to Nona's side of the table, so they could sit side by side.

She made a face, repositioned herself, and shoved her phone in her back pocket.

He fired up his tablet and swiped until he found the notes he'd made.

Even though he was giving a boring presentation to her on the laws of intestacy, he was antsy, like he'd had three Red Bulls. Sassy kept him on edge in the best way possible. He was used to women using every trick in the book to snare his attention. Not Nona. She threw up enough walls to keep him at bay, but she never slammed on the brakes entirely.

"So, were you able to find out exactly what Pastor Grant needs to prove he's an heir?"

"We don't even know who the decedent is in this case or what the relationship to the decedent is. But heir hunting firms only take cases where there isn't a will." He tapped the screen a few times. "Under the intestacy laws in Alabama, an inheritance can only pass to a select number of individuals." He swiped up.

"How does that help us?"

"We can narrow down the relationship between Pastor Grant and the unknown decedent based on how the laws work." DeMarcus reached to snatch a fry from Nona's pile.

She slapped his hand. "Fake fiancés don't get boyfriend privileges."

"Well then, I can't wait for the day I can legitimately eat some of your fries."

"In your dreams. Get back to the Probate Code."

He pretended to snore. "Since you insist. If someone dies without a will and also has not left behind a living spouse, there's a hierarchy of beneficiaries. The first individuals to inherit are the decedent's children. Obviously, it's not Pastor Grant's parents. Next, if someone outlives their children but leaves behind grandchildren, the decedent's estate goes to the grandchildren. Since Pastor Grant is nearly eighty, there is zero chance he is the heir of one of his grandparents' estates." He pointed to the next line on the statute. "After that, it's the decedent's parents. There is no chance the decedent's parents are living. Again, Pastor Grant isn't in that category." He moved his finger again on the tablet. "But here is the relationship that I think is the source of the inheritance. If the parents are dead, it is the sisters and brothers of the decedent who inherit. And if the decedent's siblings are dead but there are living nieces and nephews, the decedent's nieces and nephews inherit."

Nona screwed up her face in concentration.

"You told me Pastor Grant had at least one aunt."

"Yes. He remembered his mother had a sister. He also remembered that his father told him, at some point, his two brothers predeceased him, but he remembers nothing else." Nona moved closer to read the statute on his tablet. One of her wayward curls brushed his cheek.

"Then this estate might be for the sister of Pastor Grant's mother. In other words, his aunt. Based on Pastor Grant's age, we're looking for a decedent in her upper nineties. Maybe even one hundred. And if Pastor Grant is the only child of his mother, he's the sole surviving heir."

"You said 'if.'"

"That note you mentioned to me the other day is open to any number of interpretations, including the possibility that Pastor Grant's mother has another child out there somewhere."

"I never thought about that. Do you mean, a baby she may have given away?"

"Yes. If that's the case, Pastor Grant would still be an heir, but he'd have to split the estate."

"Okay, we've narrowed it down to the estate of a woman who was near one hundred years old, who died in or around Burnt Water, Alabama. And we cannot rule out the possibility of another heir."

Nona reached out, snagged DeMarcus's tablet, and studied the notes on the screen. "Maybe Burnt Water has a local online paper with obituaries." Her voice lifted at the end in a question.

"You might get a hit on that." His mind wandered. Probate might be the most boring area of the law ever. No. Real estate closings were the most boring. Then securities regulation, then probate estates. The sheer tedium might cause him to pop a vein. He started planning his March Madness brackets, but his attention pinged to a pigeon eating a piece of bun that had fallen on the ground. Gross. Flying rats. Black rims would have worked better on that Tesla.

Nona slid DeMarcus's tablet toward him and pulled her phone out of her pocket, and her index finger darted around on the screen. His eyes bounced off Nona's hands as she typed on her phone, searching for a local paper with online obituaries. His focus returned like a laser. "Whoa. Why are you wearing my ring backward?"

She held her left hand out in front of her and examined it. "The light bounces off it." She squinted at him. "Flipped it around so it won't blind me."

"I knew you liked my ring. All you have to do is say you like it and then I won't mention it again." She didn't have to wear the ring when they weren't with people from his firm. The fact that she had was interesting. He'd file that info away for later.

"Won't mention it again?" She scoffed. "I see I can add *liar* to my list of things I know about you."

He deployed his full smile. "Oh, I didn't say I wouldn't mention Princeton again. Just not my Princeton ring."

She dropped her head and resumed her search on the phone, but he caught her smiling.

"Besides, your dogs love me." He scratched Bruiser behind the ears. The dog licked his fingers, raised up on his hind legs, and rested his muzzle on DeMarcus's lap. He pulled a treat from the bag he'd stashed in his pocket and slipped it to him.

"Yes, well, he's fickle."

"Doesn't explain why Lady likes me."

"She's the beta. Does whatever Bruiser tells her to."

"Oh, I see." He focused his attention on Nona like a heat-seeking missile locked on its target. She attempted to squish a section of her mane of loopy curls behind her ear, but they popped right back out, stringing across her face as the wind picked up. After snatching her sunglasses off the table, she slid them over her hair as a makeshift headband.

A heavy sigh seeped out, and she placed her phone onto the table.

"What's wrong?" He leaned slightly toward her. With her mass of curls pushed back, the angles and lines of her face stood out like facets on a diamond. He'd dated many attractive women, but the steely determination on her face, the seriousness in her eyes—Nona was a woman of substance, not a plaything. He couldn't stop watching her if he tried.

"I'm not finding what I'm looking for. Also"—she pinned his gaze with hers—"it's not polite to stare, Johnson."

He lifted a shoulder, let it drop, and kept staring. He wanted Nona in his life. She challenged him and made him laugh. When the spite fence and inheritance cases were over, how was he going to get her to date him for real?

Chapter 13

Nona yawned and rubbed her eyes. She didn't need to check her watch. Ten o'clock jogger dude had made his nightly lap past her office window a minute or two earlier. She stood from her desk to drag herself to the kitchen to make some more coffee. Her sock-clad feet moved silently across the wooden floor. Lady popped up from her resting spot beside Nona's chair and trotted dutifully behind her, while Bruiser cracked open his eyes for a second, then closed them again from his perch on the occasional chair where he'd been sleeping.

In the kitchen, she took down the canister of cheap robusta, scooped a mound into the machine, and poured in the water. A message notification chimed on her phone. She rested her hip against the countertop, slid her phone from her back pocket, and swiped in her password.

It was Lemar.

> Circling back to your text.
> Did some asking around.
> Check out this site—Reality
> PAs Dish. It's a forum for
> production assistants on
> reality TV shows to gripe
> anonymously about their
> bosses. It's a long shot, but
> you might find something.

> What exactly is the job of a
> production assistant?

Gopher, chauffeur,
secretary, whipping post. 😩

Awesome! Where do I sign up?

With your attitude
and Terminator facial
expressions, you'd be fired
within an hour.

#Facts. Thanks for the info. Will
let you know if I find any leads.

Anytime, sis.

She slid her mug from beside the machine, rinsed it out at the sink, and eyed Lady, who stood tongue out in front of her empty water dish. Nona refilled her mug with water and poured it into Lady's bowl. Lady's lapping noises and the clink of her tags filled the otherwise quiet kitchen.

Nona and Nikki had always talked about getting an apartment together and having some pets. Dogs for Nona, cats for Nikki. Nikki would start her own dance studio, and Nona would find a job using her criminal justice degree. Nona's world now had everything she'd wanted, except her twin beside her to share in the dream. Her forehead tightened. She shook her head to cast the thoughts of the past out of her mind. She couldn't go down this road. Not today. Two cases needed her attention, and work was her first and only priority. There'd be plenty of time when she was wide awake at 3:00 a.m. to relive her past mistakes.

After filling her cup with coffee, she opened the cabinet and grabbed the caramel Coffee mate creamer. Cupping the mug between her hands, she made her way to her office while inhaling the rich scent. At her desk, she looked up Reality PAs Dish on her computer. The opening picture featured a woman, phone wedged between her cheek and shoulder, hands holding a Starbucks four-cup carrier filled with huge whipped cream–topped drinks, and a bulging handled bag hanging off her pinky. The woman's rumpled outfit and mismatched shoes were all displayed beneath a tagline that read "Stardom Is Just One Coffee Run Away."

After surfing around, Nona found the message board where people could anonymously post their gripes and grievances against their studio bosses or the stars they worked for. She scanned the various categories of posts. "Violating My Nondisclosure Here!" "That Moment When I Got Backstabbed." "My Boss Is Worse Than Your Boss." "Shout-Out to the Good Guys." The last section, entitled "Exit Stage Left," featured posts and videos of PAs dramatically quitting their jobs. She clicked the search bar at the top and typed in "Yo! It's the Yacoubians." A notification popped up, prompting her to create a login ID and password. She remembered back in middle school, she'd sneak copies of her mother's Janet Evanovich books and read them under the covers after bedtime. She picked Stephanie Plum for her username and used a password generator. After accepting the terms of service that no one ever read, she reentered her search query. The page populated with several threads dedicated to the Yacoubians. Lemar's tip had been spot-on. These results hadn't shown up during her searches of publicly accessible information.

She opened the first thread, titled "Yo! The Yacoubians Don't Pay Their Bills."

"Who owes me four weeks' pay for dog sitting? Mila Yacoubian, that's who. How can you go on vacation to Hawaii and leave me hanging?" Harried in Hollywood

"Drove their car to the mechanic to get it fixed. Credit card declined when I paid. Had to use my own. If you can't afford a Range Rover, don't drive one. Next time, I might ask the mechanic to leave the cap off after your oil change." Car Jockey 2002

"Did makeup and hair for photo shoot. Promised publicity and cross-promotion on their Instagram. Not even a 'thanks.' Wish I'd superglued on those lashes." Artistry by Desiree

"Had to do some quick talking with the landscaper. Yard needed cut, edge, and blow before exterior shoot for season finale. Never paid. Threatened to walk out. Did anybody thank me after?" Harried in Hollywood

The date on the last post was six months ago.

She played a hunch and limited her searches to posts made by Harried in Hollywood. The page populated with ten different topics. She started with "A to Z Rolodex," which listed referrals for everything from liposuction doctors and personal trainers to the best place to get ombré highlights. Nothing controversial there. She searched through a few more topics, finally landing on a post in the thread "Exit Stage Left."

> "Well, I did it, you guys. I quit. Thanks for encouraging me with all your likes and messages this last year. *Yo! It's the Yacoubians* is a sham!!!!! I gave Mila and Arthur everything. Sacrificed my personal life, my health. Lost my boyfriend, and for what? They made promise after promise. A producer's credit. Screen time. A raise. They reneged on all of it. I don't want to go back to Indiana with my tail between my legs, but what are my options?" Harried in Hollywood

Nona scrolled down into the comments, finding well-wishes and commiserations.

> "Hey, fellow Hoosier. I'm an assistant producer for *Pasadena Pooch*. It's a reality show that follows the life of a grandmother type, her husband, and their dog as they travel around California, antiquing and finding quirky tourist spots. Send me a private message. We need a new PA. Last one got married. Promise you, we're humans, not vampires over here." Naptown2LAX

Nona's brain started pinging in all directions. This was what she lived for when investigating. One thread of information led to another. A clue, a hint. The satisfying snap between two pieces of a puzzle. She typed "Pasadena Pooch" into the popular site that tracked movie and television productions. After a couple more clicks and some scrolling, a list of the cast and crew filled the screen. She scanned the thumbnail headshots, names, and roles or positions, looking for the production assistants. Listed under Additional Crew, she found a trainer, groomer, veterinarian, and two production assistants. She selected the first, a guy in his thirties. His bio said he was an LA native and had attended USC film school. The second bio was for a woman, Alex Morgan. Pay dirt. Nona found *Yo! It's the Yacoubians* listed as one of Alex Morgan's credits. There'd be no need for any more coffee tonight. Pure adrenaline held her eyes wide open.

She tabbed back a page. It listed *Two Dogs One Bone* as the production company for *Pasadena Pooch*. She typed that in the search engine. The company had a physical business address and a phone number, which she noted in her phone.

Nona spun her desk chair around, faced Bruiser, who still lay angled on the occasional chair. "I found her." Excitement thrummed through her.

Bruiser cracked open an eye, yawned, and readjusted himself.

She knew who would care about this discovery, but it was 1:00 a.m. Hopefully, he'd get back to her first thing in the morning. Her fingers tapped out a text message to DeMarcus "Big Head" Johnson.

> Think I found the production
> assistant for the Yacoubians.
> Want to proceed with a face-to-
> face interview tomorrow. Advise.

She powered down her computer, picked up her cup, and flipped off the light as she exited. Bruiser's snore trailed her out of the room.

In the kitchen, she rinsed out her mug, then trudged up to her bedroom. Fatigue sapped all her strength. Tossing her phone on the nightstand, she collapsed onto her bed, clothes still on, and closed her eyes. Weariness relaxed her limbs, melting her into the top comforter like butter on toast. The vibration of her phone on her bedside table roused her before she fell completely asleep. She pushed Talk.

"Sassy." A loud yawn punctuated the air through her phone's speaker. "Sup?"

"Why are you answering texts at this hour?" She couldn't restrain her laugh at his sleep-clogged voice.

"Doesn't matter the time. My fiancée is top priority."

"Whatever, Johnson." She flipped onto her side. "So if I can track her down, should I interview the witness in the morning?"

"Absolutely. Tell her you're a private investigator who needs information about the Yacoubians' business dealings. Don't mention the real estate angle."

She stifled her own yawn.

"You should hit the hay, Nona."

"You're right. Night, Johnson. Talk to you tomorrow."

"Absolutely. Sleep tight."

A smile formed on her lips as her eyelids drooped down. In horror, she yanked her eyelids back open. Absolutely no drifting off to sleep with a smile after talking to DeMarcus Johnson.

◆ ◆ ◆

Nona parked her car at the offices of Two Dogs One Bone Productions, nestled in a nondescript business park in Sherman Oaks. The one-story stucco building appeared to be an artifact from the 1990s. That entire morning, unease had plagued her. Something wasn't right. She checked her surroundings before she unlocked her car, then hustled to the front door. The handle did not yield when she jerked it. She rolled her neck to ease the tingling that crept up her spine, and checked behind herself, but nothing seemed out of order in the parking lot. Her jitters were dulling her senses; otherwise, she wouldn't have initially missed the note on the call box to the left of the wooden door, which read, "Please announce your arrival."

"Yes." A voice cracked out from the metal speaker.

"Nona Taylor. I'm here to meet with Alex Morgan."

After a buzz, Nona swung open the door. She was unprepared for the luxury of the reception area. The duotone room featured flooring in an alabaster tone and black walls. Chrome legs topped with sparkling glass stood in the center of the room and acted as a receptionist's desk. "I Want It That Way" by the Backstreet Boys drifted down softly from a hidden speaker. Nona approached a twentysomething woman with a sleek, burgundy-colored bob; a long, narrow face; and flawless skin.

"Nona Taylor, here to see Alex Morgan."

The woman stood. Nona rarely encountered a woman taller than she, so she stifled her surprise.

"I'm Alex. Nice to meet you." Alex's grip was firm and confident. She wore a nubby mock turtleneck, wide-legged jeans, and some chunky Mary Janes. "Let's go to the conference room to talk in private."

Their footsteps thudded on the marble flooring while Alex led Nona into a room off the hallway. The room was hushed by the black carpeting and had stark white walls.

"Have a seat." Alex extended her arm, gesturing to a dark leather sofa flanked by two chrome-and-glass end tables. A canvas painted with splashes and streaks of red hung behind the couch. Alex sat in a chair that was a modern take on a classic wingback. Also in black.

"This place is—"

"Over the top?" Alex offered.

Nona's shoulders dropped. She hadn't even noticed her unease. She gave a chuckle. "Yeah."

"They don't call it Tinseltown for nothing." Alex's smile was caring and transparent. "How can I help?"

"First, thank you so much for meeting with me." It had surprised Nona how readily Alex had agreed via phone for a face-to-face meeting, and Nona had assumed Alex had a major axe to grind with the Yacoubians. In person, however, it seemed like she might be straightforward and upfront by nature.

"Like I mentioned on the phone, I am trying to find out more about the Yacoubians' business dealings, and through my research, I learned you were one of their assistants."

Alex picked up an elegant bottle of overpriced spring water from the center of the table, removed the cap, and drank a swig. "Yes. It's no secret that I quit. But the Yacoubians and I worked it out as a downsizing on paper. I kept my health benefits, and I received a severance. As a condition of the settlement, I signed a nondisclosure agreement."

"Wow. You must have had some dirt on them if you quit and still received a severance package."

Alex gave a smile, but her lips remained pressed together as if holding back a torrent of words. "Let's just say, 'No comment.'"

"Hopefully, my questions will fall outside of the agreement. If I touch on any areas where you don't feel comfortable, give me the signal to move along."

Alex made a gesture with her hand, indicating Nona should proceed.

"My research has uncovered several individuals with payment disputes with the Yacoubians." No reason to tell Alex that her posts on the site for disgruntled production assistants was the source of her information. Best to let her think Nona had independently verified the info. "Do you know of any former tradesmen, landscapers, nannies who have had"—she cast around for the word she wanted to use—"contractual disputes with the Yacoubians?"

A sharp knock on the door drew both of their attention.

A man in his sixties or seventies, who wore clothing like an aging rocker, stuck half his body in the room. "Alex, the whole shoot at the flea market in Pasadena is blowing up. The city doesn't like our filming permits, says we're exceeding the scope in terms of where we can film. I need you out there right away." The rings on all his fingers clacked together as he moved his hands around in an agitated manner.

Alex puffed out a sigh, and her mouth turned down.

The man vibrated with panic-level energy and checked his watch.

"Sorry you came out here for nothing." Alex's lips thinned. "But duty calls." She stood, moved toward the door, but then turned. "Here's what I can give you. *Yo! It's the Yacoubians* is available on multiple streaming platforms. There's an episode called 'Trouble in Palisades Paradise.' Watch it. I don't know who you represent, and I don't want to know. But"—strong emotion crossed her face—"I hope you nail the Yacoubians' hides to the wall." Alex gave a crooked smile, then hustled from the room.

Nona dropped off one of her business cards as she left. Another friendly woman had replaced Alex in the reception area and buzzed Nona out of the office building. The itchy sensation like someone was watching her instantly returned as she exited. Once inside her car, she locked the doors and fired up the engine. Alex hadn't given her much to go on. She hadn't given specifics about what Nona should look for. Apprehension tightened Nona's neck, and she did a few isometric contractions to ease the strain before she backed out.

Nona turned left out of the parking lot and began reviewing what she'd learned about Alex on Reality PAs Dish. Something nagged at her, then realization hit. On the website, Alex had mentioned a landscaper who was complaining about nonpayment. It might not be the landscaper who cut the junipers, but it could be a lead. Alex may not have provided the slam-dunk information Nona needed, but she solved most cases one small step at a time, tugging on a piece of thread to see what wiggled on the other end.

At a stoplight she checked her surroundings for any police cruisers. Seeing none, she summoned Siri and spoke out a quick text to DeMarcus, letting him know her next steps.

Then she made a right and glanced at her rearview mirror. Three cars back, the same beige subcompact that had been in the parking lot at Two Dogs One Bone kept a steady speed behind her. Approaching the freeway ramp she flicked on her blinker and entered. She checked over her left shoulder. The car that had been immediately behind her didn't enter the freeway, but the one after that and the beige car did. Who would follow her? She wasn't working on any high-stakes investigations. Occasionally, a deadbeat dad or someone caught in disability fraud became irate and yelled at her, but nothing more serious.

She snapped on the radio and flipped through the channels until she landed on a throwback '90s station. She checked her gas gauge. Slow traffic might drain her quarter tank. She moved over from the center lane and took the next exit. At the traffic light at the end of the ramp, she glanced in her rearview mirror and the beige car was directly behind her. She turned off the radio and adjusted the rearview mirror. The driver had the visor down, but she made out the glowing tip of a cigarette.

She turned off her right blinker and flicked on the left. When the light changed, the beige car turned left, like she did. She drove two blocks and moved into the left lane. At the green arrow, she made another left. The beige car followed suit. One more left, and she'd be certain. She drove down three more blocks and made a left. Three really difficult-to-make left turns in a row, and the nondescript beige subcompact still dogged her every move.

She glanced up again to get the plate number. Contrary to California law, the car didn't have a front plate.

She thought through where she was and what evasive maneuvers she could make to shake the tail. Approaching the next intersection, she moved to the center lane and slowed at the yellow. When the light turned green, she continued to sit. Horns honked behind her, but she didn't move. She was first in line and craned her neck to see what the light for the cross traffic was doing. Her light turned yellow. Trap set. Several cars had swung around from behind her. Beige car still sat.

She stared at the countdown timer for the pedestrians. In three seconds the hand would stop blinking, and a second after that, she'd have a red and the cross traffic would have a green. *Please, God, don't let any pedestrians jump the gun.* She gave another quick eyeball in the rearview to the tail directly behind her. Even though the car was closer than it had been when she'd been moving, there was still nothing to see but concealing sunglasses and a hat. Her signal turned red. Pedestrians began inching off the curb. Flooring her accelerator, she shot through the crossing seconds before the late afternoon crowd filled the pedestrian lanes, blocking her tail. A quick check of the rearview again, and the driver slammed his fist on the steering wheel.

Her adrenaline crashed and fear kicked in. Who was tailing her? She was only working on two cases. Impossible to imagine she'd blown her cover with the Yacoubians. She couldn't think of a logical reason for Alex to betray her. Could it be someone from an old workers' comp case? Someone she'd busted wanting to even the score? Or was it the inheritance case? Leisure Zone Holdings had millions on the line in Burnt Water. Pastor Grant's loving face drifted through her mind. Was he in danger? The thought of that dear man being targeted because of her carelessness doused her insides like a bucket of ice water over the head. Fear chilled her. *What is going on?*

◆ ◆ ◆

The roaring of blood in Zeke's ears reverberated like crashing waves. He raised a hand to massage the tight muscles in his jaw. He sucked on his cigarette and choked on the smoke from the violent inhale. After two days, the brazen witch had figured out she was being tailed. He didn't know how. He'd tracked marks before and as far as he could tell had never blown his cover.

He'd suspected hanky-panky between her and the pastor, but her visits were so random, and some were too short, so he'd followed her. Stuffing her face with that tall dude, who she'd said was her fiancé. Then the stupid girl drove straight to her home. Kitty ran the address through some search engines for him and found the house was owned by the NGT Revocable Trust, which held the same address.

Zeke snapped his finger as realization hit. The old buzzard preacher had let the name "Nona" slip during their phone call. The N in "NGT" was her first initial. Zeke still didn't have a last name for her, but he'd figure out a way to piece it together.

While she'd been inside the building, he'd called Kitty to have her run Two Dogs One Bone. A reality show production company. He scratched his head. He'd dangled only ten grand in front of the preacher. Not logical that a production company planned to make an entire TV show about such a measly inheritance. Also, he couldn't see any connection between Two Dogs One Bone and that run-down church.

Zeke navigated back onto the freeway and drove to the dump he'd been staying at while he tried to work out another angle for securing the retainer from the pastor. The neon sign on his ratty hotel flickered. In his room, he switched on the barely functioning air-conditioning unit and shucked his shirt but kept on his yellowed tank top. His shoulders slumped as he shuffled to the mini fridge to take out a cold one.

He'd followed her to figure out what the nosy temptress was up to. Was she keeping the pastor from signing on the dotted line? Zeke was missing something, and she might be the key. Sweat pricked his underarms. Why did she know how to spot and shake a tail? Who was she, and what was she up to? How dare she run interference between him and the Right Reverend? Always popping up. There were millions at stake. Millions. All he needed was one old man's signature on a piece of paper. If Zeke could, he'd forge the retainer letter, but he and Calloway still needed Grant to show up in court and collect the inheritance. Then they'd take it right out from underneath him before he realized how much it was really worth.

Zeke strained to think straight and get his con scheme back on track, but nothing was working out as he'd planned. Every day's delay was money out of his pocket. He was done using kid gloves trying to get Grant to sign. He'd ratchet up the pressure tenfold. Grant needed a reason he *had* to sign. The desire to cause intense pain in Grant's life burned inside Zeke. He wanted to make the pastor beg to have someone help him gain the inheritance. Zeke knew all about how pain made you do things you didn't want to do. His daddy made sure Zeke learned that lesson well.

He flipped on the TV to ESPN and plopped onto the stained bedspread. He intended to smash something the pastor cared about dearly and would pay top dollar to fix. Maybe now was the time for that extortion. Zeke rummaged around in his mind.

Or maybe something worse.

Chapter 14

DeMarcus rolled to his side, grabbed the remote, and turned up the volume on his TV.

The CBS Sports Network was broadcasting the Cavs game, and ESPN2 carried the Tigers. He debated watching the Princeton game for a moment but flipped over to UVA. A game against Navy, always good for a laugh. As always he was hoping his Cavs would mop the floor with the Mids. As far as he was concerned, the only decent player the Navy ever had was David Robinson. Nona had mentioned that she'd played basketball. His brain jumped the track. Now he wanted to call her. To hear her voice. To say hi. But she'd just updated him with a text. He knew calling would irritate her. He toyed with the idea anyway.

Vibration from his cell phone jerked him out of his thoughts to the end table beside his couch. He glanced over. *Jamaria.*

"What's up, Li'l J? It's past your bedtime. Why you calling me?"

His stomach rumbled, and he checked his watch. Only six, but time to get some food. He put Jamaria on speaker and ambled to the kitchen.

"I'm calling you because it's time for you to pay up, D."

"Watchoo talkin' 'bout, Willis?"

Jamaria gave a laugh. "That show was so corny it was good."

"I know, right?" All those reruns of *Diff'rent Strokes* they'd watched together. "But seriously, what do you mean it's time for me to pay up?" He opened the fridge and eyed the meager options. He retrieved the container of milk and shifted to the cabinet beside the sink, where he took down a bowl and a box of cereal.

"You said if I received straight As on my report card, you'd get me an upgrade on my iPhone."

Jamaria had texted, DMed, and emailed him—basically haranguing him into agreeing to upgrade her phone if she racked up good grades. He'd promised, but then he'd forgotten like so many other details—minor and major. He poured out the muesli, added the milk, tossed in a handful of raisins, and walked back to the couch. "Yeah, well, I haven't seen any report card." He crunched his cereal without mercy in her ear.

"Ew, D. I see you still don't have any manners."

"That's what family's for."

"Scroll down in your inbox? I know I sent it."

"Give me a second." He put the cereal bowl down on the end table and snapped up his phone. The game in the background snared his attention. Blue streaking down the court for a layup. Typical Navy. No style at all.

"Are you paying attention to me, DeMarcus?" Jamaria's voice jerked him up short.

No. "Yes. Give me a second." He swiped up on his email icon and searched around. The notification on his iPhone said he had over eighty-five thousand unopened messages. He found the email from Jamaria, entitled "Time to Pay Up," sandwiched between unread messages from Foot Locker, the *Princeton Alumni Weekly*, and WatchTime, the timepiece aficionado website. All emails he never took the time to open. "All right, let me see here." He scanned her report card. "Excellent, J. You're taking some tough classes. The Ivies want to see rigor." He studied the information again. "I'm glad to see you're still taking art as well. You're really talented. I keep that sketch you did for me as my wallpaper on my phone."

"Seriously, D?"

"For real."

"So can I get the upgrade on the phone?"

"Well . . ."

"Don't play with me, D."

"You know you can get it."

His concentration trailed off. Did Nona have artistic ability? He checked the score on the chyron at the bottom of the screen. UVA up by ten. All was right with the world.

He forced himself to focus back in on Jamaria's words and gave a grunt to make her think he'd been listening the whole time. "How are you doing besides slaying it in class?"

Silence stretched on Jamaria's end.

"You can tell me. You know we always keep it real."

A heavy sigh drifted through the line. "There's this boy."

He readjusted on the couch and placed his arm behind his head. "What's his name?" Anxiety slithered down his back.

"His name doesn't matter. He wants to take me to the prom in the spring."

He relaxed a bit. "That's no big deal. You already conned me into getting you that dress you wanted." Jamaria was dancing around something. "Spit it out already."

More silence strung out. "He's older than me. He's a senior."

"That shouldn't be a problem."

"And he's really popular."

"O-kaaay." He drew the word out. UVA stole the ball and made a full-court run for a dunk. He stifled his cheer.

"Well, some of his friends want to get a suite after the prom."

He bolted upright on the couch. "Heck to the no." He used to be the guy who booked a suite on prom night and after homecoming, because, well, he'd been that type of guy. "I promise you, Jamaria, any dude who's thinking about that months in advance is not the one for you."

"He's a hottie. Popular too. He's a tight end on the football team."

"First, there's no reason for you to use words like *hottie*. It doesn't help your case with me. Second, football team?" He let out a snort. "Those guys have rocks for brains."

"You're so biased against any sport except basketball."

"That is correct."

"He's really smart too." She gave a sigh.

"Is he in any of your classes?"

"No."

"You're in all the top classes. If he's not in there with you, he ain't smart."

"Come on, D. I need you to back me up here. I really like him."

"I'll tell you what. Have him call me. I'll talk to him. If I like him, you can go."

"He's not gonna want to call you."

"If he doesn't want to call me, he doesn't want to go to the prom with you. Simple as that. End of discussion."

Jamaria let out a heavy huff of air on her end. "Fine. I'll tell him to call you."

"I'm not agreeing that you can go to the prom with him just because I talk to him. I will talk to him to see if you *can* go to the prom with him."

"You're worse than G'Mama."

"That's right. I am. G'Mama doesn't need another kid to take care of. She's earned the right to live in peace."

"I'm not like that, D."

"I know you're not like that, but there are guys out there who are. I used to be one."

"Used to be?" Total surprise laced her voice.

"I've turned over a new leaf. I'm a new man."

"Well, this is something I want to hear about."

"In due time, J, in due time."

"I have homework, so . . ."

"Okay, I'll be talking to you.

"And, DeMarcus . . ."

"Yes."

"Thanks."

He tossed his phone on the table. Was he a new man? That's what he'd told Jamaria. His mind pinged back to the Watch Night message. Pastor Grant had whipped out an old G'Mama verse on him. DeMarcus still had her version memorized.

"'For since the creation of the world His invisible attributes are clearly seen, being understood by the things that are made, even His eternal power and God-head, so that they are without excuse.'"

She had drilled that into his head. It was like she was on speakerphone even now. "Boy, you ain't got no excuse. 'Do not be deceived, God is not mocked; for whatever a man sows, that he will also reap.' What are you sowing, De-Marcus? You're sowing the wind, and you better believe you gonna reap the whirlwind."

He'd always found himself praying at odd times for insights when dealing with clients. He prayed for Nona too. In his head. Real quick. But lately, somehow, his ADHD brain was shifting to thinking about God when before he would have been running basketball stats.

He returned his attention to the game on the TV. What? Navy was up. "Come on, Cavs. You're embarrassing me!" He resisted the urge to throw a shoe at the television.

His phone vibrated on the table. Probably Jamaria wanting to renegotiate the deal he'd just made with her.

He snatched up the phone, pushed Talk, and held it to his ear. He didn't want her getting a word in edgewise. "Jamaria. A deal's a deal. Tell the dude to call me, then you and I will talk."

"DeMarcus, it's Nona." Panic tinged her voice.

He stood up, looked around for his shoes, and jammed his feet into them. "Where are you? I'm coming."

◆ ◆ ◆

Why had she called Johnson the hot second she'd arrived home? He plucked her last nerve. Didn't he? He was worming his way into her mind and heart like an annoying song trending on TikTok. He'd sprung into action first-responder style, reassuring her he was on the way and only hanging up once he'd gotten into his car and started navigating. By nature, she wasn't some shivering damsel in distress, but this was a whole new ball game.

Lady, sensing her agitation, tail held aloft on high alert, dogged her footsteps. Bruiser trotted in to lie in front of her desk.

Leisure Zone Holdings was a billion-dollar entertainment juggernaut. Theme parks, restaurants, live shows. They had venues in Atlantic City and Las Vegas. Organized crime thrived in these cities. Money laundering, trafficking, drugs. Was Pastor Grant's inheritance case somehow on the radar of a crime family? If so, why? She was a one-woman PI shop. She had a degree in criminal justice from UC Irvine. Her cases involved tracking down workers faking injury and scamming their employers. She wasn't equipped for this. Even worse, Pastor Grant's life might be on the line.

Nona paced around her office. Her brain kept circling back to her immediate impulse to reach out to DeMarcus. She shoved her hands into her hair and tugged—hard. Fear had short-circuited her common sense. No. She'd called because some part of her knew he would come. That he'd help her any way he could. That they were in this thing together, and he'd see it to the end.

Her phone rang.

"I'm parked in front." At the sound of DeMarcus's voice, something unknotted inside of her. They'd sit down, talk it over, and come up with a new plan.

She hustled to the entryway with Lady and Bruiser on her heels, checked the security display, and opened the front door.

In one step DeMarcus was inside. He kicked the door shut with his foot. "I'm here."

She held still in surprise at the evidence of intense worry in his eyes. His long arms wrapped around her, and he held her close, like he cared. As though he wanted to reassure not only her but himself that everything would be okay. The security of his embrace combined with the hint of his Drakkar Noir penetrated to her very core.

He stepped back, and it was as if someone had ripped away one half of herself.

She took him in from top to bottom. He had on a dry-fit athletic shirt, some running tights . . . and dress shoes.

Tears came unbidden. Tears of relief. Tears at the absurdity. Cathartic laughter bubbled out.

His brow puckered, and he put his hands on his hips. "I was worried out of my mind. What are you laughing about, woman?"

A few more chuckles escaped, but she pushed down the rest with a swallow. She gave a pointed glance at his feet, then made a small grimace.

He looked down, and a rueful smile crossed his lips. "See what happens next time you call, Sassy. I might not come so fast."

She shook her head. Inside, she knew he'd come just as fast if there ever was a next time. "You hungry? I can make a frozen pizza."

* * *

They sat at Nona's two-person dining room table with a legal pad, cans of fizzy water, and a pizza between them.

"I was spooked. I think I overreacted." She shrugged. "I've tracked people before, but no one's ever tracked me."

"And you're pretty certain it's about Pastor Grant's inheritance and not something in one of your old cases or the Yacoubians . . ." He hesitated. "A boyfriend?" His Adam's apple moved up and down with those words as if he had a hard time getting them out.

She snorted. "Boyfriend, hardly."

His brows drew together, a line forming between them.

"All the Yacoubians need to do to end this thing is trim some hedges. No need for *Mission: Impossible*–level espionage."

"Do you have a laptop we can use?"

She grabbed up their empty plates and put them in the sink, then retrieved her computer. "What are you searching for?"

"I'm going to use LexisNexis to find corporate filings for Leisure Zone Holdings." He entered the site address, then logged in. She watched him jab at the keyboard with his index fingers. Somehow even hunting and pecking he had the speed of a decent typist. "I'm going to add Alabama as an additional search parameter."

"Not Burnt Water?"

"No, I don't want to limit it."

He flipped the computer around toward Nona and then scooted his chair next to hers. Together, they scrolled past various links.

"Here's a Notice of Annual Meeting to Shareholders for last year." He opened the pdf and navigated through the table of contents.

"Here." She selected an item entitled "Anticipated Acquisitions of Land."

> With the approval of last year's proposal to acquire land to expand Leisure Zone Holdings' operations in the southeastern US, we are partnering with Southland First National Bank and Birmingham Developers to acquire one hundred fifty acres of farmland, abandoned residential land, and other tracts by purchase in Burnt Water, Alabama, to build Leisure Zone Resort. Leisure Zone Holdings is working closely with the city council of Burnt Water, spearheaded by Councilman Gavin Calloway. When completed, this entertainment complex will draw vaca-

tioners from Louisiana, Mississippi, Alabama, Georgia, and the
Florida panhandle regions.

Nona and DeMarcus spent the next several hours combing through SEC
filings, available press clippings, and articles about the proposed vacation
destination. She watched DeMarcus's lids droop repeatedly only to have his
eyes snap open as they worked. By the time they were done, she was confident Pastor Grant's inheritance had something to do with Leisure Zone
Holdings' acquisition of land in Burnt Water.

"Let's call it quits." In the morning, she'd follow up with more research
on Councilman Calloway and start combing the internet for obituaries and
probate notices in Burnt Water.

"Right, let me get my keys and my phone." He gave a giant yawn, and a
noise like Chewbacca blared out of his mouth, open so wide it could fit a
tennis ball. She eyed the man who'd agreed to a fake engagement and had
sped to her house like it was burning down around her. Nikki's face floated
before her. Nona would disintegrate into a million shards if there was another tragic car accident on her conscience.

"Sleep on the couch tonight, Johnson."

＊ ＊ ＊

Dog breath, hot and meat-scented, assailed DeMarcus's nose. He lay with
his face mashed against something that felt like upholstery-grade fabric,
and his body was on its side, folded like the letter Z. He cracked open one
eye, and it all came flooding back. Lady stood beside the couch in Nona's
living room, making long blinks and snuggling up against him.

From his vantage point he looked around. He realized one wouldn't even
know a woman lived here. Nona was no-nonsense down to her bones. The
furniture looked like Rooms To Go or someplace like that. It all matched,
but there were no plants, no art, no knickknacks.

As he was driving to her house last night, his intense concern for her had
shaken his foundation. She challenged him and made him laugh. She was
gorgeous to look at and not impressed in the least that he went to Princeton.
Nona didn't jump to do whatever he wanted, like other women did. Every

second he spent with her made him want to spend more time with her. He wanted to know what made her sob during church on New Year's Eve, to understand the things in her life that had made her so tough. He'd been telling the truth when he told G'Mama that he'd met someone special. He could see Nona as his wife.

A laugh pushed out. Lady might be the only female in this house who liked him. His mind whirled around. Nona might like him too, but his interactions with her told him she was protecting herself. He now saw her snark and jabs for what they were—her armor. Had someone hurt her emotionally? She'd scoffed when he'd asked if there was an old boyfriend in the picture. There was that Lemar dude. Still unclear on that.

DeMarcus sat up and located his loafers. Bruiser was guarding the shoes with his paws propped on them. DeMarcus checked his watch. Seven o'clock. Plenty of time to make it to his place, shower, and get to work by eight thirty. He approached the front door to exit, and the jingle of a key ring sounded from the other side. He grabbed the knob and opened the door to let Nona in.

"Hey . . ." The words died off in his throat.

Not Nona. It was Lemar.

DeMarcus felt like a fool standing there, doorknob in hand. Nona simply did not seem like the sort of woman to live this way, to have a guy in her life who had a key to her house.

DeMarcus was never jealous. Ever. But right now, purple and red spots were flashing in his mind, and he couldn't think straight. His mouth engaged before his brain. If he couldn't get answers out of Nona, he'd get them out of Lemar. "So how long have you and Nona been dating?"

"Dating?" Forehead creased, Lemar stood his ground.

That dude had heard every word DeMarcus said. He'd wait for an answer. Impulsivity flared, and he changed his mind. He had more questions. "Did Nona tell you what's going on between us?"

"Yeah, she told me all about you two. Texted me before she went to bed last night to let me know you were crashing on the couch." Lemar's face held no animosity, which meant he didn't see DeMarcus as a threat.

It made no sense. No woman of his would have a fake fiancé for even two seconds.

"Um, I need to get in and get changed." Lemar lifted a suitcase and nodded toward where DeMarcus blocked the doorway. Lemar eased his way around him without a hint of suspicion or concern. "Thanks again, man."

"Yeah, well."

"Really appreciate it."

Somehow DeMarcus had switched places with Lemar and was standing on the stoop.

"We owe you."

The door shut with a snap.

Chapter 15

AFTERNOON SUNLIGHT FILTERED through the slats of Nona's office blinds. Bruiser lay on a spot of floor soaking up the warmth from the slice of light. She logged on to her computer and typed "Yo! It's the Yacoubians stream now" into the search engine. Several pay-per-view episodes and subscription services popped up. She chose the cheapest one and searched for "Trouble in Palisades Paradise."

Her phone pinged with a message from DeMarcus.

> Mitch says the real estate market is cooling. Wants to fast-track, putting the house up for sale to lock in his gains. Any leads yet?

> Checking into landscaper angle now.

> Pls call me this afternoon to report what you find. I need Mitch off my back. He's forgotten I have other cases for paying clients. #Partners

> Aren't you trying to be a #Partner?

Irrelevant. I do my thing my
way. They've never seen a
partner like me before.

> So you intend to keep wearing
> orange bow ties with orange
> socks if you make partner?

When. Not if. And yes. Did I
forget to mention today that
I went to Princeton?

You know you love me . . .

His text caught her up short. The banter between them always stayed light and funny. But the word *love* stood out in her mind like one of the giant billboards lining Sunset Boulevard. Her shoulders scrunched up, the muscles tense. Thinking about DeMarcus gave her conflicting feelings. She actually liked him now that she knew him better, but she swatted away the positive thoughts about him. She'd seen a man like him up close. As far as love-'em-and-leave-'em types, he was in the titanium membership tier. She turned off the notifications on her phone, forcing her mind not to think about the cocky squint and a dimple she'd discovered on his left cheek when he let out a raucous laugh.

Information about the price for renting single episodes now populated the screen. She typed in her credit card number, pressed Enter, and waited while the refresh circle spun and spun. She peered out her office window to see if she spotted a beige car down the street. She'd checked on Pastor Grant a few times. Didn't want to alarm him, but she asked if everything was okay and if anything seemed out of order at his home or the church. Unflappable as ever, he'd assured her he was fine.

Right now, the retainer from Mitch and Sylvia kept her afloat. If the inheritance case panned out, she'd have the money to upgrade to a higher speed internet service provider and get a brand-new laptop. She'd also spring for a monitored alarm system, not stick-on Wi-Fi-enabled cameras.

Lady rested her head on Nona's lap while she clicked Play. Splashy graphics with the show's title and quick cuts showcasing a montage of the Yacoubians' pets, social media posts, and images of them attending B-list celebrity events rolled across the screen. The soundtrack featured the dramatic horns and percussion section that accompanied all reality shows.

Mila Yacoubian, wearing spandex yoga pants and a stretchy crop top, appeared on the screen screaming at the top of her lungs at a man dressed in standard landscaper apparel—green Dickies pants, a shirt with his name embroidered on it, and a green baseball cap.

"I told you." Red blotches marred Mila's otherwise immaculate skin. "The rockscape is supposed to be Mexican beach pebbles with gray and taupe tones, not yellow beach pebbles." Mila swept her hands back and forth, pointing to the offending stones.

The camera panned to a landscaping truck with the name Ferguson Landscaping on the side. Standing next to the truck was a middle-aged man wearing a similar but well-pressed landscaping outfit. He carried himself with an air of authority. He held a cell phone to his ear. His words were not audible over Mila's yelling, but he made sharp, punctuating motions with his hands.

"None of you listen," Mila shrieked. "Remember last year, when I told you not to trim the back junipers, and that very day, you did it anyway? Six months ago, I told you that the irrigation timers were interfering with our shooting schedule, and I also told you we needed the uplighting around the house to have a manual override for nighttime filming. Still not done." The man in front of Mila was wilting under her diatribe.

Dramatic music cut in, and the streaming service inserted a commercial. Fast-forward wasn't an option, so she searched Ferguson Landscaping. Hits pinged on fifteen different businesses. The commercial ended, and a quick bumper promo for the show came on the screen, followed by a tight shot of Mila toe to toe with the gentleman who carried himself like a supervisor. Mila pointed and yelled. The *bleep-bleep* noise used to mask obscenities repeatedly squawked out from the speaker on Nona's computer every time

Mila opened her mouth. The man was giving back as good as he got volume wise, but at least eschewed profanity.

Nona hit Pause as the camera zoomed in. Embroidered on the breast pocket of the landscaper's polo shirt, she made out the name Chester Ferguson, Proprietor. *Score!*

* * *

Nona sat parked in the lot of a one-story office building. The lawn in front was lush and low-cut, like the fairway of a golf course. A sweeping expanse of red flowers fronted a precisely trimmed row of hedges lining the front of the building. Two large planter boxes, which flanked the entrance, contained flowers in a harmonized array of yellow and cream. Leafy vines spilled over the edges. During her mental prep on the drive over, she'd imagined a quaint family-run business. At her request, DeMarcus had run Chester Ferguson, Ferguson Landscaping, and the Yacoubian name through the Lexis-Nexis database and had texted her information on an outstanding judgment against the Yacoubians. At the smoked-glass front doors, Nona assessed her outfit—black joggers and a plain black T-shirt. Thinking she'd be dealing with a mom-and-pop business, she'd dressed down. Too late now.

Goose bumps rose on her arms when she opened the front door and the chill of the air-conditioning hit her. An attractive toasty-brown woman in her late fifties, early sixties, with long hair fashioned into a bun at her nape, sat at a reception desk immediately inside the door.

"May I help you?"

"I'm Nona Taylor, here to see Chester Ferguson." She concentrated on smiling.

"Ah yes. My husband told me you were coming." The woman stood and extended her hand. "I'm Victoria Ferguson. So pleased to meet you."

After shaking hands, Nona followed the woman to a door a few steps behind her desk. Victoria gave three sharp raps with her knuckles and opened the door. "Ms. Taylor's here to see you, dear. I ordered takeout for the office. Do you want some when you're done?"

"Yes, please." Chester stood and extended his hand. "I'm hoping I can help you, Ms. Taylor." Chester had light-brown hair with a few grays and a dignified mustache. He wore a button-down shirt the shade of an evergreen tree. The breast pocket bore an orange golf ball–sized circle with *FL* embroidered on it.

Victoria exited and left the door cracked.

Chester swept a hand toward a chair in front of his desk. "Please make yourself comfortable."

Nona lowered onto the offered seat. Hanging on the wall behind Chester's desk were plaques from professional landscaping trade organizations and framed magazine articles featuring his business.

"As I mentioned on the phone, I am a private investigator assisting a law firm that needs information on the Yacoubians. Public records show your business has a default judgment against the Yacoubians for unpaid invoices." At first it had surprised her that Alex and Chester were so willing to meet with her. But having watched Mila's on-screen tirade and the trail of broken promises the Yacoubians left in their wake, the willingness of their former business associates to bury a knife in Mila's back made sense.

"Yes." Chester shook his head, his lips pressed together in a thin line. "The fact that you are here leads me to believe your client has a similar problem." His eyebrows rose in question.

"Not exactly . . ." She paused, uncertain how much to reveal. "I watched an episode of the show, with Mila Yacoubian's tirade against you."

A crimson flush crept up Chester's neck. "Her attack on me was uncalled for and damaging to my reputation. Unfortunately, I signed a waiver and release to be on the show, thinking it might bring me business. The reverse was true. There was a significant drop-off in clientele and referrals for several months after the episode aired."

"I'm so sorry to hear that."

"The Yacoubians are difficult to please and think they know better than experts like me. There's nothing like ground-level knowledge about floriculture, landscaping, soil conditions, et cetera, et cetera." He bounded to his feet. "Come. Take a walk with me."

She scrambled to stand and followed Chester, who'd already made it to the door of his office. Apparently shoptalk about landscaping had an energizing effect on him. They sailed past Chester's wife, who sat at her desk with take-out bags from P.F. Chang's. The scent of the orange chicken made her stomach growl.

"I'm on a walkabout, dear. Back in ten minutes."

Chester and Nona exited the office building through a back door to a private urban oasis. Dwarf palm trees, curving borders of ground cover, and flowers encircled a putting green complete with a flag. Off to one side was a stacked-stone waterfall that fed into a koi pond.

Chester breathed in deeply and exhaled. "Landscaping is in my blood. My father was a landscaper and gardener. So was his father before him. My crew works the turf and shrubs year-round through various seasonal conditions. I pride myself on understanding vegetation and aesthetics. My company has ten King Cab trucks, and each holds a four-man crew. I fully outfitted all my trucks with mowers, blowers, edgers—the gamut."

"So what happened between you and the Yacoubians?"

She and Chester strolled across the putting green to the pond. There was a dish on a pedestal, which held little pellets. Chester grabbed a handful and tossed them into the pond. The water frothed with the swarming of a dozen bright-orange and spotted fish.

"I have a feel for what people like. I'm almost always able to keep the particular Westside and Hollywood types happy. But Mila Yacoubian and her husband were short-tempered, grasping fame chasers." Chester gave a pointed look at the koi food.

Nona picked up some pellets and flung them in. Impatience clawed at her, but she tamped it down. Her job right now was to get Chester to tell her everything he knew about the Yacoubians and their landscaping. If he needed time to warm up to her, she'd have to give it to him. She plucked up some more pellets and chucked a fistful into the water.

"I've been slowly trying to shift my company over from office parks to residential homes, because I like the customer-level interaction. Homeowners allow more creativity than leasing offices. I mainly service Beverly Hills, Brentwood, Westwood, Pacific Palisades, Bel Air—that crowd."

Their excursion ended at a small gazebo she had not noticed, tucked behind the pond. Chester's wife was waiting there with the take-out containers, plates, and serving utensils spread out.

"Thank you, sweet wife. You know how I go on about landscaping."

"I know. I figured you'd wear out this poor girl with all your talking, so I brought lunch out here to share." Victoria gave her husband an indulgent smile.

Chester leaned in and gave his wife a brief peck.

The stinging in Nona's nose and behind her eyes caught her off guard. The understated gesture of hospitality and the genuine respect between Chester and his wife were inspiring in their sincerity. Without permission, images of Tyson and Nona's clandestine meetings popped into her mind. He'd never wanted to go out in public. Never showed her off to his friends. Everything had been secretive. Behind closed doors. Shameful. What would it be like to have a man who adored her, a relationship full of silent understanding and comprised of acts of service to one another?

Her mind pivoted to DeMarcus. Despite an outward appearance of 2,000 percent cockiness, he was always a gentleman toward her. When he was with her, he was hyperfocused on what she was saying or doing or feeling.

A spoon clacked against a plate and drew her back to the moment. Chester had placed a huge mound of steaming jasmine rice and chicken on the plate in front of her. His fatherly way reminded her of Pastor Grant.

"I put my kids, nieces, and nephews through college, and they all worked for me in the summers." Chester's bearing expanded, his pride clear. "We made money. I grew my business by hiring college graduates who majored in golf course management. Did you know Rutgers has a degree in turfgrass science?"

"I didn't know." Nona had no idea one could major in grass.

"My sons are now professional turfgrass managers for pro baseball and football teams and golf courses. My dream is to have one of my kids work with the head groundsman at Wimbledon."

Nona savored the delicious lunch while Chester waxed on about various grasses. In the last few months, with her budget constraints, she sated any craving she'd had for Chinese food with frozen dinners.

"But you came to me about the Yacoubians. I've been so angry about the whole thing, because creating artful landscaping is my life. It's what I breathe in and breathe out."

His wife gave a knowing nod.

"Anyway, the whole thing with the Yacoubians started about a year ago. They have a long row of junipers in their back yard that serve as an erosion barrier and provide privacy. Well, sometimes juniper branches droop. The Yacoubians had asked me to be less aggressive in shaping and maintaining the hedgerow. I sent in a new trainee. He was only supposed to even up the tops so they would be aesthetically pleasing, but the guy chopped off about four feet. It was a simple mix-up. That variety can repair the loss in a year. The Yacoubians went ballistic, said they'd get me blackballed right as I was transitioning over to residential. From what I've heard through the grapevine, Mila is always in a feud with somebody. One day when we were filming, she bad-mouthed the neighbors who share her backyard border. Told me she didn't want them getting any air from her land or some such nonsense. Mila also refused to pay for any of the services I'd provided that day."

Nona forced herself to sit still at the revelation. Chester Ferguson had dropped a bombshell that could blow the case wide open. If DeMarcus could get Chester to repeat his story under oath, Mitch and Sylvia would have the proof they needed to win their case, if they had to take the matter all the way to trial.

Chester took a long sip from the iced tea his wife had placed in front of him and dabbed his lips.

"Well, somehow, Chester finessed his way back into Mila's good graces." Victoria chimed in on the conversation. "And he and Mila kissed and made up." Victoria gave her husband a little wink. "She even offered to allow the production company to display his business telephone number in the show's credits. She said she'd incorporate discussions about landscaping into one of her shows."

Chester nodded. "Of course, she threw another tantrum, and everything blew up in our faces again. You saw the aftermath on that episode."

Victoria rubbed her hand along Chester's back. "She fired us and ceased all remaining payments. We're owed thousands."

"All the landscaping we did, and we never received a penny after the juniper-cutting accident. That landscaping is still around her house, like an exquisite platinum setting for a stone. We sued, but they never even answered the complaint. We have a default judgment against them. It accrues interest daily, but they've filed for bankruptcy and tied everything up in court. Meanwhile, the episode with Mila yelling at me plays endlessly on reruns and on streaming platforms, and there is nothing I can do about it."

Victoria swiped her finger beneath her eye. "That episode is humiliating. It's not about the money for Chester."

"No. For me, it's the principle. They owe the money, they humiliated me, and they should give me an apology and pay up. I provided services, and I deserve my compensation."

Nona wiped her mouth and sat back. "That food was delicious. Thank you so much."

"You're welcome." Chester regarded her warmly. "I've chewed your ear off, no doubt."

"Everything you've told me is more helpful than you can know."

"Good."

A young man in a landscaper's uniform came running from the back of the building and across the putting green, waving his arms and yelling. "Mr. Ferguson, Mr. Ferguson! The sod company called. Their irrigation systems broke over the weekend, and there's a problem with our order for the Dixon estate overhaul."

Chester stood quickly. "So sorry, I must run. My wife can see you out."

"Thank you, Mr. Ferguson." Nona's words greeted his rapidly retreating back.

As she locked herself in her car, she could not wait to fill DeMarcus in on what she'd learned. She'd hit pay dirt with this meeting. Chester's information might break the entire case wide open for DeMarcus—maybe even secure the partnership for him. A pin in her thoughts leached the air out of her elation. When the spite fence and inheritance cases ended, there'd be no need to see DeMarcus's mug ever again. Was the strain of the last few weeks causing her to crack up? She must be going soft. Otherwise, why did the thought of losing her fake fiancé with his Goodyear Blimp–sized ego deflate her?

Chapter 16

ZEKE SAT IN his car, cigarette dangling from his lips, dropping ashes onto the seat. His phone rang, and he mashed Talk. "Go."

"I have the documentation to prove Grant's relationship to Old Millie. As long as you do your job, the deal is secured." The triumphant tone in Councilman Calloway's voice had the ring of someone who thought riches would soon shower down on him. "The Bible is in terrific shape, and the genealogy goes back to some old slave, if you can believe it."

Zeke grunted. This was good news, but he hated the self-congratulatory tone in Calloway's voice. Reminded Zeke of his daddy, strutting and crowing when he thought he had the upper hand.

"Where'd you find it?" Zeke kept his voice nonchalant.

"Hidden on a shelf behind some cat-lady mysteries."

"Took you long enough."

"Don't start with me, Zeke. My patience with you is razor-thin. Good thing too, because after this, we're done."

He curbed his inclination to snap back at Calloway and shifted gears. Zeke didn't care if Calloway thought he was still the flat-footed jock from high school hiding in the quarterback's shadow, that he was the failure his daddy told everyone in town that he was. "Wait, without the Bible, how'd you figure out about Grant in the first place?"

"I told you already." Calloway's voice dripped with condescension. "Old Millie dragged out that Bible whenever I'd visit her, trying to get her to sell the land to me outright. She liked for me to read her a few verses. I saw the family history pages in the front. I started piecing together the stories I'd heard around town about how some of her family disappeared like a puff of smoke way back in the '40s. Grant's name was in there, plain as day. Had to be careful, because I didn't want to tip her off."

Yippity-yip. Blah, blah. "And why do we need it again?" Zeke couldn't wait until he never had to talk to Calloway again.

"With Old Millie over a hundred, and Grant near his eighties, I want to make sure I have the information I need in hand to show his family connection to her. Birth certificates don't record siblings, and his family left here long ago. We do not know if Grant has any proof of his own that he's related to Mildred. The only thing left is for him to sign the retainer letter, so we will control the process."

"Understand." It hurt Zeke's ears listening to the councilman explain the con yet again in his you're-an-idiot voice. So what? The stupider Calloway thought Zeke was, the sweeter the revenge would feel when the whole thing blew up in Calloway's face.

"I don't think you do," Calloway barked in a sharp tone. "You've handled this thing your way, but you're getting nowhere."

Zeke's neck and face tingled. He breathed in slowly. "It's under control. The pastor's meeting with me this afternoon. I'll have the signed retainer letter by the close of business today."

"You'd better." Calloway disconnected the call.

Zeke's gut tightened. He hated the pompous way Calloway talked to him. Zeke knew *all* of Calloway's secrets, even the ones the man thought he'd hidden. Mr. High-and-Mighty might find himself on the wrong end of some blackmail or behind bars if he continued talking down to Zeke.

At the thought of turning the tables on Calloway and exacting revenge, sweet satisfaction unfurled the knots in Zeke's gut. If only there was a way to make his daddy suffer as well.

Another hour till his meeting with the pastor. He stubbed out his butt and ratcheted back the seat. With the haze of the smoke residue surrounding him, he did what Kitty always suggested. *"Set your mind on what you want, Zeke honey. See it, then claim it."*

He squeezed his eyes shut and concentrated, so he could see Calloway. Deep satisfaction oozed through him as he fantasized about watching all the blood drain out of Calloway's face. Better yet, Calloway might wet himself like a baby.

Zeke worked out the exact words he'd say to the councilman, so they'd be a sucker punch to the gut: "I know you killed Old Millie." Just thinking about it made him happy.

Well, he didn't exactly know for sure, but he'd bluff a little.

He opened his eyes and mentally ticked off the facts he knew. Calloway was the last person to see Old Millie alive. She was found dead in her bed two days later. Kitty's best friend's sister-in-law was married to the EMT who'd done the well check and found her. That's how pillow talk with Kitty had revealed that both Millie's prescription nitroglycerin bottle and her rescue necklace were empty when they had found her.

"It's being chalked up to forgetfulness," Kitty had said. *"But it's odd, Zeke baby. She'd filled her nitro script a day before she died. I was in there getting my cholesterol meds, and Dottie Washington picked up the nitro for her. So confusing. Millie's a hundred if she's a day. Maybe she threw away all her pills by mistake. Who would kill a hundred-year-old? They're gonna die any day."*

Everything he ever wanted was falling into place. The money, the escape. He would never have to witness Big Zeke stumbling drunk down Main Street or endure his berating. He'd never have to agree to another scheme of Calloway's, where Zeke bore all the risk and Calloway reaped the lion's share of the reward. Zeke wanted out of Burnt Water. It was like a stinking dead body strapped to his back.

He'd jam Calloway up with the threat of exposing him and milk that source of income for years.

Zeke turned his mind to his meeting with Grant. He knew everywhere the old man went. His home address. His daily routine. He lived the pathetic life of a monk. Not possible anything was going on with that wild-haired witch. The pastor hit the hay at eight thirty sharp every night. Didn't matter. Zeke would shake him down with the threat of a scandal anyway. The pastor could deny until he was blue in the face, but Zeke would bet the old tambourine thumpers at the church would believe an anonymous note that said a jezebel had ensnared their beloved pastor in a honeytrap.

Zeke's phone warbled, and he saw Pastor Grant's name on the screen. About time. Zeke had been cooling his jets. It was past the agreed-upon meeting time, and still no pastor. Zeke lowered his shoulders and put on a voice he hoped came off like a paralegal.

"John Smith speaking."

"Oh, good afternoon, Mr. Smith, this is Pastor Hosea Grant."

Churning irritation scratched across Zeke's taut nerves. "Yes, sir. I'm anxious for our meeting in a few minutes."

"About that meeting, Mr. Smith." The pastor cleared his throat in apparent hesitation that torqued up the dial on Zeke's irritation. "It's not going to work for me—"

"We can meet later in the day, if you'd like."

Swallowing echoed in his ear through the crystal clear 5G phone connection. "I'm still doing my research. Trying to find the family Bible . . . Well, Nona and . . ."

A sigh traveled to Zeke's ear, and he clenched his jaw to keep from cursing at the man. "Tomorrow, then?"

"Mr. Smith. I appreciate all your help, but we still have time to decide, and we'd like to wait a little longer. You understand. God bless. Have a nice day."

The pastor dismissed him by ending the call.

Zeke gave a sharp tug on the car handle and kicked open the door. After hoisting himself out of the vehicle, he turned and shoved the door closed with his foot. He paced up the sidewalk toward the still-gated church front, his strides eating up the ground beneath him. Nobody ignored Zeke and got away with it. No. One. He reached the front security gates of the church and grabbed them with both hands, then shook them and pulled with all his strength. The rusted metal bit into his clenched hands, cutting him, and his anger ratcheted higher at the pain. He wheeled around and bowled into the cashier from the convenience store.

The guy reached out his hands and steadied Zeke. "Bro, sometimes he can't hear. You gotta go around to the back and knock." The clerk hitched his thumb over his shoulder, showing Zeke the way to go.

He stormed off without a word to the cashier, shoved himself into his car, and screamed out of the parking space, then sped to the back of the church.

He grabbed his lock-picking kit from the glove box, glanced over each shoulder, and approached the back door of the church. Then he eyed the lock and selected two tools from the kit. With a few deft jiggles of his fingers, he was in.

No alarm tripped, and carpeting hushed his footsteps. The church smelled of candle wax and musty books. Light entered the corridor from the window on the church's back door. Muffled footsteps, accompanied by quiet humming, drifted from the front of the building. *Bingo.* The pastor was alone.

The first door Zeke approached on the left had a sign that read "Nursery." Across from it, to his right, was a restroom. He approached the next door. "Pastor Hosea Grant" was on a slide-in nameplate. The room had no interior windows, but the light was on. The office was an organized mess. A haphazard stack of boxes filled one corner. The desk contained piles of papers and books. A jumble of Bibles and other theological stuff maxed out the bookcase. Zeke moved to the wall-to-wall shelves, and the sheer number of Bibles overwhelmed him. Being in this room made his skin crawl.

The retainer letter lay front and center on the desk with a sticky note affixed. "Find Birth cert and Bible. Check bxs labeled Mama."

Alarm bells clanged in his head. This was bad.

Zeke shot a glance at the boxes in the corner. Two of them said "Florence Grant." According to Calloway, that was Old Millie's sister. Zeke's mind churned, and realization hit him square between the eyes. Not one but two Bibles? Mildred had one, and Grant's mother had the other. The old man was piecing things together on his own. If Grant had a Bible with the family history in it, he didn't need Calloway, and he didn't need Zeke.

Zeke could dig through those boxes, but that was inefficient and wouldn't accomplish what he wanted, which was getting Grant to sign the retainer letter before he found what he needed to locate the estate and claim it on his own. Eliminating Grant's copy of the family Bible would force Grant to work through Zeke to claim the estate.

And—grinning, Zeke plucked the matchbook from his pocket—he could kill two birds with one flick of his wrist. Eliminate the Bible and create a need for instant money.

Today, the pastor would know pain and loss and hurt. That old man cared about only two things: this shack of a church and himself. Grant would lose his church today. When the smoke cleared, he'd come crawling to Zeke to sign the retainer letter and secure that inheritance.

Zeke made his way to the stack of boxes and slid a cigarette out of the breast pocket of his shirt. He lit the cig with the match, then tossed the match into the open box. The rising flame freed something inside him. He thought about his daddy. Zeke would like to burn down his house too. He moved to the huckster's desk, lit another match, and let it land in the center of a pile of papers. Calloway's face intruded into Zeke's thoughts. A surge of power shot through him at the thought of the havoc he was unleashing. Yellow flames built slowly, then spread to other papers and lapped up the fuel on Grant's desk. Zeke lit another match and dropped it in the wastebasket and practically skipped out the back door.

Chapter 17

NONA STOOD AS still as a post at the door of Pastor Grant's hospital room. Her leaden feet refused to carry her across the threshold. Pastor lay inert on the hospital bed, eyes covered with patches and an oxygen mask covering his mouth and nose. His brown face stood out in sharp relief against the stack of pillows, and his arms rested by his sides atop the coverlet. A blinking machine stood like a sentinel beside him.

She drew in a shuddering breath. On the screen of the hospital equipment, she made out his heart rate and blood pressure. The silence in the room was broken only by the whine that accompanied the inflation and deflation of the cuff wrapped around his arm.

Her eyes were raw from the crying she'd done already. The call from the police had been straight to the point. There'd been a fire. When scrolling through his flip phone, they'd found her name and number popped up regularly for both outgoing and incoming calls. They thought maybe she was a relative or close friend. That's why they called her. The arson squad suspected foul play. She should come to the hospital immediately.

Hot, pricking emotion pushed behind her eyelids. She'd underestimated the menacing phone calls and the veiled threats by the heir hunting firm. Even DeMarcus had urged caution. But no. After being tailed, she'd wanted to prove her toughness, her smarts. Wanted Pastor Grant and DeMarcus to think highly of her. Stupid. None of her wheel-spinning had relieved the shame so far. Because of her, Pastor Grant had nearly been killed. Painful recriminations stacked one atop another.

Pastor Grant angled slightly toward the doorway. "I know it's you, Nona. Please come in. I've been waiting." His voice lacked its normal booming pastoral resonance. His fingers flicked, and she moved to the guest chair beside his bed. "If it had been the ladies from the Mothers' Board at church, I'd have heard them from all the way down the hallway." His chuckle was genuine but weaker than usual.

Random, uncomfortable sensations ping-ponged inside her chest.

Fear. What if he took a turn and went downhill? He could have far greater injuries than she could see. The tight-lipped medical staff threw HIPAA laws back in her face when she tried to extract information.

Guilt. He'd never have been in the building if she hadn't called him and asked him to check his office one last time for his birth certificate. During the fight Nikki had screamed at her, *You push people around like chess pieces. Everything has to be your way or the highway.* Nikki had been so right. Nona had made moves and countermoves behind Nikki's back, trying to win Tyson for herself. And now . . . She regarded Pastor Grant. Once again, doing things her own way and clinging to the illusion of control had placed someone she loved in danger. Scathing recrimination wrenched her insides.

"How do you feel?" The pleasantry weighed heavily on her tongue.

"To tell the truth, I have been worse, but I've also been better. The doctors say I have first- and second-degree burns, irritation in my eyes from stuff that was in the air, and some smoke inhalation. All wrapped up in a pickle this time, huh?" An impish smile appeared on the man's lips.

Even though he couldn't see her, she forced her lips into a smile to mimic his.

"So how do I look?"

How did he look? Thankfully, she couldn't see the physical damage under the bandages on his hands and over his eyes. "I'm just thankful you're alive."

"You and me both. I still have business I want to finish down here." A grimace marred his face. "If Jaxon at the Quicky Mart hadn't smelled smoke and come to find me, I might have ended up in glory today."

"Does he know how the fire started?"

"Said he bumped into a guy, but he wasn't really paying attention. Sees so many people every day, they all blur together." A racking cough pushed out, and she winced at his obvious discomfort.

She had so many questions. Why didn't he run out of the building as the blaze and smoke bore down on him? How bad were his burns? Had he lost his sight? "How . . ." She let the words die off, as she didn't know how to ask.

"There's a closet at the front of the church." He'd sensed her timidity. "Off to the right side after you enter. We use it to hang coats. The choir robes are in there. After all this time, I remembered my wife stashed some things, so I went searching. Sure enough, there were some more boxes from Mama's house." He tentatively repositioned himself on the pillow. "Don't know why I'm such a pack rat. I think I'd intended to give some of her clothes away to people who needed them, but I never was able to get that project off the ground."

"We don't have to talk about this now—"

Pastor Grant's brow crinkled. "You're right. We'll get to that later. I need to talk to you about something else, Nona."

Her mind pushed play on her recrimination loop. *He's lost all faith in you. Why wouldn't he? You're off the case. You've ruined his chances of funding his ministry.* "Of course, anything."

"I've hesitated to talk to you before, because you always had your long-handled spoon out, pushing me away." His chuckle ended in a rattle. "Not anymore. None of us is guaranteed even one more hour, and I need to get this off my chest. Can you indulge an old man for a few minutes?"

She did not want to hear one word Pastor Grant had to say. If anyone heaped another thing on her staggering load, she'd crack. But she owed him. "I have plenty of time." She leaned forward, stuck her arm through the railing, and patted his hand. More to gin herself up for what would be a dressing-down than to reassure him.

"Nona, you need to let it all go, sweetheart." He squeezed her hand. "You're slowly killing yourself."

She let go of his hand and sat back. "What . . . what are you talking about?"

"You know what I'm talking about." He screwed up his lips the way only a skeptical old man could. "The guilt and shame, the thing that brings you to my church year after year. I don't want you to leave this earth without resolving it."

She shook her head. "You don't know what you're asking." He didn't. Her life wasn't a Disney movie. There was no way to just let it go.

"You're wrong there. I do." Lines of determination creased the sides of his mouth. "I've heard the confessions of stone-cold gangbangers who've shot toddlers in drive-bys. Women who've aborted one, two, three babies in a row. Thieves, adulterers, men who beat their wives. Not every one of them released their guilt, but I promise you, not one was sorry they told me."

A giant lump rose up, constricting her throat. She grabbed a bottle of water from the nightstand, twisted open the top, and forced down several huge gulps, hoping to shove down the emotions trying to push up. Traitorous tears came. Hard. Painful. Rolling in fat drops onto her lap. Did he know what he was asking her to do? Silence hung in the air so thick with heartache and regret, she thought she'd choke.

"Please. Don't make me do this." She set down the bottle of water with shaking hands, then fisted them on her thighs. "I'm so ashamed." Her words were a mere whisper.

He found an opening in the safety railing and patted her hand that covered his own. "Guilt can be good. It's your conscience saying you've done wrong." He released her hand and pointed to the stand beside his bed.

"Do you want your tumbler?" She assumed his gesture was pointing to the container on the table.

"Yes, please."

She lifted an oversized thermal mug, embossed with St. Mark's Hospital, that had a bendy straw sticking out. She leaned over and positioned the straw between his lips.

He swallowed several long draws of water. His Adam's apple worked and his gulps filled the room.

"Enough?"

"Yes. Thank you."

Nona deposited the tumbler on the table and sat back. After a beat, Pastor Grant sought out her hand to hold it again. She simultaneously welcomed and felt exposed by the gentle connection.

"A guilty conscience is like a smoke detector. It's ringing and ringing and ringing as a warning, and sometimes it's hard to calibrate it right. You know how a smoke detector will go off and sounds as loud for some toast burning in your kitchen as it does an actual fire. The conscience can be that way too. Blaring over some burned toast, making you think it's a five-alarm fire.

"In the life of God's children, this is where we must stop, think, and pray. People feel guilty all the time for things that aren't their fault or that they can't control. Sitting in your armchair at home, you see on the news there's been an earthquake in some far-off place, and you start feeling guilty that you aren't trapped in that earthquake. That guilt doesn't change one thing. You haven't sinned. What is there to feel guilty about? What you can do is let compassion fill your heart. Make a phone call to an aid society. Pray right there where you are sitting. Why? Feeling guilty for something you didn't do or that you couldn't prevent makes the universe revolve around you and your life, as if the fate of the world rises or falls on what you are or are not doing."

He didn't know how far she'd fallen. How wicked her betrayal had been.

She shook her head. But the strength of the hand holding hers and the intensity in his voice told her he *did* know.

"There's also a difference between feeling guilty and *being* guilty, and the Enemy wants us to feel guilty even when God's forgiven us."

She shifted. His fire-burned body had earned her attention for a few more minutes, no matter how uncomfortable she felt.

"There is guilt that comes on you when you have sinned—sinned against one of God's creatures or sinned against him."

His words held her fastened in the chair.

"What does the old psalm say, 'Against you, you only, have I sinned and done what is evil in your sight . . .'

"The 'you' in that sentence is God Almighty. Ultimately, he's the one we sin against. Good news is, God's made a way for us to cleanse our guilty consciences when we've sinned. Calls it repentance."

His words echoed things her mother had said, Lemar had said.

"But your problem is, you refuse to repent. What do you young people say? You're 'all in your feelings' about this and you 'feel some kind of way.' But I'm telling you, you're not seeing the truth, not addressing the problem. Instead, Nona, you show up year after year, hoping for a magical fix.

"You come hangdog to church once a year. Pushing people off with the hard look on your face. Like a wounded animal, biting and clawing at any-one who tries to get close enough to help. That's because you don't really *want* help. You think moping around in misery is going to pay for the sins you committed, and you're also paying for things that aren't even sins. God has the remedy so that you don't have to bear the weight of either, but you think that you have all the solutions to your own problems.

"Over there in Romans, it says, 'All have sinned and fall short of the glory of God.' 'But God demonstrates his own love for us in this: While we were still sinners, Christ died for us.'" His voice carried authority and conviction.

She turned her eyes away from him and pressed her lips firmly together. His words clanged like a ball-peen hammer on an anvil. "You don't know what I did."

"Why don't you tell me, baby girl? I can't make you, but I think you want to." He gave a slight bob of his head. "Let it out, Nona. I'll take it to my grave."

Her free hand clenched the guardrail of his hospital bed in such a tight grip, her fingers hurt. Pastor Grant repositioned himself, and his IV line made a clack when it contacted the railing. He squeezed the hand he'd been holding in a loving, grandfatherly way.

She forced herself to push out the words. "Where do I start?"

"At the beginning. Start at the beginning."

She lowered her tense shoulders from their tight clinch and blew out a breath. It was time.

◆ ◆ ◆

Nona's fight with Nikki streamed across her memory like a movie on Netflix.

In her mind, she saw herself duck sharply to the right as a hot-pink flip-flop whizzed toward her face and smacked into the wall behind her shoulder.

"How could you?" Nikki's face contorted with rage. She snatched a hairbrush from their dresser and hurled it.

The brush nailed Nona smack in the center of her chest. Anger torched the inside of her brain, incinerating all thought and charring her already wounded heart.

"You know I like Tyson." Nikki's words keened out, full of anguish. She'd gone from zero to hysterical in two seconds flat. "I finally had one thing that was only for me. The one person who saw me for myself and not like half of a whole."

Nona and Nikki had shared everything since birth. The same bedroom. Most of their clothing. They'd reveled in their twindom. Each loved the other. Hard. With unshakable twin-love. Unique and identical at the same time. Until they turned thirteen. That year, Nikki veered toward skinny jeans, ballet flats, and a wicked-hot flat iron, but Nona forged her own laid-back athletic style. A rotation of sports hoodies, *Mortal Kombat* T-shirts, and a scrunchie to hold back her mass of curls. It was the first little crack in their bond. But they'd still held firm, unbreakable.

Until freshman year of high school.

Until Tyson Foster.

Nona shoved away from the wall and squared up on Nikki. "Why do you think he belongs to you, huh?"

The spot where the brush hit stung. But Nikki's assumption that Tyson belonged to her hurt more, because Nona already knew the answer to the question she'd flung at Nikki.

All the boys belonged to Nikki. How could Nikki not see that?

It was the way of things. The men Nona loved opted not to love her back. Dad loved basketball. Mom loved the arts. Once Nona's style choices diverged from Nikki's, so did life at home. For years, Nona courted her father's favor, wanting to be his favorite. She let Nikki have all the girlie stuff. Dance squad and cheer. And all their mom's attention. Nona had paid a high price for her choice.

Even though they shared identical faces, once they started high school, guys always gravitated to Nikki with her ballerina grace and self-confidence. What guy wanted a snarky girl with a killer jump shot who threw elbows harder than he did?

When their dad ejected himself from their family, he left Nona with nothing and Nikki with everything.

"Tyson told me he loved me. He wanted to be exclusive." Nikki's nostrils flared and contracted; her breath shuddered. "You knew he and I were dating. Why did you do it?"

Why?

"I've been trying to let Nikki down easy," Tyson had recently told Nona. *"She's got a crush on me. I don't feel the same. Athletic girls are my type. We have more in common. You're different. Special . . . and I like that."*

He'd smoothed an escaped curl back from her face and tucked it behind her ear. The lyrical words, whispered low and sweet, soothed the ache in her heart. He'd said things she longed to hear since their father turned his back on them. On her. And walked away.

"He told *me* he loved *me*. That he'd talked to you and that you understood." Nona had no intention of backing down. Not over Tyson. Every second she'd stared into those mesmerizing eyes and listened to his honey-coated words, she'd fallen a little harder and worried about her sister's feelings a little less.

His beauty. The passion they shared for basketball. The way his piercing eyes consumed her. In her bones, she had known their destinies were intertwined. Guys buzzed around Nikki like drunken bees. Nikki would get over this one guy.

Tyson had to choose her. Had to. She'd given him *everything*.

In a cruel, sick twist, Tyson had fooled them all. The idea of dating twins had been irresistible. He'd bragged to a few teammates about how he planned to spend New Year's Eve with one sister and New Year's Day with the other.

But then Tyson called and begged Nikki to forgive him. Told her he'd made a mistake. She was the one he loved. And Nikki forgave him.

New Year's Eve, Nona had the scorched-earth fight with her sister. Nikki stalked to the front door, on her way to reconcile with Tyson. She yanked open the door and turned reddened eyes to Nona.

Bile and anger rose inside Nona. Her mind scrambled for a weapon that would pierce Nikki's heart as much as watching Nikki walking out the door into Tyson's arms pierced hers.

"I wish I never had a sister." Nona's cold, flat voice hit its target, and Nikki drew back like Nona had slapped her.

Nikki stormed from the house, snatched open the car door, and tore out of the driveway.

Twenty minutes later, a small sprinkle began, and a quiet unease built inside Nona's mind. Rain started pelting the street outside their house in rapid, fat drops. She called Nikki, but there was no answer. When Nona's phone finally rang, a California Highway Patrol officer upended her life.

* * *

When the words stopped falling from Nona's mouth, the room fell silent, and Pastor Grant's steady, loving presence enveloped her. The cavern where Nona's heart lived no longer ached, yet no magical lightness replaced the underlying, ever-present numbness that always lived there. She felt spent, as if she'd taken a long, exhausting run. The exertion had purged something. But a heaviness remained.

The pastor's hand still rested over hers with a firm and reassuring grip.

"Pastor Grant, I've felt guilty for so long. I got what I wished for, and I've hated myself every moment since."

"I know, Nona. I know."

"If I could unwind everything. Take it all back. Every word. Every thought."

"Was it wrong for you to tell Nikki you wished you never had a sister? Yes. Why? Because you intended to hurt her, and we should never set out to hurt one of God's children. But your words didn't cause the accident."

"Yes, but I knew she wanted to date Tyson, and I didn't care. I wanted him to myself."

"That may have been selfish." He paused and coughed. "But that didn't kill your sister either."

"She got hit because I didn't put gas in the car. She was stranded and had to walk to the station in the rain. But for me, none of that would have happened."

"It's true too. The lack of gas caused the car to stop on the road, but she didn't check. She stormed out of the house, mad, running off to see that boy. She wasn't thinking about *your* feelings either. You both had plenty of selfishness to go around about that young man."

The name of that production company floated into mind. Yes. She and Nikki had been two dogs with one bone, neither letting go, each pulling and fighting and scrapping for what they wanted.

"Everything that happens in life is a string of events. A supposed coincidence here, a change in plans there, taking one fork in the road over the other. Yes, you hurt Nikki's feelings, but you didn't kill her. What you are doing is pushing people away. You're so harsh and cynical. All balled up in your hurt. You're not living the life God has for you. You are squandering the gift he's given you by choosing to believe that holding on to the pain will somehow pay for what happened."

For some reason, Pastor Grant's words penetrated her mind. She leaned in closer to him.

"Only one thing pays for your sins," he said. "Only one thing pays for my sins. That's Jesus's death on the cross. The amazing thing is that when we repent, turn away, and renounce all our sins, and place our faith, hope, and trust in Jesus, the Good Book says, 'If we confess our sins, he is faithful and just and will forgive us our sins and purify us from all unrighteousness.' 'As far as the east is from the west, so far has he removed our transgressions from us.' He will 'tread our sins underfoot and hurl all our iniquities into the depths of the sea.'" Pastor Grant inhaled sharply, once. Then again. His body sagged farther into the bed. "Could you raise the back a little?"

She grabbed the controller and eyed the array of buttons, finally picking the one with a reclined stick figure and an arrow pointing up. After raising him six inches, she fluffed the pillows behind his head. "Better?"

"Much. Now where was I. Oh yes. God does not want to hold our sins against us, but he will because he's holy. But praise be to him, he made a way. He put the punishment for sins on his Son, Jesus. 'If you declare with your mouth, "Jesus is Lord," and believe in your heart that God raised him from the dead, you will be saved. For it is with your heart that you believe and are justified, and it is with your mouth that you profess your faith and are saved.' That's all you need to do."

Her heart pounded inside her chest. Could it be as simple as he said? For the first time in ten years, darkness gave way to light, resignation to hope. "I want that. I want it so much."

"Hold my hand, Nona, and pray along with me."

Moments of whispered prayers and unburdening passed. At Pastor's *amen*, calm resolve entered her mind. *"As far as the east is from the west."*

"Thank you, Pastor."

"Thank the Lord."

Nona swiped under her lids. Her eyes felt gummy and hot. With her free hand, she snatched a few tissues from beside Pastor's bed and dabbed under her nose.

Several moments of silence ticked by. Pastor Grant's grip on her hand slackened.

"I should be going." She stood to leave, still clasping his hand in hers, reluctant to break the connection. "Thank you again, Pastor."

He tightened his grip. "One more thing, Nona. I know it's here in this room. I can't see it." His weariness shifted to agitation.

"What is it? Let me help you figure it out."

"Top drawer of the bedside table. That's what the nurse said. The top drawer."

"What's in the top drawer?"

"What I found is in the top drawer. Get it out and take it with you."

She opened the drawer. There was a hospital gown inside, and it appeared to be wrapped around something. With care, she removed the bundle and slowly peeled back the cloth.

The scents of burned leather and ash rose to her nose. "It's a Bible." Wonder laced her voice.

"It's *the* Bible, Nona. *The* Bible."

The cover and edges bore the marks of fire damage. "I want to be careful with it. I'll open it at home. Maybe take it to an expert."

"I think that's a good plan. Call me and let me know what you find." His torso relaxed back against the bed as tension eased from his body.

She could not wait to open the Bible to see if it held the information they needed. She wrapped the Book back up, clutched it to her chest, and exited his room with a faint click of his door.

Chapter 18

IN THE HOSPITAL'S parking garage, Nona peeled back the fabric and peeked inside at the Bible. Given what she'd seen, common sense told her not to flip open the Bible and start paging through it. But she also knew Pastor Grant didn't have enough money to hire a professional conservator to examine it. As a compromise, she stopped at the hardware store to purchase some nitrile gloves and then spent the better part of the day watching videos and reading internet articles about how to handle smoke- and fire-damaged books.

It was nearly five o'clock in the evening when Nona stuffed her hands in her gloves and gathered enough courage to approach the aquamarine-colored hospital gown swaddling the Bible on the corner of her desk. Her entire office smelled like burned leather. And she was beyond exhausted. Her visit with Pastor Grant had both drained her and left her wound up at the same time.

Lady gave a low whine from the other side of the door.

Nona had locked the animals out as a precaution. She didn't want them jostling her or knocking the Book off the desk. "You can come in when I'm done, Lady."

The dog gave a yip in response.

"Here we go." Nona centered the package on the desk and, with careful hands, folded back the fabric and exposed the Book. She lifted the Bible and examined it from every angle. No wonder Pastor Grant had bandages covering both of his hands. The front cover was stiff to the touch. She slowly rotated the Book. Charring blackened the exposed edges of pages as well. She gently flipped the item over to examine the back, grateful to see some portion had sustained minimal damage.

She bowed her head and said a quick prayer. Her fingers trembled as she eased opened the leather of the back cover. Wedged inside were three undamaged, regular-sized envelopes and a folded, yellowed piece of newsprint.

She slid out the papers. The envelopes smelled of smoke but were otherwise in excellent condition. Circular postmarks said "Mobile, Alabama," with the earliest in 1946 and the last, 1992.

She lay each item on the desk in chronological order and set the newspaper article aside to review last. None of the envelopes had a return address. The name "F. Grant" at a post office box in Long Beach, California, appeared in a precise, thin cursive on the front of each envelope except one. That one had been sent to Calexico, California.

"F. Grant" had to mean "Florence Grant," since the letters were among her possessions. Given the absence of a return address and the use of PO boxes, it seemed Pastor's mother and the unknown letter writer had taken extreme measures to conceal their correspondence. Each envelope bore a slit at the top, presumably from a letter opener or a knife.

The envelope bearing the 1992 postmark triggered a memory. Nona closed her eyes and concentrated, then retrieved her phone and opened up her Notes app. Pastor's mother had died in 1992. That date might have some significance.

Her hands trembled, and she extracted the oldest letter, the one sent to Calexico.

December 1946
My Heart,
   Do not look back. Never return. Shake the dust of this forsaken
earth off your feet and be free. I am ever faithful. You can entrust your
secret to me until I return to the earth. I am now and will always be,
   Your Dearest Love

Nona turned the words over in her mind and tried to understand the connection. Pastor Grant was born in 1946. She googled Calexico, California. It was about a thirty-minute drive without traffic from there to Mexicali, where Pastor Grant was born.

She picked up the next letter. The smoky scent assaulted her nose. Her eyes stung, partially from the irritating odor but more from remembering that retrieving the Bible had nearly cost Pastor Grant his life.

April 4, 1968
My Heart,

The sorrow and agony of this day remind me why you cannot return to me. Pressures are mounting, and although I knew my silence would pain you, I drew out the time even further only for your safety and protection. Every day without reaching out to you seemed like an eternity. You cannot, you will not, make any attempt to see me. My hope is in the Lord. He knows all. I will trust that our being apart is his will and will bow my life to his. You must as well. Stay far from me and never return. We will see each other in glory. Until then, my love for you burns brighter every day.

Your Dearest Love

This letter seemed to talk passionately about romance. She bounced ideas around her mind. The most logical explanations were an unexpected pregnancy, the fallout from an unwanted baby, or a forbidden romance.

The spiky handwriting was neither feminine nor masculine. Had the writer tried to disguise their identity? She checked again—April 4, 1968, the day Martin Luther King Jr. was shot—and oddly, the lyric from that band U2 about Martin Luther King's murder entered her mind. How was the sorrow and agony of that day tied to Florence's inability to return to the one who addressed himself as "Dearest Love"? Wouldn't her marriage be the thing to keep her apart from him?

Nona picked up the next letter, postmarked March 10, 1973. Anxiety and anticipation circled inside her. Was there some other date in history as dreadful as the day Dr. King was assassinated that she wasn't remembering from school?

My Heart,

There is so much I want to say to you. So much history has passed.

Some of those who held the memories of that time have gone on to their reward. Things are changing. Perhaps I can see you? All these years without you, it is as if I am a half, not a whole. The love I have for you will never waiver, never lessen, never die.

Always and ever,

Your Dearest Love

The feelings Dearest Love held for Florence had not abated over the years. Yet, Florence remained with her husband in California and never returned to her hometown.

Nona squeezed her forehead between her thumb and index finger and massaged her temples. None of this made any sense. She rechecked the date, then ran it through the internet, searching for "on this day in history." Two deaths popped into the results. The assassination of Richard Sharples, governor of Bermuda, and the passing of Eugene "Bull" Connor. She instantly recognized Connor's nickname in the article. Bull was the southern politician who had ordered the use of fire hoses and police dogs on protesters. She'd seen pictures of his horrific use of force in her textbooks in the chapters covering nonviolent civil protests against segregation. This was now the second letter postmarked on the date of death of someone historically connected to the Civil Rights Movement.

She glanced at her notes again. Pastor Grant had mentioned that his parents never spoke about his mother's family following the death of Emmett Till. Was there a civil rights angle to the family split? Was there a murder involved?

Nausea, caused by the persistent smell left by the fire and the dates of the letters, rose in her stomach. She slid the last letter to the side and turned the Bible to the front. Her assignment from Pastor Grant was to find out the name of the long-lost relative who'd left him an inheritance, not to expose family history that should remain in the past.

Every intuition told her this indeed was the Bible Pastor Grant had been searching for. She gently loosened the front cover. She could only partially lift it without cracking away a piece. The first ten to fifteen pages, where publishers left space for the recording of genealogies and baptisms, were burned beyond recognition. She slid her fingers in and smoothed them over the remains. The front might have contained a birth certificate, but now it was lost forever.

She forced herself to put the Bible away and unfolded the final item bearing the 1992 postmark. A scan of the yellowed paper caused her chest to tighten, and cold sweat broke out on her forehead. Not a love triangle or a concealed birth. She refolded the paper, stood, and left her office. She had to get out of the house. She had to think. This was not news she wanted to break to an old man on a hospital bed. She opened the door. Lady trotted in, and Nona gave her an absent-minded pat. "No. We're not going out right now." Agitation swirled inside of her, and she had to shake it off. She donned her cross-trainers, tucked her gun into the waistband of her concealed carry leggings, and jerked open the front door. Maybe if she ran fast enough and far enough, she could outrun the horrible suspicion that held her in a vise grip.

◆ ◆ ◆

Two weeks later, Nona parked at the curb in front of Pastor Grant's tan stucco cottage, exited her vehicle, and walked up his pathway. She had spoken with him several times since his return to his home, where he continued to recuperate. But she'd deflected whenever he wanted to talk about the case specifically. Instead, she'd focused on encouraging him to build up his strength and rest, which had proven challenging for a man dedicated to service and caring for others.

His silver Lincoln Continental sat in the carport. Judging by the other homes she'd passed on the street, and the small front yard, his cottage probably topped out at three bedrooms with one bath. His grass needed a mow, which was understandable, and the flower beds under each of the front windows held some evergreen shrubs and stalky rosebushes without buds. Closer to the front door, peeling paint and exposed wood revealed the trim, and the house itself needed a fresh coat of paint and some gutter repairs. Sadness seeped into her heart. Pastor worked some mention of his wife's love of gardening and the pride she had in her housekeeping into almost every conversation.

He opened the door after one knock. While his bandage-free eyes held their customary affection, she suppressed a wince at the sparse regrowth of his singed eyebrows. She quickly averted her gaze from his face, to reel in the self-recriminations for not protecting him, and instead took in his Fruit of the Loom sweat suit—navy-blue top and matching bottoms—athletic socks, and house shoes. A total grandpa outfit, not the usual dapper pastor in a suit. Her insides squeezed with an ache of longing and realization. With all her family back east, he was the grandfather she wished she'd had.

He moved aside, and Nona stepped through the doorway straight into his vintage living room. An enormous brown overstuffed leather sectional lined the wall to her left. In front of the couch stood a pine, glass-topped coffee table cluttered with sections of newspaper. Two matching La-Z-Boy recliners upholstered in burnt orange, cream, and brown plaid sat on her right, facing the couch. Directly in front of her, on the back wall, a fifty-inch flat-screen TV hung mounted above the brick-surrounded fireplace and represented the only nod to the current millennium. Empty vases sat on each side of the television. Every piece of furniture was a testimony to his perseverance in ministry despite the loss of the love of his life.

"How are you feeling?" Nona asked.

He appeared thinner by maybe ten pounds, but his eyes had regained their sparkle.

"Feeling much better, but still a ways to go." He stretched out his arms, then tried to make fists. "Scarring has limited my motion a bit, but the doctor says I should get it all back if I keep up with my physical therapy and exercises."

His skin bore a few raw patches that glistened with some sort of ointment. She forced herself not to glance away.

He gestured toward the recliners. "Make yourself comfortable. Can I get you some coffee? Water?"

"I'm fine." Nona moved to the first chair and sat.

"Be right back." He shuffled toward a doorway near the end of the sofa.

From her position, she could see through the opening of the doorframe into a bit of the kitchen—a countertop and some cabinets.

She lifted the sports section from the pile of newspaper to scan the basketball scores for the Western Conference, and an envelope bearing the name Javit, Blatt & Steele mixed in among the other bills and mail caught her eye. At the shuffle-slap of Pastor's house slippers, she angled herself to face him squarely. "I found something when I examined the Bible, and I wanted to share it with you in person."

"Come in here, so we can sit at a table." He motioned for her to join him in the kitchen.

She followed him to the dinette table and removed all the letters from a folder in her handbag. "I think you should read these."

Pastor Grant patted his breast pocket, attempting to locate his reading glasses.

She pointed at him.

A rueful smile graced his lips, and he slid his readers down from his forehead.

Confusion marred his face as he read the letters. "This is like the first note we found."

"It is. Do the dates mean anything to you?"

"This is the date of Dr. King's assassination."

"Yes."

"This one, I don't know."

"The day Bull Connor died."

His eyes widened.

"Exactly." She pulled out one last piece of paper. "This one is not a letter." She pushed forward the newspaper clipping and spread it out in front of him.

The Burnt Water Herald—Wednesday, April 20, 1946

Sheriff's deputies found the body of Sergeant Sylvester Dillard concealed near the trash barrels in the alley behind Tippen's Drug Store, next to Sweet Time Cabaret early this morning. According to authorities, the cause of death appears to be blunt force trauma. Wounds on Dillard's body indicate there may have been an altercation between the victim and an unknown assailant. The authorities are withholding further details as the investigation is ongoing. Sergeant Dillard received a Purple Heart for his valiant service in

Operation Dragoon in the South of France. He leaves behind a
grieving widow and two children. The *Herald* will publish information about funeral arrangements once provided by the family.

"Have you ever seen this article before?" She studied the look of intense
concentration on Pastor Grant's face.

He closed his eyes, appearing to concentrate intently. Then his features
fell. "No. Never."

"Does it bring to mind any conversations your parents may have had?"

"Nothing about this is familiar."

"I'm not sure what this all means, but it tells us two important things.
First, my research is correct, and your family has roots in Burnt Water,
Alabama. Second, I think the reason there was so much secrecy about your
family history has something to do with the death of Sergeant Sylvester
Dillard."

She hesitated, not sure she should proceed, but deep affection and care
for Pastor Grant urged her to speak. "Until we get this all settled, please
take some additional precautions. Be on guard. Make sure you check your
locks, and don't open your door to strangers."

Chapter 19

Nona freed Lady and Bruiser as soon as she entered Pawsitivity Unleashed, the dog park around the corner from her house. DeMarcus had said he didn't want to meet at her office or his, because he was fidgety from being cooped up and needed an excuse to leave, get outside and stretch his legs. She flipped her wrist to check the time. Raucous barks rang out from every grass-covered corner. She squinted at the bright midday sun and slid her sunglasses down from the top of her head. The smell of carnitas and corn tortillas drifted over from one of the food trucks that parked outside the entrance, drawing adults like ice cream trucks drew sweaty kids. Vinnie, a rust-colored vizsla and a park regular, trotted up, and the trio of canines bolted for the doggy tunnel.

She spied Vinnie's owner, Eric, sidling up to talk to her. Nothing wrong with Eric. He had a great job at a midsize firm in the IT department. Owned a house. Drove a Camry.

"Nona, how about we go to that charcuterie place we talked about?" He stuffed his fists into his chino shorts and rocked back on the heels of his brown Sperry loafers. "After that, we could hit the Westside Art House for that German film."

She'd sworn off bad boys and Adonis types. Eric was neither of these. A nice guy with a friendly dog, but her mind hunted for another excuse to turn him down. "Thanks, Eric—"

"Hey, babe." DeMarcus sneaked up while Eric had distracted her. DeMarcus leaned in and pecked her on the cheek, winked, then stuck out his hand. "Hey, man, I'm DeMarcus, Nona's fiancé."

Eric stammered, trying to push out his return greeting. "Eric. Nice to meet you."

Bruiser came and stood, front and back legs slightly spread apart, beside DeMarcus like they were best friends.

"Well, um. I'll see you around, Nona. And congratulations." Eric's voice drifted up like he wasn't sure felicitations were in order, then he eased away.

Nona faced DeMarcus.

He held one hand palm up, shushing her. He raised his other hand, which gripped a bag with a yellow sombrero and the name "Street Taco Maestro" written in red letters on it. "Lunch with onions. Lots of them. Super smelly." He raised an eyebrow.

She mashed her lips into a thin line, then made her way to a bench with DeMarcus close behind.

At the table, he divvied out the food and handed her a bottle of water. He closed his eyes and opened them a few seconds later. Something was different about him. She hadn't known him long, but her gut told her he was going through something or had changed somehow.

She boxed out the thoughts. Why did she even care? Their work together would end. She'd relinquish custody of his giant ring, and they'd move on.

"What's wrong, Sassy?"

"What?" She worked to steel herself and set her facial expression to neutral.

He studied her for a long moment. "I want you to know, you can talk to me if you need to." His eyes were sincere.

Old fear welled in her heart, telling her she needed never-serious, always-joking DeMarcus to return immediately, because sensitive, understanding DeMarcus would chop up her heart like a crisscross paper shredder. Her brain fought against her heart, reminding her of Pastor Grant's admonition that she didn't have to face all of life's challenges alone.

"You called this little meeting to discuss your case, so let's talk about it, shall we." She deflected, for now. The thought of being open with DeMarcus was too new and too scary. She'd need baby steps.

Bruiser and Lady joined them at the table, and DeMarcus removed two tinfoil-covered take-out containers. He glanced up at her. "Beef is fine, right? It's unseasoned."

She gave a dismissive wave of her hand, granting him permission. Inch by inch, doggy treat by doggy treat, he was working his way into her heart.

He opened the foil and set the containers on the ground. "How's Pastor Grant holding up?"

"You know Pastor. He already wants to return to visitations. His doctor told him no. He is holding Wednesday night prayer out of his house." She made a concerned face. "Pastor Grant has limitless reserves of energy. The church has full insurance coverage, but you know how wrangling with insurance companies goes."

"Well, tell him I said hi, next time you see him. In fact, maybe I'll go visit him."

Had body snatchers come and whisked away the real DeMarcus? "I'm sure he'd like that." She forced a sincere tone into her voice.

"What are the next steps in your investigation for him?"

His question made her pause. Should she tell him she suspected Pastor Grant's parents had fled Alabama because of a murder? She didn't know if they were involved as witnesses. Maybe they were suspects? Had they run to protect their own lives? Was the murderer still alive? Were there any living witnesses? She didn't have enough evidence at this point to come to an accurate conclusion.

This investigation needed to go back to where everything started. She looked squarely at DeMarcus. "I think I need to make a trip to Alabama."

"Really? Why's that?" His eyebrows inched closer to his hairline.

"I have the names of Pastor Grant's parents, and I am pretty confident they were born in Burnt Water, Alabama. Unfortunately, I have zero familial information other than their names. The trail is cold, and Burnt Water is still in the AOL age as far as the internet is concerned. The county hasn't digitized pre-1970 courthouse records. Their library still uses microfiche."

"I was a jock. Never had to use microfiche."

"Whatever, Johnson."

The words in the letters she found floated through her mind. So full of pain and loss. "As of right now, I still need to figure out the name of the decedent and then I need to prove Pastor Grant's relationship to that person."

"Did I ever tell you I scored a one hundred in my legal research class?"

"At Princeton, no doubt."

"Of course not." He reached out a finger and tweaked her nose. "I went to UVA for law school. Did I forget to mention that? I picked my schools based on color. Princeton is black and orange. Virginia, blue and orange."

She laughed.

"Before you go hopping on a jet to go two thousand miles away, let me see what favors I can cash in. Our firm has a small satellite office in Birmingham. What's the distance from there to Burnt Water?"

Phone in hand, she checked the map. "It's almost to Mobile, so a little over two hundred miles."

"Is everything in your life this complicated?"

If he only knew. "Not at all."

"Wait, send me a text message with exactly what you need. I zoned out for a second on the specific information."

"Really, Johnson?"

He shrugged. "There was a cute dog catching Frisbees in his mouth. It distracted me."

She dashed off a text.

"Receipt confirmed. I'll work on this tomorrow. Where are we on Mitch and Sylvia's case?"

Finally, the conversation was on safe ground. "You read my email about my talk with Chester Ferguson?"

"Yes. I've reached out to him, but he won't return my calls. All Mitch needs is for the Yacoubians to cut back the junipers. If they know we've found actual spite, Mitch figures they'll cave."

"Is Mitch breathing down your neck?"

"He's in trial right now on a product defect case for our client Gimballed Industrial. Boring stuff." He grew silent, and his eyes became vacant. The assured gleam gone. "I haven't . . . He and I haven't spoken in a couple of days, but I'm worried I won't make partner. I've been getting weird looks from some stakeholders on the committee." He glanced at her, then looked the other direction, his focus trained on the frolicking dogs. "Could be my imagination."

Without permission or thought, her hands covered his. "I'm sorry, De-Marcus."

He shrugged. "We'll get these cases done, then I'll update my résumé."

She stiffened, and her lips tightened as protectiveness toward DeMarcus unfurled inside her. How could Mitch backstab him like that?

"No biggie." He jerked his chin upward. He interlaced their fingers.

Her insides felt as though hummingbirds were fighting for territory in her chest. Emotions swirled. Anger toward Mitch and Sylvia, plus emotions she chose not to examine, caused by the sensation of her hand in DeMarcus's.

He gave a quick squeeze and released it. "Anyway, try to call Mr. Ferguson. From what you told me, you two hit it off. Let's see if he'll take a call from you. I want to get his statement locked down in an affidavit for him to sign."

She nodded and placed her phone on the table in front of herself. Lady and Bruiser frolicked with newcomers to the park. After tapping the speakerphone button, she pushed the phone closer to DeMarcus so he could hear. After two rings, she hovered her finger over the disconnect button, expecting the call to roll over to voicemail.

"Ferguson Landscaping, this is Victoria."

She gave DeMarcus a thumbs-up. "Hi, Victoria, it's Nona Taylor."

"Nona, so glad to hear from you." Genuine warmth emanated across the line.

"Victoria, the lawyer I'm working for has been trying to contact Chester, to gather some additional information, but hasn't been able to reach him. I was wondering if you could help me."

Silence greeted her from Victoria's end.

"Victoria . . . ?"

"Nona." Victoria let out a long sigh. "I don't know everything that's going on, but the Yacoubians reached out to Chester the day after you met with him. Offered to pay everything they owed plus interest. Worked out an agreement to edit out the fight in the reruns of the 'Trouble in Palisades Paradise' episode."

"But, Victoria, Chester told me holding the Yacoubians responsible was a matter of principle with him."

Victoria hissed. "Aye, sweetie. Men." The sound of sucking teeth crossed the line. "Besides, business is business. Chester's going to get his own reality show. They even have a title, *Greener Grass with Chester Ferguson*. They'll follow Chester as he manages Ferguson Landscaping. He'll get to jabber on and on about different varieties of grass and soil conditions. They'll film our homelife as well, how we juggle Chester as my boss and my husband. The grandkids will even make cameos."

"Well, it sounds great for you guys." She wanted to be mad, but she really respected Chester and Victoria, honest, hardworking people. She couldn't begrudge them this opportunity.

"So sorry, Nona. We owe you a debt of gratitude. All of this came our way, because your investigation lit a fire under the Yacoubians' tails."

Nona heard insistent warbling.

"I so enjoyed meeting you. Gotta go. I have another call coming in." The call clicked off on Victoria's end, and Nona shifted position to angle herself toward DeMarcus.

He rubbed his eyes. "So are we back to square one?"

"I can—"

"Don't worry about it. We'll regroup."

"Okay." She didn't want to abandon DeMarcus's case. She wanted to hand him a win.

"Cheer up, Sassy." His scrutiny penetrated her, and she could not decipher his expression. "At this rate, our breakup is right around the corner. That's what you want. Right?"

She knew they weren't really engaged, so they couldn't actually break up. So why did his words create a leaden weight in her heart?

Chapter 20

DeMarcus sat in his office, feet propped on his desk with the miniature microphone for his speech-to-text software in his hand. The email notification on his phone dinged. He let out a sigh of relief. Anything to keep him from having to dictate this memorandum of points and authorities. He put down the mic, grabbed his phone, and swiped it open with one hand. He snared the Red Bull sitting on his desk with the other hand. His heart sped up when Nona's name popped up on the screen.

Merry Christmas nine months early, Johnson. Maybe God's listening to your prayers, after all. :-)

He smiled. Contact from Nona had that effect on him. He gulped a swig from the can and plunked it down on his desk.

After scrolling to the bottom of the email, he read the name of the attachment. "YITY-S02E15 Raw Footage." He clicked the attachment, and the voice of a screaming woman filled his office. He used the volume controller to rein in the screeching Mila Yacoubian, manically gesticulating while wearing spandex exercise pants and a crop top. Not one hair had escaped her tight ponytail, and her flawless skin appeared stretched by surgery or plumped by filler injections.

"I never want him on my property again." Mila shouted at a thirtysomething dude dressed in a T-shirt that said Production Crew, and jeans.

"There's nothing wrong with how it looks, Mila," the man said. "It doesn't affect the—"

"I don't care how it looks. I care what they can see, and I don't want them seeing anything but my juniper trees when they look out their back windows."

"Who and what are we talking about, Mila? I don't understand."

"You're not paid to understand. You're paid to produce this show."

"We're already behind schedule. If you'd calm down—"

"Calm down? Calm down?" Mila's arms flailed like someone swatting away a bee, and orange blotches mottled her face.

"Those people"—she pointed toward Mitch and Sylvia's house behind the junipers—"deserve everything coming to them. They ruined my reputation on Beverly Hills Undercover, and Bespoke Pooch Clothier reneged on their sponsorship of our clothing line."

The beleaguered producer stepped closer to Mila, gentling his voice as though talking to a feral animal. "You can't know that, Mila. Besides, it has nothing to do with—"

"This is not about the show. It's about those two-faced liars, who claimed to be our friends but told everyone about an accident at our groomers." Tears streamed down Mila's face. "It was all blown out of proportion. I was so humiliated."

"Can't we talk about this later?" The camera zoomed out to a wide shot, capturing an image of the Ferguson Landscaping truck. And based on the pictures DeMarcus had seen of Chester Ferguson on the company's website, the owner himself paced in front of the truck having his own intense conversation on his cell phone.

"I told him." Mila stabbed her index finger in Chester's direction. "I don't want one molecule of air—I don't want one particle of light—leaching onto Mitch and Sylvia Meyer's property from my property. Not now. Not as long as we own this house. As a matter of fact, we're not moving. Ever." The last words were at a decibel that might break glass.

"Wait! Are you filming this? Cut!" Mila sliced her hand across her throat. "Cut it now."

The screen went blank, and DeMarcus shot to his feet. Over nine months early, but this was the best Christmas gift anyone had ever given him.

He clicked over to Nona's number. "Nona!"

A dog barked in the background.

"Volume, Johnson. Volume. The dogs can hear you in the other room." She laughed.

"Where'd you get the video? It's exactly what we need. Mitch and Sylvia can sell their house."

"The video came to me anonymously from a disposable email account, but I suspect Alex or Chester. Probably Chester."

"Under that crusty exterior, Sassy, you're a dude magnet. Had Chester eating out of your hand all along." His elation flagged for a moment at the thought she was truly a dude magnet and already involved with Lemar.

"Aren't you going to have a hard time getting the video admitted into evidence?"

"What? Sorry. Say that again." His brain had spun off on the wrong track when it hit the Lemar speed bump.

"I was asking how we authenticate the video so that it's admissible? We don't know if it's even real."

The intricacies of Nona's love life were far more interesting than the evidence code. He downed another gulp of his energy drink, hoping to speed up its effect. "Doesn't matter. The goal is to get the Yacoubians to maintain their trees until after the sale of the property. By the time any lawsuit winds its way through the court, the market might be cold. This video is exactly what we need to show that the Yacoubians continued to let the shrubs grow with spiteful intent. Now we can force a settlement. We're hoping this thing never sees a courtroom. We're going to lay all the cards on the table before we file and see if we can get the other side to the table to dispose of this thing before litigation costs start to mount. If they balk, Mitch and Sylvia will put the house on the market ASAP and turn around and file for a preliminary injunction, citing the exigent circumstances of the cooling market. Might sue the HOA also, for failure to enforce their own rules, as additional leverage against the Yacoubians. Under the board chair's influence, all oversight has collapsed. People are looking for a way to cash in, and they've all let Mila and Arthur slide. Then we can fast-track discovery with a deposition of Chester Ferguson and get the producer to authenticate the video."

"Looks like you have it all figured out." Her voice didn't hold its usual sarcasm, and the sincere compliment unexpectedly moved him.

"It's a slam dunk, thanks to you, Nona." He swallowed hard. "We're a good team."

Silence stretched out.

"Well," she said, "you did go to Princeton."

"That I did. We're going out tonight to celebrate."

"We are, are we?"

"Absolutely. Wear some—"

"Watch it, Johnson."

"I was going to say 'gym shorts,' so I can school you on the basketball court, but if you want to wear a slinky dress, I'm fine with that too."

"You wish."

"You are correct."

She laughed.

A knock on the door distracted him from whatever Nona was saying. "Gotta go. Later, Sassy."

"Later, Johnson."

Maxine cracked the door, and he waved her in. Sheathed in her scandalous outfit of the day, Maxine's fire-engine red fingernails on the hand clutching a manila envelope matched the hue of the skin-tight sweater she wore atop skinny pants. DeMarcus shook his head. Maxine's clothing was more appropriate for a late-night meetup at a club than an eight-thirty morning briefing. While her outfit hurt his still-groggy brain, the worry lines imprinted on her forehead caused warning flares to shoot off in his mind.

"What's wrong?" He'd only seen the normally unflappable Maxine this agitated once before, when her little grandbaby spent a week in the NICU. Devastation for her had rocked him.

"Is it one of your kids? Grandkids? You can talk to me." He stood up to usher Maxine to a chair, so she could sit and fill him in.

"No." She turned away momentarily and blew out a breath. Looking at him gently, she slid the envelope onto his desk. "It's not my kids."

He reached for the envelope, unable to think of anything that Maxine might know that would cause her to act so strangely.

"Mitch's secretary and I were talking in the copy room. You know Mitch is up in San Jose in that trial?" Maxine's throat worked as she swallowed hard. "Anyway, I went to make those copies of that brief you wanted. When she left, there was an error light and a jam or something. I found what's in that envelope crinkled up in the back of the machine."

Maxine stared at him with glassy eyes. "I'm sorry, DeMarcus. I'll pull this shut behind me, and I'll hold all your calls."

The click of his door closing snapped him out of the daze that had overcome him. He sat and eyed the envelope. Was it a sexual harassment claim? He didn't flirt at the office. Ever. Friendly to everyone. Over the years, various coaches had drilled into him that there were certain lines you didn't cross, and he'd received the messages loud and clear.

Maybe a ruling had come in on the arbitration from the previous month. Thad Livingston could have called and let DeMarcus know immediately. Had he blown a statute of limitations? Committed malpractice? He'd had some close calls with deadlines, but Maxine and the paralegals helped compensate for his tendency to forget minor details. Still, things slipped through the cracks from time to time.

He focused on his chaotic desk, and ice water ran through his veins. Bile filled his gut. The envelope practically glowed.

Suck it up, Johnson. His teammates hadn't called him Professor Clutch for nothing. DeMarcus placed two fingers on top of the envelope and dragged it to the edge of the desk. He unwound the red string on the reusable clasp and slid out one sheet of paper.

To: The Partnership Nomination Subcommittee
From: Thad Livingston, Partnership Committee Chair
Re: Partnership Straw Vote

In conjunction with the Nomination Committee, the Partnership Committee has agreed to scale back on the partnership offers for the rising class of senior associates. The upcoming class is larger than usual. There's been a falloff in our construction litigation department, and there has been a downward slide in billable hours. Hence, our per-partner distributions have decreased.

After an anonymous straw vote, we've created a short list of those we think should receive an invitation into the partnership. We will offer any senior associate whose name is not on the list an of counsel position, or we will encourage them to make a lateral move to another firm. We will offer exit packages contingent upon the signing of customary waivers and releases. The straw vote is not final but advisory. If any partner thinks there's been a serious miscarriage, he or she should bring their concerns to the Nomination Subcommittee.

He flipped the page with shaking fingers and scanned the alphabetical list. His name should fall between Lisa Henry and Charlie Keener. Charlie's name didn't appear, and DeMarcus's own name was missing.

He lurched so quickly to his feet, his chair tipped over. A cold sweat broke out on his back. He snatched up the memo and stalked to a corner near his window. He'd lost important basketball games—championships—before. But they were never more than games, means to an end.

Partnership had been the end. The years of running and gunning. Two-a-day practices. Tutoring. G'Mama's sacrifices to cover out-of-pocket expenses for Princeton, which didn't offer athletic scholarships, only financial aid based on need. He'd been busting his gut here at Livingston, Meyer & Kendrick for years, and now he teetered on the brink of getting pushed out? A low growl forced its way from deep inside.

He reread the sentence about billable hours dropping off. Never should have taken that spite fence case for Mitch. Here he'd thought helping Mitch would gain him the inside edge, but it may have cost him the partnership. He raked his hand from his forehead to his nape.

"We Are Family" blasted from the corner of his desk. He'd given Jamaria and G'Mama the same ringtone. The avalanche of stimulation made him want to crawl out of his skin. He marched over to his desk and eyed the caller ID. Not G'Mama. He stabbed the Decline button and sent the call straight to voicemail. The last thing he needed right now was to deal with his little cuz's teenage foolishness.

He righted his overturned chair and collapsed onto the seat. Leaning back, he tossed a forearm over his eyes to close out the world and think. Sister Sledge sang out again, slicing into his concentration. He leaned forward and declined Jamaria. Again. He checked his watch. Twelve forty-five, East Coast time. She should be in school, not bothering him.

Think, Johnson. He leaned his elbows on the desk and held his head in his hands. A ballpoint pen in the cup on his desk snared his attention and his ire. He clicked and clicked and clicked until the button that worked the retractable tip popped off. He chucked the pen to the corner of the room, then resolve set in.

He'd appeal to Mitch, the partner with whom he had the best relationship. Mitch knew the quality of DeMarcus's work. Plus, his efforts on Mitch's personal case had to count for something, right?

Two knocks sounded, and Maxine entered, wrinkles formed between her brows. "I'm so sorry to disturb you . . ." She cleared her throat. "A young lady named Jamaria has called three times. I told her you were unavailable and asked to take a message. She insisted I let you know she called."

His plans about how to handle the partnership short list collapsed. Jamaria knew the rule. Never, ever use the office number unless life and death hung in the balance. He gave a dismissive wave, and Maxine backed out of the office. He pivoted toward his cell, grabbed it, and dialed.

Jamaria answered before the first ring finished. "G'Mama's on a train to California."

◆ ◆ ◆

"I'm taking the rest of the day off." DeMarcus stormed by Maxine's desk and stalked toward the elevators.

Maxine scampered after him. "Mitch just called. What should I tell him?"

"Tell him I'm taking a sick day." He hadn't taken a sick day in the seven years he'd been at the firm. "Tell them whatever you want. I'm not taking calls." He jammed his thumb repeatedly on the Down elevator button and entered swiftly when the doors opened.

He pressed and held the Close button. *Come on. Come on.*

"Hold the elevator."

He caught sight of a blazer and tie between the closing doors. He didn't care who wanted this elevator car. It was going down without them. The doors sealed shut.

His phone rang. Mitch's secretary. He turned on Do Not Disturb. Exiting the parking deck, his wheels spun, throwing up acrid smoke behind him as he tore down Lower Grand Avenue.

Jamaria's words had tumbled out like a Jenga tower crashing down. Something about G'Mama's time getting short. Wanting to sightsee along the way. A two-week trip across America. Hoping to meet DeMarcus's girl-friend before it was too late.

He'd talked to G'Mama three or four days ago. She hadn't said a word to him about her plan because, he suspected, she knew he'd try to stop her.

He slammed his hand on the steering wheel, then throttled back the speed. Given his mood, a run-in with the cops might end up with him in jail. He pointed his car south and drove down the 110.

"Hey, Siri, call G'Mama." His Bluetooth speakers kicked in, but his call went straight to G'Mama's voicemail.

"Morning glory and evening grace. This is Hattie Johnson. Please leave a message, and, Lord willing, I'll get back to you as soon as I can."

"This is D, G'Mama. Call me when you get this."

He flipped on the blinker and exited at MLK on autopilot. At a traffic signal, he pushed the button for the convertible roof, and the low whine of the motor filled his ears. Maybe he'd drive to the Santa Monica Pier and clear his mind.

What did his life amount to anyway? Did people take him seriously, or did they see him as a big joke? A law workhorse and a has-been basketball player? He scoured his thoughts for answers but could not form anything cohesive. The partnership catastrophe and the horror of his seventy-five-year-old grandmother on some bucket list trip banged into each other, crowding out clarity.

Nona's face sprang into his mind out of nowhere, like a pop-up ad on a website. He let out a grunt. G'Mama put herself on a marathon train ride to meet someone who didn't like him and under no circumstances wanted to be his fake fiancée or his actual girlfriend. Nona didn't have him on a pedestal, took every chance she could to stick it to him, and deployed blunt force trauma–level honesty. Truth be told, that's why he knew he could trust her. His temples throbbed, trying to process the unfolding scene be-tween G'Mama and Nona. Definitely not tea and crumpets. It might be like a dinner at Medieval Times, complete with jousting.

The clock on the dash read ten thirty. Way too early to drink. Normally, he treated his body like a machine. Minimal alcohol at firm functions and only one beer when out with the guys. But right now, he wanted to get wasted. Obliterate all the neurons in his skull. He slid into a parking space and killed the ignition. His stomach cramped, and his mind convulsed with a jumble of emotions.

He reclined the seat back twenty degrees, closed his eyes, and let the sun beat down on his face. After dragging air into his lungs through his nose, he held it for a three count, then forced the air out of his mouth. Another three-count hold and release. And another and another. The whirling, crashing thoughts slowed down. He opened his eyes, and the boarded-up storefront to Mount Zion faced off against him. Charred areas peeked out from behind the plywood, and a heavy chain secured by a padlock wound around the security gating.

His gaze rose to the neon cross atop the fire-damaged church signage. Was this entire day a cosmic joke? Was he being punked by God? Of all the places to end up, he'd come to Mount Zion without thinking. He just arrived.

He could hear G'Mama in his mind. *"Nah, baby. You didn't just arrive. God says before he formed you in your mama's womb, he knew you. He knows your end from your beginning. Ain't no accidents."*

If God cared so much, why was G'Mama talking about not having much time? Why was his entire partnership bid on the skids?

"Boy, God said to Job, 'Where were you when I laid the foundations of the earth?'" The little G'Mama sitting on his shoulder, whispering in his ear, always had a comeback. *"Do you think you know better than him? 'Who has known the mind of the Lord?' Definitely not you."*

All through his growing up, G'Mama spoke half regular English, half New King James Version of the Bible. She always had a quote, a song, or something from a sermon. Even now, her words were transmitting loud and clear in his mind, directly from some state in the Midwest.

With the money from the partnership, he'd planned to set up G'Mama for the rest of her life. She'd turned him down flat every time he'd asked her to move to LA to be near him, so he'd asked Maxine to research and find a nice independent-adult living facility close to her church. He'd wanted to take care of G'Mama until the end, but in his mind *the end* didn't play out like this. What was so important that she'd climbed aboard a giant soda can to ride for two weeks to get to him? If G'Mama was dying, if there was no partnership in his future, why was he even doing all of this?

"*What he wants from you, DeMarcus, is for you to live the way he wants. For you to want the things he wants you to have. Only then will you truly have your best life. He doesn't promise sunshine and rainbows every day, but he promises he'll never leave or forsake you.*

"*What have you got now? That fancy car. Pretty girls ringing your phone every day. That huge watch and giant ring, but you don't have peace, do you, DeMarcus? 'What will it profit a man if he gains the whole world, and loses his own soul?'*"

G'Mama would have been a good attorney. She'd let DeMarcus off the hook, then circle back around to the topic like an old fox trying to steal chickens from a coop.

What did he want from his life?

"*Vanities. Baby, it's all vanity. You can't take any of it with you. Don't store up your treasure 'where moth and rust destroy and where thieves break in and steal.'*"

He knew what he needed to do right now. G'Mama had already shown him the way. That year, when his cousin Quinton was on trial for dealing drugs, and the government shut down G'Mama's in-home day care because of his activities, she'd shoved all her clothes aside in her bedroom closet and put down a pillow to kneel on. Beside the pillow, she had a little boom box and a stack of ancient CDs of her favorite gospel singers. G'Mama disappeared into that closet for hours at a time. The sound of some tabernacle choir or another, and sometimes crying and fussing, would flow out. G'Mama emerged from her closet different from when she went in.

All DeMarcus's grasping for achievement and diversions had made him one tight ball of chaotic mess. And the only answer was to trust that God was big enough and loved him enough to fix the broken parts and work it all out.

If he couldn't have the partnership, if he were going to lose G'Mama, if Nona wouldn't have him, at least he'd have God. G'Mama used to say, "*God plus one is a majority. He'll never leave you or forsake you. And he's enough.*"

DeMarcus closed his eyes, hunting in his mind to find the right words.

He returned the back of his seat to upright, rested his forehead against the steering wheel, started listing off his sins and failures to God, and relinquished all the fake control he'd thought he'd had all these years to the King of the Universe.

Chapter 21

NONA SAT INSIDE the smoothie shop and sipped her pineapple island chiller. She opened her laptop and squeezed her eyes shut as brain freeze hit between her eyes like a spike driven into the ground. She winced and put the drink down to give herself a moment to recover. The savory smells of green onions and ham floating up from the quiche bites on her plate prompted her to take a nibble before she dug into work for the day.

DeMarcus said he'd arrange for the satellite office to file the legal paperwork to claim the estate, so that part was completed. But there was still a ton of important information missing before local counsel could file the forms. Top of the list—the name of the decedent. She massaged the spot between her eyes. Every time she and Pastor Grant moved two steps forward, obstacles out of left field pushed them back a whole city block.

She checked her action list. She'd make her reservation to fly to Birmingham after she called the Williams County Public Library. The population of the town of Burnt Water topped out at about seven thousand people, but the surrounding county had enough residents to support a library. She plopped the final morsel of her breakfast in her mouth and reached toward her phone to dial. The phone rang in her hand. The caller ID showed a number with the 424 LA area code but not a name. Her insides skittered as she debated answering. Several nights in a row, the buzzing phone had awakened her. When she'd answered, the caller had hung up. This call rang until her voicemail picked up.

She placed the phone down and blew out a long, controlled breath. She'd spoken with the fire department, and the chief was certain arson caused the fire at Mount Zion. They'd pinpointed the fire's origin to Pastor Grant's office.

Her initial thoughts had attributed the fire to someone with Leisure Zone Holdings. But now she remembered the news clipping about the murder of Sylvester Dillard and the carefully worded letters she'd found. Giant corporations settled matters in the courtroom, not with stakeouts and burning down buildings. Was the heir hunting letter a ruse to flush out Sylvester Dillard's murderer? Anyone trying to solve the crime would know that it happened so long ago, the odds of finding the murderer alive were slim.

The call spooked her a bit. What if the killer himself was still alive? Or someone who had knowledge about the crime? Someone related to the killer might be trying to protect them. The passage of time didn't mean all traces of the murderer's identity had vanished. Her phone rang again, and she ignored it. Was someone hunting down Pastor Grant to destroy evidence about the crime and silence the last person alive who might know something? Had someone tracked down Pastor Grant not to shower him with a windfall but to neutralize him?

The insistent ringing of her phone stopped her musings. It was the same number from the 424 area code. Her temper flared, and the desire to shield Pastor Grant from anyone who wanted to hurt him simmered inside. She hit the Talk button and raised the phone to her ear.

"I will do whatever it takes to make sure you go to prison for what you did to Hosea Grant. Do I make myself clear?" Her voice came out in a clipped staccato.

"Nona?"

"Who is this?" Anger laced her words.

"Nona, it's Mitchell Meyer. You know, Mitch and Sylvia. Glad I reached you."

"Mitch, I'm so sorry. One of my cases . . ."

"No worries, Nona. I only have a five-minute break from this trial up here in San Jose. A witness needed to use the little boy's room." Mitch chuckled. "Anyway, this is a secret, but a partnership is DeMarcus's if he likes. I want to take DeMarcus out to dinner to tell him, but I want to keep it hush-hush."

She struggled to shift gears and engage with Mitch's words. "What are you saying?"

"What I'm saying is, once this trial is over, we'll take you guys out someplace swanky, and we'll make the partnership announcement. I expect another week up here, but clear out some dates on your calendar at the end of the month."

"Okay." Her tongue felt thick in her mouth. "Um, sure. I'll do that."

"And remember, DeMarcus knows nothing about this. None of the associates do. He'll think it's one more of Sylvia's little dinner parties."

"I understand."

Muffled noises entered her ear. Mitch carried on a conversation with someone on his end. "Sorry about that. I need to run, but before I go, I want to tell you that you did a fantastic job on that spite fence case. DeMarcus sent me an email about what you dug up, and I think this thing will resolve itself as soon as I get back." More muffled talking came through the line. "Don't forget, Nona. Mum's the word." The call dropped.

The dramatic turn in her thoughts caused cognitive whiplash. She'd been puzzling out clues to a murder, and now her fingers itched to dial up DeMarcus and congratulate him. A laugh escaped. When DeMarcus finally learned he made partner, his ego would inflate and float around like a Macy's Thanksgiving Day Parade balloon.

A smile made its way onto her lips. After all this time working with Johnson, she saw beneath the puffery. DeMarcus didn't take himself seriously. The bragging about Princeton was a schtick, a routine he used to amuse himself and others, while also letting them know he wasn't someone they could trifle with. She shoved the thoughts away. She needed to get her focus back on determining if there even was an inheritance waiting for Pastor Grant in Burnt Water or if someone had set a trap for them.

◆ ◆ ◆

"Williams County Public Library. This is Ms. Loretta Adams. How may I direct your call?"

Nona stumbled for words. She'd expected a phone tree, not a live person. An automated answering service would have listed a series of departments, helping her to narrow down what she was searching for. Now she had to rummage in her own brain to figure out the exact type of help she needed.

"Hi. I live in California, and I'm helping an older relative do some genealogical research about his family in Burnt Water, Alabama." She swallowed. For ten years, she'd pushed the man away, and now, in her heart, she viewed Pastor Grant as a grandfather. He'd never pressured, never touched her tender spots, until the time was right. Even then, he'd been so gentle. The man was a gift to her, and she'd do anything to protect him. Plus, telling the librarian she was a private detective might get back to whoever was trying to track him down, and she couldn't risk a leak if the heir hunting thing was actually something nefarious. "Is there a reference librarian who might assist me?"

"Absolutely, sweetie. I'm the director of library services. We have some part-time assistants, but I'm the trained researcher."

"I'd like to start by finding out if the *Burnt Water Herald* is still your local paper, and if so, does it carry obituaries?"

"That's easy. Yes, it does. The *Herald*. It's published once a week and delivered free to every address. We keep hard copies on hand for a year, and everything else is sent off-site."

Surprise filtered through her. She checked her notes. The date on the article about the murder of Sylvester Dillard was nearly eighty years old. Amazing that the *Burnt Water Herald* was still in production after all this time. She contemplated, then rejected, the idea of reaching out to the newspaper directly. A random person calling might tip off someone about a potential story. Plus, since the original article about the murder came from the paper, she didn't want to request copies directly from its offices. The odds were small, but it still might throw up a warning flare.

"It was a distant relative, so he's not sure of the name. Is it possible to have copies of the obituaries for the last year mailed to me?"

"Bless your heart. Honey, I don't have time to make all those copies. Tell you what I can do. I can have a research assistant do it. She's my niece Chloe. She's working on her Girl Scout Gold Award by helping us modernize the library. Anyway, I can have her pull the papers for the last year and read the obituaries to you over the phone. Burnt Water is so small, about sixty to seventy deaths in a year. Won't take too long."

"How much would that cost?"

"No charge. All we ask for is a photocopy fee and postage if we find the one you want."

"May I set up an appointment?"

"Call after three o'clock our time. She comes straight from school."

"That would be fantastic. How long do you think it would take for her to get back to me?"

"She could do it tomorrow. She'll sit in the stacks and pull them one by one. Will that work for you?"

"Absolutely, and thank you so much."

"Sure thing, honey."

Click. Click. Click. The pieces of the puzzle snapped themselves into place. Nona had the town and, by tomorrow, the name of the decedent. She said a quick prayer that the path she went down led to an inheritance for Pastor Grant and not the reopening of a cold case murder investigation.

◆ ◆ ◆

After spending time in LA, being back in Burnt Water made Zeke's skin crawl. He sat in Kitty's dining room, staring at the burned toast and watery grits she'd served him. Kitty was an idiot and a terrible cook. It tasted exactly like the food he'd had in prison, but it beat having to make something himself. He looked around at the clean but overly female interior of her double-wide. The woman loved the color pink. He felt like he was sitting inside a Pepto-Bismol bottle with all the watermelon-colored pillows and little flamingo knickknacks on every flat surface. Thankfully, he didn't have to listen to Kitty's yammering on and on this evening, since she'd gone to work. He'd park himself in front of her computer and follow up on a few things.

All the time he'd spent in Los Angeles pursuing Grant had eaten up his savings. He flicked his eyes to the cash Kitty left for him. Wasn't having Calloway advance him one dime of expenses on this job. He'd run it his way and get the payout he deserved.

Kitty's home phone rang twice. Stopped. Rang once. Stopped. And when it rang again, he answered. Didn't want to pick up the phone and accidentally talk to Calloway.

"Hey, doll." He'd pour it on thick for her until he disappeared for good. Make her think he loved her and that he was taking her along for the ride.

"Hey, Zeke baby. Want me to pick up those pictures from the drugstore for you?"

"They're not ready yet. I'll get 'em tomorrow." Truth was, he didn't want Kitty to know his plans. He opened his phone and swiped through the pictures he'd uploaded and intended to pick up. He clicked on the juiciest. Grant hugging the female cop wannabe. The two of them eating lunch. The photo before the Watch Night service looked particularly salacious. A young thing like her, all dressed up, visiting an old man so late at night, with no one else on the premises. Holy Rollers scandalized easily, so it wouldn't take much to compromise the pastor. Kitty had a big mouth, and he didn't want her seeing the pictures. The less she knew, the better.

"What do you want for dinner?"

"Why don't you surprise me?" Didn't matter what she made. He'd hate it.

"All right, Zeke. See you later."

He shook a cigarette out of the pack and lit up. Kitty hated it when he smoked inside. So what? He flicked his ashes in the bowl holding the grits, then startled when his phone rang in his pocket. He checked the caller ID. In a town as small as Burnt Water, he couldn't hide forever.

"Calloway." He laced his voice with as much disdain as possible. No more rolling over for Gavin. No more listening to his insults. No more depending on him for a living. Zeke reached into his pocket and extracted his burner phone. He turned on its voice recorder and then put Calloway's call on speaker.

"Am I on speaker? Are you alone?" Suspicion undercut with irritation filled Calloway's voice.

"Yeah, you're on speaker. The phone makes my ear all sweaty. Stop worrying. Nobody's here. I'm at Kitty's, and she's at work."

"Fine. You've been dodging my calls." Zeke chaffed at Calloway's snippety tone. "I'm not taking the fall for this if it goes south."

The councilman couldn't be more wrong. Zeke suppressed a laugh. Sitting in a cramped economy seat flying from LA to Birmingham, he'd figured it all out. A no-lose proposition for himself, with Calloway catching all the repercussions. Zeke had three avenues of attack—two with the pastor and one with Calloway himself. Zeke would cover all the angles. Nothing to do but rake in the money.

"All that time and effort, and you *still* don't have a signed retainer agreement."

"Don't worry. I'll get your precious retainer letter." And he'd still work on that angle. It was the least complicated option, one that left a clean paper trail. But if it didn't work . . .

"If you can't get it into my hands by the end of the week, I'm bringing in someone new."

Threats? Calloway thought he could scare Zeke? Dismiss him?

"Who?" Zeke kept his voice cool.

"Don't you worry about that."

White-hot fury zigged through him, and it required every ounce of will-power to suppress it. "I don't care who you bring in. I'm still getting my cut." No way he was letting Calloway one-up him ever again. "You flip that last Leisure Zone parcel without me, and I'm telling everything I know."

Silence, like the grave, settled over the call.

"What do you think you know, Zeke?"

"Let's just say, I know what happened to Old Millie."

"You do? And exactly what is it you think happened to her?" Calloway's words came out clipped and low.

Lightheaded glee overtook Zeke as he launched the words he'd been running through his mind for months. The epic takedown he'd been wanting to give Calloway for years. "I know how you killed her, and I have proof."

"Let's talk about this in person, Zeke." Calloway was a hard man to fluster, but Zeke heard the strain in his voice.

"I want to talk about it now." Anger at Calloway's high-handedness overwhelmed Zeke. He practiced Kitty's mantra and envisioned what he wanted in his mind. "I want to flip the split of the proceeds. In fact, now I get 75 percent, and you get 25."

"And what do I get?"

"My lifetime of silence."

"What assurances do I have?"

"My word."

Calloway laughed at that.

Rage, black and consuming, coiled in Zeke's gut.

"Zeke, Zeke, Zeke. Leave all the thinking up to me. Remember how I fixed things back for you in college?"

Calloway had fixed things for him, all right. Once Zeke had lost his football scholarship, Calloway found illegal ways for Zeke to earn money, which coincidentally ended up lining Calloway's pockets as well. And eventually landed Zeke in lockup for eighteen months.

"Yeah. I remember everything." No way he was doing time for Calloway again. Somehow Calloway always ended up with the girls and the money. Gavin had also kept his freedom. Said he couldn't risk associating with Zeke when Zeke went away. Gavin promised to help out if Zeke kept his mouth shut and did the time. What did Zeke have to show for his loyalty? Nothing.

But not anymore.

"You're the muscle, and I'm the smarts. We complement each other. We each have strengths and weaknesses. Calm yourself down, and we'll talk about this tomorrow."

Gavin always employed his politician voice on Zeke when he was trying to get his way. Fine, let Calloway think Zeke was still the fool the councilman thought he was. "Sure, Gavin. You're right."

"So we'll talk in the morning?"

"Absolutely."

"See you then, Zeke."

The phone clicked off, and Zeke turned off the recorder. He emailed the recording to himself at the new email address he'd created. He loved the name: getoutofjailfree@tracefreemail.com.

Calloway thought Zeke was an idiot. Wrong. He was a genius. The stupid retainer no longer mattered at all. He was glad he'd burned down that church. Now that it was a pile of ash, the pastor felt the same suffering as Zeke. The old man wanted his building repaired, and Zeke wanted his money. The pastor would be on his knees, ready to do whatever Zeke wanted to get his precious congregation back under that ramshackle roof.

Zeke checked to make sure he'd dropped the folder with the doctored bank account statements in his duffel. His running buddy, Tommy, had really come through on that. Recommended his nephew, who'd served time for identity theft, to create fake statements in Grant's name, which made it look like Grant was siphoning money from his rinky-dink church. He'd shine Calloway on, blackmail him, then Zeke would turn around and blackmail the pastor too. Zeke would be the only one who ended up with any money from the inheritance.

He stood and moved toward the bedroom. Time to bug out of Burnt Water and lie low. If he drove fast enough, he could be in Atlanta right after lunchtime. His thoughts turned to Suzanna, a redheaded firecracker, who lived there. She'd let him crash at her place for a few days. He grabbed Kitty's laptop, went to her sock drawer, and cleaned out the rest of her cash. After grabbing his revolver and the box of ammo from the nightstand, he stuffed everything, along with his shave kit and change of boxers, into his duffel bag. He'd outfit himself at Walmart in Atlanta and leave the rest of his stuff here. He might need to come back, but even if he didn't, he needed Kitty to think he was.

Calloway thought he was stupid? Well, who'd been smart enough to line up the name of a reporter who loved snatching the covers off philandering pastors? Who'd been smart enough to follow Grant everywhere so that he knew which little old ladies in white dresses to mail the photos to? Who'd thought up the idea of threatening to send the dummied bank statements to the IRS to scare the pastor to death? Not Calloway. Zeke thought up those ideas. He had all the power and control now. He controlled Kitty. He controlled the pastor and his meddling she-cat. Now he also controlled Calloway. When that pastor rolled into town to collect his inheritance, Zeke would be right there to take every dime from him. Everyone in town would find out how Zeke was living large once this was over. The cars, the houses, the women—he'd be a bigger man than Big Zeke ever was. Zeke stuck out his chest, shoved the duffel bag under his arm, and slammed the door closed behind him as he left.

◆ ◆ ◆

Sun filtered into Nona's office, highlighting the floating dust motes in the air. Bruiser lay snoring on the couch, and Lady pressed herself against Nona's leg, providing quiet reassurance. She checked her watch. Half past three. She swiped her phone open and entered the number for the library.

"Williams County Public Library, this is Ms. Lorretta Adams. How may I assist you?"

"Hi, Ms. Adams. It's Nona Taylor again."

"Oh, Miss Taylor, great timing. Grab a piece of paper and jot down Chloe's number." Loretta rattled off the number for her niece's cell phone. "She's back in the stacks, where the newspapers are."

"Thank you, Ms."—Nona hesitated—"Ms. Lorretta."

"You're welcome, dear. Hope you find what you need."

Nona hung up and immediately called Chloe. "Hi, Chloe. This is Nona Taylor."

"Hi, Miss Nona. I can't wait to help you. It's exciting talking to someone from Los Angeles. Have you ever seen any movie stars?"

"Please call me Nona, and yes. Three or four times a year."

"Really?" Chloe's voice held the breathless exuberance of a teen who'd just spotted Taylor Swift.

"The movie industry and television companies support the Los Angeles economy. The city is where a lot of the actors, producers, and directors live." Nona suppressed a sigh. Having popped in on her brother, Lemar, at various film locations, the tedium of waiting around and prepping for production siphoned off much of the illusion of glamour.

"Who's the most famous person you ever saw?"

She thought for a moment. Other than paparazzi, the whole LA vibe was to pretend you didn't see the people. She rummaged through her mind for the last time Lemar escorted her onto a set. "I saw Tom Holland one day."

"Spider-Man? No. Way."

"Yes, he was on the next soundstage over from where my brother was on set as an extra."

"Your brother's an actor?"

"Yes."

"Awesome."

With Chloe's enthusiasm, Nona's hopes for a productive call increased.

"My aunt told me you're looking for obituaries. Do you have any clues that might help narrow it down?"

"I think the person I am looking for was close to one hundred when they died—a Black woman of that age, specifically. So if the obituaries have pictures, that will help rule out some people immediately."

"Okay. How far back should we start?"

"Let's do it in reverse. Start in January of this year and work backward."

"Sounds like a plan."

The noise of rustling papers scritched in Nona's ear. "In January of this year, no reported deaths."

More shuffling of papers. "I have the edition for the last week of December. Two people died, both men. Third week of December, one woman. There's a picture. She's Caucasian."

They worked their way back until they reached November from the prior year.

"There are two Black women who died in November. One woman was thirty-five and died in a car accident. Wait . . . I think I found it."

The excitement in Chloe's voice upped her volume several notches.

"'Carter, Mildred Elizabeth "Lizzie" (née Hall) died on November 14 of natural causes. She was one hundred and three years old. A lifelong resident of Burnt Water, Mildred was predeceased by her husband, Edward Carter; her daughter Geraldine Anne Carter, former Williams County head librarian; her son, Ellis "Skip" Carter, killed in action in Vietnam; and her sister, Mrs. Florence (née Hall) Grant of Los Angeles, California.

"'Mildred was an active member of Bethel African Methodist Episcopal where, over the years, she taught Sunday school; served on the missions committee, the prayer team, and the hospitality ministry; and oversaw various other offices in the church.

"'Funeral services will take place on Saturday at Bethel AME, with interment to follow thereafter in the church cemetery. In lieu of flowers, the family requests friends make donations to the Pan-African Liberian Outreach Fund.'"

An achy lump formed in Nona's throat, clogging any words. She'd found the decedent. Mrs. Mildred Hall Carter.

"Can you . . ." She pushed out a cough and downed some water from a nearby bottle. "Can you take a picture of that and send it to me?"

"Sure thing."

"Would it be too much to ask for you to fax it to someone as well?"

"Not a problem at all."

Nona looked up the number for the UPS Store where Pastor Grant had temporarily forwarded the church's mail and where he could receive a fax.

"Miss Nona, I recognize the name Geraldine Anne Carter. We have a little section here in the library named after her. She was the first Black librarian in Williams County, and she set up a special display of memorabilia from her family."

The hairs stood up on the back of Nona's neck.

"Could you send me some pictures of the display?"

"My pleasure."

Nona hesitated. This favor could lead her to information Pastor Grant might not want to know, but she had to determine if Sylvester Dillard's murder was why Pastor Grant was in danger.

Did she dare have Chloe dig even deeper into the past? She said a brief prayer and plunged ahead.

"Chloe, how hard would it be to research something in the *Burnt Water Herald* from 1946?"

"Not too hard. You'd have to wait a few days for the storage service to retrieve them from the archives."

Nona did a quick calculation. "With once-a-week publication, it shouldn't be too much. Are you willing to pull all the *Burnt Water Herald* papers from April 1946 to April 1947?"

"Sure thing. I'll call you when they come in."

Excitement and trepidation warred for supremacy inside of Nona. It was unclear which emotion accurately reflected how she should feel.

Chapter 22

TABLET IN HAND, electricity zinged through Nona's insides as she examined the photographs Chloe had sent her. Chloe's text named the exhibit "The Geraldine Carter Archives and Special Collection. Burnt Water, Alabama, from 1869 to 1968." The first picture showed a glass display case, about six feet tall by four feet wide. Nona zoomed in on a stubby ceramic item, which might be a stemless pipe, that rested on a stand. Displayed on a headless mannequin torso was a tattered and stained shirt made from rough cloth. She pinched and spread her fingers on the tablet screen to get a clearer view of a document inside an eight-by-ten frame. She couldn't read the wisp-thin cursive letters on the yellowed paper. A small placard identified the document as a sharecropper agreement between Mr. Walter Williams and Bankston Williams, freedman. June 6, 1869.

The last photo from Chloe showed both a doll with a description plate dated circa 1930s and a report card from Calhoun Colored School in Lowndes County, Alabama, for Florence Hall. Beside the report card was a Bible with a black cover. A brass plate affixed to the display case read:

THIS DISPLAY IS A LOVING TRIBUTE TO
SARA HALL, MILDRED HALL CARTER &
FLORENCE HALL GRANT
DONATED BY GERALDINE CARTER, HEAD
LIBRARIAN, WILLIAMS COUNTY LIBRARY

Goose bumps rose on Nona's arms. The fire in Pastor Grant's church destroyed key parts of Florence's Bible. She didn't know if Mildred had a copy of the family Bible when she died. But there, behind glass, was another Bible that might contain a family tree.

Nona checked her watch. After six o'clock in Burnt Water. Library closed an hour ago. She debated texting Chloe after hours but fired off a text anyway.

> Hi, Chloe. Thanks again for the pictures. There is a Bible in one of them. I'm hoping to ask you a few questions about it the next time you're on duty.

> Sure thing. The copies of the Herald should be in Thursday, and I'm working that day.

> Thanks. Talk to you then.

Nona should call Pastor Grant. Her fingers danced around the screen, not doing what she had commanded them to do. They dialed DeMarcus instead of the pastor. She hovered her finger over the red hang-up button to disconnect, but before she could hit it, his voice boomed through the line.

"Sassy."

Grrrrrr. Her courage had failed, but DeMarcus had been too fast on the draw. "Johnson."

"Wow. Is that what we're doing? Calling me and dismissing me at the same time? I thought we were friends. First-name basis."

"Whatever, Johnson." She laughed. "I had a development in Pastor Grant's case."

"I'm all ears."

She launched into describing the Burnt Water library and Mildred's obituary.

DeMarcus let out a groan. "You're killing me."

"Are you even paying attention to me?" She heard the distinctive horn signaling the halftime of a basketball game.

"Sorry, the 76ers are down by fourteen at the half."

"76ers. I figured you for a Wizards fan."

"Girl, please. I watch basketball games, not tiddlywinks."

Everything DeMarcus said made her laugh. "There you go, using those long words again."

"You are correct. And let the record reflect, I'm always paying attention to you." He cleared his throat. "By the way, Mitch called me from his trial up in San Jose. Says he needs to meet with us both for dinner tomorrow to talk. I was going to put him off. Don't feel like meeting with him on that low-profile personal case right now. Need to ramp up my billable hours. But are you free for dinner tomorrow?"

Her cheeks heated and happiness for him suffused her. The partnership announcement. A smile forced its way onto her face without her permission. *Ugh.* No being happy for Johnson. "Sure. What time?"

"I'll get back to you on that."

DeMarcus started humming along with the jingle of a fast-food commercial playing in the background.

"So anyway, Johnson, if I can get the last piece of information I need this week, I plan to fly to Alabama as soon as possible. Is everything all set with the attorney in Birmingham?"

"We've been trading voicemails, but I'm on top of it."

A calm silence settled between them.

Lady poked her nose on Nona's thigh, asking for a pat.

"Did I mention my grandma's coming to see me?" His words buzzed with nervous energy.

"Really?"

"She wants to meet you."

"Why would she want to do that?"

"I told her about you."

Why in the world would DeMarcus talk to his grandmother about Nona? They were working some cases together, no big deal. Their conversations did not need grandma-level security clearance.

"I told her we met at church and that you can't stand me."

"You told her I can't stand you. Does she want to meet me so she can tell me how horrible I am for not liking her grandson?"

"Oh, she loves the fact that you knock me down a peg or two every chance you get."

Exactly how many times had he and his grandmother talked about her?

"You told her we're working a case together, right? She knows there's nothing going on between us?

"She knows we're working on a case. I didn't tell her about our engagement, though."

"We're not engaged."

"Mitch and Sylvia think we're engaged."

"You know what I mean."

"Dog park dude thinks we're engaged."

He'd actually helped her out there by telling Eric they were engaged. "He and I aren't even friends."

"Do you have a boyfriend, Nona?" Suddenly, jocular DeMarcus disappeared. In his place was a man asking a serious question in a low, intense voice. The question hung in the air like smoke needing to clear.

"A boy . . . a boyfriend?" He'd reduced her to stammering. "Why are you asking?"

"You know why I'm asking, Sassy."

His skill as an attorney became crystal clear. Flirt, charm, laugh, then go in for the kill.

"Is Lemar your boyfriend?"

"Lemar?"

"When a witness repeats a question, it means they're stalling for time. Time's up, Nona."

She squeezed her eyes shut and opened them. She'd tried in vain not to like DeMarcus Johnson, but now she saw he'd had her checkmated ten moves earlier, and she'd never seen it coming.

"I can't."

"Because of Lemar?"

Why did he keep bringing up Lemar? "Lemar's not an issue."

"He comes and goes as he pleases. He has a key."

Realization hit. "Is that what you think of me?"

"I'm asking a straightforward question so that I understand."

"I'm insulted."

"You're not insulted. You're scared. If you're not seeing Lemar, just say so. Roommate? Old friend?"

She didn't like his persistence and how he was penetrating her force field.

In quiet moments, when she was honest with herself, she'd always known their fake engagement had the potential to become something more. But her battered heart wasn't ready.

"There are things about me you don't know. Things I'm not ready to share."

"You're right. But I was there beside you at church. I know it's serious and painful." He gave a sigh. "I need to talk to you about something as well. Things at work I've been going through. But even with what's going on at work, I don't recognize myself anymore. I've changed. I'm not the guy you met on New Year's Eve. God did that. He wiped away some old stuff that I was hanging on to and is turning me into a better man. If he did it for me, he can do it for you."

She wanted to make a smart retort and shift the conversation back to their usual banter. She wanted to push back the desire to tell him everything and have him comfort her. Tyson's face rose like a specter in her mind. She'd lowered her defenses with a man once before, and her life had spiraled down the drain. Could she risk it again?

"Well, Johnson. If your grandmother ends up hating me, I'm toast anyway." She shifted back to their usual banter. It was safer that way. Easier.

"We'll table this conversation for now, but we'll come back to it." He hesitated for a beat. "I've been talking to God about you, Sassy."

Her mouth hung open. It was the most intimate thing any man had ever said to her, and it terrified her. The thought of fidgety, confident DeMarcus reaching out to God on her behalf moved her with the force of an earthquake. She needed to retrench immediately. "Don't throw your back out or anything doing that, Johnson."

"I'll talk to you tomorrow, Nona." His voice, sure and determined, reached her ears.

"Okay." She ended the call, panic and elation warring in her heart.

Chapter 23

Nona sat at Pastor Grant's dining room table with her laptop open and the video chat feature displayed on the screen, ready for a teleconference with Chloe. Nona slid her tablet from her knapsack and opened up the snapshots from the library display. Dressed for a full day of ministry—slacks, a crisp shirt, and a bow tie—Pastor Grant shuffled from the kitchen on feet still encased in house shoes, balancing a cup of coffee and a plate with the Sara Lee cheese Danish he'd promised her. She placed the paper plate to the side of all her gear, plucked up the Danish, and savored a lemony bite. The gooey filling reminded her of the snack her mother used to give her and Nikki after school, and a wave of nostalgia washed over her.

The afternoon before, Chloe had given her a summary of what she'd found, but Nona had stopped her midsentence when she had realized what the documents in the display case revealed. She wanted to share the information with Pastor Grant in real time.

She turned to him. "Are you ready?"

"As ready as I'll ever be." His eyes sparkled with hope and anticipation as he sat beside her.

Her heart thudded in her chest, surprising her with the intensity of how badly she wanted this estate case to turn out in Pastor Grant's favor. She pushed Start Chat on her laptop, and a series of warbling rings pulsed out.

"Hi, Nona." Chloe's face filled the screen of the computer, and the girl's chipper voice made Nona smile.

"Hi, Chloe. I have Pastor Grant here with me. Can you see him?"

"Sure can. Hi, Pastor Grant. Nice to meet you." Chloe waved.

He gave a broad smile and waved back. "Nice to meet you too, Chloe."

"I'm so glad to do this, Pastor Grant, but I need to warn you, I'm in a rush. Calculus test tomorrow."

At the word *calculus*, Nona gave a mock shiver.

Chloe laughed.

"That's fine, Chloe," Pastor Grant said. "You've already helped us so much."

Chloe wore gloves, and on the table in front of her was a black, leather-bound book, which Nona presumed was the Bible from the display case. "My aunt gave me permission to remove the Book from the case. We don't have a rare books librarian, and we don't have the funds to keep the display temperature controlled and all that stuff, like they do at university libraries, but I figured, at least I could wear some gloves. Picked 'em up at the bridal shop."

Chloe slowly opened the front cover. "My aunt inspected it first and said it's in worn but good condition for a ninety-year-old book. It opens all the way easily, without stiffness. Like someone opened to this page many times before."

"I received your snapshots of the interior covers, but the text is hard to read with the shadowing."

"Yeah, sorry about that. I don't have the equipment to take great photos on my phone."

"We'll work with what we've got." Nona positioned the tablet so it sat side by side with the laptop screen. "We'll look at the photo as you read to us what you see on your end."

"Absolutely. The inside of the front cover has white paper glued to it, and I see the handwriting of two different people. At the top, it says, 'This Bible belongs to Sara Hall and is one of three family Bibles given to commemorate the baptisms of Florence, age twelve, and Mildred, age nine, this Easter Sunday, 1930.'"

"Amazing." Pastor Grant's eyes widened. "My mother told me about her baptism on Resurrection Sunday when she was twelve years old."

"That handwriting differs from the writing that follows. Under what I just read to you, it says, 'This is my remembrance of my family, starting with Pappy Bankston, born a slave on the plantation of Mr. Walter Williams, and my mammy, Polly, born there about 1847.'"

Pastor Grant swiped under his eyes.

"Under that, it says, 'Mammy and Pappy sharecropped on the Williams land, 1869. Buys some of they own land with they Sunday moneys.'"

Nona made a note to google the term *Sunday moneys*. "Go on."

Chloe squinted and drew the Bible closer to herself. "After that, it says 'Me, Sara, marries Jacob, June 22, 1884. Jacob helps with the sharecropping. Pappy buys more land with moneys he and Mammy gets from selling eggs, milk, doing washing.'"

"This is amazing, Chloe." The words Chloe had spoken transported Nona to the 1800s as if by a time machine.

"I agree. We didn't study stuff like this in my history class. This information is going somewhere into my project. Okay, after that, it says, 'March 25, 1918, Florence Hall born,' then 'Mildred Elizabeth Hall, born October 29, 1921.'"

Nona held her tablet closer to Pastor Grant. He adjusted his reading glasses and peered at the glowing screen, and his Adam's apple bobbed up and down. "I can make that out in the picture. Florence was my mother. And Mildred, the auntie I heard about but never knew."

"Yes. It was Mildred's obituary I showed you the other day," Nona reminded Pastor Grant. "Since her children both died before Mildred did, under the law, you inherit Mildred's estate as the child of her sister."

Pastor Grant shook his head. "I never met any relatives. It pains me."

Nona patted his hand and then clasped his icy fingers. She had a painful history. Pastor had a complicated family background. Both had suffered loss from the absence of family. The letters plus the newspaper article about the murder in Burnt Water had to be the reason Pastor Grant never met his relatives. Tension wound tightly inside of her, and her heart gave a squeeze. If a murder had driven Pastor's mother to California, would it be better not to dig under that rock from the past lest something horrible slither out?

Chloe continued. "Next, it says, 'Bankston Williams, 1845 to January 13, 1905.' Written beside that entry are the initials 'S.H.'"

"My guess is that Sara made that entry." Nona turned toward Pastor Grant.

He nodded in agreement. "Seems reasonable to me."

Chloe smiled, then looked back down to the Bible. "Under that, if you can read it, is, 'November 14, 1908, Mammy Polly dies.' Again, there are the initials 'S.H.'"

"Okay, I think I can read the next entry." Pastor Grant held the tablet gently, as if the digital screen contained something precious. "It says, 'April 20, 1930, Florence and Millie baptized Easter morning,' followed by the initials 'S.H.' again." A satisfied smile lifted Pastor's lips.

Nona inched the tablet closer to herself and examined the photo on the screen. She pinched her fingers and expanded them to zoom in on various sections. "Since the Bible itself says the girls received them on their baptismal day, I assume the entries dated before April 1930 were transcriptions of someone else's memories combined with info collected from obituaries."

Chloe nodded. "That's what I think too. I think it was Sara who wrote the history in the Bible."

"The next entry is, 'Millie marries Edward Carter, March 5, 1938.' Am I seeing that clearly?" Nona asked.

"Yes. I need to go soon, so let's skip some stuff for now," Chloe interjected. "It gets better. If you look down, you can see your own birth, Pastor. It says, 'Roscoe Hosea Grant, born December 18, 1946.'"

"All this time, I thought my parents wanted nothing to do with their family back home. But now I see my family back in Burnt Water knew about me. A telegram? A letter? Something went back to them to let them know I'd been born." He slapped his knee. "Well, I'll be."

Nona scoured her mind to retrieve what she'd read in the *Burnt Water Herald* about Sylvester Dillard's murder. It had been April 1946. Pastor was born just shy of eight months later.

"Did your mother ever tell you that your birth was premature?"

A smile made his face crinkle all over. "Just the opposite. She told me she thought I'd never get here. Called it the longest nine months of her life."

Given this information, Pastor Grant's birth did not appear directly related to the murder, but intuition told her the timing of his parents' departure from Burnt Water wasn't a coincidence.

"And after my birth, there are no more entries in the Bible that I can see in the photo." Tears slid down Pastor Grant's face, and he didn't hide them. "Miss Chloe, thank you so much." He sniffled a few times. "I can't wait to meet you and take you out for an ice cream cone as soon as we get to Alabama."

Chloe nodded and laughed. "Deal. I can't wait. Bye, Nona. Bye, Pastor Grant." She waved. "I'm excited to meet you both soon."

"Chloe," Nona spoke up quickly to catch her before she signed off. "Let's keep this information between us until we can take the Bible to the courthouse."

"Sure thing. I won't tell anyone."

The video chat screen went blank.

Pastor Grant sat silently, shaking his head, disbelief on his face. He wiped his eyes with his hands.

Nona hoped the girl would keep her promise. Burnt Water was a small town, and no doubt, news traveled fast. When Nona and Pastor Grant arrived, the first thing she'd do would be to secure the Bible, then she'd go through the back issues of the *Burnt Water Herald* for more information about the murder.

She turned to Pastor Grant. "I have the tickets. We're headed that way in about a week. Are you ready?"

"Health wise, I feel almost back to my old self. A few twinges here and there. Nothing I can't handle. I will say, all this information has been overwhelming. But yes, I'm ready. Do we know what the inheritance is?"

"We've figured out who the decedent is. Date of birth, date of death. Now I can run her name through some databases. I probably won't find out any bank account information, but real property and property tax records are publicly available."

"Nona, I don't know how to thank you for everything you've done for me." The look Pastor Grant gave her was full of love and, more than that, acceptance. His care for her was a balm to her battered heart. She *was* lovable. *Not* damaged beyond repair. He didn't need to thank her. She should be thanking *him*.

"Well, we need to see this through. There are no guarantees, but I'm hopeful there is something substantial for you at the end.

"Lord willing."

Amen to that.

* * *

The next morning Nona stood in her entryway shuffling through some bills in the mail basket and running the plans for her Alabama trip through her mind.

Lemar exited the guest room, sidled up to her, and placed his arm on her shoulder. "Need to leave for my audition in about fifteen minutes, but brief me again on the timetable? I'm watching the dogs for how long?"

"Pastor Grant and I will be in Alabama for four days. We're going to file papers with the court, and we're going to do some investigation—contacting relatives, trying to find out more family history, to piece together his past."

"Got it."

"I need you to drop us at LAX for the outbound flight and pick us up when we get back."

"Check. Later, sis." Lemar sauntered away, and Lady entered.

"Hey, girl, how are you this morning?" A scratch under Lady's chin was rewarded with an appreciative snort. She walked to her office and sank into the couch. She picked up her laptop and tried to start it. The video chat had drained the battery, so she booted up the tablet instead. Then she found the Williams County tax commissioner's office and clicked the property and vehicles tab. That gave her the choice to search by parcel ID, account number, or street address. She didn't have any of that information.

She backtracked, opened PeopleFinderUSA.com, and entered "Mildred Hall Carter." Her birth date, phone number, and street address popped up—542 Mill Rd, Burnt Water, Alabama. Nona shook her head. Easy to find someone once you knew where they'd been hiding.

Back at the tax page, she entered the address. The parcel ID was hyperlinked, and she clicked. Her pulse quickened. She'd located Mildred's residence. A quick scan of the tax history showed the current fair market value at $42,000. She needed to see the house. She popped the address into the Map app and hoped the company had sent their crazy car with all the cameras as far away as Burnt Water. Nope. A satellite view from the top, with the house obscured by trees.

She typed the street address into a general search engine. Results for random real estate sites popped up with autofilled information taken from publicly accessible sources. She flipped through. Five pages into her search, a link for minutes to a Burnt Water City Council meeting appeared. She hit Ctrl+F and entered 542 Mill Rd. The screen autoscrolled up.

> With Councilwoman Wilma Davis abstaining, the Burnt Water City Council approves the sale of those parcels of land to Burnt Water via eminent domain.

She skimmed down.

> . . . to Leisure Zone Holdings, a California Corporation ALSO EXCEPTING THEREFROM the *Parcel of land* described in the Deed from Sara Hall to Mildred Hall Carter, dated November 30, 1946, recorded January 15, 1947, in Book 1696 of Williams County Official Records at Page 211, Instrument No. 14344.

She stood, paced to the door and back to her computer. Bruiser trotted in, curled up in a corner, and watched her. She strode back to her desk and collapsed into the chair. Upon opening the drawer, she removed the documents she'd found in Pastor Grant's Bible and laid them out in chronological order.

According to the *Burnt Water Herald*, someone murdered Sylvester Dillard on April 20, 1946. In December 1946, Dearest Love sent My Heart the "Do not look back. Never return" letter. Connecting Florence to the murder somehow, as the assailant or witness, made sense, because Pastor Grant was born about eight months after his parents left Burnt Water, never to return. Was there also a connection between Sylvester Dillard's murder and Leisure Zone Holdings? Didn't seem likely. Yet someone had torched Pastor Grant's church.

Nona worked her way through two plausible scenarios. First, Leisure Zone Holdings hired the arsonist for financial gain, using the fire to shove Pastor Grant out of the way to snatch up Mildred Hall's property. She shook her head. Seemed far-fetched. More likely, burning the church was personal—either a witness to Sylvester Dillard's murder, someone seeking revenge for the murder, or the murderer himself. Regardless of the exact reason, given what she'd seen, she was confident she'd find the answer to who set fire to Mount Zion in Burnt Water. Hopefully, before anyone else was hurt.

Chapter 24

DeMarcus maneuvered his car into a parallel parking spot in front of Nona's townhome. He felt jittery, keyed up. With the official partnership decision still hanging out there unannounced and Mitch's having been out of pocket in trial for the last two weeks, DeMarcus had been in suspended animation. But today came his big letdown. He appreciated Mitch's doing it privately, outside the office. Glad Nona was going to be there too. She knew how hard he'd worked on Mitch's case. Didn't know why, but DeMarcus knew she'd support and encourage him, albeit in her own sarcastic way. She'd even agreed to let him drive her like a proper date. He didn't want to go, but he'd need a good recommendation from Mitch as he searched for a new job. He'd just suck it up. All he wanted tonight was to get through the dinner without having to shovel his pride off the floor.

He plucked up the bag holding the peanut-butter-and-yogurt dog munchies he'd purchased for Bruiser and Lady. He fiddled with the three hydrangea blooms he'd tucked in a separate bag, which were surrounded by that flimsy paper girls liked to have sticking out.

At his knock, Bruiser started up with a racket from behind the door. DeMarcus's heart thudded heavily, and he squirmed in his suit, which now felt electrically heated. The door opened. Lady and Bruiser, wagging their traitorous tails, stood beside Lemar. Disappointment, raw and grating, sloughed away all DeMarcus's nervous anticipation.

"Hey, man. DeMarcus, right?" Lemar gave his head an upward jerk in greeting. "Nona will be down in a second."

DeMarcus swallowed his pride and stuck out his free hand. "Good to see you again, Lemar."

"Come in." Lemar stood aside and let DeMarcus enter the foyer.

He heard a noise and looked up. Nona stood at the top of the stairs. The light shining from behind her in the stairwell made her honey-gold curls glow like they were lit from within. Her dress was the color of a tangerine and had a V-neck, ruffled sleeves, and other flouncy stuff around the bottom.

She descended the stairs in a fluid motion, the small slit in the dress making way for her long legs and high, wedge-shaped shoes as she came down.

"Wow, sis. You look fantastic."

DeMarcus's head swiveled with a snap toward Lemar, who stood there with brotherly love shining in his eyes. DeMarcus turned to face Nona, and a shy smile with a little snark hiding behind it played across her lips.

At the landing, she sailed past him and gave Lemar a hug. "Thanks, bro."

"I gotta work on my lines. Good to see you again, DeMarcus." Lemar disappeared into a doorway down the hall.

Nona approached DeMarcus.

"Lemar's your"—sudden dryness in his throat held back the word for a moment—"brother?" His nervousness returned. He'd been hoping to shoot his shot for so long with Nona, now that he had the ball and the lane was open, he didn't want to choke.

She regarded him squarely. "Yes."

Her expression baffled him. It appeared both bashful and defiant at the same time.

Her glance fell to the bag in his hand.

"Some snacks for the dogs. I picked the flowers because of the colors. Light blue and gold for UC Irvine." He lifted and dropped his shoulder. "You could have told me Lemar was your brother."

She reached out to take the bag from him, and her fingers brushed his. "So now you know."

"That is correct."

Her face continued to send him mixed signals. She was interested but wary. He reached out and encircled her wrist, stopping her movement away from him. His attention dropped to her hand. She had his ring on her thumb. Everything was crystal clear now. Nona liked him. Was she afraid? Yes. But behind the fear, she cared for him. The knot of tension in his chest loosened a millimeter.

He moved his gaze and stared boldly into her eyes. "I won't hurt you, Nona."

Rose tinted her cheeks, and she broke the connection between them. "Let me put these flowers in some water." She turned and walked down the hall, her dogs faithfully following behind.

When she returned, she waltzed past him, picked up a small handbag, and reached for the door handle. "Well, don't keep standing there, Johnson. We have a dinner to attend."

◆ ◆ ◆

In the car, he selected an urban oldies station on his streaming service. The smooth crooning of Luther Vandross filled the interior, and he maneuvered into traffic.

"What's the latest on Pastor Grant's case?"

As her light floral scent wafted from her side of the car over to him, his attention drifted from the words she was saying, and he lost himself in the moment of being with her. Navigating through traffic, he realized he had a gap in his understanding of what she'd been telling him. "Wait. When are you going to Alabama?"

"We're leaving Monday, first thing."

The partnership memo Maxine had found had distracted him. He was also grappling with G'Mama's imminent arrival. And he hadn't yet nailed down the details on getting local counsel in Birmingham to assist Nona. He was juggling all the plates at once, and something was bound to come crashing down.

"You were telling me about the Bible you found?"

"Yes. There's a standing display with some family memorabilia dating to the Reconstruction era. Pastor Grant's grandmother had a Bible. The family genealogy was recorded inside the front cover and starts with the generation that was enslaved at the time of the Emancipation Proclamation."

"Nona, that's amazing." He flicked on his blinker and entered the parking deck for his office.

"Where is dinner tonight?"

"A little spot tucked beside the Museum of Contemporary Art." He parked the car, killed the ignition, and turned to her. "The spite fence case is all but done. A few loose ends on the paperwork are all that's left. I wanted to thank you for everything. All the hard work on the case against the Yacoubians. Letting me string out the engagement so I could try to secure the partnership bid. And for busting my chops every chance you could." He chuckled. "I've never met anyone like you before, and I wanted to get that out before the dinner."

There was so much more he wanted to say. Words that spoke of a life together—forever. But this wasn't the time. There might never be a time. When Mitch brought an end to DeMarcus's run-up to partnership, his entire future as a lawyer would be up in the air. Firms did not want an associate passed over for partnership, and he didn't have a plan B.

Her eyes held compassion and care. He wanted to splay his fingers in that riot of curls, wrap her up close to his heart, and kiss her for an hour straight. But he was going down in flames tonight with Mitch, and she didn't know. He didn't want to start something now that she wouldn't want to finish later. Maybe if God answered his prayers, if he landed on his feet, perhaps in the future she might consider him as a prospect for real. For tonight, it would be one last evening of pretending the woman he wanted was already his.

He exited the car and scooted around to help her out. Her willowy frame rose until she stood beside him. He interlaced their fingers, and he strode with her to the elevator. The innocent gesture felt profound and intimate. At the entrance to the restaurant, he swung open the door, and the succulent smell of seafood drenched in garlic butter caused his stomach to growl.

"You need to eat three squares a day, Johnson. Keep the hunger beast at bay."

"Duly noted." He gave her hand a squeeze, and he spied Mitch and Sylvia seated at a table across the room. Mitch waved him over. Gratitude that DeMarcus had Nona on his arm on the night his career was going down in total defeat steadied his nerves.

Mitch stood at their approach.

With reluctance, DeMarcus withdrew his hand from Nona's and reached out to shake with Mitch.

Mitch reeled him in for a couple of backslaps.

Sylvia patted the chair next to herself. "Sit, Nona. Sit." Her face was beaming with happiness, and the festive mood jarred him. He wished Mitch had simply called him into the office, said, "Close the door behind you," and told him straight-out that he hadn't made it. Mitch was drawing the blade out at a slow, agonizing pace.

They sat, ordered, and made small talk. The wine steward appeared, held out a corked bottle, and presented it to Mitch. "The champagne you ordered, sir."

Champagne. DeMarcus wanted Mitch to rip off the Band-Aid and stop torturing him. The food hadn't even arrived. If it weren't for Nona's presence beside him, he might bolt.

"Fill all the glasses," Mitch told the sommelier.

The scene unfolding before DeMarcus felt like a bizarre horror movie in which the plot twist revealed at the end was that he himself was the entrée they'd be eating for dinner.

He coughed. He'd been a star player, Professor Clutch. Time to take control of his own future. "What are we celebrating, Mitch?"

"Yes, right, right." Mitch lifted his glass. "A threefold toast. First, to my dear Sylvia. I promised you I'd slow down, and we'd do some traveling. Well, thanks to DeMarcus and Nona, our house is on the market, and there is a small bidding war. I'm going into semiretirement after I wind down some things at the firm."

"Oh, Mitch." Sylvia gave a watery smile.

"Second, to DeMarcus and Nona, on your engagement. You two make a wonderful couple, and Syl and I are expecting front-row invitations to your wedding." DeMarcus shot a surreptitious glance at Nona. She had the fakest smile on her face. He reached out and squeezed her hand, transmitting his thanks to her. She'd been a trouper throughout this whole thing.

"And finally, to DeMarcus, the man of the hour and one of the newest partners at Livingston, Meyer & Kendrick. The firm is elevating an outstanding lawyer into ownership."

Nona, Mitch, and Sylvia lifted their glasses toward the center of the table and clinked them together, and everyone except DeMarcus tipped their flute. He sat glued to his seat, flabbergasted.

"Mitch, I don't know what to say." He didn't. Not a single coherent sentence would form in his mind.

"I know how you feel, DeMarcus. I felt the same way when the firm announced my partnership." Mitch beamed at Nona. "You did a great job keeping my secret."

DeMarcus cut a glance at Nona, who gave him a timid smile.

Their food arrived, and he ate dinner via muscle memory. The conversation drifted around him, but he absorbed next to nothing. Nona chatted on, filling in Sylvia on every detail of the investigation and the methods she'd used to track down the evidence Mitch had needed. By the time dessert arrived, DeMarcus had wrestled himself into composure.

He watched Mitch fork a piece of cherry cheesecake into his mouth, and DeMarcus worked up the courage to ask about the partnership decision. "Mitch, I'm at a loss for words."

"Oh, I know we still need to go into the weeds on the partnership agreement. Our obligations, your obligations. Don't worry. We'll hash it all out in the next few weeks."

"When did you have the final vote?"

"Funny you should ask that. They conducted a straw vote while I was gearing up for that San Jose trial, but things skidded off the rails during my trial prep. Somebody forgot to reach out to me for my thoughts on the candidates. We had to have an emergency partnership meeting over the phone to get everything back on track. They tallied the final votes while I was in trial."

Mitch had DeMarcus's back all along. Guilt over the deception he and Nona continued to perpetuate struck him. "Mitch—"

Nona grabbed his hand under the table midsentence and gave it a squeeze. "DeMarcus and I need to discuss some things, Mitch. But I want you to know, as an investigator, it's been fantastic working with him."

"Your work's been top-notch, Nona, and we won't forget it. Anything we can do to help you professionally." Mitch nodded. "I mean it."

◆ ◆ ◆

A band tucked in a corner of the restaurant struck up a number. DeMarcus stood. "May I have this dance?"

Nona shot a glance at Mitch and Sylvia, who were already making their way to the small parquet floor near the band. She recognized the song as "(Everything I Do) I Do It for You" when the gravelly male vocalist crooned out the lyrics.

DeMarcus's signature—and now understated—Drakkar Noir mesmerized her. He held her so near she could feel his heart thudding against her.

She twisted herself into a knot, trying to put together a sentence. "What do you think you'll do with the bonus Mitch mentioned?"

He gave her an enigmatic smile but said nothing.

Her hand in his felt secure, and his face lost the guarded and anxious appearance he'd had when he picked her up. He locked his gaze on hers. As the song progressed, she saw his self-assurance return. Gentleness also filled his perusal. Realization dawned. He hadn't been certain he had a lock on the partnership. She could not stop staring at him. She wanted his eyes to take her in like this forever. His unflinching affection pierced her, and cold apprehension crept back in. Would she ever be free of her fear that men would hurt her? Resignation deflated her mood.

"DeMarcus, after we close Pastor Grant's case, we need to break the engagement publicly." She felt so vulnerable, certain her face betrayed every emotion she was feeling.

His brow creased. "We can talk about that later. Let's try to enjoy tonight."

"Our business will be done. No more cases or need to see each other again." Anxiety set off her mouth at a mile-a-minute pace.

"We make a great team, Nona." He drew her closer. "Let's table this for another day. After we've taken care of Pastor Grant."

The singer's raspy voice whispered to her that she should try for love. Fight for it. But could she? Did she have anything worthwhile to give? She leveraged some space between DeMarcus and herself. Physically. Emotionally. "No, I don't want to draw it out." She feared her battle-scarred heart would never recover if DeMarcus wasn't the man she thought he was.

"Nona. Look at me." He gently tipped up her chin.

She didn't want to. If she did, she'd never want him to leave her.

"I'm the man you've been waiting for." His voice held conviction. He bent down and moved in slowly.

She had every chance to back away, but she didn't.

Then he pressed a gentle kiss to her lips as the song faded, and every defense she'd ever erected shattered into a million pieces. She kissed him back with all the love that was in her heart. It would be their first and last kiss, because she knew that tonight was the end.

Chapter 25

FINALLY. BURNT WATER, Alabama. Nona rubbed her eyes and choked back a yawn. After a forty-five-minute go-around with TSA and the gate agent about checking her firearm, the cross-country flight from LAX to Birmingham, then the three-plus-hour drive from Birmingham to Burnt Water, exhaustion dogged Nona's every step. Neither Nona nor Pastor Grant had the funds for a protracted stay, and with the clock ticking on Pastor Grant's heirship claim, Nona needed this one trip to cover everything.

Now in the lobby of the motel, they munched on snacks from the vending machine to tide them over until dinner, and she coached Pastor Grant—again—about her objectives. Top of the list, assemble all the paperwork to file the probate claim. Only then, and if there was any time remaining, she'd help him find and meet distant relatives. He'd literally vibrated with anticipation as he gulped down his coffee and oatmeal, and she couldn't blame him. A lot was riding on the next few days. Pastor Grant would either inherit or not. Worse, she'd leave Burnt Water as a failure if she didn't file. She wasn't sure she could face him if their mission went down in defeat.

She'd parked her rental car in a spot on the main drag. In a town as small as Burnt Water, an educated guess told Nona to stop by the beauty salon to find someone who knew Mildred Hall. From what she'd seen when they drove into town, Dottie May's Beauty Parlor was their target. Nona and Pastor Grant entered the front door, and time careened backward sixty years. A bank of hooded dryers, occupied by senior citizens, lined the wall. The *click-clack* of stove-heated curling irons competed with the chatter of the patrons. Posters of famous Black singers from the 1960s and '70s hung on the wall.

Nona stood in the center of the room, straightened her back, and launched in. "Hi, everyone. I'm Nona Taylor, and this is Pastor Hosea Grant. We're here trying to locate anyone who knew Mildred Hall Carter."

"Child, we know who you are." A jovial, brown-skinned beautician chuckled as she stood over the shampoo bowl and kneaded the scalp of a woman reclined on the seat.

"Don't get many visitors," someone piped up from the adjacent shampoo bowl.

"Excepting those slicksters who came out here sniffing about Mildred's property a few months back." The beautician shampooing at the bowl spoke up again.

"They weren't sniffing, Earlene. They was surveying around there." A woman at a manicurist station in the corner scoffed. "Didn't you see the orange vests they was wearing? If y'all attended a city council meeting every once in a while, you'd know what's going on round here."

"You think you know everything, Cela." The beautician turned from the shampoo bowl, her hands covered in suds.

"I do. I'm minding my business and yours too, Earlene."

The whole salon cracked up at the banter between the two ladies.

"Y'all should go over to the church." Earlene looked at her watch. "Millie's friends are always over there on Monday evenings for prayer. They should be wrapping it up any minute now."

A woman festooned with pink plastic rollers, held in place with metal clips, pointed to her right. "Go down the street, then turn right on Church Street. Can't miss it. White building, about the size of a house. There's a sign. Says 'Bethel' on it."

"Before you go, you single, Pastor?" A thin, hawkish woman, with skin the color of graham crackers and a fresh French roll hairstyle, stood paying at the reception desk.

"Yes, ma'am. I lost my sweet wife a while back."

"Well, my name is Alva, and I own the Burnt Water Café, back up the road a ways. You and Miss Taylor stop by this evening, and I'll feed you both chicken and dumplings so tasty, you'll never go back to where you came from." Alva gave a smile.

"We'll make sure we do that." Pastor Grant gave a little bow.

Nona exited the salon, and Pastor Grant followed on her heels. She felt her ears burning when they climbed inside the rental car. She and Pastor Grant would be the talk of the town for weeks to come.

Nona drove down the central drag of Burnt Water. Shops lined the street—an Ace Hardware, a drugstore, a dry cleaner, a bait and tackle shop.

"I bet there's some good fishing out here." Pastor Grant paid wistful attention to the fishing supply store. "One thing my daddy did talk about from the past was all the fishing he did as a boy. There're places to fish in LA. He always told me they weren't as good."

Five minutes down the road, she rolled into the gravel parking lot for Bethel. The woman at the salon had accurately described the building. It resembled a small house except for the steeple over the doorway. Grave markers and headstones dotted one side of the lawn. In the lot were a silver Ford LTD and a PT Cruiser.

Nona gave the door a gentle push, and she and Pastor Grant entered. Two columns of a dozen wooden pews flanked a center aisle. The red carpeting of the aisle drew her gaze to the front of the church, where three steps led to the chancel and a pulpit. Whispered prayers drew her attention. In the very first row, three women, heads bowed, sat close together.

Nona motioned for Pastor Grant to sit on the back pew, and she joined him.

A hearty chorus of amens echoed from the front of the church, and the ladies rose.

"Well, I'll be. Y'all come on down here." A woman with a slight build, gentle eyes, and wearing a tan beret gestured for them to step forward. "You must be the people here from Hollywood, come to ask about Millie."

Nona suppressed a smile. Like the kids' game of telephone, the details about their visit were morphing into urban legends.

"We're here trying to find information about Pastor Grant's family." She pointed to him. "He's Mildred Hall Carter's only remaining heir. There'll be some paperwork with the court, but he also wants to know more about his family history."

"I see it in you. In the nose and in the brow. You have those Hall eyes with the pretty lashes and the Carter forehead, all wide and smooth."

"Thank you." Pastor Grant ducked his head.

"Let me introduce us. I'm Edna. That there's Pearly."

Pearly wore a matching pants-and-top ensemble in sky blue.

"And that's Bernice."

"Nice to meet y'all." Bernice gave a toothy smile. Her brown skin had pink undertones and no wrinkles.

"We were about the closest thing Millie had to family. When she couldn't make it to prayer, we'd go to her. All her people died. Husband, daughter. Son died back in Vietnam, years ago."

"Tell you what." Pearly snapped her finger. "We always have a late supper at the Burnt Water Café after prayer. Why don't y'all join us, and we'll talk."

"Excellent," Pastor Grant said. "And dinner is my treat."

"Oh, we like you already." Edna emitted a cackling laugh.

◆　◆　◆

Nona swallowed down the last bite of what may have been the best meal of her life. Sweet corn bread slathered with butter; collard greens with pieces of pork and diced onions; and a juicy, fried pork chop. She'd ordered the same thing as Pastor Grant, who'd asked for another piece of corn bread, which he tucked into a napkin.

"For later," he said. "Mama used to cook like this." He gulped a generous amount of his sweet tea and dabbed his lips with his napkin.

Pearly pointed a finger at him. "Of course she did. That's 'cause your great-grandmammy Polly was the best cook hereabouts. Polly taught your grandmother Sara everything she knew, and Sara passed it on down to your mama and your auntie, Mildred."

"Uh-huh. Sara was born on old Mr. Williams's plantation right before slavery ended." Edna placed her knife and fork across her plate. "They named this county after his kinfolk."

Pearly nodded up and down. "Half the people in this town, Black and White, share the last name Williams."

"Millie had always been so proud of her family," Bernice said. "They'd been one of the few who was able to buy the land they'd sharecropped and some surrounding parcels as well."

Pastor Grant pushed the lever on the toothpick dispenser, took one, and chewed on it.

"You see that, Bernice?" Edna gestured toward Pastor Grant. "Same thing his cousin Ellis used to do when he was a boy."

"You right, Pearly. Spittin' image." Bernice cracked a wide smile.

"I heard about Ellis. Do you have more information?" Nona looked between the women.

"Saddest thing. Ellis was Millie's son. He went off to war in '65. Didn't make it more than a few months. He's buried over at the military cemetery in Mobile."

Nona didn't know what a busy day at the café looked like, but nearly every table had two or three people, and there were a couple of patrons at the counter as well. Senior citizens. Some construction workers. At one table in the opposite corner were men dressed in shirts and ties. Some had doffed their jackets.

She'd researched the crime stats. No murder in years. No robberies either. A low rate of assaults. Mostly property crimes. Thefts, drunk and disorderlies. Domestic abuse and child welfare cases. Drugs.

No one, present or in the history she'd learned, seemed out of place or a threat to Pastor Grant.

She turned her attention back to the conversation at her table, searched for her phone in her bag, then opened her Notes app. Pastor Grant sat enraptured by the family stories, and she intended to make the memories as permanent as she could, so he could have them for later.

Bernice sat back in her chair. "Lemme see, your daddy's people are still here. The Carters. Most of them are one county over, but I know them."

"Do you think we could visit them while we're here?" Pastor Grant looked around the table expectantly.

"'Course. I'd be happy to make the introduction."

"There's something else we want to know about." Lines creased Pastor Grant's brow. "Nona, show them the article."

Nona removed a folder from her purse and took out a photocopy of the article about Sylvester Dillard's murder and slid it across the table.

Bernice handed it to Pearly. Edna, Pearly, and Bernice exchanged looks.

Pearly stood and nodded at Edna. "This is something y'all best talk to

Bernice about." Pearly gave Pastor Grant a sad smile. She gave a brief wave as she and Edna left the café.

The crowd started to thin out. The businessmen and construction workers drifted away. Nona could now make out the strains of smooth jazz playing in the background.

Bernice motioned to the waitress to return to the table.

The young server approached. "Y'all want coffee?" She held a pot aloft. Nona nodded.

Bernice let out a sigh. "Mildred and me were best friends. Knowed each other for sixty years. I'll be seventy-five and a half next month."

"I'm only a little older than that myself." Pastor smiled at her.

"Round 'bout a month or so before Mildred died, me and her went down to Mobile for a ladies' conference. There was a wonderful speaker. Had the ladies crying and testifying."

The waitress poured them each a cup of coffee, then one by one, she removed three plates of apple pie à la mode from a tray and placed a dish in front of each of them.

"Where was I? Oh, right. On the drive home, I could tell Millie was fretting about something." Bernice grabbed two artificial sweetener packets, ripped them open simultaneously, and poured them in her coffee. She then stirred, clacking the spoon against the side.

Pastor Grant remained silent. Nona knew from experience what a good listener he was.

"She told me she'd been keeping a secret. Not about something she'd done, but a secret for somebody else." Bernice forked a piece of the pie, swirled the morsel around in the melting ice cream, and savored the bite.

Nona sipped her coffee and, even though her stomach might burst, tried some of the pie herself. Her eyes rolled backward at the flaky crust and tart filling.

Bernice leaned forward. "Mildred told me that her sister, Florence, killed a man who attacked her."

Clanging bells sounded in Nona's mind. Finally. The payoff for the weeks of research. She glanced at Pastor Grant. He sat rock-still.

"Your parents was out for a walk that evening and your daddy ran into the drugstore to buy some gum." Bernice stared off into the distance as she pulled the details about the conversation from her memory. "When he came out of the drugstore, Florence was gone. He heard a commotion in the alley right next to the store. He ran round the corner in time to pry off a man trying to violate Florence. The man and your daddy got to fighting, and your mama found something and hit the attacker over the head with it. A brick or rock, she wasn't sure. He was still alive when they left him, but they found out the next day he had died." Bernice swiped moisture from her eyes with a finger. Her shoulders relaxed as the burden of carrying the secret fell from her.

The gravity of Bernice's revelation momentarily stunned Nona. She forced herself to speak. "Did she say why she didn't go to the police and explain she was defending herself and her husband?"

Pastor Grant placed his hand on top of hers to stop her line of questioning. "He was a White man, wasn't he?"

"Yes, he was. A soldier, like Mildred's husband."

Weary lines creased Pastor Grant's face. He shook his head. "My daddy told me once that after he came back from France, some people treated him worse when he was in uniform than when he was out. I can only imagine how terrified my parents were, even if it was self-defense."

Bernice reached over and squeezed Pastor Grant's arm. "Over the years, Mildred had me mail letters for her when I went to visit my people in Mobile. Said she didn't want anybody from Burnt Water knowing her business, which I understand, 'cause we a town full of busybodies. I opened up a post office box in Mobile as well, to collect the letters Flo sent to Mildred. Millie said the letters were to a friend of hers from the teacher's school, who needed privacy."

Bernice pushed away the plate in front of her. "I took her word for it. Never met her sister, 'cause I'm so much younger than Millie. Never suspected anything illegal. Thought it was something personal, and I like to respect people's privacy."

"Nineteen forty-six Alabama." Pastor Grant pursed his lips and sighed. "I can see how this would have been a difficult situation. The article says the man received a Purple Heart. Florence and her husband probably feared she wouldn't get a fair trial."

"That's what Millie thought." Bernice gave a resolute nod. "Said they panicked and dragged him behind a trash can in the alley, thinking he'd shake it off and walk out of there under his own steam. After they heard he died, they lay low for a while and left town about a month later. We've kept it between ourselves all this time."

"Now things are starting to make sense. Daddy said even though some people stayed back home, he didn't want any child of his born under Jim Crow. Mama had to be pregnant with me when this all happened." Pastor Grant read the article again and counted on his fingers. "Maybe four, five weeks. Probably gave them another reason to run." He pushed back his chair and dropped his arms to his sides.

"They never told me. They carried that secret to their graves." A stricken expression overcame Pastor Grant's face. Sorrow deflated his whole countenance. "Even when I was an adult, they said nothing."

Nona mulled over the gravity of what Bernice had shared. "There's no statute of limitations on murder. Running from a crime is circumstantial evidence of a guilty conscience. And if they'd slipped even once, they might have revealed something. Makes sense that they never came back."

"Can anybody get in trouble now?" Bernice directed her question to Nona.

"I don't think so. I don't know the law here, but I think everyone the current prosecutor could charge with the crime or as an accessory is deceased." Nona would ask DeMarcus if there was any way Bernice could be charged as an accessory after the fact. She began typing a text message.

"That poor family." Sorrow filled Pastor Grant's voice.

She lifted her head in surprise. "Whose?"

"Sylvester Dillard's family. They have never known all these years what happened to their loved one. Here one day, gone the next."

"But—"

"No buts, Nona. I believe what Mildred told Bernice, but it still hurts to lose a loved one to violence. The man's kids. His widow. 'Red and yellow, black and white.' Jesus loves them all. I want to find Dillard's kin and talk to them."

Chapter 26

DeMarcus sat at his desk and stared at his blank computer screen. Mitch had briefed him on a new client the firm was taking on and had told De-Marcus that he was Mitch's first and only choice for point man. Scrambling and hustling his whole life to get to this place in his career, but all he could think about was his kiss with Nona. Nervous energy had his leg jiggling double time, and he stopped before he busted a spring on his chair. He'd kissed Nona. Not a long kiss, not super passionate, but enough to know that unless it was Nona, he never wanted to kiss another woman ever again.

He stood and prowled around his office. The morning sun glinted off the high-rise across from him, and he levered his blinds closed. He'd get to pack up soon and move to Partners' Row. He'd put in for Phil Kelly's office. With Phil's upcoming retirement, DeMarcus might snag the best view in the building, albeit with a smaller footprint than his current office. From his desk, he grabbed the electrolyte drink with added caffeine. His mind was drifting to Nona again, but he needed to focus right now. He held himself back from calling her and checked his watch. She and Pastor Grant were in Burnt Water. DeMarcus had looked up the motel where they planned to stay. It ranked one notch up from the Bates Motel in *Psycho*. He wanted her out of that town as soon as possible.

DeMarcus sat and flipped through the notes Mitch had given him. He willed his fingers to draft the rough outline of what he wanted in the complaint, so he could shoot it over to a junior associate, but his focus pinged all over the place. Kissing Nona had tripped a mental circuit breaker.

As soon as Nona returned to town, he was cementing their relationship in stone. No loopholes, no fake rings. To do that, he had to clear the decks this week, so he could take her out on a proper first date when she returned.

He put on his wireless headphones and turned on some background static to drown out the cacophony in his brain and drill down on his work. If he paced himself, he'd have the entire weekend to wine and dine Nona to convince her to give him a chance for real.

DeMarcus angled his head back and forth, stretching out the tight muscles in his neck and shoulders. He typed his last thoughts into a quick outline of the complaint and entered the email address for one of the junior associates. She was the lucky winner of a week's worth of drudge work, including drafting the full complaint and assembling the accompanying documentation. He clicked Send and swung his chair around from the side computer stand and over to his main desk. He went to click off Do Not Disturb on his desk phone and saw a blinking message light.

Maxine stood in his doorway, hands on her hips, her face stamped with irritation. And beside her stood G'Mama. The reality of G'Mama's presence jolted him like a shot from a stun gun. He blinked twice to recover.

"Why didn't you tell me G'Mama was coming, DeMarcus?" Maxine's furious scowl could strip the paint off a wall. "You made your own grandmother take a taxi from Union Station." She pointed at him and shook her finger.

"I—"

"It's all right, Maxine." G'Mama patted the irate secretary on the shoulder. "I didn't let him know when I'd get here. Wanted to surprise him."

Oh, she'd surprised him all right. She'd been sending his calls straight to voicemail on her grand tour of America via an Amtrak sleeper car. Jamaria had assured him she was fine and had been checking in. His gut wrenched. Was the news G'Mama wanted to share so bad that she had to travel across the entire country to tell him face-to-face?

He worked to regain his composure and appear professional in front of Maxine. "Thank you, Maxine. Would you mind bringing G'Mama a cup of tea and some peanut butter crackers from the break room?"

Maxine rolled her eyes so hard he could see the veins in the corners. She gave a slight wring of her neck and closed the door with a firm click behind her.

He felt like an idiot standing there. He rounded the desk and wrapped G'Mama up in a bear hug.

"DeMarcus, DeMarcus. It's so good to see you too, baby."

He held her close and inhaled the scent of the Jean Naté body splash she loved.

"Aw, baby. That's enough now. Gonna make me cry. It's been so long."

It had been too long. Work, distance, distractions.

He released her and ushered her to one of his guest chairs.

Maxine returned with a foam cup with a Lipton tea bag in it and a package of crackers.

"Thank you, Maxine." G'Mama gave Maxine the loving smile she gave almost everyone. "It's so good to meet you in person after talking to you on the phone so many times."

"I feel the same, G'Mama."

"And thanks for keeping an eye on my boy for me."

"Of course."

"You meet his Nona yet?"

Maxine gave him the stink eye. "I have. Only briefly. A"—she hesitated—"sweet young lady."

"Well, I can't wait to meet her."

Maxine excused herself, and DeMarcus sat behind his desk, soaking up G'Mama's presence. She wore standard-issue G'Mama attire: Her Sunday wig, which she liked, because it was almost like one that Patti LaBelle wore. A white-collared blue dress with flowers on it. Cinnamon-colored compression stockings supported her diabetic legs, while orthopedic sneakers with Velcro closures encased her feet. She was never more radiant.

First things first. "You're staying with me, right? You didn't make reservations at a hotel?"

"Nah, baby, I knew you'd put me up in style at your place."

He didn't know about *style*, but the monthly housekeeper had come to clean a few days ago, so it should be fine. "Of course, I will." He snatched up an ink pen and started absentmindedly clicking the retractable tip in and out. He didn't know how to get G'Mama to talk about her reason for traveling all the way to California. She'd get around to it, so he might as well sit back and let her tell him when she was ready. "You hungry?"

"I think I could eat. Why don't you take me someplace famous out here, like the Cheesecake Factory?" She sounded as excited as a teenager.

"G'Mama, they have those in Baltimore."

"True, but we might see someone famous out here."

"Cheesecake Factory it is." He knew better than to explain to G'Mama that no stars hung out at the Cheesecake Factory, but he'd take her to the one in Marina del Rey, and they could look out over the water while they ate and caught up. G'Mama rose, not as agile as she had been the last time he'd seen her but better than he'd hoped. He stood and ushered G'Mama out.

◆ ◆ ◆

"That lunch was de-li-cious." G'Mama sat back with a satisfied smile on her face. She and DeMarcus sat at a window facing the marina, with a piece of tiramisu cheesecake between them. He wasn't a coffee lover, but G'Mama had seen someone eating tiramisu on one of her TV shows and wanted to try it.

"Have another bite. I'm stuffed."

"Tell you what, let's box it up to go. I hate to do this, but I need to run back to the office, then I can take you to my house." He'd enjoyed getting caught up with G'Mama on all the lady deacons back home and even on the sad news about some of the guys he'd grown up with. But her inexplicable visit had distracted him. Like a dripping faucet, the thought that he was supposed to remember something important kept blinking in his brain. He couldn't pin it down. It danced out of reach every time he tried to recall it. He cycled through his thoughts. Was it someone he was supposed to call? Something he meant to look at? He waved it out of his brain. Maxine would help him figure it out.

He held G'Mama's elbow and steadied her as he lowered her into his car. "Do you want the top down?"

"Boy, you know my wig might fly off with all that wind. Best to leave it up."

No need to tell her convertibles didn't work that way. He dialed up the AC and started backing out of the parking lot. His phone rang, and he answered over Bluetooth while attempting to avoid hitting someone rollerblading down the street.

"This is DeMarcus Johnson."

"DeMarcus, can you hear me?"

"Sassy! So glad you—"

"There's no local counsel here in Alabama to help me. I called the name you gave me. She said she has a hearing today, and she hadn't heard back from you, so she assumed the whole thing was off. I don't know any attorneys in Alabama. I don't know what I need to do next, and we're leaving here the day after tomorrow."

He grimaced, swallowed hard, and rubbed the back of his neck. "Nona, I'm so sorry. I'm on my way back to my office now. Let me call you as soon as I get there, and I'll work something out."

"Okay, we'll wait to hear from you."

Nona didn't sound panicked, but he could hear the stress in her voice. He disconnected the call to concentrate on speeding and gunning it through yellow lights.

"Everything okay, baby?" G'Mama clutched her shoulder belt as the car bumped over a pothole.

"No, G'Mama. I messed up big-time."

"It'll be all right."

G'Mama had arranged for him to be tested, lined up a special tutor, even had him on medication for a while. He'd worked out systems to organize his mind and keep the things he needed sorted out, but when the plates he juggled came crashing down, feelings of incompetence racked him.

G'Mama patted his hand. "Your brain likes to fight you from time to time, but you always come out on top in the end."

Ninety percent of the time he beat his ADHD into submission, but when that 10 percent came around to bite him, it bit him in the hind parts so hard, he wanted to scream. The next yellow light turned red, so he stopped the car before the crosswalk.

He turned to G'Mama. "I need to go to Alabama for a day or two, and I want you to stay put in my apartment. I'll have Maxine plan a sightseeing trip for you, with a shuttle pickup and everything." The light changed to green, and he shot into the intersection.

"Nuh-uh." G'Mama shook her head vigorously, causing her earrings to jiggle around. "You goin', I'm goin'." She folded her arms across her bosom.

He suppressed a growl. "You know I love you." His skyrocketing stress was making his driving too aggressive. He eased his foot off the gas. "G'Mama, you rode a train out here because you don't fly. Plus, what am I going to do with you? I can't babysit."

"I can be your assistant. Watch you in court. Always wanted to see you making an argument in front of a judge."

"I can't have you underfoot, G'Mama. Don't know what I'm going to have to do while I'm there."

"Didn't you tell me that Pastor Grant is in Alabama? I'd like to meet him, maybe have lunch. He's been such a wonderful influence on you."

DeMarcus had told G'Mama about the case, Nona's involvement, and Pastor Grant's inheritance over lunch.

"Besides, I'm still packed. All my luggage is ready to go in the trunk of this car."

He blew out a breath. Sneaky old woman was using his information against him and making arguments like a judo master taking down an opponent.

He screeched into his parking spot and killed the ignition.

G'Mama put a hand on his shoulder before he could exit. "I'm through living scared, baby. My time left is too short to go around in fear. God has not given me 'a spirit of fear, but of power and of love and of a sound mind.'" She gave a resolute nod. "I'm going to get on that plane with you *despite* the fact that I'm scared. I'm going to step out in faith that the same God who's been holding planes up in the sky since the Wright brothers will hold our plane up when we fly. Been cooped up in Baltimore my whole life, and before I go, I want to see a little more of God's creation."

Her eyes held a thin sheen of unshed tears. He couldn't deny her anything.

"All right, old lady. Come on up to my office while I straighten things out."

They exited the car, and he snatched out his cell phone to call before he caught the elevator to his floor.

"Maxine, I didn't follow up to nail down all the details, and now Nona doesn't have counsel in Alabama."

"What can I do to help?" Ever-supportive Maxine.

Emotion clogged his throat. Maxine, G'Mama, Nona. Wonderful, strong, loving women surrounded him. How did he get so blessed? He swallowed hard to clear out the intensity of his feelings.

"I need you to book two tickets to Alabama. We need to go ASAP. Get a car and two hotel rooms as well. I'm taking G'Mama to Burnt Water."

Chapter 27

"You're fired." Calloway's voice rang cold and hard in Zeke's ear. "While you're off doing whatever it is you're doing in Atlanta, Hosea Grant is here. Right now. In Burnt Water, trying to collect that inheritance."

Zeke checked the clock. Five thirty. He repositioned himself on the bed he'd been lounging on all day, flipping between the station showing NASCAR and the one with the golf tournament, and stubbed out his cigarette in the ashtray. How did Calloway get this new burner number? Only Kitty had it. Zeke had been stringing her along about his return date, telling her his job in Atlanta was taking longer than he'd hoped. Kitty believed everything he told her.

He willed himself to play it cool. Calloway always knew how to get under Zeke's skin, ever since junior high. "I don't care."

A harsh laugh traveled across the phone line. "You should care. What if something unfortunate happens to you? Something permanent. Wouldn't want that, would you?"

"I'm not afraid of you, Calloway. I have insurance."

"What insurance do you think you have, Zeke, hmm? Have you been making little recordings? Taking pictures? Emailing things to yourself?" Calloway scoffed. "Kitty wasn't happy at all when she came home and found all her money gone and her laptop missing."

"Leave Kitty out of this. She don't know nothing."

"No, Zeke. It's you who knows nothing. Do you think I'd let you traipse off to Los Angeles without keeping tabs on you? Go off to Atlanta without knowing where you are and who you're with? You're as stupid as Big Zeke always said you were and will always be an insignificant, low-level, bit player in a game too complex for your little brain."

Zeke, in his boxers, shot to his feet and prowled the floor of the trailer.

"You always told me Kitty was a whiz with the computer. That came in handy when I wanted to know where you were and what you were doing. You hurt her, Zeke. Badly. And what do they say about a woman scorned?"

He couldn't believe Kitty betrayed him. Ungrateful. Untrustworthy, just like the pastor's she-witch. After all the promises Zeke made to Kitty. He'd lied and told her he was going to share his millions with her, and she tossed it all away. Grabbing his pants off the back of a chair and shoving his legs in, he cradled the phone between his ear and shoulder. The snakelike sound of Calloway's voice ignited firecrackers of anger inside him.

"She's smarter than you give her credit for. You've been having her search for things on her computer, and you're using her computer now. With your emails on it. Your search results saved in the history. Because of smart little Kitty, everything you've done, I now have."

Zeke curled his hand around his cell phone so tightly, the buttons on the case bit into his flesh.

"But today's your lucky day. I'm feeling generous. You have one last chance to bring that pastor to heel. I still need him to flip the property to me, and he can't do that if he can't prove his identity. You did one thing right when you burned down his church. You destroyed his paperwork."

"How do you know that?"

"Think, Zeke. Think. If he had documentation of his identity, he'd have filed it with the court already."

"What do you think I'm going to do for you?"

Calloway may have slipped off his hook, but Zeke could still get to the pastor. All Calloway gained was access to the pictures Zeke had downloaded to the laptop. Calloway couldn't get to the old man like Zeke could. Couldn't scare him. Calloway didn't know Grant's pressure points. Zeke rolled his eyes. Calloway was still droning on. Still thinking he had everything figured out. Zeke would help the pastor secure the inheritance but then would get Grant to sign the whole thing over to him.

Zeke took a breath to steady his nerves. "Tell me what the plan is."

"My niece is friends with a young lady named Chloe Jenkins, and at the cookout earlier this evening, she went on and on about Chloe's Girl Scout

Gold Award project. Turns out, there's another Grant family Bible at the Williams County Public Library, and it also has the entire genealogy for Hosea Grant in it. It's a duplicate of the Bible I found at Old Millie's home. The Jenkins girl made my niece promise not to tell anyone else, but after I told Bella that family like me didn't count and that I wouldn't tell a soul, she spilled the secret. The Bible the pastor's been rooting around for is out in the open, if you can imagine. In a generic trophy case. Even you can jimmy the lock with your eyes closed."

"What's that got to do with me?"

"You get back to Burnt Water. Tonight. You get that Bible, and you bring it to me. I'll tell you how the handoff is going to work later. You get this right, and you might not go to prison. You double-cross me, and you'll spend the rest of your sorry life in Holman with the other death-row inmates."

"I never killed anybody, and you know it."

"That's not what I heard. As I understand it, *you* killed Old Millie. You went to her house and stole all her heart medication. Then you left her to die. Kitty will testify that's what you told her. She's so wounded by what you've done to her, she's willing to accept some consolation from me in the form of cash and that mink coat you reneged on."

Zeke swore.

"I'll also testify you told me the exact same thing. Who do you think they'll believe? A councilman or a convict?" Calloway tsk-tsked.

"Even if it were true, which you know good and well it isn't, anything you two say is hearsay. Not admissible."

"Wrong again, Zeke. Statements against penal interest are admissible. Especially if both the witness offering his testimony and the circumstances seem credible. I'm very credible, Zeke." Calloway's tone was low and menacing.

A snarl worked its way up Zeke's throat, but he held it back. "Fine." He'd string Calloway along this one last time, but Zeke would not let him win. "I'll get the Bible. Then I'm done with you forever."

"Yes, you and I will part ways forever."

The call ended, and Zeke stared at the blackened screen, fury lighting his insides aflame.

◆ ◆ ◆

"Coffee is disgusting." DeMarcus sat in the Burnt Water Café, shoveling teaspoon after teaspoon of sugar into the mug in front of him. There wasn't a word in the dictionary to describe how physically draining the last twelve hours had been. But somehow seeing Nona revived his spirits.

Nona grimaced, sipped from her cup, and eyed him, while he furiously stirred in his sugar. He'd called her at eight thirty in the morning, telling her to meet him at the café. Hadn't even told her he was coming to Alabama, and definitely didn't tell her his grandmother was sleeping in the same horror-movie motel where Nona and Pastor Grant were staying.

The TV in the corner broadcast a morning show based out of Birmingham, with the weatherman forecasting temperatures in the high eighties with 70 percent humidity. Sweat broke out under DeMarcus's arms just looking at the numbers. He returned his attention to Nona.

"You in your pajamas, Sassy?" He gave her a wink.

She'd stuffed her hair into a scrunchie at the nape, and she had a baseball cap secured low on her head. She wore a UC Irvine T-shirt and some joggers. Before Nona, he'd always preferred women who dressed up, did their nails, and wore makeup. Half the time, Nona dressed like someone on her way to play a half-court game of basketball. It made her seem genuine. She wasn't dressing to impress him, and he liked that.

"Tell me again why you're here in Burnt Water, Johnson?" Her words jostled him out of his own head.

He wanted to say he was the cavalry, here to save the day. That he'd planned some epic, grand gesture to win her over. He squeezed his eyes shut and pushed out the truth. "I messed up, Nona. I didn't nail down all the arrangements I was supposed to, so I came here to correct the mistake myself. I want to oversee everything personally and make sure I get it right." He hunched his shoulders. He hated losing at basketball and losing cases. Best to take the L head-on. Rip off the Band-Aid, suffer the sting, and keep moving.

"I talked to you around lunchtime yesterday. How'd you arrange all this?"

He wagged his index finger back and forth. "I told you before, a magician never tells his secrets, woman."

She gave a small laugh. "That's . . ." Nona blinked a few times.

He thought he detected the sheen of moisture in her eyes.

"Thanks, DeMarcus."

He gave a dip of his head. "Of course. Anything." The low-pitched words were gravelly. He downed the last drops of the disgusting coffee to clear his throat.

No need to tell her he and G'Mama had traveled into the night and early this morning. They'd slept propped up against each other at the Atlanta airport to catch the first flight out to Mobile. Then they rented a car and drove to Burnt Water. He could tell Nona was beat. She had shadows under her eyes, and she'd suppressed a yawn. Always hard to travel east from the West Coast, because of the time jump.

"I did get one thing right," DeMarcus said. "Once we figured out Mildred Carter was the decedent, I had our Birmingham branch file a motion for me to appear pro hac vice in Alabama, so that's already taken care of."

"'Pro hac' what?" Creases appeared between her brows.

"In layman's terms, I'm allowed to appear in court here in Alabama on a very limited basis and for this specific purpose, as long as I am associated with the firm up in Birmingham."

He could wake up every day staring at her bleary-eyed, cranky face.

"What's that goofy smile for, Johnson?"

"Don't worry about it."

A waitress appeared with two plates of scrambled eggs, a platter of sausage patties and bacon for them to share, and a stack of buttermilk pancakes for DeMarcus.

He bowed his head and said a silent grace. When he looked up, Nona was still praying.

"I see starting our relationship in church was the right move." He gave Nona a teasing wink.

"Relationship? We're more like coworkers."

He saw the twinkle in her eye. "You keep telling yourself that." He hoisted a forkful of eggs to his mouth.

"Anyway, what do we need to get Pastor Grant certified as Mildred's heir?"

"We're going to file an affidavit with the court. I know he doesn't have a birth certificate, but his driver's license, the family Bible with the genealogy, and his sworn statement, hopefully, will suffice. Computers and digital storage didn't exist when he was born. Plus, fires and flooding of courthouses were more common the farther back in time we go."

Nona nodded. "Based on what I've seen on the internet, almost eleven million citizens don't have certified copies of their birth certificates."

"That's what I found as well. I think we have a credible case on this point." His leg jiggled in time to the oldies song "Could It Be I'm Falling in Love." He suppressed a smile. No *could* about it.

"We'll get the librarian to submit paperwork detailing how the library obtained the Bible, how Geraldine gave it to them, et cetera. It's not a slam dunk, but we also have Pastor Grant himself to testify about who his parents were, if necessary."

The bell above the door tinkled, and DeMarcus choked on the water he was drinking. There in the doorway stood G'Mama, mouth wide open, giving her gusty laugh, while on the arm of Pastor Grant.

G'Mama caught his attention and waved at him like she hadn't a care in the world. She had on her good wig, a burgundy velour tracksuit, and Skechers, like she stepped out of a 1980s exercise video. She and Pastor Grant approached the table where DeMarcus and Nona sat.

"Hey, baby." G'Mama's smile stretched from ear to ear. "Look who I ran into at the vending machine, while I was trying to get some peanut butter crackers." She smiled in Pastor Grant's direction.

"We started talking and realized we had something in common." Pastor Grant patted DeMarcus on the back and gave Nona a side hug, then slid back a chair for G'Mama.

G'Mama then lowered herself onto the chair beside DeMarcus and Pastor Grant sat beside Nona. A waitress scurried over, and the senior citizens accepted the woman's offer of coffee and two menus.

DeMarcus chanced a peek at Nona.

She stared at him blankly, speechless.

He reached across the table and grasped the fingers Nona was using to fiddle with her flatware. "Nona, this is my grandmother." He nodded in G'Mama's direction. "G'Mama, this is . . . ." His reckless thoughts and hopes for the future ran away from him, but he reeled them back in. "Nona."

"Nona, what a lovely name," G'Mama said kindly. "I'm so glad to meet you."

Nona wrinkled her brows like she was solving trigonometry in her head. "DeMarcus, where did your grandmother come from?" The muddled question matched the look on her face.

"G'Mama arrived unexpectedly"—he stressed the last word and gave his grandmother a pointed stare—"yesterday. I offered to have her stay at my place for a few days, to do some sightseeing in LA, but she refused." She still hadn't told him why she'd traveled across the country to see him and had jettisoned her fear of flying at the snap of the fingers.

"Nice to meet you, Mrs.—"

"Baby, everybody calls me G'Mama." His grandmother gave Nona a smile.

"Okay, G'Mama."

The waitress arrived. "Y'all ready to order something?"

"You go first, Hattie."

Hattie? Exactly when did she become "Hattie" to Pastor Grant? Those two were as cozy as two bugs in a rug, as G'Mama used to say.

"Thank you, Hosea. I'll have a bowl of oatmeal with some brown sugar and butter." G'Mama was nothing if not consistent. She loved hot oatmeal.

"And I'll have one egg, scrambled, and some bacon." Pastor Grant handed back the menu to the waitress. "I told Hattie all about the case on the way over. What are we doing today?"

DeMarcus nodded toward Nona, urging her to speak. He wanted her to show off her investigation skills to G'Mama.

Nona let out a quiet, cleansing breath to focus her mind. "Today we'll finalize the preparation of all the documents, which will prove who you are, and file those with the court. The library opens at nine o'clock, so you two can sit here and finish your breakfast, and DeMarcus and I will come back and fill you both in."

"Oh no," G'Mama piped up. "We going too. Isn't that right, Hosea?"

"Yes, it is, Hattie. The food will be here any minute. We'll be quick and then we can all go."

"There's no need," Nona interjected.

Pastor Grant held up his hand. "It seems like I've been waiting all my life to find out who I am, who my people are. I'm here now, where it all started, and I don't want to miss one moment of it."

"Amen to that." G'Mama made a satisfied sound.

Nona's phone rang. She slid her fingers around the screen and held it to her ear. Her mouth opened wide, and her face blanched. "No. Please no. Okay."

DeMarcus bounded to his feet and circled the table. He bent to one knee beside her and put his arm around her shoulder, then pulled her close to whisper in her ear. "Nona, what is it? Is everything okay?"

She turned her face toward him, her eyes vacant. "There's been a break-in at the library."

Chapter 28

NONA STOOD STOCK-STILL in the Williams County Public Library, not daring to breathe, hoping somehow she'd awaken from the horrible nightmare unfolding before her eyes. She moved one step forward, and glass crunched under her feet. Pastor Grant, G'Mama, and DeMarcus all stood silent as well, as if beside a desecrated grave.

Tears sprang to Nona's eyes. This was to be Pastor Grant's first time seeing his family's precious memories in person—the history denied him because of a tragedy in an alley nearly eighty years prior.

Someone had ruthlessly destroyed all the precious items in the case. The cotton shirt that had belonged to Pastor Grant's great-grandfather lay on the floor, rent into a half dozen pieces. The few buttons she'd seen in the picture had been stripped away. One rested next to her shoe. Her soul ached for Pastor Grant. He'd dressed up in his Sunday best for this day. To be so close and to have it all lay in ruins must be devastating.

G'Mama stood, clutching Pastor Grant's arm for support. She dabbed her lids with a limp handkerchief.

DeMarcus walked toward her. His normally vibrating presence was subdued. He stooped over the remnants of the stemless clay pipe.

Nona reached out an arm to stop him. "There may be fingerprints."

Beside the pipe, scraps of the report card lay ripped into shreds.

She backed away.

Ms. Lorretta stood near the circulation desk. "Nona, I'm so sorry."

"Nona, is it . . . ? Is the . . . ?" Pastor Grant slumped slightly toward G'Mama, as if her presence were holding him up.

Nona knew what he was asking. Squatting down on her haunches, she was careful not to disturb anything. Her heart held out a sliver of hope that on the floor, underneath the glass and shredded dreams, they'd find the Bible. She used her hands to push against her knees and stand. No trace of the Book, which was key to proving his family history. "We need to call the police."

"Already did." Ms. Lorretta wrung her hands.

Chloe, gasping and sweaty, entered the library like a whirlwind. "They called me out of class." She rushed toward Nona.

"Stop!" Nona threw an arm out to halt the girl's forward progress.

Chloe found a chair and sat down. Shuddering breaths jerked her shoulders. "Nona, I'm so sorry." The girl's eyes were red-rimmed and full of tears. "This is all my fault. I only told one person, my best friend, Bella. I told her not to tell anyone." Chloe wiped her nose on her sleeve. "We started in Girl Scouts as Brownies together. We've known each other our whole lives."

"You told Isabella Calloway?" Ms. Lorretta stared at Chloe incredulously. "You know that girl can't keep a secret. And what with her uncle's being a councilman? No telling who's heard about what Nona and Pastor Grant are doing."

Tension tightened the muscles between Nona's shoulder blades, and her awareness pricked. The name Calloway connected with being a councilman sounded an alarm in her mind. She needed to focus and bring her investigatory skills to the crime scene. She moved over to Chloe and sat beside her.

"Chloe, I know what it's like to say words you wish you could take back, but we're human. Never going to be perfect." Nona stepped out of her comfort zone and reached out to Chloe, rubbing her back in circles. "Tell me everything you told Bella."

Fat tears rolled down Chloe's cheeks. "I told her about how Pastor Grant was the long-lost relative of Old Millie and that he grew up never knowing about her." She sniffed and shuddered.

Nona rubbed her back some more. "Anything else?"

"I told her that the Bible had his genealogy and that you were going to take it to court and use it, so he could get his inheritance." Chloe started shaking. "I was so proud and excited about helping you and Pastor Grant." Her entire body drooped.

Nona gave her shoulder a squeeze.

Pastor Grant walked over and sat on the other side of Chloe. "Baby girl, look at me."

Chloe lifted her head.

"God is still on his throne. He knows the beginning from the end, and he is sovereign. Sometimes, what appears to be a mistake from our point of view is something God is using to do what he intended all along."

G'Mama scooted a chair in front of Chloe as well and patted her hand.

Chloe's trembling lessened, and Nona stood. Chloe had revealed everything about the crucial evidence to another teenager. Nona pinched the bridge of her nose and pushed back irritation. This wasn't Chloe's fault. Nona had asked a kid to keep a secret most adults would jump to spill. In her own eagerness, she'd abandoned all investigative protocols.

She focused her mind on working through the case in front of her. "When was this conversation, and where?"

"Early last evening. It was at a cookout at Bella's house. The whole family was there. Her little brother. Her mom and dad. And Councilman Calloway. Bella's dad is Councilman Calloway's brother."

Nona used her phone to find a picture of the Burnt Water City Council. She recognized Calloway from the charity ball. She squinted. He'd been at the Burnt Water Café when Bernice had revealed her long-held secret. Had he tailed her in California? Burned down Pastor Grant's church? If so, why? Every time she thought she was close to solving Pastor Grant's case, another issue popped up. At every turn, something thwarted her. And now the root of the problem was clear. All the attempts to block her investigation had nothing to do with Sylvester Dillard's murder. It all had to do with Pastor Grant and his inheritance. Someone in Burnt Water didn't want Pastor Grant to prove his heirship. Maybe it was Calloway. Maybe it was someone else. Her heart thudded. Was Pastor's life in danger here in Burnt Water?

DeMarcus called her name, and she walked over from where she'd been questioning Chloe.

DeMarcus had circled around and was standing at the side of the case. He gave an upward jerk of his head, and she backtracked, then joined him. On the floor was the brass plate with the tribute to the Hall family. She pointed toward the front of the case and saw scratch marks. The perp had come with tools. Something caught her eye on the floor, and she backed away with jerky steps, her legs unsteady.

Beside the brass plate was a cigarette butt.

After the police wrapped up taking statements and getting everyone's contact information, overwhelm and fatigue crashed over Nona like a wave. She stood outside the library, planning her next moves, her nerves taut as a piano string.

"Will you be okay?" DeMarcus stood beside her.

"Yes. I think so." She wrapped her arms around herself and ran her hands up and down, even though it was a balmy day.

He gathered her in slowly, gently. And he kissed her forehead.

She examined his face. "I see a little cockiness around the edges, Johnson." A faint smile eased onto her lips.

"I'm a package. You get the good with the cocky."

A genuine smile pulled out then.

She turned and entered the rental car while DeMarcus rounded up G'Mama and Pastor Grant.

Fifteen minutes of aimless driving around town, down side streets and past neighborhoods, she found herself at Bethel. She opened the car door, and the sound of screeching insects filled her ears, and the scent of freshly mown grass permeated the air. Her feet crunched on the gravel in the parking lot, and she made her way to the small cemetery beside the church. A low iron fence enclosed an area with weathered headstones and fire ant hills. In the back corner of the graveyard, a tree, with a base as large as a dining room table and two stories tall, stretched its leafy limbs out over the plots, covering them in shade.

She lingered, running her fingers over the tops of the cool granite markers, reading the names. Her gaze jerked back to the last grave she'd passed. Modern, freshly cut stone stood out in the old churchyard.

MILDRED ELIZABETH HALL CARTER
WIFE, MOTHER, SISTER

Prone to wander, Lord, I feel it,
prone to leave the God I love;
here's my heart; O take and seal it;
seal it for thy courts above.

Tears, hot and stinging, sprang into her eyes. She was here—the place where everything began and, now, where it all ended. Mildred and Florence, sisters bound by love and fierce loyalty, were torn apart by tragic circumstances. Consequences had reverberated across time, but their love for each other had never wavered. For the first time since Nikki's death, the memories of the love Nona's twin and she shared only filled her with affection without the recrimination that previously had always washed ashore to dash the fond remembrance. Was sisterhood messy and complicated? Yes. But she would press forward, letting the thoughts of the good overtake the hurt, pain, and guilt. She would no longer diminish her sister's love for her by letting one moment in time, one fight, erase the years of love they'd had for one another. From today forward, Nona would cling to the happy thoughts and see the time she'd had with Nikki as the precious gift it had been. A laugh and a sob escaped simultaneously, and images of the good times they'd shared washed over her.

At the crunch of gravel, she turned, startled. Lost in the past, she'd let down her guard and had missed the sound of a car parking. A woman in her fifties approached. Her blond hair had frosted highlights. She wore tight capri pants and a hot-pink peasant blouse. She had a large woven handbag over her shoulder, and silver bracelets festooned her arms.

Nona blanked out her face to mask her thoughts, and the woman stood beside her. Even though a slight breeze moved through the churchyard, the scent of the woman's perfume made Nona want to sneeze.

"Everybody in this town loved Old Millie." The woman let out a sigh. "Everybody in town also knows you and that good-looking guy are from Hollywood and that you're here to settle Millie's estate." The bracelets on the woman's arms clicked and clacked as she adjusted the bulging bag she carried.

Nona nodded. The speculation in Burnt Water ran rampant, and the gossip mill was working overtime, but the essence of the facts was true.

"I'm Jacqueline." The woman extended her hand. "But everybody around here calls me Kitty."

Nona paused for a beat but shook the woman's hand, not offering her own name, and inspected the woman. The heavy concealer on her face couldn't hide Kitty's black eye, and the lipstick didn't diminish the swollenness of the bruised lip. Nona clamped back harsh words for whoever did this to her.

Kitty turned and faced Mildred's grave. "I've seen that man you're with. He is some kind of pretty." She sucked her teeth. "The pretty ones will break your heart." She shrugged. "So will the ugly ones."

There had been a time when Kitty's statement would have earned a hearty *amen* from Nona. But DeMarcus had shown himself to be faithful. She didn't owe this stranger anything, but the beating the woman had taken deserved something.

"They're not all like that, Kitty."

"Yeah, well, that kind seems to find me." Kitty glanced over her shoulders, reached into her oversized bag, and extracted a hefty expandable folder secured by an elastic band. "Maybe if I do what's right, God will forgive me." She extended the package to Nona, turned, and with an air of resignation walked to her car.

At her vehicle, Kitty looked back over her shoulder. Nona gave her a single wave, and Kitty returned it with a sad smile.

Kitty drove away, and Nona shifted the package in her arms, testing its weight and size. In her rental car, she locked the door, removed the rubber cord, and opened the flap that concealed the contents. She reached inside and removed a sheet of paper. The sharecropper agreement. With trembling hands, she pulled out the only other item. The Bible.

Chapter 29

EVERY INCH OF space between Zeke's ears ached, and his mouth tasted like an ashtray. He forced his sleep-crusted eyes open, trying to figure out where he was and what he'd done the night before. He cast about in his mind. Hazy impressions came back. He'd reached Burnt Water around eight and went straight to Dougan's for a cold one. The cover band had finished its set, and someone had fired up the jukebox. Didn't know how long he'd sat there, talking to the bartender. Mike kept filling his pint, yacking on about Alabama's football prospects. Zeke remembered watching the late-night sports scores on the evening news plus some spring training highlights on the flat-screen mounted in the corner. After that, everything started going fuzzy.

He'd driven to the library. Didn't break the glass to get in, but his brain remembered shards everywhere. He hated libraries. When he was little, he'd once asked Big Zeke to take him to get some books. He wanted his daddy to read him a story at bedtime, like he'd heard some other daddies did. Big Zeke told him only losers and punks jammed their noses in books and that no one would find him dead in a girlified place like that. He pushed down the humiliating memory. As he replayed the evening, he saw himself taking the Bible from the display case. Then he'd driven to Kitty's house. He didn't know what time. But he remembered pounding on her door until she let him in. She'd ranted and raved about something, arms flailing around. But he'd shut her up. Hard. Then his memory blacked out.

He scanned Kitty's bedroom. The sun streaming in from the window hurt his eyes. Looked like a tornado had ripped through the place. Broken containers, plus smears of powder and goop, covered her makeup vanity. There were half-open drawers with clothing spilling out and a broken lamp in the corner.

"Kitty." She didn't come when he called. "Kitty!" His throat felt raw. "Get your sorry hide in here, and bring some coffee with you." She was worthless. His mama was worthless too. Nausea boiled in his stomach.

Silence greeted him.

"Don't make me come out there. You'll regret it." Maybe she'd gone to work or out for groceries. He hauled himself out of the bed and squatted to fish around for his pants on the ground. The floor undulated beneath him like a boat on choppy water. He planted his hands by his sides and steadied himself. Still had on his socks from last night. He stumbled to the living room. Still no sign of Kitty.

He'd deal with her when she came back. He had bigger things to handle. Now that he had the Bible, he had the power. Calloway thought he'd just give it over? Not a chance.

He went to the coat closet to rummage through all the shoes. Kitty had a million pairs, and that had always been his hiding place. He reached the bottom of the pile, but his bag wasn't there. Maybe he'd put it somewhere else.

He trudged to the kitchen and reached for a glass to fill with water to take an aspirin for his headache. *Think.* Of course. Under the bed. He went back into Kitty's room, lay on the floor, worked his face beneath the dust ruffle so he could see, and swept a hand back and forth as far as he could reach. Nothing. Fury momentarily blurred his vision. He checked the knickknack closet next to the bathroom. That little . . . He swore. When he got his hands on her, she would never, ever double-cross him again. An intense growl emanated from his gut. The ringing of the phone pulled him to his feet to search around for his everyday cell.

"You better be on your way back here, Kitty, or I swear—"

"It's me. Where is it? You were supposed to meet me this morning." Calloway's voice was low and tight. "Don't know how I'm going to clean this mess up after you. You couldn't simply sneak out the book, could you? Had to trash the place in your wake. That's how you've always been, Zeke. Sloppy and stupid."

"Shut up, Calloway." Heat flushed Zeke's skin, and red dots of light danced in his vision as fury clawed at his brain and overcame his reason.

"Know what? You're not getting your precious book." His gut told him Kitty had made off with it to get even. Pounding a woman until he got what he wanted was one lesson his daddy had taught him well. He'd track her down and get it, but a new plan formed.

"Zeke, Zeke, Zeke. I'm worried about you. I really am. You're losing touch with reality. Are you thinking of harming yourself?" Calloway laughed. "If you disappear, who would miss you, Zeke? Hmm? No one, that's who." He released a sigh. "I'm coming to get what you promised me. I'll have a little something for you for all our trouble when I get there. Then we're done. No more business or communications between us. Ever. Do you understand?"

Calloway must think Zeke a complete fool. He knew he couldn't trust a single word slithering out of that snake's mouth. Steely determination overcame Zeke. "Yup. I'll be waiting right here for you at Kitty's house."

He disconnected the phone and found his jacket on the floor. After removing his gun from the pocket, he tested the weight in his hands. He turned it over and smiled. He reached in the other pocket for the bullets, but another thought occurred to him. A bullet was too merciful for Calloway. Soft Calloway. Big shot Calloway. He'd never make it in prison the way Zeke had. The cons in gen pop at Holman would eat the councilman alive. Oh, what Zeke wouldn't give to be there as Calloway begged and pleaded for protection behind bars. The humiliation. The pain.

Zeke recalled all the illegal deals he'd brokered for Calloway. Zeke had enough dirt on the councilman that he could pick and choose which enforcement agency he wanted to have haul off Calloway to prison. Call the FBI? Nope. No federal prosecution with cushy prison time at Club Fed. Local police? They were all on Calloway's payroll. Zeke wanted everyone in Burnt Water to witness how the high-and-mighty Gavin Calloway had fallen, watch him as he was frog-marched down Main Street in handcuffs.

Zeke lifted his phone and looked up the number for the Williams County Sheriff's Office. After he made his call, he'd head straight over to visit that she-cat. If he was going to have to do hard time for selling out Calloway and implicating himself, he may as well get something he wanted out of it. It would be worth a few more years if that meddling woman suffered. When he rolled on Calloway, and punished the girl, he'd tie everything up with such a pretty little bow the prosecutors would beg him to cut a deal.

✦ ✦ ✦

Nona and DeMarcus sat with G'Mama and Pastor Grant in Bernice's living room. In the corner, a timeworn boom box played a cassette of gospel music. Bernice lived in a small bungalow. The sitting area featured a matching set of cream-colored easy chairs and a sofa with a plastic slipcover. An ache thudded in Nona's heart. Edna and Pearly were at the house as well. The people Nona had met in Burnt Water weren't flashy or well-to-do, but their down-to-earth hospitality and genuine warmth stirred an unexpected envy, a longing for connection, inside her.

She smooshed an errant curl behind her ear and exhaled a stream of air. Although Kitty hadn't ratted out her attacker when she'd turned over the Bible to Nona, the bruises on Kitty's face solved the mystery of who trashed the display at the library. Domestic violence and destruction of government property charges would mean real prison time if Kitty worked up her courage and pushed for prosecution. Hopefully, with the Bible now secured and the leverage over Pastor Grant gone, the snake—whoever he was—would spend years in a penitentiary.

Bernice shooed out her rangy mutt, Otis, onto her front porch. Otis sat yowling from his spot on the welcome mat, then settled down when Bernice opened the door and tossed him a large chew toy. Bernice ambled back to join her guests.

"Your aunt was some kind of woman." Bernice lifted a cup of coffee to her lips, blew gently, then took a tentative sip. "She taught third grade in Burnt Water for forty years."

Edna held aloft her piece of pound cake and gestured toward Nona. "Sure did. Those kids loved her." She nibbled a bite of the treat. "When she retired"—Edna's mouth worked around the cake—"we rounded up every kid we could find. Some were grandparents themselves. Whoo-whee we had a good time. Mildred made a big impact on the children around here."

Nona watched Pastor Grant. His face glowed as if lit from inside. She shook out her hands to work off the tension. Unease still niggled at her. The police had not arrested anyone, and estate proceedings took a while to unwind. Had Nona and DeMarcus eliminated all threats to Pastor Grant? She forced herself to push down the disquiet, willing herself to turn off her PI skills to focus on Pastor Grant's joy.

"Bernice, tell 'em 'bout her trip to Liberia," Pearly chimed in.

"She traveled all over the world. Went to Liberia for a week of missions work at a school. For her seventieth birthday, she did a one-year term as an English teacher in Japan." Bernice chuckled.

Edna leaned forward. "Her health stayed good for a long time, until her mideighties. She slowed down a little then. Started teaching women's Sunday school. Then, when she was ninety, she transitioned to the prayer and pastor support teams, stuff that didn't take too much physical effort. All the while, she baked her famous sweet corn bread for the sick and shut-in and crocheted baby booties and blankets for new mothers here in Burnt Water and the rest of Williams County."

"We saw photographs of papers and mementos that were on display in the library." Pastor Grant dropped his head and gave a sorrowful shake. "Some things are still missing, but we did get the sharecropper agreement back." Pastor Grant cast his gaze around at the Bethel ladies. "Do any of you know its significance?"

"We all do. Lots of people here in town know." Pearly stroked her chin. "Mildred and Florence's family started sharecropping right about the time of Reconstruction. Williams County received its name from the family that owned the biggest plantation around. Lost all three of their sons in battle. Your family signed that formal agreement with him a few years later. They worked the land and somehow managed not to get behind on what they owed for seed, tools, and whatnot. The Williams, meanwhile, fell on hard times. Gambling. Grief. Thank the Lord, your family always did know how to turn what few pennies they had into dollars." Pearly cackled and gave an appreciative nod. "Bit by bit, Mr. Williams kept selling off pieces of his property, and your grandparents kept buying up a little here and a little there."

"More coffee, anyone? Cake?" Bernice stood from her place on the couch.

Nona hated cooking, but she wanted the recipe to Bernice's lemon loaf. The creamy icing and moist cake tasted better than any she'd ever had in California. Something about this Alabama cooking put West Coast fusion cooking to shame.

"You, DeMarcus, want some more? You're still a growing boy."

DeMarcus lounged back on one end of the couch, his long legs stretched out in front of him, a satisfied smirk on his face. "I'm about to go into a food coma. Everything you all have been feeding me is the best grub I've ever had in my entire life." He winked at Nona, and she rolled her eyes. He had all the women in Burnt Water swooning.

"I saw that, DeMarcus." G'Mama cackled. "I'm loving hearing all these stories. Reminds me of my family in Mississippi." She folded her hands over her belly and rocked back and forth in time to the hushed music floating over the room.

A question popped into Nona's thoughts. "When I was helping Pastor Grant research, I was looking for towns with odd names. Burnt Water jumped out at me. Do any of you know why the town is called that?"

"Sure do," Edna spoke up. "They taught us in school. Sometime early in Williams County history, there was a huge textile mill. Cotton. Had a gin too. The whole thing, gin and mill, burned to the ground about 1820, 1830, something like that. Lightning strike. Anyway, with the residue from the fire leaching down into the water table and the runoff into the river, people started saying the water tasted burnt. Doesn't taste like that now, but the name Burnt Water stuck."

Nona glanced at each lady and weighed how best to ask her question. "Why didn't Florence receive any land? Is it because she moved to California?"

"Oh no." Pearly made an animated gesture with her hands. "Florence and Mildred's parents made a deal. They paid for Flo to go to that Calhoun Colored School in Lowndes County. Back then, it was an enormous sacrifice for a family to send an able-bodied child off to school. Plus, the tuition."

"That's right," Bernice chimed in.

"Mildred stayed home and helped on the land, so the family agreed the land would be hers. Mildred and Florence's parents always called the property 'the parcels.' Talked about having a legacy to pass down to their children and great-grandchildren. Little did Mildred know, she'd outlive her husband and both her kids."

* * *

Otis gave some yappy barks, and a knock rattled Bernice's storm door. "Niecy, it's me. Let me in."

"Who it is knocking so loud on my door?"

"You know it's me, Bernice—Luther. I brought Tiny with me. We coming in to meet our cousin."

Two men tumbled into the house in a flurry of excitement. One had Pastor Grant's bearing. The other man was giant, both in height and girth, with a smile that lit the room.

Pastor Grant stood to greet them. Water gathered in his eyes.

Luther grabbed Pastor Grant up in a smothering bear hug. "I'm your cousin Luther Jr. Your uncle Edward, Mildred's husband, was my daddy's brother. That makes us cousins by marriage. I was a little itty-bitty thing when your mama and daddy left, but I still remember how pretty she was. Always smelled like roses."

"She sure did." Pastor Grant and Luther gave each other a tight hug.

Tiny stepped forward. "I'm family on your granddaddy Grant's side. Booker's daddy. My grandfather and your grandfather were brothers, so we have both of our great-grandparents in common. They were slaves, and we don't know nothing about them, but I know we're kin."

DeMarcus stood and motioned to Nona, then pointed at the front door. They exited, leaving the senior citizens inside to reminisce.

Bernice's spacious front porch had a swing, supported by heavy-duty chains, with two decorative pillows. A row of tall hedges ran in front. Potted ferns stood guard over the center stairway.

DeMarcus sat and patted the seat next to him. She hesitated. He gave a tender smile, which broke the fragile wall she was clinging to, and she sat. He draped his long arm across the back of the swing and started rocking with a gentle push of his foot. Otis ambled up to investigate but returned to a sunny spot closer to the front door.

She gave him a surreptitious glance. He'd paired some khaki pants with a polo. Of course there was a tiger embroidered on the right side of the chest. She returned her attention to his face and caught him smirking at her.

"Now that you have the Bible, we have everything we need to file the papers for Pastor Grant to be named heir." He moved his hand and rested it on her nape. When she didn't shrug him off, he slowly kneaded away the stress she didn't even know was there.

"Tomorrow I'll reach out to my connection in Birmingham at the satellite office again and get someone to work with me to get all the right paperwork on file to open an estate and have Pastor Grant named as the heir. I can't do it overnight, but I'll ensure there's a team in place here in Alabama to take care of it, and I'll check in with them regularly. Not going to drop that ball again."

The rhythmic press of his fingers on her tight muscles relaxed her. She let the walls come down and reclined against his shoulder. His chest moved up and down, rhythmic and soothing. "I'm going to go to the tax offices tomorrow and confirm my suspicions about Leisure Zone Holdings. My guess is, Mildred's property shares a boundary with the land they intend to use for their development. Her tract might even be landlocked by it. If my hunch is right, what she owned is worth millions."

DeMarcus reached out his arm and gathered her closer to him. His old-man cologne stole her breath away. How could she ever have thought she didn't like it?

He turned his head and scrutinized her eyes radiating emotions she worked to decode. "I think G'Mama is in hog heaven here. Pastor Grant too. They'll be fine hanging out for a day or two while we put everything in place."

His chest expanded, and he blew out a slow breath. "You did a great job on all of this plus Mitch's case. He's offering you a job as a staff investigator, if you want it. You wouldn't be working for me directly, so no problem there. Gold-plated insurance. Dental and vision. Expense reimbursement."

A salary, benefits. Lunches with DeMarcus.

They stared into each other's eyes. Finally, the pieces clicked into place. She could see sincerity shining in his face. Determination. Care. Commitment.

She held up her hand and his ring glinted. "You want to wear it? I'm sure you miss it . . ." She waggled her thumb in front of him. "Like Gollum."

He reared back and laughed, deep, rumbling. Tears gathered in his eyes. Chuckles kept bubbling out of him. After about thirty seconds, he finally marshaled control over himself.

She had his number coming and going.

He looked at her face, and tracked his gaze over her, taking her in. "Like Frodo, I have my flaws." He stretched out his hand and dared to touch one of her curls.

She did not object in the least.

"Do I mess up? Sure. Do I get blinded by bling and style? Sometimes. But I'm loyal and determined, single-minded." A series of emotions played across his features. "I'm not that guy who hurt you. What's more . . ." He peered closely at her. "You know it."

Moisture clouded her vision. She sat silently, blinking. He held still, giving her time. He inclined his head, keeping his eyes open, gauging her approval. She had no plans to stop him as he drew within a hair's breadth.

Low growling from Bernice's dog, Otis, pulled her attention. A reflective surface flashed in her sight, partially obscured by the tall hedges that flanked the wraparound porch. Apprehension crawled up her neck. A figure emerged from behind the bushes and began charging up the porch stairs, flailing an arm in the air. All her mind could take in were the eyes—crazed, pulled wide—and the gun, a snub-nosed stainless-steel revolver.

The porch swing jerked. DeMarcus sprang to his feet and in one motion hurled himself toward the charging man. His momentum toppled the guy, and they both tumbled down the porch stairs. DeMarcus had the wild man in a bear hug, trapping the assailant's arms, hands and the gun between their two bodies. The dude writhed beneath DeMarcus, who was attempting to wrestle the man's hands, and the gun, out from between them. The guy had a freakish superstrength. His face was a mask of insane rage, his eyes wild and bloodshot.

"If I can't have what *I* want"—the guy pushed out between grunts, thrashing his body—"you can't have what *you* want."

Otis dove off the porch and latched on to the creep. The fight shifted, and the grunting became screams as the man jerked his leg, attempting to shake Otis loose. "Get it off!"

DeMarcus wrenched the gun free and pulled away.

"Heel, Otis." Nona scrambled down from the porch. She stood with her gun pointed at the man. "Freeze, dirtbag. Don't even twitch."

She recognized the creep from the Valentine's ball out in LA. Burgundy-colored splotches mottled his face, and he twisted on the ground, clutching his leg. He looked feral, like he was high on drugs or in need of psychiatric care.

Bernice and G'Mama, eyes wide, stood in the doorway.

"I called the police," Bernice shouted out. "Hold him a little longer."

It seemed like an eternity until squealing tires and sirens echoed from down the street of the quiet residential neighborhood. DeMarcus faced the cops and tossed the dude's gun on the ground, far away from his reach.

"Lower your weapon, ma'am. We'll take it from here."

Nona lowered her gun and engaged the safety.

The perp struggled and jerked as the police worked the cuffs onto his wrists.

Nona holstered her weapon and stepped closer to DeMarcus. "Babe, you okay?" She reached out and ran her hands over his face, smoothing his cheeks. She traced her touch over his shoulders, checking him for injuries.

He appeared stunned. Incredulity shadowed his eyes followed by a grin. "Woman, you know I had it under control."

"I had it under control." She smiled, but the smile faltered.

He held her gaze. "You called me 'babe.'"

"Yes, I did." Shyness overcame her. "I love you, Big Head Johnson."

"I love you, Sassy."

He pressed his lips to hers, a promise to cherish, love, and protect her always.

Epilogue

One Year Later

DeMarcus, Nona, and Pastor Grant each stood holding a gold-colored shovel and wearing hard hats alongside suit-and-tie-clad executives from Leisure Zone Holdings. Cameras snapped, and Nona willed the sweat that trickled down her forehead to retreat mid-drip. The groundbreaking ceremony scheduled two weeks after the closing of Mildred's estate had resulted from a multimillion-dollar deal DeMarcus brokered with Leisure Zone Holdings on Pastor Grant's behalf. The mouthwatering scent of catering from the Burnt Water Café drifted to her nose. An arch with black and orange balloons stood against a backdrop of trees overgrown with kudzu and the screech of cicadas.

After a photo op where the assembled dignitaries pretended to dig a scoop of dirt, a PR rep for Leisure Zone Holdings gathered up the shovels, and the photographer took more candid shots. An executive then moved to the microphone at a podium off to the side. Nona tuned out as he droned on and on about what a boon the development would be for Alabama in general and Burnt Water in particular. The CEO gestured for Pastor Grant to approach the podium.

He stood there, dignified in a three-piece suit despite the heat. He adjusted the microphone and consulted some index cards.

"Friends, I stand here today on land sharecropped by my great-grandparents, Bankston and Polly Williams. Through grit and hard work, they successfully farmed this land and purchased parcels as far as your eyes can see in any direction. Now, this land, combined with about three hundred acres already owned by Leisure Zone Holdings, will become a vacation destination for families from around the world."

A smattering of applause broke out. He raised his hand to quiet down everyone.

Nona thought her heart would burst. Pastor Grant was safe. Zeke and Calloway were both behind bars, Zeke in federal prison in Talladega for his cooperation in nailing Calloway, and Calloway in the Williams County Jail awaiting trial for Mildred's murder, as his attorneys dragged out the proceedings with motions and continuances. Leisure Zone Holdings had known nothing about the pair's shady dealings and had cooperated fully, assisting the authorities with their investigation of Calloway.

Pastor Grant's extended family had made time to come to the ground-breaking. Watching him interact with his father's side of the family and relatives by marriage filled Nona's heart with joy for him. She focused her attention on his words.

"What pleases me the most is Leisure Zone Holdings' commitment to funding summer camps and retreats for underprivileged children traveling here from within the United States and even from abroad. I am also grati-fied by the company's determination to preserve a natural environment of twenty-five acres to provide an authentic camp experience for city kids, es-pecially children from Los Angeles and Baltimore."

Pastor Grant motioned with his hand that he needed a drink of water, and someone hustled forward and handed him a bottle. "You know what they say. It's not the heat, it's the humidity."

The crowd gave him an appreciative laugh.

"God caused this wonderful gift to fall into my lap." He chuckled. "I'm what's known as a laughing heir. And I want to use the money as he would have me use it. As the Bible says, 'From everyone who has been given much, much will be demanded.'"

G'Mama gave a hearty "amen" from her position in the audience as she stood beside Pastor Grant and beamed. To be near Jamaria at UCLA, she'd moved to Los Angeles. G'Mama went on and on about how she felt revital-ized by helping the Mothers' Board at Mount Zion and taking walks in the California sunshine.

"An additional component of the summer camp will be the Nikki Taylor Dance Studio, with residencies for some of the finest dance teachers in the nation plus mentorships for girls and boys who want to explore pursuing dance as a career."

Louder clapping followed this announcement.

"Everyone knows you should never give a pastor a microphone."

The crowd laughed some more.

"I'll say grace, and we can eat that delicious food."

After the "amen," Nona sidled up to DeMarcus. "You didn't tell me about the dance studio named after my sister."

"Consider it a wedding present from me."

"What? We're not even engaged for real."

He grabbed her hand and led her over to the balloon arch. "I plan to take care of that right here, right now."

The PR photographer was already in place.

"You planned this, didn't you?"

He smirked. "Of course I did. Do you not see the balloons in Princeton colors? Who do you think you're dealing with?"

Her cheeks hurt, she was smiling so hard.

DeMarcus knelt. "Nona, will you do me the honor of marrying me?" He opened his fist and revealed an oval cut solitaire as large as a lima bean.

She had no words.

"What? Too big? Too much?"

"Always too much."

"I am who I am." He shrugged. "But you'll marry me?"

"You know my answer."

He stood and scanned her face. His countenance, dead serious, and his eyes held the promise of forever. Then a slow smile. Infernal. Gloating. "You are correct. I know the answer. But you have to say it." He stood and stepped closer to her.

The force of her emotions shook her. "Yes, I'll—"

He captured her lips in a kiss, cutting off her words. When he pulled away, she was breathless. He winked.

"Now that we've settled the matter . . ." He kissed her again, with a gentleness that said he cherished her.

God had restored her crushed heart, giving her hope. Hope for a future, not just existence, here in this life and hope for her eternal future. Gratitude for the precious second chance God had given her overwhelmed her.

Lord my God, I called to you for help,
and you healed me.
You, Lord, brought me up from the realm of the dead;
you spared me from going down to the pit.

Sing the praises of the Lord, you his faithful people;
praise his holy name.

Psalm 30:2–4

Acknowledgments

THANK YOU TO my husband for supporting me every step of the way. You are 110 percent behind the cause. Thank you to my kids for championing me and for hyping me up. Thank you to the budding writer in my house. It has been a joy blabbing on and on with you about the craft and business of writing. Finally, thank you to my mom for the support, excitement, and enthusiasm.

To the "Inklings," as my husband calls you—Kimberley Woodhouse, Becca Whitham, Jocelyn Green, Darcie Gudger, Jaime Jo Wright, and Tracie Peterson—your wholehearted embrace has been kind beyond words, and I am so thankful.

To my agent, Tamela Hancock Murray, thank you for believing in my work, for encouraging me, and for finding a home for this book.

Janyre Tromp, thank you for championing my book and for believing in my writing. I am so blessed to have you on my side.

The Kregel Publications team, Catherine DeVries, Rachel Kirsch, Andrea Renee Cox, Sarah Cross, Barb Barnes, Kayliani Shi, Emily Irish, and Caroline Cahoon. I had no idea how many people it takes to bring a book into the world. I am grateful, thankful, and humbled by your belief in my work, and by the collective effort of everyone at Kregel in bringing my story to life. Thank you.

To Tina Radcliffe, words cannot express how dear to me your encouragement has been and how it has carried me. Thank you very much.

To Carla and Liz, besties over the decades, thank you for reading early manuscripts and cheering me on, for all the prayers over the years, and for all the love.

ACKNOWLEDGMENTS

To my prayer partner, Pam, thank you for twenty years of steadfast prayer for me and for covering this project in prayer as well.

To Miriam Pace, thank you for pouring into me for months as a mentor. This book would not exist without you.

Jenelle Hovde, critique partner extraordinaire, thank you for reading every word of this book and for always being available to share words of encouragement via audio chat. Your help has been invaluable.

To the internet writer tribe that brings me pure joy, encouragement, and laughs: Rosey Lee, Joy K. Massenburge, Lotice Greene, Robin W. Pearson, Michelle Stimpson, and Rebekah Millet, thank you all.

To my early beta readers, Letha, Chelsea, and Jill, thank you for your gentle reading of my rough first attempts at writing.

A shout-out to Terry Franklin and JKM for answering my Instagram callout for help naming a character. Tyson Foster owes his name to you both.

To "the Slayer." Surprise! Thank you for telling me about NaNoWriMo and for the two-hundred-thirty-plus games of Wordfeud. There is no way statistically to catch up to your win record, but I have fun trying.

Finally, to my readers. Thank you for taking time out of your real life to spend it with my imaginary characters. I hope you enjoyed reading this book as much as I enjoyed writing it.

Both Burnt Water and Williams County are entirely fictional places. The law and legal matters in this book are used fictitiously and solely for your entertainment and enjoyment. Nothing in here should be considered legal advice. Please consult an attorney if you have legal questions.

Dear Lord, "here's my heart; O take and seal it; seal it for thy courts above."

About the Author

JAYNA BREIGH IS A retired attorney living in the Southeast United States. She brings to her writing over a decade of experience in trust and estate litigation in Los Angeles. She speaks at Christian women's conferences, hosts Bible studies, and homeschools her children. When not writing, she enjoys word puzzles and British period dramas. This is her debut novel. Connect with her at jaynabreigh.com.